THE MINISTRY OF HEALING

ELLEN G. WHITE

THE MINISTRY OF HEALING

Printed in the United Kingdom
by The Stanborough Press Limited
Alma Park, Grantham, Lincs, NG31 9SL

ISBN 0-904748-86-3

To the Physicians and Nurses
of every land, who, as co-workers
with the Chief Physician,
the great Medical Missionary,
are labouring bravely and unselfishly
to heal the sick,
to comfort the afflicted,
and to teach the way of life,
this book is dedicated.

Preface

The world is sick, and wherever the children of men dwell, suffering abounds. On every hand there is a seeking for relief.

It is not the creator's purpose that mankind shall be weighed down with a burden of pain, that his activities shall be curtailed by illness, that his strength wane, and his life be cut short by disease. But all too frequently the laws established by God to govern the life are flagrantly transgressed; sin enters the heart, and man loses sight of his dependence upon God, the source of life and health. Then follow the penalties of transgression – pain, sickness, death.

To understand the physical laws governing the body and to bring the life practices into harmony with these laws is a duty of first importance. There is a need for an understanding of the many factors contributing to true happiness – a cheerful home, obedience to the laws of life, proper relationship to one's fellow men.

When sickness comes, it is essential that we employ the varied agencies which, in co-operation with nature's efforts, will build up the body and restore the health. There is, also, a larger and more vitally important question – that of our relationship to the Creator who originally gave man his life, who made every provision for his continued happiness, and who today is interested in his welfare.

In this volume, the author, a woman of large experience in the practical affairs of life, and one particularly favoured with rare insight and knowledge, has brought within the reach of every father and mother, every man and woman, lay and professional, a vast fund of information on life and its laws, on health and its requisites, on disease and its remedies, on the sickness of the soul and the healing balm of Gilead.

The book is written in clear, simple, beautiful

language instructive to the learner, hopeful to the despondent, cheering to the sick, and restful to the weary. Through several decades it has conveyed its helpful message to hundreds of thousands, as it has been issued and reissued in many lands, in a dozen of the world's leading languages.

That this work, which presents a better way, revealing to us a simpler, sweeter life, full of joy and gladness, with room for that helpful service which "it is more blessed to give than to receive," may fully accomplish its mission is the sincere hope of the publishers and

THE TRUSTEES OF THE
ELLEN G. WHITE PUBLICATIONS

The bracketed numbers at the foot of each page co-ordinate this edition with the pagination of the standard hardback printings.

Contents

To preach good tidings unto the meek; . . . to bind up the brokenhearted to proclaim liberty to the captives, and the opening of the prison to them that are bound; to proclaim the year of Jehovah's favour; . . . to comfort all that mourn."

THE TRUE MEDICAL MISSIONARY

Our Example

Our Lord Jesus Christ came to this world as the unwearied servant of man's necessity. He "took our infirmities, and bare our sicknesses," that He might minister to every need of humanity. Matthew 8:17. The burden of disease and wretchedness and sin He came to remove. It was His mission to bring to men complete restoration; He came to give them health and peace and perfection of character.

Varied were the circumstances and needs of those who besought His aid, and none who came to Him went away unhelped. From Him flowed a stream of healing power, and in body and mind and soul men were made whole.

The Saviour's work was not restricted to any time or place. His compassion knew no limit. On so large a scale did He conduct His work of healing and teaching that there was no building in Palestine large enough to receive the multitudes that thronged to Him. On the green hill slopes of Galilee, in the thoroughfares of travel, by the seashore, in the synagogues, and in every other place where the sick could be brought to Him, was to be found His hospital. In every city, every town, every village, through which He passed, He laid His hands upon the afflicted ones and healed them. Wherever there were hearts ready to receive His message, He comforted them with the assurance of their heavenly Father's love. All day He ministered to those who came to Him; in the evening He gave attention to such as through the day must toil to earn a pittance for the support of their families.

Jesus carried the awful weight of responsibility for the salvation of men. He knew that unless there was a decided change in the principles and purposes of the human race, all would be lost. This was the burden of His soul, and none could appreciate the weight that rested upon Him. Through childhood, youth, and manhood He walked alone. Yet it was heaven to be in His presence. Day by day He met trials and temptations; day by day He was brought into contact with evil and witnessed its power upon those whom He was seeking to bless and to save. Yet He did not fail or become discouraged.

In all things He brought His wishes into strict abeyance to His mission. He glorified His life by making everything in it subordinate to the will of His Father. When in His youth His mother, finding Him in the school of the rabbis, said, "Son, why hast Thou thus dealt with us?" He answered — and His answer is the keynote of His lifework — "How is it that ye sought Me? wist ye not that I must be about My Father's business?" Luke 2:48, 49.

His life was one of constant self-sacrifice. He had no home in this world except as the kindness of friends provided for Him as a wayfarer. He came to live in our behalf the life of the poorest and to walk and work among the needy and the suffering. Unrecognized and unhonoured, He walked in and out among the people for whom He had done so much.

He was always patient and cheerful, and the afflicted hailed Him as a messenger of life and peace. He saw the needs of men and women, children and youth, and to all He gave the invitation, "Come unto Me."

During His ministry, Jesus devoted more time to healing the sick than to preaching. His miracles testified to the truth of His words, that He came not to destroy, but to save. Wherever He went, the tidings of His mercy preceded Him. Where He had passed, the objects of His compassion were rejoicing in health and making trial of their new-found powers. Crowds were collecting around them to hear from their lips the works that the Lord had wrought. His voice was the first sound that many had ever heard, His name the first word they had ever spoken, His face the first they had ever looked upon. Why should they not love Jesus and sound His praise? As He passed through the towns and cities He was like a vital current, diffusing life and joy.

"The land of Zebulun and the land of Naphtali,
Toward the sea, beyond the Jordan,
Galilee of the nations,
The people that sat in darkness
Saw a great light,
And to them that sat in the region and shadow of death,
To them did light spring up."
Matthew 4:15, 16, ARV, margin.

The Saviour made each work of healing an occasion for implanting divine principles in the mind and soul. This was the purpose of His work. He imparted earthly blessings, that He might incline the hearts of men to receive the gospel of His grace.

Christ might have occupied the highest place among the teachers of the Jewish nation, but He preferred rather to take the gospel to the poor. He went from place to place, that those in the highways and byways might hear the words of truth. By the sea, on the mountainside, in the streets of the city, in the synagogue, His voice was heard explaining the Scriptures. Often He taught in the outer court of the temple, that the Gentiles might hear His words.

So unlike the explanations of Scripture given by the scribes and Pharisees was Christ's teaching, that the attention of the people was arrested. The rabbis dwelt upon tradition, upon human theory and speculation. Often that which men had taught and written about the Scripture was put in place of the Scripture itself. The subject of Christ's teaching was the word of God. He met questioners with a plain, "It is written," "What saith the Scripture?" "How readest thou?" At every opportunity when an interest was awakened by either friend or foe, He presented the word. With clearness and power He proclaimed the gospel message. His words shed a flood of light on the teachings of patriarchs and prophets, and the Scriptures came to men as a new revelation. Never before had His hearers perceived in the word of God such depth of meaning.

Never was there such an evangelist as Christ. He was the Majesty of heaven, but He humbled Himself to take our nature, that He might meet men where they were. To all people, rich and poor, free and bond, Christ, the Messenger of the covenant, brought the tidings of salvation. His fame as the Great Healer spread throughout Palestine. The sick came to the places through which He would pass, that they might call on Him for help. Hither, too, came many anxious to hear His words and to receive a touch of His hand. Thus He went from city to city, from town to town, preaching the gospel and healing the sick — the King of glory in the lowly garb of humanity.

He attended the great yearly festivals of the nation, and to the multitude absorbed in outward ceremony He spoke of heavenly things, bringing eternity within their view. To all He brought treasures from the storehouse of wisdom. He spoke to them in language so simple that they could not fail of understanding. By methods peculiarly His own, He helped all who were in sorrow and affliction. With tender, courteous grace He ministered to the sin-sick soul, bringing healing and strength.

The prince of teachers, He sought access to the people by the pathway of their most familiar associations. He presented the truth in such a way that ever after it was to His hearers intertwined with their most hallowed recollections and sympathies. He taught in a way that made them feel the completeness of His identification with their interests and happiness. His instruction was so direct, His illustrations were so appropriate, His words so sympathetic and cheerful, that His hearers were charmed. The simplicity and earnestness with which He addressed the needy, hallowed every word.

What a busy life He led! Day by day He might have been seen entering the humble abodes of want and sorrow, speaking hope to the downcast and peace to the distressed. Gracious, tenderhearted, pitiful, He went about lifting up the bowed-down and comforting the sorrowful. Wherever He went, He carried blessing.

While He ministered to the poor, Jesus studied also to find ways of reaching the rich. He sought the acquaintance of the wealthy and cultured Pharisee, the Jewish nobleman, and the Roman ruler. He accepted their invitations, attended their feasts, made Himself familiar with their interests and occupations, that He might gain access to their hearts, and reveal to them the imperishable riches.

Christ came to this world to show that by receiving power from on high, man can live an unsullied life. With unwearying patience and sympathetic helpfulness He met men in their necessities. By the gentle touch of grace He banished from the soul unrest and doubt, changing enmity to love, and unbelief to confidence.

He could say to whom He pleased, "Follow Me," and the one addressed arose and followed Him. The spell of the world's enchantment was broken. At the sound of His voice the spirit of greed and ambition fled from the heart, and men arose, emancipated, to follow the Saviour.

Brotherly Love

Christ recognized no distinction of nationality or rank or creed. The scribes and Pharisees desired to make a local and a national benefit of the gifts of heaven and to exclude the rest of God's family in the world. But Christ came to break down every wall of partition. He came to show that His gift of mercy and love is as unconfined as the air, the light, or the showers of rain that refresh the earth.

The life of Christ established a religion in which there is no caste, a religion by which Jew and Gentile, free and bond, are linked in a common brotherhood, equal before God. No question of policy influenced His movements. He made no difference between neighbours and strangers, friends and enemies. That which appealed to His heart was a soul thirsting for the waters of life.

He passed by no human being as worthless, but sought to apply the healing remedy to every soul. In whatever company He found Himself He presented a lesson appropriate to the time and the circumstances. Every neglect or insult shown by men to their fellow men only made Him more conscious of their need of His divine-human sympathy. He sought to inspire with hope the roughest and most unpromising, setting before them the assurance that they might become blameless and harmless, attaining such a character as would make them manifest as the children of God.

Often He met those who had drifted under Satan's control, and who had no power to break from his snare. To such a one, discouraged, sick, tempted, fallen, Jesus would speak words of tenderest pity, words that were needed and could be understood. Others He met who were fighting a hand-to-hand battle with the adversary of souls. These He encouraged to persevere, assuring them that they would win; for angels of God were on their side and would give them the victory.

At the table of the publicans He sat as an honoured guest, by His sympathy and social kindliness showing that He recognized the dignity of humanity; and men longed to become worthy of His confidence. Upon their thirsty hearts His words fell with blessed, life-giving power. New impulses were awakened, and to these outcasts of society there opened the possibility of a new life.

Though He was a Jew, Jesus mingled freely with the Samaritans, setting at nought the Pharisaic customs of His nation. In face of their prejudices He accepted the hospitality of this despised people. He slept with them under their roofs, ate with them at their tables — partaking of the food prepared and served by their hands — taught in their streets, and treated them with the utmost kindness and courtesy. And while He drew their hearts to Him by the tie of human sympathy, His divine grace brought to them the salvation which the Jews rejected.

Personal Ministry

Christ neglected no opportunity of proclaiming the gospel of salvation. Listen to His wonderful words to that one woman of Samaria. He was sitting by Jacob's well, as the woman came to draw water. To her surprise He asked a favour of her. "Give Me to drink," He said. He wanted a cool draft, and He wished also to open the way whereby He might give to her the water of life. "How is it," said the woman, "that Thou, being a Jew, askest drink of me, which am a woman of Samaria? for the Jews have no dealings with the Samaritans." Jesus answered, "If thou knewest the gift of God, and who it is that saith to thee, Give Me to drink; thou wouldest have asked of Him, and He would have given thee living water. . . . Whosoever drinketh of this water shall thirst again: but whosoever drinketh of the water that I shall give him shall never thirst; but the water that I shall give him shall be in him a well of water springing up into everlasting life." John 4:7-14.

How much interest Christ manifested in this one woman! How earnest and eloquent were His words! When the woman heard them, she left her waterpot, and went into the city, saying to her friends, "Come, see a man, which told me all things that ever I did: is not this the Christ?" We read that "many of the Samaritans of that city believed on Him." Verses 29, 39. And who can estimate the influence which these words have exerted for the saving of souls in the years that have passed since then?

Wherever hearts are open to receive the truth, Christ is ready to instruct them. He reveals to them the Father, and the service acceptable to Him who reads the heart. For such He uses no parables. To them, as to the woman at the well, He says, "I that speak unto thee am He."

Days of Ministry

In the fisherman's home at Capernaum the mother of Peter's wife is lying sick of "a great fever," and "they tell Him of her." Jesus "touched her hand, and the fever left her," and she arose and ministered to the Saviour and His disciples. Luke 4:38; Mark 1:30; Matthew 8:15.

Rapidly the tidings spread. The miracle had been wrought upon the Sabbath, and for fear of the rabbis the people dared not come for healing until the sun was set. Then from the homes, the shops, the market places, the inhabitants of the city pressed toward the humble dwelling that sheltered Jesus. The sick were brought upon litters, they came leaning upon staffs, or, supported by friends, they tottered feebly into the Saviour's presence.

Hour after hour they came and went; for none could know whether tomorrow would find the Healer still among them. Never before had Capernaum witnessed a day like this. The air was filled with the voice of triumph and shouts of deliverance.

Not until the last sufferer had been relieved did Jesus cease His work. It was far into the night when the multitude departed and silence settled down upon the home of Simon. The long, exciting day was past, and Jesus sought rest. But while the city was wrapped in slumber, the Saviour, "rising up a great while before day," "went out, and departed into a solitary place, and there prayed." Mark 1:35.

Early in the morning Peter and his companions came to Jesus, saying that already the people of Capernaum were seeking Him. With surprise they heard Christ's words, "I must preach the kingdom of God to other cities also: for therefore am I sent." Luke 4:43.

In the excitement which then pervaded Capernaum there was danger that the object of His mission would be lost sight of. Jesus was not satisfied to attract attention to Himself merely as a wonder-worker or as a healer of physical disease. He was seeking to draw men to Him as their Saviour. While the people were eager to believe that He had come as a king to establish an earthly reign, He desired to turn their minds from the earthly to the spiritual. Mere worldly success would interfere with His work.

And the wonder of the careless crowd jarred upon His spirits. No self-assertion mingled with His life. The homage which the world gives to position, wealth, or talent was foreign to the Son of man. None of the means that men employ to win allegiance or command homage did Jesus use. Centuries before His birth it had been prophesied of Him, "He shall not cry, nor lift up, nor cause His voice to be heard in the street. A bruised reed shall He not break, and the dimly burning flax shall He not quench: He shall bring forth judgement unto truth." Isaiah 42:2, 3, margin.

The Pharisees sought distinction by their scrupulous ceremonialism and the ostentation of their worship and their charities. They proved their zeal for religion by making it the theme of discussion. Disputes between opposing sects were loud and long, and it was not unusual to hear on the streets the voice of angry controversy from learned doctors of the law.

In marked contrast to all this was the life of Jesus. In that life no noisy disputation, no ostentatious worship, no act to gain applause, was ever witnessed. Christ was hid in God, and God was revealed in the character of His Son. To this revelation Jesus desired the minds of the people to be directed.

The Sun of Righteousness did not burst upon the world in splendour, to dazzle the senses with His glory. It is written of Christ, "His going forth is prepared as the morning." Hosea 6:3. Quietly and gently the daylight breaks upon the earth, dispelling the darkness and waking the world to life. So did the Sun of Righteousness arise, "with healing in His wings." Malachi 4:2.

"Behold My Servant, whom I uphold;
Mine Elect, in whom My soul delighteth."
Isaiah 42:1.

"Thou hast been a strength to the poor,
A strength to the needy in his distress,
A refuge from the storm, a shadow from the heat."
Isaiah 25:4.

"Thus saith God the Lord,
He that created the heavens, and stretched them out;
He that spread forth the earth, and that which cometh out of it;
He that giveth breath unto the people upon it,
And spirit to them that walk therein:
I the Lord have called Thee in righteousness,
And will hold Thine hand,
And will keep Thee, and give Thee for a covenant of the people,
For a light of the Gentiles;
To open the blind eyes,
To bring out the prisoners from the prison,
And them that sit in darkness out of the prison house."
Isaiah 42:5-7.

"I will bring the blind by a way that they knew not;
I will lead them in paths that they have not known:
I will make darkness light before them,
And crooked things straight.
These things will I do unto them, and not forsake them."
Verse 16.

"Sing unto the Lord a new song,
And His praise from the end of the earth,
Ye that go down to the sea, and all that is therein;
The isles, and the inhabitants thereof.
Let the wilderness and the cities thereof lift up the voice,
The villages that Kedar doth inhabit:
Let the inhabitants of the rock sing,
Let them shout from the top of the mountains.
Let them give glory unto the Lord,
And declare His praise in the islands."
Verses 10-12.

"Sing, O ye heavens; for the Lord hath done it:
Shout, ye lower parts of the earth:
Break forth into singing, ye mountains,
O forest, and every tree therein:
For the Lord hath redeemed Jacob,
And glorified Himself in Israel."
Isaiah 44:23.

From Herod's dungeon, where in disappointment and perplexity concerning the Saviour's work, John the Baptist watched and waited, he sent two of his disciples to Jesus with the message:

"Art Thou He that should come, or do we look for another?" Matthew 11:3.

The Saviour did not at once answer the disciples' question. As they stood wondering at His silence, the afflicted were coming to Him. The voice of the Mighty Healer penetrated the deaf ear. A word, a touch of His hand, opened the blind eyes to behold the light of day, the scenes of nature, the faces of friends, and the face of the Deliverer. His voice reached the ears of the dying, and they arose in health and vigour. Paralyzed demoniacs obeyed His word, their madness left them, and they worshipped Him. The poor peasants and labourers, who were shunned by the rabbis as unclean, gathered about Him, and He spoke to them the words of eternal life.

Thus the day wore away, the disciples of John seeing and hearing all. At last Jesus called them to Him, and bade them go and tell John what they had seen and heard, adding, "Blessed is he, whosoever shall not be offended in Me." Verse 6. The disciples bore the message, and it was enough.

John recalled the prophecy concerning the Messiah, "Jehovah hath anointed Me to preach good tidings unto the meek; He hath sent Me to bind up the broken-hearted, to proclaim liberty to the captives, and the opening of the prison to them that are bound; to proclaim the year of Jehovah's favour, and . . . to comfort all that mourn." Isaiah 61:1, 2, ARV. Jesus of Nazareth was the Promised One. The evidence of His divinity was seen in His ministry to the needs of suffering humanity. His glory was shown in His condescension to our low estate. The works of Christ not only declared Him to be the Messiah, but showed in what manner His kingdom was to be established. To John was opened the same truth that had come to Elijah in the desert, when "a great and strong wind rent the mountains, and brake in pieces the rocks before the Lord; but the Lord was not in the wind: and after the wind an earthquake; but the Lord was not in the earthquake: and after the earthquake a fire; but the Lord was not in the fire:" and after the fire, God spoke to the prophet by a still, small voice. 1 Kings 19:11, 12. So Jesus was to do His work, not by the overturning of thrones and kingdoms, not with pomp and outward display, but through speaking to the hearts of men by a life of mercy and self-sacrifice.

The kingdom of God comes not with outward show. It comes through the gentleness of the inspiration of His word, through the inward working of His Spirit, the fellowship of the soul with Him who is its life. The greatest manifestation of its power is seen in human nature brought to the perfection of the character of Christ.

The followers of Christ are to be the light of the world; but God does not bid them make an effort to shine. He does not approve of any self-satisfied endeavour to display superior goodness. He desires that their souls shall be imbued with the principles of heaven; then, as they come in contact with the world, they will reveal the light that is in them. Their steadfast fidelity in every act of life will be a means of illumination.

Wealth or high position, costly equipment, architecture or furnishings, are not essential to the advancement of the work of God; neither are achievements that win applause from men and administer to vanity. Worldly display, however imposing, is of no value in God's sight. Above the seen and temporal, He values the unseen and eternal. The former is of worth only as it expresses the latter. The choicest productions of art possess no beauty that can compare with the beauty of character, which is the fruit of the Holy Spirit's working in the soul.

When God gave His Son to our world, He endowed human beings with imperishable riches — riches compared with which the treasured wealth of men since the world began is nothingness. Christ came to the earth and stood before the children of men with the hoarded love of eternity, and this is the treasure that, through our connection with Him, we are to receive, to reveal, and to impart.

Human effort will be efficient in the work of God just according to the consecrated devotion of the worker — by revealing the power of the grace of Christ to transform the life. We are to be distinguished from the world because God has placed His seal upon us, because He manifests in us His own character of love. Our Redeemer covers us with His righteousness.

In choosing men and women for His service, God does not ask whether they possess worldly wealth, learning, or eloquence. He asks, "Do they walk in such humility that I can teach them My way? Can I put My words into their lips? Will they represent Me?"

God can use every person just in proportion as He can put His Spirit into the soul temple. The work that He will accept is the work that reflects His image. His followers are to bear, as their credentials to the world, the ineffaceable characteristics of His immortal principles.

"He Shall Gather the Lambs With His Arm."

As Jesus ministers in the streets of the cities, mothers with their sick and dying little ones in their arms press through the throng, seeking to come within reach of His notice.

Behold these mothers, pale, weary, almost despairing, yet determined and persevering. Bearing their burden of suffering, they seek the Saviour. As they are crowded back by the surging throng, Christ makes His way to them step by step, until He is close by their side. Hope springs up in their hearts. Their tears of gladness fall as they catch His attention, and look into the eyes expressing such pity and love.

Singling out one of the group, the Saviour invites her confidence, saying, "What shall I do for thee?" She sobs out her great want, "Master, that Thou wouldest heal my child." Christ takes the little one from her arms, and disease flees at His touch. The pallor of death is gone; the life-giving current flows through the veins; the muscles receive strength. Words of comfort and peace are spoken to the mother; and then another case, just as urgent, is presented. Again Christ exercises His life-giving power, and all give praise and honour to Him who doeth wonderful things.

We dwell much on the greatness of Christ's life. We speak of the wonderful things that He accomplished, of the miracles that He wrought. But His attention to things accounted small is even higher proof of His greatness.

Among the Jews it was customary for children to be brought to some rabbi, that he might lay his hands upon them in blessing; but the disciples thought the Saviour's work too important to be interrupted in this way. When the mothers came desiring Him to bless their little ones, the disciples looked on them with disfavour. They thought these children too young to be benefited by a visit to Jesus, and concluded that He would be displeased at their presence. But the Saviour understood the care and burden of the mothers who were seeking to train their children according to the word of God. He had heard their prayers. He Himself had drawn them into His presence.

One mother with her child had left her home to find Jesus. On the way she told a neighbour her errand, and the neighbour wished to have Jesus bless her children. Thus several mothers came here together, with their little ones. Some of the children had passed beyond the years of infancy to childhood and youth. When the mothers made known their desire, Jesus heard with sympathy the timid, tearful request. But He waited to see how the disciples would treat them. When He saw the disciples reproving the mothers and sending them away, thinking to do Him a favour, He showed them their error, saying, "Suffer the little children to come unto Me, and forbid them not: for of such is the kingdom of God." Mark 10:14. He took the children in His arms, He laid His hands upon them, and gave them the blessings for which they came.

The mothers were comforted. They returned to their homes strengthened and blessed by the words of Christ. They were encouraged to take up their burden with new cheerfulness and to work hopefully for their children.

Could the afterlife of that little group be opened before us, we should see the mothers recalling to the minds of their children the scene of that day, and repeating to them the loving words of the Saviour. We should see, too, how often, in after years, the memory of these words kept the children from straying from the path cast up for the ransomed of the Lord.

Christ is today the same compassionate Saviour as when He walked among men. He is as verily the helper of mothers now as when He gathered the little ones to His arms in Judea. The children of our hearths are as much the purchase of His blood as were the children of long ago.

Jesus knows the burden of every mother's heart. He who had a mother that struggled with poverty and privation, sympathizes with every mother in her labours. He who made a long journey in order to relieve the anxious heart of a Canaanite woman will do as much for the mothers of today. He who gave back to the widow of Nain her only son, and in His agony upon the cross remembered His own mother, is touched today by the mother's sorrow. In every grief and every need, He will comfort and help.

Let mothers come to Jesus with their perplexities. They will find grace sufficient to aid them in the care of their children. The gates are open for every mother who would lay her burdens at the Saviour's feet. He who said, "Suffer the little children to come unto Me, and forbid them not" (Mark 10:14), still invites mothers to bring their little ones to be blessed by Him.

In the children who were brought in contact with Him, Jesus saw the men and women who should be heirs of His grace and subjects of His kingdom, and some of whom would become martyrs for His sake. He knew that these children would listen to Him and accept Him as their Redeemer far more readily than would grown-up people, many of whom were the worldly-wise and hardhearted. In teaching, He came down to their level. He, the Majesty of heaven, answered their questions and simplified His important lessons to meet their childish understanding. He planted in their minds the seeds of truth, which in after years would spring up and bear fruit unto eternal life.

When Jesus told the disciples not to forbid the children to come to Him, He was speaking to His followers in all ages — to officers of the church, ministers, helpers, and all Christians. Jesus is drawing the children, and He bids us, "Suffer them to come;" as if He would say, They will come, if you do not hinder them.

Let not your unChristlike character misrepresent Jesus. Do not keep the little ones away from Him by your coldness and harshness. Never give them cause to feel that heaven would not be a pleasant place to them if you were there. Do not speak of religion as something that children cannot understand, or act as if they were not expected to accept Christ in their childhood. Do not give them the false impression that the religion of Christ is a religion of gloom, and that in coming to the Saviour they must give up all that makes life joyful.

As the Holy Spirit moves upon the hearts of the children, co-operate with His work. Teach them that the Saviour is calling them, that nothing can afford Him greater joy than for them to give themselves to Him in the bloom and freshness of their years.

Parental Responsibility

The Saviour regards with infinite tenderness the souls whom He has purchased with His blood. They are the claim of His love. He looks upon them with unutterable longing. His heart is drawn out, not only to the best-trained and most attractive children, but to those who by inheritance and through neglect have objectionable traits of character. Many parents do not understand how much they are responsible for these traits in their children. They have not the tenderness and wisdom to deal with the erring ones whom they have made what they are. But Jesus looks upon these children with pity. He traces from cause to effect.

The Christian worker may be Christ's agent in drawing these faulty and erring ones to the Saviour. By wisdom and tact he may bind them to his heart, he may give courage and hope, and through the grace of Christ may see them transformed in character, so that of them it may be said, "Of such is the kingdom of God."

Five Small Barley Loaves Feed the Multitude

All day the people had thronged the steps of Christ and His disciples as He taught beside the sea. They had listened to His gracious words, so simple and so plain that they were as the balm of Gilead to their souls. The healing of His divine hand had brought health to the sick and life to the dying. The day had seemed to them like heaven on earth, and they were unconscious of how long it had been since they had eaten anything.

The sun was sinking in the west, and yet the people lingered. Finally the disciples came to Christ, urging that for their own sake the multitude should be sent away. Many had come from far and had eaten nothing since morning. In the surrounding towns and villages they might be able to obtain food. But Jesus said, "Give ye them to eat." Matthew 14:16. Then, turning to Philip, He questioned, "Whence shall we buy bread, that these may eat?" John 6:5.

Philip looked over the sea of heads and thought how impossible it would be to provide food for so great a company. He answered that two hundred pennyworth* of bread would not be enough to divide among them so that each might have a little.

Jesus inquired how much food could be found among the company. "There is a lad here," said Andrew; "which hath five barley loaves, and two small fishes:

---

* About £10

but what are they among so many?" Verse 9. Jesus directed that these be brought to Him. Then He bade the disciples seat the people on the grass. When this was accomplished, He took the food, "and looking up to heaven, He blessed, and brake, and gave the loaves to His disciples, and the disciples to the multitude. And they did all eat, and were filled: and they took up of the fragments that remained twelve baskets full." Matthew 14:19, 20.

It was by a miracle of divine power that Christ fed the multitude; yet how humble was the fare provided — only the fishes and barley loaves that were the daily fare of the fisher-folk of Galilee.

Christ could have spread for the people a rich repast, but food prepared merely for the gratification of appetite would have conveyed no lesson for their good. Through this miracle Christ desired to teach a lesson of simplicity. If men today were simple in their habits, living in harmony with nature's laws, as did Adam and Eve in the beginning, there would be an abundant supply for the needs of the human family. But selfishness and the indulgence of appetite have brought sin and misery, from excess on the one hand, and from want on the other.

Jesus did not seek to attract the people to Him by gratifying the desire for luxury. To that great throng, weary and hungry after the long, exciting day, the simple fare was an assurance both of His power and of His tender care for them in the common needs of life. The Saviour has not promised His followers the luxuries of the world; their lot may be shut in by poverty; but His word is pledged that their need shall be supplied, and He has promised that which is better than earthly good — the abiding comfort of His own presence.

After the multitude had been fed, there was an abundance of food left. Jesus bade His disciples, "Gather up the fragments that remain, that nothing be lost." John 6:12. These words meant more than putting the food into baskets. The lesson was twofold. Nothing is to be wasted. We are to let slip no temporal advantage. We should neglect nothing that would serve to benefit a human being. Let everything be gathered up that will relieve the necessities of earth's hungry ones. With the same carefulness are we to treasure the bread from heaven to satisfy the needs of the soul. By every word of God we are to live. Nothing that God has spoken is to be lost. Not one word that concerns our eternal salvation are we to neglect. Not one word is to fall useless to the ground.

The miracle of the loaves teaches dependence upon God. When Christ fed the five thousand, the food was not nigh at hand. Apparently He had no means at His command. There He was, with five thousand men, besides women and children, in the wilderness. He had not invited the multitude to follow Him thither. Eager to be in His presence, they had come without invitation or command; but He knew that after listening all day to His instruction they were hungry and faint. They were far from home, and the night was at hand. Many of them were without means to purchase food. He who for their sake had fasted forty days in the wilderness, would not suffer them to return fasting to their homes.

The providence of God had placed Jesus where He was, and He depended on His heavenly Father for means to relieve the necessity. When we are brought into strait places, we are to depend on God. In every emergency we are to seek help from Him who has infinite resources at His command.

In this miracle, Christ received from the Father; He imparted to the disciples, the disciples to the people, and the people to one another. So all who are united to Christ will receive from Him the bread of life, and impart it to others. His disciples are the appointed means of communication between Christ and the people.

When the disciples heard the Saviour's direction, "Give ye them to eat," all the difficulties arose in their minds. They questioned, "Shall we go into the villages to buy food?" But what said Christ? "Give *ye* them to eat." The disciples brought to Jesus all they had; but He did not invite them to eat. He bade them serve the people. The food multiplied in His hands, and the hands of the disciples, reaching out to Christ, were never unfilled. The little store was sufficient for all. When the multitude had been fed, the disciples ate with Jesus of the precious, heaven-supplied food.

As we see the necessities of the poor, the ignorant, the afflicted, how often our hearts sink. We question, "What avail our feeble strength and slender resources to supply this terrible necessity? Shall we not wait for someone of greater ability to direct the work, or for some organization to undertake it?" Christ says, "Give *ye* them to eat." Use the means, the time, the ability, you have. Bring your barley loaves to Jesus.

Though your resources may not be sufficient to feed thousands, they may suffice to feed one. In the hand of Christ they may feed many. Like the disciples, give what you have. Christ will multiply the gift. He will reward honest, simple reliance upon Him. That which seemed but a meagre supply will prove to be a rich feast.

"He that soweth sparingly shall reap also sparingly; and he that soweth with blessings shall reap also with blessings. . . . God is able to make all grace abound unto you; that ye, having always all sufficiency in everything, may abound unto every good work: as it is written,

> "He hath scattered abroad, He hath given to the poor;
> His righteousness abideth forever.

"And He that supplieth seed to the sower and bread for food, shall supply and multiply your seed for sowing, and increase the fruits of your righteousness: ye being enriched in everything unto all liberality." 2 Corinthians 9:6-11, RV, margin.

With Nature and With God

The Saviour's life on earth was a life of communion with nature and with God. In this communion He revealed for us the secret of a life of power.

Jesus was an earnest, constant worker. Never lived there among men another so weighted with responsibilities. Never another carried so heavy a burden of the world's sorrow and sin. Never another toiled with such self-consuming zeal for the good of men. Yet His was a life of health. Physically as well as spiritually He was represented by the sacrificial lamb, "without blemish and without spot." 1 Peter 1:19. In body as in soul He was an example of what God designed all humanity to be through obedience to His laws.

As the people looked upon Jesus, they saw a face in which divine compassion was blended with conscious power. He seemed to be surrounded with an atmosphere of spiritual life. While His manners were gentle and unassuming, He impressed men with a sense of power that was hidden, yet could not be wholly concealed.

During His ministry He was continually pursued by crafty and hypocritical men who were seeking His life. Spies were on His track, watching His words, to find some occasion against Him. The keenest and most highly cultured minds of the nation sought to defeat Him in controversy. But never could they gain an advantage. They had to retire from the field, confounded and put to shame by the lowly Teacher from Galilee. Christ's teaching had a freshness and a power such as men had never before known. Even His enemies were forced to confess, "Never man spake like this Man." John 7:46.

The childhood of Jesus, spent in poverty, had been uncorrupted by the artificial habits of a corrupt age. Working at the carpenter's bench, bearing the burdens of home life, learning the lessons of obedience and toil, He found recreation amidst the scenes of nature, gathering knowledge as He sought to understand nature's mysteries. He studied the word of God, and His hours of greatest happiness were found when He could turn aside from the scene of His labours to go into the fields, to meditate in the quiet valleys, to hold communion with God on the mountainside or amid the trees of the forest. The early morning often found Him in some secluded place, meditating, searching the Scriptures, or in prayer. With the voice of singing He welcomed the morning light. With songs of thanksgiving He cheered His hours of labour and brought heaven's gladness to the toilworn and disheartened.

During His ministry Jesus lived to a great degree an outdoor life. His journeys from place to place were made on foot, and much of His teaching was given in the open air. In training His disciples He often withdrew from the confusion of the city to the quiet of the fields, as more in harmony with the lessons of simplicity, faith, and self-abnegation He desired to teach them. It was beneath the sheltering trees of the mountainside, but a little distance from the Sea of Galilee, that the Twelve were called to the apostolate and the Sermon on the Mount was given.

Christ loved to gather the people about Him under the blue heavens, on some grassy hillside, or on the beach beside the lake. Here, surrounded by the works of His own creation, He could turn their thoughts from the artificial to the natural. In the growth and development of nature were revealed the principles of His kingdom. As men should lift their eyes to the hills of God and behold the wonderful works of His hand, they could learn precious lessons of divine truth. In future days the lessons of the divine Teacher would thus be repeated to them by the things of nature. The mind would be uplifted and the heart would find rest.

The disciples who were associated with Him in His

work, Jesus often released for a season, that they might visit their homes and rest; but in vain were their efforts to draw Him away from His labours. All day He ministered to the throngs that came to Him, and at eventide, or in the early morning, He went away to the sanctuary of the mountains for communion with His Father.

Often His incessant labour and the conflict with the enmity and false teaching of the rabbis left Him so utterly wearied that His mother and brothers, and even His disciples, feared that His life would be sacrificed. But as He returned from the hours of prayer that closed the toilsome day, they marked the look of peace upon His face, the freshness and life and power that seemed to pervade His whole being. From hours spent alone with God He came forth, morning by morning, to bring the light of heaven to men.

It was just after the return from their first missionary tour that Jesus bade His disciples, Come apart, and rest awhile. The disciples had returned, filled with the joy of their success as heralds of the gospel, when the tidings reached them of the death of John the Baptist at the hand of Herod. It was a bitter sorrow and disappointment. Jesus knew that in leaving the Baptist to die in prison He had severely tested the disciples' faith. With pitying tenderness He looked upon their sorrowful, tear-stained faces. Tears were in His own eyes and voice as He said, "Come ye yourselves apart into a desert place, and rest awhile." Mark 6:31.

Near Bethsaida, at the northern end of the Sea of Galilee, was a lonely region, beautiful with the fresh green of spring, that offered a welcome retreat to Jesus and His disciples. For this place they set out, going in their boat across the lake. Here they could rest, apart from the confusion of the multitude. Here the disciples could listen to the words of Christ, undisturbed by the retorts and accusations of the Pharisees. Here they hoped to enjoy a short season of fellowship in the society of their Lord.

Only a short time did Jesus have alone with His

beloved ones, but how precious to them were those few moments. They talked together regarding the work of the gospel and the possibility of making their labour more effective in reaching the people. As Jesus opened to them the treasures of truth, they were vitalized by divine power and inspired with hope and courage.

But soon He was again sought for by the multitude. Supposing that He had gone to His usual place of retirement, the people followed Him thither. His hope to gain even one hour of rest was frustrated. But in the depth of His pure, compassionate heart the Good Shepherd of the sheep had only love and pity for these restless, thirsting souls. All day He ministered to their needs, and at evening dismissed them to go to their homes and rest.

In a life wholly devoted to the good of others, the Saviour found it necessary to turn aside from ceaseless activity and contact with human needs, to seek retirement and unbroken communion with His Father. As the throng that had followed Him depart, He goes into the mountains, and there, alone with God, pours out His soul in prayer for these suffering, sinful, needy ones.

When Jesus said to His disciples that the harvest was great and the labourers were few, He did not urge upon them the necessity of ceaseless toil, but bade them, "Pray ye therefore the Lord of the harvest, that He will send forth labourers into His harvest." Matthew 9:38. To His toil-worn workers today as really as to His first disciples He speaks these words of compassion, "Come ye yourselves apart, . . . and rest awhile."

All who are under the training of God need the quiet hour for communion with their own hearts, with nature, and with God. In them is to be revealed a life that is not in harmony with the world, its customs, or its practices; and they need to have a personal experience in obtaining a knowledge of the will of God. We must individually hear Him speaking to the heart. When every other voice is hushed, and in quietness we wait before Him, the silence of the soul makes more distinct the voice of God. He bids us, "Be still, and know that I am God." Psalm 46:10. This is the effectual preparation for all labour for God. Amidst the hurrying throng, and the strain of life's intense activities, he who is thus refreshed will be surrounded with an atmosphere of light and peace. He will receive a new endowment of both physical and mental strength. His life will breathe out a fragrance, and will reveal a divine power that will reach men's hearts.

The Touch of Faith

"If I may but touch His garment, I shall be whole." Matthew 9:21. It was a poor woman who spoke these words — a woman who for twelve years had suffered from a disease that made her life a burden. She had spent all her means upon physicians and remedies, only to be pronounced incurable. But as she heard of the Great Healer, her hopes revived. She thought, "If only I could get near enough to speak to Him, I might be healed."

Christ was on His way to the home of Jairus, the Jewish rabbi who had entreated Him to come and heal his daughter. The heartbroken petition, "My little daughter lieth at the point of death: I pray Thee, come and lay Thy hands on her, that she may be healed" (Mark 5:23), had touched the tender, sympathetic heart of Christ, and He at once set out with the ruler for his home.

They advanced but slowly; for the crowd pressed Christ on every side. In making His way through the multitude, the Saviour came near to where the afflicted woman was standing. Again and again she had tried in vain to get near Him. Now her opportunity had come. She could see no way of speaking to Him. She would not seek to hinder His slow advance. But she had heard that healing came from a touch of His garments; and, fearful of losing her one chance for relief, she pressed forward, saying to herself, "If I may but touch His garment, I shall be whole."

Christ knew every thought of her mind, and He was making His way to where she stood. He realized her great need, and He was helping her to exercise faith.

As He was passing, she reached forward and succeeded in barely touching the border of His garment. That moment she knew that she was healed. In that one touch was concentrated the faith of her life, and instantly her pain and feebleness disappeared. Instantly she felt the thrill as of an electric current passing through every fibre of her being. There came over her a sensation of perfect health. "She felt in her body that she was healed of that plague." Verse 29.

The grateful woman desired to express her thanks to the Mighty Healer, who had done more for her in one touch than the physicians had done in twelve long years; but she dared not. With a grateful heart she tried to withdraw from the crowd. Suddenly Jesus stopped, and looking round He asked, "Who touched Me?"

Looking at Him in amazement, Peter answered, "Master, the multitude throng Thee and press Thee, and sayest Thou, Who touched Me?" Luke 8:45.

"Somebody hath touched Me," Jesus said; "for I perceive that virtue is gone out of Me." Verse 46. He could distinguish the touch of faith from the casual touch of the careless throng. Someone had touched Him with a deep purpose and had received answer.

Christ did not ask the question for His own information. He had a lesson for the people, for His disciples, and for the woman. He wished to inspire the afflicted with hope. He wished to show that it was faith which had brought the healing power. The woman's trust must not be passed by without comment. God must be glorified by her grateful confession. Christ desired her to understand that He approved her act of faith. He would not have her depart with a half blessing only. She was not to remain in ignorance of His knowledge of her suffering, or of His compassionate love and of His approval of her faith in His power to save to the uttermost all who come to Him.

Looking toward the woman, Christ insisted on knowing who had touched Him. Finding concealment vain, she came forward trembling, and cast herself at His feet. With grateful tears she told Him, before all the people, why she had touched His garment, and how she had been immediately healed. She feared that her act in touching His garment had been one of presumption; but no word of censure came from Christ's lips. He spoke only words of approval. They came from a heart of love, filled with sympathy for human woe. "Daughter," He said gently, "be of good comfort: thy faith hath made thee whole; go in peace." Verse 48. How cheering were these words to her. Now no fear that she had given offence embittered her joy.

To the curious crowd pressing about Jesus there was imparted no vital power. But the suffering woman who touched Him in faith received healing. So in spiritual things does the casual contact differ from the touch of faith. To believe in Christ merely as the Saviour of the world can never bring healing to the soul. The faith that is unto salvation is not a mere assent to the truth of the gospel. True faith is that which receives Christ as a personal Saviour. God gave His only-begotten Son, that *I,* by believing in Him, "should not perish, but have everlasting life." John 3:16. When I come to Christ, according to His word, I am to believe that I receive His saving grace. The life that I now live, I am to "live by the faith of the Son of God, who loved *me,* and gave Himself for *me.*" Galatians 2:20.

Many hold faith as an opinion. Saving faith is a transaction, by which those who receive Christ join themselves in covenant relation with God. A living faith means an increase of vigour, a confiding trust, by which, through the grace of Christ, the soul becomes a conquering power.

Faith is a mightier conqueror than death. If the sick can be led to fix their eyes in faith upon the Mighty Healer, we shall see wonderful results. It will bring life to the body and to the soul.

In working for the victims of evil habits, instead of pointing them to the despair and ruin toward which they are hastening, turn their eyes away to Jesus. Fix them upon the glories of the heavenly. This will do more for the saving of body and soul than will all the terrors of the grave when kept before the helpless and apparently hopeless.

"According to His Mercy He Saved Us."

A centurion's servant was lying sick of the palsy. Among the Romans the servants were slaves, bought and sold in the market places, and often treated with abuse and cruelty; but the centurion was tenderly attached to his servant, and greatly desired his recovery. He believed that Jesus could heal him. He had not seen the Saviour, but the reports he had heard inspired him with faith. Notwithstanding the formalism of the Jews, this Roman was convinced that their religion was superior to his own. Already he had broken through the barriers of national prejudice and hatred that separated the conquerors from the conquered people. He had manifested respect for the service of God and had shown kindness to the Jews as His worshippers. In the teaching of Christ, as it had been reported to him, he found that which met the need of the soul. All that was spiritual within him responded to the Saviour's words. But he thought himself unworthy to approach Jesus, and he appealed to the Jewish elders to make request for his servant's healing.

The elders present the case to Jesus, urging that "he was worthy for whom He should do this: for he loveth our nation, and he hath built us a synagogue." Luke 7:4, 5.

But on the way to the centurion's home, Jesus receives a message from the officer himself, "Lord, trouble not Thyself: for I am not worthy that Thou shouldest enter under my roof." Verse 6.

Still the Saviour keeps on His way, and the centurion comes in person to complete the message, saying, "Neither thought I myself worthy to come unto Thee," "but speak the word only, and my servant shall be healed. For I am a man under authority, having soldiers under me: and I say to this man, Go, and he goeth; and to another, Come, and he cometh; and to my servant, Do this, and he doeth it." Verse 7; Matthew 8:8, 9.

"I represent the power of Rome, and my soldiers recognize my authority as supreme. So dost Thou represent the power of the infinite God, and all created things obey Thy word. Thou canst command the disease to depart, and it shall obey Thee. Speak but the word, and my servant shall be healed."

"As thou hast believed," Christ said, "so be it done unto thee. And his servant was healed in the selfsame hour." Verse 13.

The Jewish elders had commended the centurion to Christ because of the favour he had shown to "our nation." He is worthy, they said, for "he hath built us a synagogue." But the centurion said of himself, "I am not worthy." Yet he did not fear to ask help from Jesus. Not to his own goodness did he trust, but to the Saviour's mercy. His only argument was his great need.

In the same way every human being can come to Christ. "Not by works of righteousness which we have done, but according to His mercy He saved us." Titus 3:5. Do you feel that because you are a sinner you cannot hope to receive blessing from God? Remember that Christ came into the world to save sinners. We have nothing to recommend us to God; the plea that we may urge now and ever is our utterly helpless condition, which makes His redeeming power a necessity. Renouncing all self-dependence, we may look to the cross of Calvary and say:

> "In my hand no price I bring;
> Simply to Thy cross I cling."

"If thou canst believe, all things are possible to him that believeth." Mark 9:23. It is faith that connects us with heaven and brings us strength for coping with the powers of darkness. In Christ, God has provided means for subduing every evil trait and resisting every temptation, however strong. But many feel that they lack faith, and therefore they remain away from Christ. Let these souls, in their helpless unworthiness, cast themselves upon the mercy of their compassionate Saviour. Look not to self, but to Christ. He who healed the sick and cast out demons when He walked among men is still the same mighty Redeemer. Then grasp His promises as leaves from the tree of life: "Him that cometh to Me I will in no wise cast out." John 6:37. As you come to Him, believe that He accepts you, because He has promised. You can never perish while you do this — never.

"God commendeth His love toward us, in that, while we were yet sinners, Christ died for us." Romans 5:8.

And "if God be for us, who can be against us? He that spared not His own Son, but delivered Him up for us all, how shall He not with Him also freely give us all things?" Romans 8:31, 32.

"I am persuaded, that neither death, nor life, nor angels, nor principalities, nor things present, nor things to come, nor powers, nor height, nor depth, nor any other creation, shall be able to separate us from the love of God, which is in Christ Jesus our Lord." Verses 38, 39, ARV, margin.

"Thou Canst Make Me Clean."

Of all the diseases known in the East the leprosy was most dreaded. Its incurable and contagious character, and its horrible effect upon its victims, filled the bravest with fear. Among the Jews it was regarded as a judgement on account of sin, and hence was called "the stroke," "the finger of God." Deep-rooted, ineradicable, deadly, it was looked upon as a symbol of sin.

By the ritual law the leper was pronounced unclean. Whatever he touched was unclean. The air was polluted by his breath. Like one already dead, he was shut out from the habitations of men. One who was suspected of having the disease must present himself to the priests, who were to examine and decide his case. If pronounced a leper, he was isolated from his family, cut off from the congregation of Israel, and doomed to associate with those only who were similarly afflicted. Even kings and rulers were not exempt. A monarch attacked by this terrible disease must yield up the sceptre and flee from society.

Away from his friends and his kindred the leper must bear the curse of his malady. He was obliged to publish his own calamity, to rend his garments, and sound the alarm, warning all to flee from his contaminating presence. The cry, "Unclean! unclean!" coming in mournful tones from the lonely exile, was a signal heard with fear and abhorrence.

In the region of Christ's ministry were many of these sufferers, and as the news of His work reached them, there is one in whose heart faith begins to spring up. If he could go to Jesus he might be healed. But how can he find Jesus? Doomed as he is to perpetual isolation, how can he present himself to the Healer? And will Christ heal him? Will He not, like the Pharisees, and even the physicians pronounce a curse upon him and warn him to flee from the haunts of men?

He thinks of all that has been told him of Jesus. Not one who has sought His help has been turned away. The wretched man determines to find the Saviour. Though shut out from the cities, it may be that he can cross His path in some byway along the mountain roads, or find Him as He is teaching outside the towns. The difficulties are great, but this is his only hope.

Standing afar off, the leper catches a few words from the Saviour's lips. He sees Him laying His hands upon the sick. He sees the lame, the blind, the paralytic, and those dying of various maladies rise up in health, praising God for deliverance. His faith strengthens. Nearer and yet nearer he approaches to the listening throng. The restrictions laid upon him, the safety of the people, the fear with which all men regard him, are alike forgotten. He thinks only of the blessed hope of healing.

He is a loathsome spectacle. The disease has made frightful inroads, and his decaying body is horrible to look upon. At sight of him the people fall back. In their terror they crowd upon one another to escape from contact with him. Some try to prevent him from approaching Jesus, but in vain. He neither sees nor hears them. Their expressions of loathing are lost upon him. He sees only the Son of God, he hears only the voice that speaks life to the dying.

Pressing to Jesus, he casts himself at His feet with the cry, "Lord, if Thou wilt, Thou canst make me clean."

Jesus replies, "I will; be thou clean," and lays His hand upon him. Matthew 8:2, 3.

Immediately a change passes over the leper. His blood becomes healthy, the nerves sensitive, the muscles firm. The unnaturally white, scaly surface peculiar to leprosy disappears; and his flesh becomes as the flesh of a little child.

Should the priests learn the facts concerning the healing of the leper, their hatred of Christ might lead them to render a dishonest sentence. Jesus desired that an impartial decision be secured. He therefore bids the man tell no one of the cure, but without delay present himself at the temple with an offering before any rumours concerning the miracle should be spread abroad. Before the priests could accept such an offering, they were required to examine the offerer and certify his complete recovery.

This examination was made. The priests who had condemned the leper to banishment testified to his cure. The healed man was restored to his home and society. He felt that the boon of health was very precious. He rejoiced in the vigour of manhood and in his restoration to his family. Notwithstanding the caution of Jesus, he could no longer conceal the fact of his cure, and joyfully he went about proclaiming the power of the One who had made him whole.

When this man came to Jesus, he was "full of leprosy," Its deadly poison permeated his whole body. The disciples sought to prevent their Master from touching him; for he who touched a leper became himself unclean. But in laying His hand upon the leper, Jesus received no defilement. The leprosy was cleansed. Thus it is with the leprosy of sin — deep-rooted, deadly, impossible to be cleansed by human power. "The whole head is sick, and the whole heart faint. From the sole of the foot even unto the head there is no soundness in it; but wounds, and bruises, and putrefying sores." Isaiah 1:5, 6. But Jesus, coming to dwell in humanity, receives no pollution. His presence was healing virtue for the sinner. Whoever will fall at His feet, saying in faith, "Lord, if Thou wilt, Thou canst make me clean," shall hear the answer, "I will; be thou clean."

In some instances of healing, Jesus did not at once grant the blessing sought. But in the case of leprosy no sooner was the appeal made than it was granted. When we pray for earthly blessings, the answer to our prayer may be delayed, or God may give us something other than we ask; but not so when we ask for deliverance from sin. It is His will to cleanse us from sin, to make us His children, and to enable us to live a holy life. Christ "gave Himself for our sins, that He might deliver us from this present evil world, according to the will of God and our Father." Galatians 1:4. "And this is the confidence that we have in Him, that, if we ask anything according to His will, He heareth us: and if we know that He hear us, whatsoever we ask, we know that we have the petitions that we desired of him." 1 John 5:14, 15.

Jesus looked upon the distressed and heart-burdened those whose hopes were blighted, and who with earthly joys were seeking to quiet the longing of the soul, and He invited all to find rest in Him.

"Ye Shall Find Rest."

Tenderly He bade the toiling people, "Take My yoke upon you, and learn of Me; for I am meek and lowly in heart: and ye shall find rest unto your souls." Matthew 11:29.

In these words, Christ was speaking to every human being. Whether they know it or not, all are weary and heavy-laden. All are weighed down with burdens that only Christ can remove. The heaviest burden that we bear is the burden of sin. If we were left to bear this burden, it would crush us. But the Sinless One has taken our place. "The Lord hath laid on Him the iniquity of us all." Isaiah 53:6.

He has borne the burden of our guilt. He will take the load from our weary shoulders. He will give us rest. The burden of care and sorrow also He will bear. He invites us to cast all our care upon Him; for He carries us upon His heart.

The Elder Brother of our race is by the eternal throne. He looks upon every soul who is turning his face toward Him as the Saviour. He knows by experience what are the weaknesses of humanity, what are our wants, and where lies the strength of our temptations; for He was "in all points tempted like as we are, yet without sin." Hebrews 4:15. He is watching over you, trembling child of God. Are you tempted? He will deliver. Are you weak? He will strengthen. Are you ignorant? He will enlighten. Are you wounded? He will heal. The Lord "telleth the number of the stars;" and yet "He healeth the broken in heart, and bindeth up their wounds." Psalm 147:4, 3.

Whatever your anxieties and trials, spread out your case before the Lord. Your spirit will be braced for endurance. The way will be open for you to disentangle yourself from embarrassment and difficulty. The weaker and more helpless you know yourself to be, the stronger will you become in His strength. The heavier your burdens, the more blessed the rest in casting them upon your Burden Bearer.

Circumstances may separate friends; the restless waters of the wide sea may roll between us and them. But no circumstances, no distance, can separate us from the Saviour. Wherever we may be, He is at our right hand, to support, maintain, uphold, and cheer. Greater than the love of a mother for her child is Christ's love for His redeemed. It is our privilege to rest in His love, to say, "I will trust Him; for He gave His life for me."

Human love may change, but Christ's love knows no change. When we cry to Him for help, His hand is stretched out to save.

"The mountains may depart,
And the hills be removed;
But My loving-kindness shall not depart from thee,
Neither shall My covenant of peace be removed,
Saith Jehovah that hath mercy on thee."
Isaiah 54:10, ARV.

Healing of the Soul

Many of those who came to Christ for help had brought disease upon themselves, yet He did not refuse to heal them. And when virtue from Him entered into these souls, they were convicted of sin, and many were healed of their spiritual disease as well as of their physical maladies.

Among these was the paralytic at Capernaum. Like the leper, this paralytic had lost all hope of recovery. His disease was the result of a sinful life, and his sufferings were embittered by remorse. In vain he had appealed to the Pharisees and doctors for relief; they pronounced him incurable, they denounced him as a sinner and declared that he would die under the wrath of God.

The palsied man had sunk into despair. Then he heard of the works of Jesus. Others, as sinful and helpless as he, had been healed, and he was encouraged to believe that he, too, might be cured if he could be carried to the Saviour. But hope fell as he remembered the cause of his malady, yet he could not cast away the possibility of healing.

His great desire was relief from the burden of sin. He longed to see Jesus and receive the assurance of forgiveness and peace with heaven. Then he would be content to live or to die, according to God's will.

There was no time to lose; already his wasted flesh bore signs of death. He besought his friends to carry him on his bed to Jesus, and this they gladly undertook to do. But so dense was the crowd that had assembled in and about the house where the Saviour was, that it was impossible for the sick man and his friends to reach Him, or even to come within hearing of His voice. Jesus was teaching in the home of Peter. According to their custom, His disciples sat close about Him, and "there were Pharisees and doctors of the law sitting by, who were come out of every village of Galilee and Judea and Jerusalem." Luke 5:17, ARV. Many of these had come as spies, seeking an accusation against Jesus. Beyond these thronged the promiscuous multitude, the eager, the reverent, the curious, and the unbelieving. Different nationalities and all grades of society were represented. "And the power of the Lord was present to heal." Verse 17. The Spirit of life brooded over the assembly, but Pharisees and doctors did not discern His presence. They felt no sense of need, and the healing was not for them. "He hath filled the hungry with good things; and the rich He hath sent empty away." Luke 1:53.

Again and again the bearers of the paralytic tried to push their way through the crowd, but in vain. The sick man looked about him in unutterable anguish. How could he relinquish hope when the longed-for help was so near? At his suggestion his friends bore him to the top of the house and, breaking up the roof, let him down at the feet of Jesus.

The discourse was interrupted. The Saviour looked upon the mournful countenance and saw the pleading eyes fixed upon Him. Well He knew the longing of that burdened soul. It was Christ who had brought conviction to his conscience when he was yet at home. When he repented of his sins and believed in the power of Jesus to make him whole, the mercy of the Saviour had blessed his heart. Jesus had watched the first glimmer of faith grow into a conviction that He was the sinner's only helper, and had seen it grow stronger with every effort to come into His presence. It was Christ who had drawn the sufferer to Himself. Now, in words that fell like music on the listener's ear, the Saviour said, "Son, be of good cheer; thy sins be forgiven thee." Matthew 9:2.

The burden of guilt rolls from the sick man's soul. He

cannot doubt. Christ's words reveal His power to read the heart. Who can deny His power to forgive sins? Hope takes the place of despair, and joy of oppressive gloom. The man's physical pain is gone, and his whole being is transformed. Making no further request, he lay in peaceful silence, too happy for words.

Many were watching with breathless interest every movement in this strange transaction. Many felt that Christ's words were an invitation to them. Were they not soul-sick because of sin? Were they not anxious to be freed from this burden?

But the Pharisees, fearful of losing their influence with the multitude, said in their hearts, "He blasphemeth: who can forgive sins but One, even God?" Mark 2:7, RV.

Fixing His glance upon them, beneath which they cowered and drew back, Jesus said, "Wherefore think ye evil in your hearts? For whether is easier, to say, Thy sins be forgiven thee; or to say, Arise, and walk? But that ye may know that the Son of man hath power on earth to forgive sins," He said, turning to the paralytic, "Arise, take up thy bed, and go unto thine house." Matthew 9:4-6.

Then he who had been borne on a litter to Jesus rose to his feet with the elasticity and strength of youth. And immediately he "took up the bed, and went forth before them all; insomuch that they were all amazed, and glorified God, saying, We never saw it on this fashion." Mark 2:12.

It required nothing less than creative power to restore health to that decaying body. The same voice that spoke life to man created from the dust of the earth, had spoken life to the dying paralytic. And the same power that gave life to the body had renewed the heart. He who at creation "spake, and it was," who "commanded, and it stood fast" (Psalm 33:9), had spoken life to the soul dead in trespasses and sins. The healing of the body was an evidence of the power that had renewed the heart. Christ bade the paralytic arise and walk, "that ye may know," He said, "that the Son of man hath power on earth to forgive sins."

The paralytic found in Christ healing for both the soul and the body. He needed health of soul before he could appreciate health of body. Before the physical malady could be healed, Christ must bring relief to the mind, and cleanse the soul from sin. This lesson should not be overlooked. There are today thousands suffering from physical disease who, like the paralytic, are longing for the message, "Thy sins are forgiven." The burden of sin, with its unrest and unsatisfied desires, is the foundation of their maladies. They can find no relief until they come to the Healer of the soul. The peace which He alone can impart would restore vigour to the mind and health to the body.

The effect produced upon the people by the healing of the paralytic was as if heaven had opened and revealed the glories of the better world. As the man who had been cured passed through the throng, blessing God at every step and bearing his burden as if it were a feather's weight, the people fell back to give him room and with awe-stricken faces gazed upon him, whispering softly among themselves, "We have seen strange things today." Luke 5:26.

In the home of the paralytic there was great rejoicing when he returned to his family, carrying with ease the couch upon which he had been slowly borne from their presence but a short time before. They gathered round with tears of joy, hardly daring to believe their eyes. He stood before them in the full vigour of manhood. Those arms that they had seen lifeless were quick to obey his will. The flesh that had been shrunken and leaden-hued was now fresh and ruddy. He walked with a firm, free step. Joy and hope were written in every lineament of his countenance, and an expression of purity and peace had taken the place of the marks of sin and suffering. Glad thanksgiving went up from that home, and God was glorified through His Son, who had restored hope to the hopeless and strength to the stricken one. This man and his family were ready to lay down their lives for Jesus. No doubt dimmed their faith, no unbelief marred their fealty to Him who had brought light into their darkened home.

> "Bless the Lord, O my soul:
> And all that is within me, bless His holy name.
> Bless the Lord, O my soul,
> And forget not all His benefits:
> Who forgiveth all thine iniquities;
> Who healeth all thy diseases;
> Who redeemeth thy life from destruction; . . .
> So that thy youth is renewed like the eagle's.
> The Lord executeth righteousness
> And judgement for all that are oppressed. . . .
> He hath not dealt with us after our sins;
> Nor rewarded us according to our iniquities. . . .
> Like as a father pitieth his children,
> So the Lord pitieth them that fear Him.
> For He knoweth our frame;
> He remembereth that we are dust."
> Psalm 103:1-14.

"Wilt Thou Be Made Whole?"

"Now there is at Jerusalem by the sheep market a pool, which is called in the Hebrew tongue Bethesda, having five porches. In these lay a great multitude of impotent folk, of blind, halt, withered, waiting for the moving of the water." John 5:2, 3.

At certain seasons the waters of this pool were agitated, and it was commonly believed that this was the result of supernatural power, and that whoever first after the troubling of the pool stepped into the waters, would be healed of whatever disease he might have. Hundreds of sufferers visited the place; but so great was the crowd when the water was troubled that they rushed forward, trampling underfoot men, women, and children, weaker than themselves. Many could not get near the pool. Many who had succeeded in reaching it died upon its bank. Shelters had been erected about the place, that the sick might be protected from the heat by the day and the chilliness of the night. There were some who spent the night in these porches, creeping to the edge of the pool day after day, in the vain hope of relief.

Jesus was at Jerusalem. Walking alone in apparent meditation and prayer, He came to the pool. He saw the wretched sufferers watching for that which they supposed to be their only chance of cure. He longed to exercise His healing power and make every sufferer whole. But it was the Sabbath day. Multitudes were going to the temple for worship, and He knew that such an act of healing would so excite the prejudice of the Jews as to cut short His work.

But the Saviour saw one case of supreme wretchedness. It was that of a man who had been a helpless cripple for thirty-eight years. His disease was in a great degree the result of his own evil habits and was looked upon as a judgement from God. Alone and friendless, feeling that he was shut out from God's mercy, the sufferer had passed long years of misery. At the time when it was expected that the water would be troubled, those who pitied his helplessness would bear him to the porches. But at the favoured moment he had no one to help him in. He had seen the rippling of the water, but had never been able to get farther than the edge of the pool. Others stronger than he would plunge in before him. The poor, helpless sufferer was unable to contend successfully with the scrambling, selfish crowd. His persistent efforts toward the one object, and his anxiety and continual disappointment, were fast wearing away the remnant of his strength.

The sick man was lying on his mat and occasionally lifting his head to gaze at the pool, when a tender, compassionate face bent over him, and the words, "Wilt thou be made whole?" arrested his attention. Hope came to his heart. He felt that in some way he was to have help. But the glow of encouragement soon faded. He remembered how often he had tried to reach the pool, and now he had little prospect of living till it should again be troubled. He turned away wearily, saying, "Sir, I have no man, when the water is troubled, to put me into the pool: but while I am coming, another steppeth down before me."

Jesus bids him, "Rise, take up thy bed, and walk." Verses 6-8. With a new hope the sick man looks upon Jesus. The expression of His countenance, the tones of His voice, are like no other. Love and power seem to breathe from His very presence. The cripple's faith takes hold upon Christ's word. Without question he sets his will to obey, and, as he does this, his whole body responds.

Every nerve and muscle thrills with new life, and healthful action comes to his crippled limbs. Springing to his feet, he goes on his way with firm, free step, praising God and rejoicing in his new-found strength.

Jesus had given the palsied man no assurance of divine help. The man might have said, "Lord, if Thou wilt make me whole, I will obey Thy word." He might have stopped to doubt, and thus have lost his one chance of healing. But no, he believed Christ's word, believed that he was made whole; immediately he made the effort, and God gave him the power; he willed to walk, and he did walk. Acting on the word of Christ, he was made whole.

By sin we have been severed from the life of God. Our souls are palsied. Of ourselves we are no more capable of living a holy life than was the impotent man capable of walking. Many realize their helplessness; they are longing for that spiritual life which will bring them into harmony with God, and are striving to obtain it. But in vain. In despair they cry, "O wretched man that I am! who shall deliver me from this body of death?" Romans 7:24, margin. Let these desponding, struggling ones look up. The Saviour is bending over the purchase of His blood, saying with inexpressible tenderness and pity, "Wilt thou be made whole?" He bids you arise in health and peace. Do not wait to feel that you are made whole. Believe the Saviour's word. Put your will on the side of Christ. Will to serve Him, and in acting upon His word you will receive strength. Whatever may be the evil practice, the master passion which through long indulgence binds both soul and body, Christ is able and longs to deliver. He will impart life to the soul that is "dead in trespasses." Ephesians 2:1. He will set free the captive that is held by weakness and misfortune and the chains of sin.

The sense of sin has poisoned the springs of life. But Christ says, "I will take your sins; I will give you peace. I have bought you with My blood. You are Mine. My grace shall strengthen your weakened will; your remorse for sin I will remove." When temptations assail you, when care and perplexity surround you, when, depressed and discouraged, you are ready to yield to despair, look to Jesus, and the darkness that encompasses you will be dispelled by the bright shining of His presence. When sin struggles for the mastery in your soul, and burdens the conscience, look to the Saviour. His grace is sufficient to subdue sin. Let your grateful heart, trembling with uncertainty, turn to Him. Lay hold on the hope set before you. Christ waits to adopt you into His family. His strength will help your weakness; He will lead you step by step. Place your hand in His, and let Him guide you.

Never feel that Christ is far away. He is always near. His loving presence surrounds you. Seek Him as One who desires to be found of you. He desires you not only to touch His garments, but to walk with Him in constant communion.

"Go, and Sin No More."

The Feast of Tabernacles had just ended. The priests and rabbis at Jerusalem had been defeated in their plottings against Jesus, and, as evening fell, "every man went unto his own house. Jesus went unto the Mount of Olives." John 7:53; 8:1.

From the excitement and confusion of the city, from the eager crowds and the treacherous rabbis, Jesus turned away to the quiet of the olive groves, where He could be alone with God. But in the early morning He returned to the temple; and as the people gathered about Him, He sat down and taught them.

He was soon interrupted. A group of Pharisees and scribes approached Him, dragging with them a terror-stricken woman, whom with hard, eager voices they accused of having violated the seventh commandment. Pushing her into the presence of Jesus, they said, with a hypocritical display of respect, "Master, this woman was taken in adultery, in the very act. Now Moses in the law commanded us, that such should be stoned: but what sayest Thou?" Verses 4, 5.

Their pretended reverence veiled a deep-laid plot for His ruin. Should Jesus acquit the woman, He might be charged with despising the law of Moses. Should He declare her worthy of death, He could be accused to the Romans as one who assumed authority belonging only to them.

Jesus looked upon the scene — the trembling victim in her shame, the hard-faced dignitaries, devoid of even human pity. His spirit of stainless purity shrank from the spectacle. Giving no sign that He had heard the question, He stooped and, fixing His eyes upon the ground, began to write in the dust.

Impatient at His delay and apparent indifference the accusers drew nearer, urging the matter upon His attention. But as their eyes, following those of Jesus, fell upon the pavement at His feet, their voices were silenced. There, traced before them, were the guilty secrets of their own lives.

Rising, and fixing His eyes upon the plotting elders, Jesus said, "He that is without sin among *you,* let him first cast a stone at her." Verse 7. And, stooping down, He continued writing.

He had not set aside the Mosaic law nor infringed upon the authority of Rome. The accusers were defeated. Now, their robes of pretended holiness torn from them, they stood, guilty and condemned, in the presence of infinite purity. Trembling lest the hidden iniquity of their lives should be laid open to the multitude, with bowed heads and downcast eyes they stole away, leaving their victim with the pitying Saviour.

Jesus arose and, looking upon the woman, said, "Where are those thine accusers? hath no man condemned thee? She said, No man, Lord. And Jesus said unto her, Neither do I condemn thee: go, and sin no more." Verses 10, 11.

The woman had stood before Jesus, cowering with fear. His words, "He that is without sin among you, let him first cast a stone," had come to her as a death sentence. She dared not lift her eyes to the Saviour's face, but silently awaited her doom. In astonishment she saw her accusers depart speechless and confounded; then those words of hope fell upon her ear, "Neither do I condemn thee: go, and sin no more." Her heart was melted, and, casting herself at the feet of Jesus, she sobbed out her grateful love and with bitter tears confessed her sins.

This was to her the beginning of a new life, a life of purity and peace, devoted to God. In the uplifting of this fallen soul, Jesus performed a greater miracle than in healing the most grievous physical disease; He cured the spiritual malady which is unto death everlasting. This penitent woman became one of His most steadfast followers. With self-sacrificing love and devotion she showed her gratitude for His forgiving mercy. For this erring woman the world had only contempt and scorn, but the Sinless One pitied her weakness and reached to her a helping hand. While the hypocritical Pharisees denounced, Jesus bade her, "Go, and sin no more."

Jesus knows the circumstances of every soul. The greater the sinner's guilt, the more he needs the Saviour. His heart of divine love and sympathy is drawn out most of all for the one who is the most hopelessly entangled in the snares of the enemy. With His own blood He has signed the emancipation papers of the race.

Jesus does not desire those who have been purchased at such a cost to become the sport of the enemy's temptations. He does not desire us to be overcome and perish. He who curbed the lions in their den, and walked with His faithful witnesses amid the fiery flames, is just as ready to work in our behalf to subdue every evil in our nature. Today He is standing at the altar of mercy, presenting before God the prayers of those who desire His help. He turns no weeping, contrite one away. Freely will He pardon all who come to Him for forgiveness and restoration. He does not tell to any all that He might reveal, but He bids every trembling soul take courage. Whosoever will, may take hold of God's strength, and make peace with Him, and He will make peace.

The souls that turn to Him for refuge, Jesus lifts above the accusing and the strife of tongues. No man or evil angel can impeach these souls. Christ unites them to His own divine-human nature. They stand besides the great Sin Bearer in the light proceeding from the throne of God.

The blood of Jesus Christ cleanses "from all sin." 1 John 1:7.

"Who shall lay anything to the charge of God's elect? It is God that justifieth. Who is he that condemneth? It is Christ that died, yea rather, that is risen again, who is even at the right hand of God, who also maketh intercession for us." Romans 8:33, 34.

Over the winds and the waves, and over men possessed of demons, Christ showed that He had absolute control. He who stilled the tempest and calmed the troubled sea spoke peace to minds distracted and overborne by Satan.

In the synagogue at Capernaum, Jesus was speaking of His mission to set free the slaves of sin. He was interrupted by a shriek of terror. A madman rushed forward from among the people, crying out, "Let us alone; what have we to do with Thee, Thou Jesus of Nazareth? art Thou come to destroy us? I know Thee who Thou art, the Holy One of God." Mark 1:24.

Jesus rebuked the demon, saying, "Hold thy peace, and come out of him. And when the devil had thrown him in the midst, he came out of him, and hurt him not." Luke 4:35.

The cause of this man's affliction also was in his own

life. He had been fascinated with the pleasures of sin and had thought to make life a grand carnival. Intemperance and frivolity perverted the noble attributes of his nature, and Satan took entire control of him. Remorse came too late. When he would have sacrificed wealth and pleasure to regain his lost manhood he had become helpless in the grasp of the evil one.

In the Saviour's presence he was roused to long for freedom, but the demon resisted the power of Christ. When the man tried to appeal to Jesus for help, the evil spirit put words into his mouth, and he cried out in an agony of fear. The demoniac partially comprehended that he was in the presence of One who could set him free; but when he tried to come within reach of that mighty hand, another's will held him, another's words found utterance through him.

The conflict between the power of Satan and his own desire for freedom was terrible. It seemed that the tortured man must lose his life in the struggle with the foe that had been the ruin of his manhood. But the Saviour spoke with authority and set the captive free. The man who had been possessed stood before the wondering people in the freedom of self-possession.

With glad voice he praised God for deliverance. The eye that had so lately glared with the fire of insanity now beamed with intelligence and overflowed with grateful tears. The people were dumb with amazement. As soon as they recovered speech they exclaimed one to another, "What is this? a new teaching! with authority He commandeth even the unclean spirits, and they obey Him." Mark 1:27, RV.

There are multitudes today as truly under the power of evil spirits as was the demoniac of Capernaum. All who wilfully depart from God's commandments are placing themselves under the control of Satan. Many a man tampers with evil, thinking that he can break away at pleasure; but he is lured on and on, until he finds himself controlled by a will stronger than his own. He cannot escape its mysterious power. Secret sin or master passion may hold him a captive as helpless as was the demoniac of Capernaum.

Yet his condition is not hopeless. God does not control our minds without our consent; but every man is free to choose what power he will have to rule over him. None have fallen so low, none are so vile, but that they may find deliverance in Christ. The demoniac, in place of prayer, could utter only the words of Satan; yet the heart's unspoken appeal was heard. No cry from a soul in need, though it fail of utterance in words, will be unheeded. Those who consent to enter into covenant with God are not left to the power of Satan or to the infirmity of their own nature.

"Shall the prey be taken from the mighty, or the lawful captive delivered? . . . Thus saith the Lord, Even the captives of the mighty shall be taken away, and the prey of the terrible shall be delivered: for I will contend with him that contendeth with thee, and I will save thy children." Isaiah 49:24, 25.

Marvellous will be the transformation wrought in him who by faith opens the door of the heart to the Saviour.

"I Give Unto You Power."

Like the twelve apostles, the seventy disciples whom Christ sent forth later received supernatural endowments as a seal of their mission. When their work was completed, they returned with joy, saying, "Lord, even the devils are subject unto us through Thy name." Jesus answered, "I beheld Satan as lightning fall from heaven." Luke 10:17, 18.

Henceforth Christ's followers are to look upon Satan as a conquered foe. Upon the cross, Jesus was to gain the victory for them; that victory He desired them to accept as their own. "Behold," He said, "I give unto you power to tread on serpents and scorpions, and over all the power of the enemy: and nothing shall by any means hurt you." Verse 19.

The omnipotent power of the Holy Spirit is the defence of every contrite soul. No one who in penitence and faith has claimed His protection will Christ permit to pass under the enemy's power. It is true that Satan is a powerful being; but, thank God, we have a mighty Saviour, who cast out the evil one from heaven. Satan is pleased when we magnify his power. Why not talk of Jesus? Why not magnify His power and His love?

The rainbow of promise encircling the throne on high is an everlasting testimony that "God so loved the world, that He gave His only-begotten Son, that whosoever believeth in Him should not perish, but have everlasting life." John 3:16. It testifies to the universe that God will never forsake His children in the struggle with evil. It is an assurance to us of strength and protection as long as the throne itself shall endure.

Saved to Serve

It is morning on the Sea of Galilee. Jesus and His disciples have come to shore after a tempestuous night on the water, and the light of the rising sun touches sea and land as with the benediction of peace. But as they step upon the beach they are greeted with a sight more terrible than the storm-tossed sea. From some hiding place among the tombs two madmen rush upon them as if to tear them in pieces. Hanging about these men are parts of chains which they have broken in escaping from confinement. Their flesh is torn and bleeding, their eyes glare out from their long and matted hair, the very likeness of humanity seems to have been blotted out. They look more like wild beasts than like men.

The disciples and their companions flee in terror; but presently they notice that Jesus is not with them, and they turn to look for Him. He is standing where they left Him. He who stilled the tempest, who has before met Satan and conquered him, does not flee before these demons. When the men, gnashing their teeth and foaming at the mouth, approach Him, Jesus raises that hand which has beckoned the waves to rest, and the men can come no nearer. They stand before Him, raging but helpless.

With authority He bids the unclean spirits come out of them. The unfortunate men realize that One is near who can save them from the tormenting demons. They fall at the Saviour's feet to entreat His mercy; but when their lips are opened, the demons speak through them, crying, "What have we to do with Thee, Jesus,

Thou Son of God? art Thou come hither to torment us?" Matthew 8:29.

The evil spirits are forced to release their victims, and a wonderful change comes over the demoniacs. Light shines into their minds. Their eyes beam with intelligence. The countenances so long deformed into the image of Satan become suddenly mild, the bloodstained hands are quiet, and the men lift their voices in praise to God.

Meanwhile the demons, cast out from their human habitation, have entered into the swine and driven them to destruction. The keepers of the swine hurry away to publish the news, and the whole population flock to meet Jesus. The two demoniacs have been the terror of the country. Now these men are clothed and in their right mind, sitting at the feet of Jesus, listening to His words, and glorifying the name of Him who has made them whole. But those who behold this wonderful scene do not rejoice. The loss of the swine seems to them of greater moment than the deliverance of these captives of Satan. In terror they throng about Jesus, beseeching Him to depart from them, and He complies, taking ship at once for the opposite shore.

Far different is the feeling of the restored demoniacs. They desire the companionship of their Deliverer. In His presence they feel secure from the demons that have tormented their lives and wasted their manhood. As Jesus is about to enter the boat they keep close to His side, kneel at His feet, and beg to remain near Him, where they may listen to His words. But Jesus bids them go home and tell what great things the Lord has done for them.

Here is a work for them to do — to go to a heathen home and tell of the blessings they have received from Jesus. It is hard for them to be separated from the Saviour. Great difficulties will beset them in association with their heathen countrymen. And their long isolation from society seems to have disqualified them for this work. But as soon as He points out their duty, they are ready to obey.

Not only did they tell their own households and neighbours about Jesus, but they went throughout Decapolis, everywhere declaring His power to save and describing how He had freed them from the demons.

Though the people of Gergesa had not received Jesus, He did not leave them to the darkness they had chosen. When they bade Him depart from them, they had not heard His words. They were ignorant of that which they were rejecting. Therefore He sent the light to them, and by those to whom they would not refuse to listen.

In causing the destruction of the swine, it was Satan's purpose to turn the people away from the Saviour and prevent the preaching of the gospel in that region. But this very occurrence roused the country as nothing else could have done, and directed attention to Christ. Though the Saviour Himself departed, the men whom He had healed remained as witnesses to His power. Those who had been mediums of the prince of darkness became channels of light, messengers of the Son of God. When Jesus returned to Decapolis, the people flocked about Him, and for three days thousands from all the surrounding country heard the message of salvation.

The two restored demoniacs were the first missionaries whom Christ sent to teach the gospel in the region of Decapolis. For a short time only, these men had listened to His words. Not one sermon from His lips had ever fallen upon their ears. They could not instruct the people as the disciples who had been daily with Christ were able to do. But they could tell what they knew; what they themselves had seen, and heard, and felt of the Saviour's power. This is what everyone can do whose heart has been touched by the grace of God. This is the witness for which our Lord calls, and for want of which the world is perishing.

The gospel is to be presented, not as a lifeless theory, but as a living force to change the life. God would have His servants bear testimony to the fact that through His grace men may possess Christlikeness of character and may rejoice in the assurance of His great love. He would have us bear testimony to the fact that He cannot be satisfied until all who will accept salvation are reclaimed and reinstated in their holy privileges as His sons and daughters.

Even those whose course has been most offensive to Him He freely accepts. When they repent, He imparts to them His divine Spirit, and sends them forth into the camp of the disloyal to proclaim His mercy. Souls that have been degraded into instruments of Satan are still, through the power of Christ, transformed into messengers of righteousness and are sent forth to tell how great things the Lord hath done for them and hath had compassion on them.

"My Praise Shall Be Continually of Thee."

After the woman of Capernaum had been healed by the touch of faith, Jesus desired her to acknowledge the blessing she had received. The gifts which the gospel offers are not to be secured by stealth or enjoyed in secret

> "Ye are My witnesses, saith the Lord,
> That I am God."
>
> Isaiah 43:12.

Our confession of His faithfulness is Heaven's chosen agency for revealing Christ to the world. We are to acknowledge His grace as made known through the holy men of old; but that which will be most effectual is the testimony of our own experience. We are witnesses for God as we reveal in ourselves the working of a power that is divine. Every individual has a life distinct from all others, and an experience differing essentially from theirs. God desires that our praise shall ascend to Him, marked with our own individuality. These precious acknowledgements to the praise of the glory of His grace, when supported by a Christlike life, have an irresistible power that works for the salvation of souls.

It is for our own benefit to keep every gift of God fresh in our memory. By this means faith is strengthened to claim and to receive more and more. There is greater encouragement for us in the least blessing we ourselves receive from God than in all the accounts we can read of the faith and experience of others. The soul that responds to the grace of God shall be like a watered garden. His health shall spring forth speedily; his light shall rise in obscurity, and the glory of the Lord shall be seen upon him.

"What shall I render unto the Lord
For all His benefits toward me?
I will take the cup of salvation,
And call upon the name of the Lord.
I will pay my vows unto the Lord,
Yea, in the presence of all His people."

"I will sing unto the Lord as long as I live:
I will sing praise to my God while I have my being.
My meditation of Him shall be sweet:
I will be glad in the Lord."

"Who can utter the mighty acts of the Lord?
Who can show forth all His praise?"

"Call upon His name;
Make known among the peoples His doings.
Sing unto Him, sing praises unto Him:"
"Talk ye of all His wondrous works.
Glory ye in His holy name:
Let the heart of them rejoice that seek the Lord."

"Because Thy loving-kindness is better than life,
My lips shall praise Thee. . . .
My soul shall be satisfied as with marrow and fatness;
And my mouth shall praise Thee with joyful lips;
When I remember Thee upon my bed,
And meditate on Thee in the night watches.
For Thou hast been my help,
And in the shadow of Thy wings will I rejoice."

"In God have I put my trust, I will not be afraid;
What can man do unto me?
Thy vows are upon me, O God:
I will render thank offerings unto Thee.
For Thou hast delivered my soul from death:
Hast Thou not delivered my feet from falling,
That I may walk before God in the light of the living?"

"O Thou Holy One of Israel.
My lips shall greatly rejoice when I sing unto Thee;
And my soul, which Thou hast redeemed.

My tongue also shall talk of Thy righteousness all
the day long."

"Thou art my trust from my youth. . . .
My praise shall be continually of Thee."
"I will make Thy name to be remembered: . . .
Therefore shall the people praise Thee."

Psalms 116:12-14, RV; 104:33, 34; 106:2; 105:1, 2 (ARV), 2, 3; 63:3-7, ARV; 56:11-13, ARV; 71:22-24, 5, 6; 45:17.

"Freely Ye Have Received, Freely Give."

The gospel invitation is not to be narrowed down and presented only to a select few, who, we suppose, will do us honour if they accept it. The message is to be given to all. When God blesses His children, it is not alone for their own sake, but for the world's sake. As He bestows His gifts on us, it is that we may multiply them by imparting.

The Samaritan woman who talked with Jesus at Jacob's well had no sooner found the Saviour than she brought others to Him. She proved herself a more effective missionary than His own disciples. The disciples saw nothing in Samaria to indicate that it was an encouraging field. Their thoughts were fixed upon a great work to be done in the future. They did not see that right around them was a harvest to be gathered. But through the woman whom they despised a whole cityful were brought to hear Jesus. She carried the light at once to her countrymen.

This woman represents the working of a practical faith in Christ. Every true disciple is born into the kingdom of God as a missionary. No sooner does he come to know the Saviour than he desires to make others acquainted with Him. The saving and sanctifying truth cannot be shut up in his heart. He who drinks of the living water becomes a fountain of life. The receiver becomes a giver. The grace of Christ in the soul is like a spring in the desert, welling up to refresh all, and making those who are ready to perish eager to drink of the water of life. In doing this work a greater blessing is received than if we work merely to benefit ourselves. It is in working to spread the good news of salvation that we are brought near to the Saviour.

Of those who receive His grace the Lord says:

"I will make them and the places round about My hill a blessing; and I will cause the shower to come down in its season; there shall be showers of blessing." Ezekiel 34:26, ARV.

"On the last day, the great day of the feast, Jesus stood and cried, saying, If any man thirst, let him come unto Me and drink. He that believeth on Me, as the scripture hath said, from within him shall flow rivers of living water." John 7:37, 38, ARV.

Those who receive are to impart to others. From every direction are coming calls for help. God calls upon men to minister gladly to their fellow men. Immortal crowns are to be won; the kingdom of heaven is to be gained; the world, perishing in ignorance, is to be enlightened.

"Say not ye, There are yet four months, and then cometh harvest? behold, I say unto you, Lift up your eyes, and look on the fields; for they are white already to harvest. And he that reapeth receiveth wages, and gathereth fruit unto life eternal." John 4:35, 36.

For three years the disciples had before them the wonderful example of Jesus. Day by day they walked and talked with Him, hearing His words of cheer to the weary and heavy-laden, and seeing the manifestations of His power in behalf of the sick and afflicted. When the time came for Him to leave them, He gave them grace and power to carry forward His work in His name. They were to shed abroad the light of His gospel of love and healing. And the Saviour promised that His presence would be always with them. Through the Holy Spirit He would be even nearer to them than when He walked visibly among men.

The work which the disciples did, we also are to do. Every Christian is to be a missionary. In sympathy and compassion we are to minister to those in need of help, seeking with unselfish earnestness to lighten the woes of suffering humanity.

All may find something to do. None need feel that there is no place where they can labour for Christ. The Saviour identifies Himself with every child of humanity. That we might become members of the heavenly family, He became a member of the earthly family. He is the Son of man, and thus a brother to every son and daughter of Adam. His followers are not to feel themselves detached from the perishing world around them. They are a part of the great web of humanity, and heaven looks upon them as brothers to sinners as well as to saints.

Millions upon millions of human beings, in sickness and ignorance and sin, have never so much as heard of Christ's love for them. Were our condition and theirs to be reversed, what would we desire them to do for us? All this, so far as lies in our power, we are to do for them. Christ's rule of life by which every one of us must stand or fall in the judgement is, "Whatsoever ye would that men should do to you, do ye even so to them." Matthew 7:12.

By all that has given us advantage over another – be it education and refinement, nobility of character, Christian training, religious experience – we are in debt to those less favoured; and, so far as lies in our power, we are to minister unto them. If we are strong, we are to stay up the hands of the weak.

Angels of glory that do always behold the face of the Father in heaven, joy in ministering to His little ones. Angels are ever present where they are most needed, with those who have the hardest battles with self to fight, and whose surroundings are the most discouraging. Weak and trembling souls who have many objectionable traits of character are their special charge. That which selfish hearts would regard as humiliating service, ministering to those who are wretched and in every way inferior in character, is the work of the pure, sinless beings from the courts above.

Jesus did not consider heaven a place to be desired while we were lost. He left the heavenly courts for a life of reproach and insult, and a death of shame. He who was rich in heaven's priceless treasure became poor, that through His poverty we might be rich. We are to follow in the path He trod.

He who becomes a child of God should henceforth look upon himself as a link in the chain let down to save the world, one with Christ in His plan of mercy, going forth with Him to seek and save the lost.

Many feel that it would be a great privilege to visit the scenes of Christ's life on earth, to walk where He trod, to look upon the lake beside which He loved to teach, and the hills and valleys on which His eyes so often rested. But we need not go to Nazareth, to Capernaum, or to Bethany, in order to walk in the steps of Jesus. We shall find His footprints beside the sickbed, in the hovels of poverty, in the crowded alleys of the great cities, and in every place where there are human hearts in need of consolation.

We are to feed the hungry, clothe the naked, and comfort the suffering and afflicted. We are to minister to the despairing, and to inspire hope in the hopeless.

The love of Christ, manifested in unselfish ministry, will be more effective in reforming the evildoer than will the sword or the court of justice. These are necessary to strike terror to the lawbreaker, but the loving missionary can do more than this. Often the heart that hardens under reproof will melt under the love of Christ.

The missionary can not only relieve physical maladies, but he can lead the sinner to the Great Physician, who can cleanse the soul from the leprosy of sin. Through His servants, God designs that the sick, the unfortunate, and those possessed of evil spirits shall hear His voice. Through His human agencies He desires to be a comforter such as the world knows not.

The Saviour has given His precious life in order to establish a church capable of ministering to the suffering, the sorrowful, and the tempted. A company of believers may be poor, uneducated, and unknown; yet in Christ they may do a work in the home, in the community, and even in "the regions beyond," whose results shall be as far-reaching as eternity.

To Christ's followers today, no less than to the first disciples, these words are spoken:

"All power is given unto Me in heaven and in earth. Go ye therefore, and teach all nations." "Go ye into all the world, and preach the gospel to every creature." Matthew 28:18, 19; Mark 16:15.

And for us also is the promise of His presence, "Lo, I am with you alway, even unto the end of the world." Matthew 28:20.

Today no curious multitudes flock to the desert places to see and hear the Christ. His voice is not heard in the busy streets. No cry sounds from the wayside, "Jesus of Nazareth passeth by." Luke 18:37. Yet this word is true today. Christ walks unseen through our streets. With messages of mercy He comes to our homes. With all who are seeking to minister in His name, He waits to co-operate. He is in the midst of us, to heal and to bless, if we will receive Him.

"Thus saith Jehovah, In an acceptable time have I answered thee, and in a day of salvation have I helped thee; and I will preserve thee, and give thee for a covenant of the people, to raise up the land, to make them inherit the desolate heritages; saying to them that are bound, Go forth; to them that are in darkness, Show yourselves."

> "How beautiful upon the mountains are the feet of him that bringeth good tidings, that publisheth peace;
> That bringeth good tidings of good, that publisheth salvation;
> That saith unto Zion, Thy God reigneth!"
>
> Isaiah 49:8, ARV; 52:7.

> "Break forth into joy, sing together, ye waste places: . . .
> For the Lord hath comforted His people. . . .
> The Lord hath made bare His holy arm
> In the eyes of all the nations;
> And all the ends of the earth
> Shall see the salvation of our God."
>
> Verses 9, 10.

THE WORK OF THE PHYSICIAN

The Co-working of the Divine and the Human

In the ministry of healing the physician is to be a co-worker with Christ. The Saviour ministered to both the soul and the body. The gospel which He taught was a message of spiritual life and of physical restoration. Deliverance from sin and the healing of disease were linked together. The same ministry is committed to the Christian physician. He is to unite with Christ in relieving both the physical and spiritual needs of his fellow men. He is to be to the sick a messenger of mercy, bringing to them a remedy for the diseased body and for the sin-sick soul.

Christ is the true head of the medical profession. The chief Physician, He is at the side of every God-fearing practitioner who works to relieve human suffering. While the physician uses nature's remedies for physical disease, he should point his patients to Him who can relieve the maladies of both the soul and the body. That which physicians can only aid in doing, Christ accomplishes. They endeavour to assist nature's work of healing; Christ Himself is the healer. The physician seeks to preserve life; Christ imparts life.

The Source of Healing

The Saviour in His miracles revealed the power that is continually at work in man's behalf, to sustain and to heal him. Through the agencies of nature, God is working, day by day, hour by hour, moment by moment, to keep us alive, to build up and restore us. When any part of the body sustains injury, a healing process is at once begun; nature's agencies are set at work to restore soundness. But the power working through these agencies is the power of God. All life-giving power is from Him. When one recovers from disease, it is God who restores him.

Sickness, suffering, and death are work of an antagonistic power. Satan is the destroyer; God is the restorer.

The words spoken to Israel are true today of those who recover health of body or health of soul. "I am the Lord that healeth thee." Exodus 15:26.

The desire of God for every human being is expressed in the words, "Beloved, I wish above all things that thou mayest prosper and be in health, even as thy soul prospereth." 3 John 2.

He it is who "forgiveth all thine iniquities; who healeth all thy diseases; who redeemeth thy life from destruction; who crowneth thee with loving-kindness and tender mercies." Psalm 103:3, 4.

When Christ healed disease, He warned many of the afflicted ones, "Sin no more, lest a worse thing come unto thee." John 5:14. Thus He taught that they had brought disease upon themselves by transgressing the laws of God, and that health could be preserved only by obedience.

The physician should teach his patients that they are to co-operate with God in the work of restoration. The physician has a continually increasing realization of the fact that disease is the result of sin. He knows that the laws of nature, as truly as the precepts of the Decalogue, are divine, and that only in obedience to them can health be recovered or preserved. He sees many suffering as the result of hurtful practices who might be restored to health if they would do what they might for their own restoration. They need to be taught that every practice which destroys the physical, mental, or spiritual energies is sin, and that health is to be secured through obedience to the laws that God has established for the good of all mankind.

When a physician sees a patient suffering from

disease caused by improper eating and drinking or other wrong habits, yet neglects to tell him of this, he is doing his fellow being an injury. Drunkards, maniacs, those who are given over to licentiousness, all appeal to the physician to declare clearly and distinctly that suffering results from sin. Those who understand the principles of life should be in earnest in striving to counteract the causes of disease. Seeing the continual conflict with pain, labouring constantly to alleviate suffering, how can the physician hold his peace? Is he benevolent and merciful if he does not teach strict temperance as a remedy for disease?

Let it be made plain that the way of God's commandments is the way of life. God has established the laws of nature, but His laws are not arbitrary exactions. Every "Thou shalt not," whether in physical or in moral law, implies a promise. If we obey it, blessing will attend our steps. God never forces us to do right, but He seeks to save us from the evil and lead us to the good.

Let attention be called to the laws that were taught to Israel. God gave them definite instruction in regard to their habits of life. He made known to them the laws relating to both physical and spiritual well-being; and on condition of obedience He assured them, "The Lord will take away from thee all sickness." Deuteronomy 7:15. "Set your hearts unto all the words which I testify among you this day." "For they are life unto those that find them, and health to all their flesh." Deuteronomy 32:46; Proverbs 4:22.

God desires us to reach the standard of perfection made possible for us by the gift of Christ. He calls upon us to make our choice on the right side, to connect with heavenly agencies, to adopt principles that will restore in us the divine image. In His written word and in the great book of nature He has revealed of the principles of life. It is our work to obtain a knowledge of these principles, and by obedience to co-operate with Him in restoring health to the body as well as to the soul.

Men need to learn that the blessings of obedience, in their fullness, can be theirs only as they receive the grace of Christ. It is His grace that gives man power to obey the laws of God. It is this that enables him to break the bondage of evil habit. This is the only power that can make him and keep him steadfast in the right path.

When the gospel is received in its purity and power, it is a cure for the maladies that originated in sin. The Sun of Righteousness arises, "with healing in His wings." Malachi 4:2. Not all this world bestows can heal a broken heart, or impart peace of mind, or remove care, or banish disease. Fame, genius, talent — all are powerless to gladden the sorrowful heart or to restore the wasted life. The life of God in the soul is man's only hope.

The love which Christ diffuses through the whole being is a vitalizing power. Every vital part — the brain, the heart, the nerves — it touches with healing. By it the highest energies of the being are roused to activity. It frees the soul from the guilt and sorrow, the anxiety and care, that crush the life forces. With it come serenity and composure. It implants in the soul, joy that nothing earthly can destroy — joy in the Holy Spirit — health-giving, life-giving joy.

Our Saviour's words, "Come unto Me, . . . and I will give you rest" (Matthew 11:28), are a prescription for the healing of physical, mental, and spiritual ills. Though men have brought suffering upon themselves by their own wrongdoing, He regards them with pity. In Him they may find help. He will do great things for those who trust in Him.

Although for ages sin has been strengthening its hold on the human race, although through falsehood and artifice Satan has cast the black shadow of his interpretation upon the word of God, and has caused men to doubt His goodness; yet the Father's mercy and love have not ceased to flow earthward in rich currents. If human beings would open the windows of the soul heavenward, in appreciation of the divine gifts, a flood of healing virtue would pour in.

The physician who desires to be an acceptable co-worker with Christ will strive to become efficient in every feature of his work. He will study diligently, that he may be well qualified for the responsibilities of his profession, and will constantly endeavour to reach a higher standard, seeking for increased knowledge, greater skill, and deeper discernment. Every physician should realize that he who does weak, inefficient work is not only doing injury to the sick, but is also doing injustice to his fellow physicians. The physician who is satisfied with a low standard of skill and knowledge not only belittles the medical profession, but does dishonour to Christ, the Chief Physician.

Those who find that they are unfitted for medical work should choose some other employment. Those who are well adapted to care for the sick, but whose education and medical qualifications are limited, would do well to take up the humbler parts of the work, ministering faithfully as nurses. By patient service under skilful physicians they may be constantly learning, and by improving every opportunity to acquire knowledge they may in time become fully qualified for the work of a physician. Let the younger physicians, "as workers together with Him (the Chief Physician), . . . receive not the grace of God in vain, . . . giving no offence in anything, that the ministry (of the sick) be not blamed: but in all things approving ourselves as the ministers of God." 2 Corinthians 6:1-4.

God's Purpose for us is that we shall ever move upward. The true medical missionary physician will be an increasingly skilful practitioner. Talented Christian physicians, having superior professional ability, should be sought out and encouraged to engage in the service of God in places where they can educate and train others to become medical missionaries.

The Physician should gather to his soul the light of the word of God. He should make continual growth in grace. With him, religion is not to be merely one influence among others. It is to be an influence dominating all others. He is to act from high, holy motives — motives that are powerful because they proceed from the One who gave His life to furnish us with power to overcome evil.

If the physician faithfully and diligently strives to make himself efficient in his profession, if he consecrates himself to the service of Christ, and takes time to search his own heart, he will understand how to grasp the mysteries of his sacred calling. He may so discipline and educate himself that all within the sphere of his influence will see the excellence of the education and wisdom gained by the one who is connected with the God of wisdom and power.

In no place is a closer fellowship with Christ needed than in the work of the physician. He who would rightly perform the physician's duties must daily and hourly live a Christian life. The life of the patient is in the hands of the physician. One careless diagnosis, one wrong prescription, in a critical case, or one unskilful movement of the hand in an operation, even by so much as a hair's breadth, and a life may be sacrificed, a soul launched into eternity. How solemn the thought! How important that the physician shall be ever under the control of the divine Physician!

The Saviour is willing to help all who call upon Him for wisdom and clearness of thought. And who needs wisdom and clearness of thought more than does the physician, upon whose decisions so much depends? Let the one who is trying to prolong life look in faith to Christ to direct his every movement. The Saviour will give him tact and skill in dealing with difficult cases.

Wonderful are the opportunities given to the guardians of the sick. In all that is done for the restoration of the sick, let them understand that the physician is seeking to help them co-operate with God in combating disease. Lead them to feel that at every step taken in harmony with the laws of God, they may expect the aid of divine power.

The sick and suffering will have much more confidence in the physician who they are confident loves and fears God. They rely upon his words. They feel a sense of safety in the presence and administration of that physician.

Knowing the Lord Jesus, it is the privilege of the Christian practitioner by prayer to invite His presence in the sickroom. Before performing a critical operation, let the physician ask for the aid of the Great Physician. Let him assure the suffering one that God can bring him safely through the ordeal, that in all times of distress He is a sure refuge for those who trust in Him. The physician who cannot do this loses case after case that otherwise might have been saved. If he could speak words that would inspire faith in the sympathizing Saviour, who feels every throb of anguish, and could present the needs of the soul to Him in prayer, the crisis would oftener be safely passed.

Only He who reads the heart can know with what trembling and terror many patients consent to an operation under the surgeon's hand. They realize their peril. While they may have confidence in the physician's skill they know that it is not infallible. But as they see the physician bowed in prayer, asking help from God, they are inspired with confidence. Gratitude and trust open the heart to the healing power of God, the energies of the whole being are vitalized, and the life forces triumph.

To the physician also the Saviour's presence is an element of strength. Often the responsibilities and possibilities of his work bring dread upon the spirit. The feverishness of uncertainty and fear would make the hand unskilful. But the assurance that the divine Counsellor is beside him, to guide and to sustain, imparts quietness and courage. The touch of Christ upon the physician's hand brings vitality, restfulness, confidence, and power.

When the crisis is safely passed, and success is apparent, let a few moments be spent with the patient in prayer. Give expression to your thankfulness for the life that has been spared. As words of gratitude flow from the patient to the physician, let the praise and thanksgiving be directed to God. Tell the patient his life has been spared because he was under the heavenly Physician's protection.

The physician who follows such a course is leading his patient to the One upon whom he is dependent for life, the One who can save to the uttermost all who come to Him.

Into the medical missionary work should be brought a deep yearning for souls. To the physician equally with the gospel minister is committed the highest trust ever committed to man. Whether he realizes it or not, every physician is entrusted with the cure of souls.

In their work of dealing with disease and death, physicians too often lose sight of the solemn realities of the future life. In their earnest effort to avert the peril of the body, they forget the peril of the soul. The one to whom they are ministering may be losing his hold on life. Its last opportunities are slipping from his grasp. This soul the physician must meet again at the judgement seat of Christ.

Often we miss the most precious blessings by neglecting to speak a word in season. If the golden opportunity is not watched for, it will be lost. At the bedside of the sick no word of creed or controversy should be spoken. Let the sufferer be pointed to the One who is willing to save all that come to Him in faith. Earnestly, tenderly strive to help the soul that is hovering between life and death.

The physician who knows that Christ is his personal Saviour, because he himself has been led to the Refuge, knows how to deal with the trembling, guilty, sin-sick souls who turn to him for help. He can respond to the inquiry, "What must I do to be saved?" He can tell the story of the Redeemer's love. He can speak from experience of the power of repentance and faith. In simple, earnest words he can present the soul's need to God in prayer and can encourage the sick one also to ask for and accept the mercy of the compassionate Saviour. As he thus ministers at the bedside of the sick, striving to speak words that will bring help and comfort, the Lord works with him and through him. As the mind of the sufferer is directed to the Saviour, the peace of Christ fills his heart, and the spiritual health that comes to him is used as the helping hand of God in restoring the health of the body.

In attending the sick, the physician will often find opportunity for ministering to the friends of the afflicted one. As they watch by the bed of suffering, feeling powerless to prevent one pang of anguish, their hearts are softened. Often grief concealed from others is expressed to the physician. Then is the opportunity to point these sorrowing ones to Him who has invited the weary and heavy-laden to come unto Him. Often prayer can be offered for and with them, presenting their needs to the Healer of all woes, the Soother of all sorrows.

God's Promises

The physician has precious opportunities for directing his patients to the promises of God's word. He is to bring from the treasure house things new and old, speaking here and there the words of comfort and instruction that are longed for. Let the physician make his mind a storehouse of fresh thoughts. Let him study the word of God diligently, that he may be familiar with its promises. Let him learn to repeat the comforting words that Christ spoke during His earthly ministry when giving His lessons and healing the sick. He should talk of the works of healing wrought by Christ, of His tenderness and love. Never should he neglect to direct the minds of his patients to Christ, the Chief Physician.

The same power that Christ exercised when He walked visibly among men is in His word. It was by His word that Jesus healed disease and cast out demons; by His word He stilled the sea and raised the dead, and the people bore witness that His word was with power. He spoke the word of God, as He had spoken to all the prophets and teachers of the Old Testament. The whole Bible is a manifestation of Christ.

The Scriptures are to be received as God's word to us,

not written merely, but spoken. When the afflicted ones came to Christ, He beheld not only those who asked for help, but all who throughout the ages should come to Him in like need and with like faith. When He said to the paralytic, "Son, be of good cheer; thy sins be forgiven thee;" when He said to the woman of Capernaum, "Daughter, be of good comfort: thy faith hath made thee whole; go in peace," He spoke to other afflicted, sin-burdened ones who should seek His help. Matthew 9:2; Luke 8:48.

So with all the promises of God's word. In them He is speaking to us individually, speaking as directly as if we could listen to His voice. It is in these promises that Christ communicates to us His grace and power. They are leaves from that tree which is "for the healing of the nations." Revelation 22:2. Received, assimilated, they are to be the strength of the character, the inspiration and sustenance of the life. Nothing else can have such healing power. Nothing besides can impart the courage and faith which give vital energy to the whole being.

To one who stands trembling with fear on the brink of the grave, to the soul weary of the burden of suffering and sin, let the physician as he has opportunity repeat the words of the Saviour — for all the words of Holy Writ are His:

"Fear not: for I have redeemed thee, I have called thee by thy name; thou art Mine. When thou passest through the waters, I will be with thee; and through the rivers, they shall not overflow thee: when thou walkest through the fire, thou shalt not be burned; neither shall the flame kindle upon thee. For I am the Lord thy God, the Holy One of Israel, thy Saviour. . . . Since thou wast precious in My sight, thou hast been honourable, and I have loved thee." "I, even I, am He that blotteth out thy transgressions for Mine own sake, and will not remember thy sins." "Fear not: for I am with thee." Isaiah 43:1-4, 25, 5.

"Like as a father pitieth his children, so the Lord pitieth them that fear Him. For He knoweth our frame; He remembereth that we are dust." Psalm 103:13, 14.

"Only acknowledge thine iniquity, that thou hast transgressed against the Lord thy God." "If we confess our sins, He is faithful and just to forgive us our sins, and to cleanse us from all unrighteousness." Jeremiah 3:13; 1 John 1:9.

"I have blotted out, as a thick cloud, thy transgressions, and, as a cloud, thy sins: return unto Me; for I have redeemed thee." Isaiah 44:22.

"Come now, and let us reason together, saith the Lord: though your sins be as scarlet, they shall be as white as snow; though they be red like crimson, they shall be as wool. If ye be willing and obedient, ye shall eat the good of the land." Isaiah 1:18, 19.

"I have loved thee with an everlasting love: therefore with loving-kindness have I drawn thee." "I hid My face from thee for a moment; but with everlasting kindness will I have mercy on thee." Jeremiah 31:3; Isaiah 54:8.

"Let not your heart be troubled." "Peace I leave with you, My peace I give unto you: not as the world giveth, give I unto you. Let not your heart be troubled, neither let it be afraid." John 14:1, 27.

"A Man shall be as an hiding place from the wind, and a covert from the tempest; as rivers of water in a dry place, as the shadow of a great rock in a weary land." Isaiah 32:2.

"When the poor and needy seek water, and there is none, and their tongue faileth for thirst, I the Lord will hear them, I the God of Israel will not forsake them." Isaiah 41:17.

"Thus saith the Lord that made thee": "I will pour water upon him that is thirsty, and floods upon the dry ground: I will pour My Spirit upon thy seed, and My blessing upon thine offspring." Isaiah 44:2, 3.

"Look unto Me, and be ye saved, all the ends of the earth." Isaiah 45:22.

"Himself took our infirmities, and bare our sicknesses." "He was wounded for our transgressions, He was bruised for our iniquities: the chastisement of our peace was upon Him; and with His stripes we are healed." Matthew 8:17; Isaiah 53:5.

The Physician, an Educator

The true physician is an educator. He recognizes his responsibility, not only to the sick who are under his direct care, but also to the community in which he lives. He stands as a guardian of both physical and moral health. It is his endeavour not only to teach right methods for the treatment of the sick, but to encourage right habits of living, and to spread a knowledge of right principles.

Need of Education in Health Principles

Education in health principles was never more needed than now. Notwithstanding the wonderful progress in so many lines relating to the comforts and conveniences of life, even to sanitary matters and to the treatment of disease, the decline in physical vigour and power of endurance is alarming. It demands the attention of all who have at heart the well-being of their fellow men.

Our artificial civilization is encouraging evils destructive of sound principles. Custom and fashion are at war with nature. The practices they enjoin, and the indulgences they foster, are steadily lessening both physical and mental strength, and bringing upon the race an intolerable burden. Intemperance and crime, disease and wretchedness, are everywhere.

Many transgress the laws of health through ignorance, and they need instruction. But the greater number know better than they do. They need to be impressed with the importance of making their knowledge a guide of life. The physician has many opportunities both of imparting a knowledge of health principles and of showing the importance of putting them in practice. By right instruction he can do much to correct evils that are working untold harm.

A practice that is laying the foundation of a vast amount of disease and of even more serious evils is the free use of poisonous drugs. When attacked by disease, many will not take the trouble to search out the cause of their illness. Their chief anxiety is to rid themselves of pain and inconvenience. So they resort to patent nostrums, of whose real properties they know little, or they apply to a physician for some remedy to counteract the result of their misdoing, but with no thought of making a change in their unhealthful habits. If immediate benefit is not realized, another medicine is tried, and then another. Thus the evil continues.

People need to be taught that drugs do not cure disease. It is true that they sometimes afford present relief, and the patient appears to recover as the result of their use; this is because nature has sufficient vital force to expel the poison and to correct the conditions that caused the disease. Health is recovered in spite of the drug. But in most cases the drug only changes the form and location of the disease. Often the effect of the poison seems to be overcome for a time, but the results remain in the system and work great harm at some later period.

By the use of poisonous drugs, many bring upon themselves lifelong illness, and many lives are lost that might be saved by the use of natural methods of healing. The poisons contained in many so-called remedies create habits and appetites that mean ruin to both soul and body. Many of the popular nostrums called patent medicines, and even some of the drugs dispensed by physicians, act a part in laying the foundation of the liquor habit, the opium habit, the morphine habit, that are so terrible a curse to society.

The only hope of better things is in the education of the people in right principles. Let physicians teach the people that restorative power is not in drugs, but in nature. Disease is an effort of nature to free the system from conditions that result from a violation of the laws of health. In case of sickness, the cause should be ascertained. Unhealthful conditions should be changed, wrong habits corrected. Then nature is to be assisted in her effort to expel impurities and to re-establish right conditions in the system.

Natural Remedies

Pure air, sunlight, abstemiousness, rest, exercise, proper diet, the use of water, trust in divine power – these are the true remedies. Every person should have a knowledge of nature's remedial agencies and how to apply them. It is essential both to understand the principles involved in the treatment of the sick and to have a practical training that will enable one rightly to use this knowledge.

The use of natural remedies requires an amount of care and effort that many are not willing to give. Nature's process of healing and upbuilding is gradual, and to the impatient it seems slow. The surrender of hurtful indulgences requires sacrifice. But in the end it will be found that nature, untrammelled, does her work wisely and well. Those who persevere in obedience to her laws will reap the reward in health of body and health of mind.

Too little attention is generally given to the preservation of health. It is far better to prevent disease than to know how to treat it when contracted. It is the duty of every person, for his own sake, and for the sake of humanity, to inform himself in regard to the laws of life and conscientiously to obey them. All need to become acquainted with that most wonderful of all organisms, the human body. They should understand the functions of the various organs and the dependence of one upon another for the healthy action of all. They should study the influence of the mind upon the body, and of the body upon the mind, and the laws by which they are governed.

Training for Life's Conflict

We cannot be too often reminded that health does not depend on chance. It is a result of obedience to law.

This is recognized by the contestants in athletic games and trials of strength. These men make the most careful preparation. They submit to thorough training and strict discipline. Every physical habit is carefully regulated. They know that neglect, excess, or carelessness, which weakens or cripples any organ or function of the body, would ensure defeat.

How much more important is such carefulness to ensure success in the conflict of life. It is not mimic battles in which we are engaged. We are waging a warfare upon which hang eternal results. We have unseen enemies to meet. Evil angels are striving for the dominion of every human being. Whatever injures the health, not only lessens physical vigour, but tends to weaken the mental and moral powers. Indulgence in any unhealthful practice makes it more difficult for one to discriminate between right and wrong, and hence more difficult to resist evil. It increases the danger of failure and defeat.

"They which run in a race run all, but one receiveth the prize." 1 Corinthians 9:24. In the warfare in which we are engaged, all may win who will discipline themselves by obedience to right principles. The practice of these principles in the details of life is too often looked upon as unimportant — a matter too trivial to demand attention. But in view of the issues at stake, nothing with which we have to do is small. Every act casts its weight into the scale that determines life's victory or defeat. The scriptures bids us, "So run, that ye may obtain." Verse 24.

With our first parents, intemperate desire resulted in the loss of Eden. Temperance in all things has more to do with our restoration to Eden than men realize.

Pointing to the self-denial practiced by the contestants in the ancient Greek games, the apostle Paul writes: "Every man that striveth for the mastery is temperate in all things. Now they do it to obtain a corruptible crown; but we an incorruptible. I therefore so run, not as uncertainly; so fight I, not as one that beateth the air: but I keep under my body, and bring it into subjection: lest that by any means, when I have preached to others, I myself should be a castaway." Verses 25-27.

The progress of reform depends upon a clear recognition of fundamental truth. While, on the one hand, danger lurks in a narrow philosophy and a hard, cold orthodoxy, on the other hand there is great danger in a careless liberalism. The foundation of all enduring reform is the law of God. We are to present in clear, distinct lines the need of obeying this law. Its principles must be kept before the people. They are as everlasting and inexorable as God Himself.

One of the most deplorable effects of the original apostasy was the loss of man's power of self-control. Only as this power is regained can there be real progress.

The body is the only medium through which the mind and the soul are developed for the upbuilding of character. Hence it is that the adversary of souls directs his temptations to the enfeebling and degrading of the physical powers. His success here means the surrender to evil of the whole being. The tendencies of our physical nature, unless under the dominion of a higher power, will surely work ruin and death.

The body is to be brought into subjection. The higher powers of the being are to rule. The passions are to be controlled by the will, which is itself to be under the control of God. The kingly power of reason, sanctified by divine grace, is to bear sway in our lives.

The requirements of God must be brought home to the conscience. Men and women must be awakened to the duty of self-mastery, the need of purity, freedom from every depraving appetite and defiling habit. They need to be impressed with the fact that all their powers of mind and body are the gift of God, and are to be preserved in the best possible condition for His service.

In that ancient ritual which was the gospel in symbol, no blemished offering could be brought to God's altar. The sacrifice that was to represent Christ must be spotless. The word of God points to this as an illustration of what His children are to be — "a living sacrifice," "holy and without blemish," "well-pleasing to God." Romans 12:I, RV, margin; Ephesians 5:27.

Apart from divine power, no genuine reform can be effected. Human barriers against natural and cultivated tendencies are but as the sandbank against the torrent. Not until the life of Christ becomes a vitalizing power in our lives can we resist the temptations that assail us from within and from without.

Christ came to this world and lived the law of God, that man might have perfect mastery over the natural inclinations which corrupt the soul. The Physician of soul and body, He gives victory over warring lusts. He has provided every facility, that man may possess completeness of character.

When one surrenders to Christ, the mind is brought under the control of the law; but it is the royal law, which proclaims liberty to every captive. By becoming one with Christ, man is made free. Subjection to the will of Christ means restoration to perfect manhood.

Obedience to God is liberty from the thralldom of sin, deliverance from human passion and impulse. Man may stand conqueror of himself, conqueror of his own inclinations, conqueror of principalities and powers, and of "the rulers of the darkness of this world," and of "spiritual wickedness in high places." Ephesians 6:12.

In no place is such instruction as this more needed, and nowhere will it be productive of greater good, than in the home. Parents have to do with the very foundation of habit and character. The reformatory movement must begin in presenting to them the principles of the law of God as bearing upon both physical and moral health. Show that obedience to God's word is our only safeguard against the evils that are sweeping the world to destruction. Make plain the responsibility of parents, not only for themselves, but for their children. They are giving to their children an example either of obedience or of transgression. By their example and teaching, the destiny of their households is decided. The children will be what their parents make them.

If parents could be led to trace the result of their action, and could see how, by their example and teaching, they perpetuate and increase the power of sin or the power of righteousness, a change would certainly be made. Many would turn away from tradition and custom, and accept the divine principles of life.

Power of Example

The physician who ministers in the homes of the people, watching at the bedside of the sick, relieving their distress, bringing them back from the borders of the grave, speaking hope to the dying, wins a place in their confidence and affection, such as is granted to few others. Not even to the minister of the gospel are committed possibilities so great or an influence so far-reaching.

The physician's example, no less than his teaching, should be a positive power on the right side. The cause of reform calls for men and women whose life practice is an illustration of self-control. It is our practice of the principles we inculcate that gives them weight. The world needs a practical demonstration of what the grace of God can do in restoring to human beings their lost kingship, giving them mastery of themselves. There is nothing that the world needs so much as a knowledge of the gospel's saving power revealed in Christlike lives.

The physician is continually brought into contact with those who need the strength and encouragement of a right example. Many are weak in moral power. They lack self-control and are easily overcome by temptation. The physician can help these souls only as he reveals in his own life a strength of principle that enables him to triumph over every injurious habit and defiling lust. In his life must be seen the working of a power that is divine. If he fails here, however forcible or persuasive his words may be, his influence will tell for evil.

Many seek medical advice and treatment who have become moral wrecks through their own wrong habits. They are bruised and weak and wounded, feeling their folly and their inability to overcome. Such ones should have nothing in their surroundings to encourage a continuance of the thoughts and feelings that have made them what they are. They need to breathe an atmosphere of purity, of high and noble thought. How terrible the responsibility when those who should give them a right example are themselves enthralled by hurtful habits, their influence affording to temptation an added strength!

The Physician and the Temperance Work

Many come under the physician's care who are ruining soul and body by the use of tobacco or intoxicating drink. The physician who is true to his responsibility must point out to these patients the cause of their suffering. But if he himself is a user of tobacco or intoxicants, what weight will be given to his words? With the consciousness of his own indulgence before him, will he not hesitate to point out the plague spot in the life of his patient? While using these things himself, how can he convince the youth of their injurious effects?

How can a physician stand in the community as an example of purity and self-control, how can he be an effectual worker in the temperance cause, while he himself is indulging a vile habit? How can he minister acceptably at the bedside of the sick and the dying, when his very breath is offensive, laden with the odour of liquor or tobacco?

While disordering his nerves and clouding his brain by the use of narcotic poisons, how can one be true to the trust reposed in him as a skilful physician? How impossible for him to discern quickly or to execute with precision!

If he does not observe the laws that govern his own being, if he chooses selfish gratification above soundness of mind and body, does he not thereby declare himself unfit to be entrusted with the responsibility of human lives?

However skilled and faithful a physician may be, there is in his experience much of apparent discouragement and defeat. Often his work fails of accomplishing that which he longs to see accomplished. Though health is restored to his patients, it may be no real benefit to them or to the world. Many recover health, only to repeat the indulgences that invited disease. With the same eagerness as before, they plunge again into the round of self-indulgence and folly. The physician's work for them seems like effort thrown away.

Christ had the same experience, yet He did not cease His efforts for one suffering soul. Of the ten lepers who were cleansed, only one appreciated the gift, and he was a stranger and a Samaritan. For the sake of that one, Christ healed the ten. If the physician meets with no better success than the Saviour had, let him learn a lesson from the Chief Physician. Of Christ it is written, "He shall not fail nor be discouraged." "He shall see of the travail of His soul, and shall be satisfied." Isaiah 42:4; 53:11.

If but one soul would have accepted the gospel of His grace, Christ would, to save that one, have chosen His life of toil and humiliation and His death of shame. If through our efforts one human being shall be uplifted and ennobled, fitted to shine in the courts of the Lord, have we not cause for rejoicing?

The duties of the physician are arduous and trying. In order to perform them most successfully he needs to have a strong constitution and vigourous health. A man that is feeble or diseased cannot endure the wearing labour incident to the physician's calling. One who lacks perfect self-control cannot become qualified to deal with all classes of disease.

Often deprived of sleep, neglecting even to take food, cut off in great degree from social enjoyment and religious privileges, the physician's life seems to lie under a continual shadow. The affliction he beholds, the dependent mortals longing for help, his contact with the depraved, make the heart sick, and well-nigh destroy confidence in humanity.

In the battle with disease and death every energy is taxed to the limit of endurance. The reaction from this terrible strain tests the character to the utmost. Then it is that temptation has greatest power. More than men in any other calling, is the physician in need of self-control, purity of spirit, and that faith which takes hold on heaven. For the sake of others and for his own sake, he cannot afford to disregard physical law. Recklessness in physical habits tends to recklessness in morals.

The physician's only safety is, under all circumstances, to act from principle, strengthened and ennobled by a firmness of purpose found only in God. He is to stand in the moral excellence of His character. Day by day, hour by hour, moment by moment, he is to live as in the sight of the unseen world. As did Moses, he must endure "as seeing Him who is invisible."

Righteousness has its root in godliness. No man can steadily maintain before his fellow men a pure, forceful life unless his life is hid with Christ in God. The greater the activity among men, the closer must be the communion of the heart with heaven.

The more urgent his duties and the greater his responsibilities, the greater the physician's need of divine power. Time must be redeemed from things temporal, for meditation upon things eternal. He must resist an encroaching world, which would so press upon him as to separate him from the Source of strength. Above all other men should he, by prayer and the study of the Scriptures, place himself under the protecting shield of God. He is to live in hourly contact and conscious communion with the principles of truth, righteousness, and mercy that reveal God's attributes within the soul.

Just to the degree in which the word of God is received and obeyed will it impress with its potency and touch with its life every spring of action, every phase of character. It will purify every thought, regulate every desire. Those who make God's word their trust will quit themselves like men and be strong. They will rise above all baser things into an atmosphere free from defilement.

When man is in fellowship with God, that unswerving

purpose which preserved Joseph and Daniel amidst the corruption of heathen courts will make his a life of unsullied purity. His robes of character will be spotless. In his life the light of Christ will be undimmed. The bright and morning Star will appear shining steadfastly above him in changeless glory.

Such a life will be an element of strength in the community. It will be a barrier against evil, a safeguard to the tempted, a guiding light to those who, amidst difficulties and discouragements, are seeking the right way.

MEDICAL MISSIONARIES AND THEIR WORK

Teaching and Healing

When Christ sent out the twelve disciples on their first missionary tour, He bade them, "As ye go, preach, saying, The kingdom of heaven is at hand. Heal the sick, cleanse the lepers, raise the dead, cast out devils: freely ye have received, freely give." Matthew 10:7, 8.

To the Seventy sent forth later He said: "Into whatsoever city ye enter, . . . heal the sick that are therein, and say unto them, The kingdom of God is come nigh unto you." Luke 10:8, 9. The presence and power of Christ was with them, "and the Seventy returned again with joy, saying, Lord, even the devils are subject unto us through Thy name." Verse 17.

After Christ's ascension the same work was continued. The scenes of His own ministry were repeated. "Out of the cities round about" there came a multitude "unto Jerusalem, bringing sick folks, and them which were vexed with unclean spirits: and they were healed every one." Acts 5:16.

And the disciples "went forth, and preached everywhere, the Lord working with them." "Philip went down to the city of Samaria, and preached Christ unto them. And the people with one accord gave heed unto those things which Philip spake. . . . For unclean spirits . . . came out of many that were possessed with them: and many taken with palsies, and that were lame, were healed. And there was great joy in that city." Mark 16:20; Acts 8:5-8.

Work of the Disciples

Luke, the writer of the Gospel that bears his name, was a medical missionary. In the Scriptures he is called "the beloved physician." Colossians 4:14. The apostle Paul heard of his skill as a physician, and sought him out as one to whom the Lord had entrusted a special work. He secured his co-operation, and for some time Luke accompanied him in his travels from place to place. After a time, Paul left Luke at Philippi, in Macedonia. Here he continued to labour for several years, both as a physician and as a teacher of the gospel. In his work as a physician he ministered to the sick, and then prayed for the healing power of God to rest upon the afflicted ones. Thus the way was opened for the gospel message. Luke's success as a physician gained for him many opportunities for preaching Christ among the heathen. It is the divine plan that we shall work as the disciples worked. Physical healing is bound up with the gospel commission. In the work of the gospel, teaching and healing are never to be separated.

The work of the disciples was to spread a knowledge of the gospel. To them was committed the work of proclaiming to all the world the good news that Christ brought to men. That work they accomplished for the people of their time. To every nation under heaven the gospel was carried in a single generation.

The giving of the gospel to the world is the work that God has committed to those who bear His name. For earth's sin and misery the gospel is the only antidote. To make known to all mankind the message of the grace of God is the first work of those who know its healing power.

When Christ sent forth the disciples with the gospel message, faith in God and His word had well-nigh departed from the world. Among the Jewish people, who professed to have a knowledge of Jehovah, His word had been set aside for tradition and human speculation. Selfish ambition, love of ostentation, greed of gain, absorbed men's thoughts. As reverence for God departed, so also departed compassion toward men. Selfishness was the ruling principle, and Satan worked his will in the misery and degradation of mankind.

Satanic agencies took possession of men. The bodies

of human beings, made for the dwelling place of God, became the habitation of demons. The senses, the nerves, the organs of men were worked by supernatural agencies in the indulgence of the vilest lust. The very stamp of demons was impressed upon the countenances of men. Human faces reflected the expression of the legions of evil with which men were possessed.

What is the condition in the world today? Is not faith in the Bible as effectually destroyed by the higher criticism and speculation of today as it was by tradition and rabbinism in the days of Christ? Have not greed and ambition and love of pleasure as strong a hold on men's hearts now as they had then? In the professedly Christian world, even in the professed churches of Christ, how few are governed by Christian principles. In business, social, domestic, even religious circles, how few make the teachings of Christ the rule of daily living. Is it not true that "justice standeth afar off: . . . equity cannot enter. . . . And he that departeth from evil maketh himself a prey"? Isaiah 59:14, 15.

We are living in the midst of an "epidemic of crime," at which thoughtful, God-fearing men everywhere stand aghast. The corruption that prevails, it is beyond the power of the human pen to describe. Every day brings fresh revelations of political strife, bribery, and fraud. Every day brings its heart-sickening record of violence and lawlessness, of indifference to human suffering, of brutal, fiendish destruction of human life. Every day testifies to the increase of insanity, murder, and suicide. Who can doubt that satanic agencies are at work among men with increasing activity to distract and corrupt the mind, and defile and destroy the body?

And while the world is filled with these evils, the gospel is too often presented in so indifferent a manner as to make but little impression upon the consciences or the lives of men. Everywhere there are hearts crying out for something which they have not. They long for a power that will give them mastery over sin, a power that will deliver them from the bondage of evil, a power that will give health and life and peace. Many who once knew the power of God's word have dwelt where there is no recognition of God, and they long for the divine presence.

The world needs today what it needed nineteen hundred years ago — a revelation of Christ. A great work of reform is demanded, and it is only through the grace of Christ that the work of restoration, physical, mental, and spiritual, can be accomplished.

Christ's method alone will give true success in reaching the people. The Saviour mingled with men as one who desired their good. He showed His sympathy for them, ministered to their needs, and won their confidence. Then He bade them, "Follow Me."

There is need of coming close to the people by personal effort. If less time were given to sermonizing, and more time were spent in personal ministry, greater results would be seen. The poor are to be relieved, the sick cared for, the sorrowing and the bereaved comforted, the ignorant instructed, the inexperienced counselled. We are to weep with those that weep, and rejoice with those that rejoice. Accompanied by the power of persuasion, the power of prayer, the power of the love of God, this work will not, cannot, be without fruit.

We should ever remember that the object of the medical missionary work is to point sin-sick men and women to the Man of Calvary, who taketh away the sin of the world. By beholding Him, they will be changed into His likeness. We are to encourage the sick and suffering to look to Jesus and live. Let the workers keep Christ, the Great Physician, constantly before those to whom disease of body and soul has brought discouragement. Point them to the One who can heal both physical and spiritual disease. Tell them of the One who is touched with the feeling of their infirmities. Encourage them to place themselves in the care of Him who gave His life to make it possible for them to have life eternal. Talk of His love; tell of His power to save.

This is the high duty and precious privilege of the medical missionary. And personal ministry often prepares the way for this. God often reaches hearts through our efforts to relieve physical suffering.

Medical missionary work is the pioneer work of the gospel. In the ministry of the word and in the medical missionary work the gospel is to be preached and practiced.

In almost every community there are large numbers who do not listen to the preaching of God's word or attend any religious service. If they are reached by the gospel, it must be carried to their homes. Often the relief of their physical needs is the only avenue by which they can be approached. Missionary nurses who care for the sick and relieve the distress of the poor will find many opportunities to pray with them, to read to them from God's word, and to speak of the Saviour. They can pray with and for the helpless ones who have not strength of will to control the appetites that passion has degraded. They can bring a ray of hope into the lives of the defeated and disheartened. Their unselfish love, manifested in acts of disinterested kindness, will make it easier for these suffering ones to believe in the love of Christ.

Many have no faith in God and have lost confidence in man. But they appreciate acts of sympathy and helpfulness. As they see one with no inducement of earthly praise or compensation come into their homes, ministering to the sick, feeding the hungry, clothing the naked, comforting the sad, and tenderly pointing all to Him of whose love and pity the human worker is but the messenger — as they see this, their hearts are touched. Gratitude springs up. Faith is kindled. They see that God cares for them, and they are prepared to listen as His word is opened.

Whether in foreign missions or in the home field, all missionaries, both men and women, will gain much more ready access to the people, and will find their usefulness greatly increased, if they are able to minister to the sick. Women who go as missionaries to heathen lands may thus find opportunity for giving the gospel to the women of these lands, when every other door of access is closed. All gospel workers should know how to give the simple treatments that do so much to relieve pain and remove disease.

Teaching Health Principles

Gospel workers should be able also to give instruction in the principles of healthful living. There is sickness everywhere, and most of it might be prevented by attention to the laws of health. The people need to see the bearing of health principles upon their well-being, both for this life and for the life to come. They need to be awakened to their responsibility for the human habitation fitted up by their Creator as His dwelling place, and over which He desires them to be faithful stewards. They need to be impressed with the truth conveyed in the words of Holy Writ:

"Ye are the temple of the living God; as God hath said, I will dwell in them, and walk in them; and I will be their God, and they shall be My people." 2 Corinthians 6:16.

Thousands need and would gladly receive instruction concerning the simple methods of treating the sick — methods that are taking the place of the use of poisonous drugs. There is great need of instruction in regard to dietetic reform. Wrong habits of eating and the use of unhealthful food are in no small degree responsible for the intemperance and crime and wretchedness that curse the world.

In teaching health principles, keep before the mind the great object of reform — that its purpose is to secure the highest development of body and mind and soul. Show that the laws of nature, being the laws of God, are designed for our good; that obedience to them promotes happiness in this life, and aids in the preparation for the life to come.

Lead the people to study the manifestation of God's love and wisdom in the works of nature. Lead them to study that marvellous organism, the human system, and the laws by which it is governed. Those who perceive the evidences of God's love, who understand something of the wisdom and beneficence of His laws, and the results of obedience, will come to regard their duties and obligations from an altogether different point of view. Instead of looking upon an observance of the laws of health as a matter of sacrifice or self-denial, they will regard it, as it really is, as an inestimable blessing.

Every gospel worker should feel that the giving of instruction in the principles of healthful living is a part of his appointed work. Of this work there is great need, and the world is open for it.

Everywhere there is a tendency to substitute the work of organizations for individual effort. Human wisdom tends to consolidation, to centralization, to the building up of great churches and institutions. Multitudes leave to institutions and organizations the work of benevolence; they excuse themselves from contact with the world, and their hearts grow cold. They become self-absorbed and unimpressible. Love for God and man dies out of the soul.

Christ commits to His followers an individual work — a work that cannot be done by proxy. Ministry to the sick and the poor, the giving of the gospel to the lost, is not to be left to committees or organized charities. Individual responsibility, individual effort, personal sacrifice, is the requirement of the gospel.

"Go out into the highways and hedges, and compel them to come in," is Christ's command, "that My house may be filled." He brings men into touch with those whom they seek to benefit. "Bring the poor that are cast out to thy house," He says. "When thou seest the naked, that thou cover him." "They shall lay hands on the sick, and they shall recover." Luke 14:23; Isaiah 58:7; Mark 16:18. Through direct contact, through personal ministry, the blessings of the gospel are to be communicated.

In giving light to His people anciently, God did not work exclusively through any one class. Daniel was a prince of Judah. Isaiah also was of the royal line. David was a shepherd boy, Amos a herdsman, Zechariah a captive from Babylon, Elisha a tiller of the soil. The Lord raised up as His representatives prophets and princes, the noble and the lowly, and taught them the truths to be given to the world.

To everyone who becomes a partaker of His grace the Lord appoints a work for others. Individually we are to stand in our lot and place, saying, "Here am I; send me." Isaiah 6:8. Upon the minister of the word, the missionary nurse, the Christian physician, the individual Christian, whether he be merchant or farmer, professional man or mechanic — the responsibility rests upon all. It is our work to reveal to men the gospel of their salvation. Every enterprise in which we engage should be a means to this end.

Those who take up their appointed work will not only be a blessing to others, but they will themselves be blessed. The consciousness of duty well done will have a reflex influence upon their own souls. The despondent will forget their despondency, the weak will become strong, the ignorant intelligent, and all will find an unfailing helper in Him who has called them.

The church of Christ is organized for service. Its watchword is ministry. Its members are soldiers, to be trained for conflict under the Captain of their salvation. Christian ministers, physicians, teachers, have a broader work than many have recognized. They are not only to minister to the people, but to teach them to minister. They should not only give instruction in right principles, but educate their hearers to impart these principles. Truth that is not lived, that is not imparted, loses its life-giving power, its healing virtue. Its blessing can be retained only as it is shared.

The monotony of our service for God needs to be broken up. Every church member should be engaged in some line of service for the Master. Some cannot do so much as others, but everyone should do his utmost to roll back the tide of disease and distress that is sweeping over our world. Many would be willing to work if they were taught how to begin. They need to be instructed and encouraged.

Every church should be a training school for Christian workers. Its members should be taught how to give Bible readings, how to conduct and teach Sabbath-school classes, how best to help the poor and to care for the sick, how to work for the unconverted. There should be schools of health, cooking schools, and classes in various lines of Christian help work. There should not only be teaching, but actual work under experienced instructors. Let the teachers lead the way in working among the people, and others, uniting with them, will learn from their example. One example is worth more than many precepts.

Let all cultivate their physical and mental powers to the utmost of their ability, that they may work for God where His providence shall call them. The same grace that came from Christ to Paul and Apollos, that distinguished them for spiritual excellencies, will today be imparted to devoted Christian missionaries. God desires His children to have intelligence and knowledge, that with unmistakable clearness and power His glory may be revealed in our world.

Educated workers who are consecrated to God can do service in a greater variety of ways and can accomplish more extensive work than can those who are uneducated. Their discipline of mind places them on vantage ground. But those who have neither great talents nor extensive education may minister acceptably to others. God will use men who are willing to be used. It is not the most brilliant or the most talented persons whose work produces the greatest and most lasting results. Men and women are needed who have heard a message from heaven. The most effective workers are those who respond to the invitation, "Take My yoke upon you, and learn of Me." Matthew 11:29.

It is heart missionaries that are needed. He whose heart God touches is filled with a great longing for those who have never known His love. Their condition impresses him with a sense of personal woe. Taking his life in his hand, he goes forth, a heaven-sent, heaven-inspired messenger, to do a work in which angels can co-operate.

If those to whom God has entrusted great talents of intellect put these gifts to a selfish use, they will be left, after a period of trial, to follow their own way. God will take men who do not appear to be so richly endowed, who have not large self-confidence, and He will make the weak strong, because they trust in Him to do for them that which they cannot do for themselves. God will accept the wholehearted service, and will Himself make up the deficiencies.

The Lord has often chosen for His colabourers men who have had opportunity to obtain but a limited school education. These men have applied their powers most diligently, and the Lord has rewarded their fidelity to His work, their industry, their thirst for knowledge. He has witnessed their tears and heard their prayers. As His blessing came to the captives in the courts of Babylon, so does He give wisdom and knowledge to His workers today.

Men deficient in school education, lowly in social position, have, through the grace of Christ, sometimes been wonderfully successful in winning souls for Him. The secret of their success was their confidence in God. They learned daily of Him who is wonderful in counsel and mighty in power.

Such workers are to be encouraged. The Lord brings them into connection with those of more marked ability, to fill up the gaps that others leave. Their quickness to see what is to be done, their readiness to help those in need, their kind words and deeds, open doors of usefulness that otherwise would remain closed. They come close to those in trouble, and the persuasive influence of their words has power to draw many trembling souls to God. Their work shows what thousands of others might do, if they only would.

A Broader Life

Nothing will so arouse a self-sacrificing zeal and broaden and strengthen the character as to engage in work for others. Many professed Christians, is seeking church relationship, think only of themselves. They wish to enjoy church fellowship and pastoral care. They become members of large and prosperous churches, and are content to do little for others. In this way they are robbing themselves of the most precious blessings. Many would be greatly benefited by sacrificing their pleasant, ease-conducing associations. They need to go where their energies will be called out in Christian work and they can learn to bear responsibilities.

Trees that are crowded closely together do not grow healthfully and sturdily. The gardener transplants them that they may have room to develop. A similar work would benefit many of the members of large churches. They need to be placed where their energies will be called forth in active Christian effort. They are losing their spiritual life, becoming dwarfed and inefficient, for want of self-sacrificing labour for others. Transplanted to some missionary field, they would grow strong and vigourous.

But none need wait until called to some distant field before beginning to help others. Doors of service are open everywhere. All around us are those who need our help. The widow, the orphan, the sick and the dying, the heartsick, the discouraged, the ignorant, and the outcast are on every hand.

We should feel it our special duty to work for those living in our neighbourhood. Study how you can best help those who take no interest in religious things. As you visit your friends and neighbours, show an interest in their spiritual as well as in their temporal welfare. Speak to them of Christ as a sin-pardoning Saviour. Invite your neighbours to your home, and read with them from the precious Bible and from books that explain its truths. Invite them to unite with you in song and prayer. In these little gatherings, Christ Himself will be present, as He has promised, and hearts will be touched by His grace.

Church members should educate themselves to do this work. This is just as essential as to save the benighted souls in foreign countries. While some feel the burden for souls afar off, let the many who are at home feel the burden of precious souls who are around them, and work just as diligently for their salvation.

Many regret that they are living a narrow life. They themselves can make their life broad and influential if they will. Those who love Jesus with heart and mind and soul, and their neighbour as themselves, have a wide field in which to use their ability and influence.

Little Opportunities

Let none pass by little opportunities, to look for larger work. You might do successfully the small work, but fail utterly in attempting the larger work, and fall into discouragement. It is by doing with your might what you find to do that you will develop aptitude for larger work. It is by slighting the daily opportunities, by neglecting the little things right at hand, that so many become fruitless and withered.

Do not depend upon human aid. Look beyond human beings to the One appointed by God to bear our griefs, to carry our sorrows, and to supply our necessities. Taking God at His word, make a beginning wherever you find work to do, and move forward with unfaltering faith. It is faith in Christ's presence that gives strength and steadfastness. Work with unselfish interest, with painstaking effort, with persevering energy.

In fields where the conditions are so objectionable and disheartening that many are unwilling to go to them, remarkable changes have been wrought by the efforts of self-sacrificing workers. Patiently and perseveringly they laboured, not relying upon human power, but upon God, and His grace sustained them. The amount of good thus accomplished will never be known in this world, but blessed results will be seen in the great hereafter.

Self-supporting Missionaries

In many places self-supporting missionaries can work successfully. It was as a self-supporting missionary that the apostle Paul laboured in spreading the knowledge of Christ throughout the world. While daily teaching the gospel in the great cities of Asia and Europe, he wrought at the trade of a craftsman to sustain himself and his companions. His parting words to the elders of Ephesus, showing his manner of labour, have precious lessons for every gospel worker:

"Ye know," he said, "after what manner I have been with you at all seasons: . . . and how I kept back nothing that was profitable unto you, but have showed you, and have taught you publicly, and from house to house. . . . I have coveted no man's silver, or gold, or apparel. Yea, ye yourselves know, that these hands have ministered unto my necessities, and to them that were with me. I have showed you all things, how that so labouring ye ought to support the weak, and to remember the words of the Lord Jesus, how He said, It is more blessed to give than to receive." Acts 20:18-35.

Many today, if imbued with the same spirit of self-sacrifice, could do a good work in a similar way. Let two or more start out together in evangelistic work. Let them visit the people, praying, singing, teaching, explaining the Scriptures, and ministering to the sick. Some can sustain themselves as canvassers; others, like the apostle, can labour at some handicraft or in other lines of effort. As they move forward in their work, realizing their helplessness, but humbly depending upon God, they gain a blessed experience. The Lord Jesus goes before them, and among the wealthy and the poor they find favour and help.

Those who have been trained for medical missionary work in foreign countries should be encouraged to go without delay where they expect to labour, and begin work among the people, learning the language as they work. Very soon they will be able to teach the simple truths of God's word.

Throughout the world, messengers of mercy are needed. There is a call for Christian families to go into communities that are in darkness and error, to go to foreign fields, to become acquainted with the needs of their fellow men, and to work for the cause of the Master. If such families would settle in the dark places of the earth, places where the people are enshrouded in spiritual gloom, and let the light of Christ's life shine out through them, what a noble work might be accomplished.

This work requires self-sacrifice. While many are waiting to have every obstacle removed, the work they might do is left undone, and multitudes are dying without hope and without God. Some for the sake of commercial advantage, or to acquire scientific knowledge, will venture into unsettled regions and cheerfully endure sacrifice and hardship; but how few for the sake of their fellow men are willing to move their families into regions that are in need of the gospel.

To reach the people, wherever they are, and whatever their position or condition, and to help them in every way possible — this is true ministry. But such effort you may win hearts and open a door of access to perishing souls.

In all you work remember that you are bound up with Christ, a part of the great plan of redemption. The love of Christ, in a healing, life-giving current, is to flow through your life. As you seek to draw others within the circle of His love, let the purity of your language, the unselfishness of your service, the joyfulness of your demeanour, bear witness to the power of His grace. Give to the world so pure and righteous a representation of Him, that men shall behold Him in His beauty.

It is of little use to try to reform others by attacking what we may regard as wrong habits. Such effort often results in more harm than good. In His talk with the Samaritan woman, instead of disparaging Jacob's well, Christ presented something better. "If thou knewest the gift of God," He said, "and who it is that saith to thee, Give Me to drink; thou wouldest have asked of Him, and He would have given thee living water." John 4:10. He turned the conversation to the treasure He had to bestow, offering the woman something better than she possessed, even living water, the joy and hope of the gospel.

This is an illustration of the way in which we are to work. We must offer men something better than that which they possess, even the peace of Christ, which passeth all understanding. We must tell them of God's holy law, the transcript of His character, and an expression of that which He wishes them to become. Show them how infinitely superior to the fleeting joys and pleasures of the world is the imperishable glory of heaven. Tell them of the freedom and rest to be found in the Saviour. "Whosoever drinketh of the water that I shall give him shall never thirst," He daclared. Verse 14.

Lift up Jesus, crying, "Behold, the Lamb of God, that taketh away the sin of the world!" John 1:29, ARV. He alone can satisfy the craving of the heart and give peace to the soul.

Of all people in the world, reformers should be the most unselfish, the most kind, the most courteous. In their lives should be seen the true goodness of unselfish deeds. The worker who manifests a lack of courtesy, who shows impatience at the ignorance on waywardness of others, who speaks hastily or acts thoughtlessly, may close the door to hearts so that he can never reach them.

As the dew and the still showers fall upon the withering plants, so let words fall gently when seeking to win men from error. God's plan is first to reach the heart. We are to speak the truth in love, trusting in Him to give it power for the reforming of the life. The Holy Spirit will apply to the soul the word that is spoken in love.

Naturally we are self-centred and opinionated. But when we learn the lessons that Christ desires to teach us, we become partakers of His nature; henceforth we live His life. The wonderful example of Christ, the matchless tenderness with which He entered into the feelings of others, weeping with those who wept, rejoicing with those who rejoiced, must have a deep influence upon the character of all who follow Him in sincerity. By kindly words and acts they will try to make the path easy for weary feet.

"The Lord Eternal hath given me a tongue for teaching." "That I should know how to speak a word in season to him that is weary." Isaiah 50:4, Leeser; AV.

All around us are afflicted souls. Here and there, everywhere, we may find them. Let us search out these suffering ones and speak a word in season to comfort their hearts. Let us ever be channels through which shall flow the refreshing waters of compassion.

In all our associations it should be remembered that in the experience of others there are chapters sealed from mortal sight. On the pages of memory are sad histories that are sacredly guarded from curious eyes. There stand registered long, hard battles with trying circumstances, perhaps troubles in the home life, that day by day weaken courage, confidence, and faith. Those who are fighting the battle of life at great odds may be strengthened and encouraged by little attentions that cost only a loving effort. To such the strong, helpful grasp of the hand by a true friend is worth more than gold or silver. Words of kindness are as welcome as the smile of angels.

There are multitudes struggling with poverty, compelled to labour hard for small wages, and able to secure but the barest necessities of life. Toil and deprivation, with no hope of better things, make their burden very heavy. When pain and sickness are added, the burden is almost insupportable. Careworn and oppressed, they know not where to turn for relief. Sympathize with them in their trials, their heartaches, and disappointments. This will open the way for you to help them. Speak to them of God's promises, pray with and for them, inspire them with hope.

Words of cheer and encouragement spoken when the soul is sick and the pulse of courage is low — these are regarded by the Saviour as if spoken to Himself.

As hearts are cheered, the heavenly angels look on in pleased recognition.

From age to age the Lord has been seeking to awaken in the souls of men a sense of their divine brotherhood. Be co-workers with Him. While distrust and alienation are pervading the world, Christ's disciples are to reveal the spirit that reigns in heaven.

Speak as He would speak, act as He would act. Constantly reveal the sweetness of His character. Reveal that wealth of love which underlies all His teachings and all His dealings with men. The humblest workers, in co-operation with Christ, may touch chords whose vibrations shall ring to the ends of the earth and make melody throughout eternal ages.

Heavenly intelligences are waiting to co-operate with human instrumentalities, that they may reveal to the world what human beings may become, and what, through union with the Divine, may be accomplished for the saving of souls that are ready to perish. There is no limit to the usefulness of one who, putting self aside, makes room for the working of the Holy Spirit upon his heart and lives a life wholly consecrated to God. All who consecrate body, soul, and spirit to His service will be constantly receiving a new endowment of physical, mental, and spiritual power. The inexhaustible supplies of heaven are at their command. Christ gives them the breath of His own Spirit, the life of His own life. The Holy Spirit puts forth its highest energies to work in mind and heart. Through the grace given us we may achieve victories that because of our own erroneous and preconceived opinions, our defects of character, our smallness of faith, have seemed impossible.

To everyone who offers himself to the Lord for service, withholding nothing, is given power for the attainment of measureless results. For these God will do great things. He will work upon the minds of men so that, even in this world, there shall be seen in their lives a fulfilment of the promise of the future state.

"The wilderness and the solitary place shall be glad for
them;
And the desert shall rejoice, and blossom as the rose.
It shall blossom abundantly, and rejoice even with joy
and singing;
The glory of Lebanon shall be given unto it,
The excellency of Carmel and Sharon,
They shall see the glory of the Lord,
And the excellency of our God.

"Strengthen ye the weak hands,
And confirm the feeble knees.
Say to them that are of a fearful heart, Be strong, fear
not;
Behold, your God. . . .

"Then the eyes of the blind shall be opened,
And the ears of the deaf shall be unstopped.
Then shall the lame man leap as an hart,
And the tongue of the dumb sing:
For in the wilderness shall waters break out,
And streams in the desert.

"And the parched ground shall become a pool,
And the thirsty land springs of water. . . .
And an highway shall be there, and a way,
And it shall be called The way of holiness;
The unclean shall not pass over it;
But it shall be for those:
The wayfaring men, though fools, shall not err therein.

"No lion shall be there,
Nor any ravenous beast shall go up thereon,
It shall not be found there;
But the redeemed shall walk there:
And the ransomed of the Lord shall return,
And come to Zion with songs
And everlasting joy upon their heads:
They shall obtain joy and gladness,
And sorrow and sighing shall flee away."

Isaiah 35:1-10.

Helping the Tempted

Not because we first loved Him did Christ love us; but "while we were yet sinners" He died for us. He does not treat us according to our desert. Although our sins have merited condemnation, He does not condemn us. Year after year He has borne with our weakness and ignorance, with our ingratitude and waywardness. Notwithstanding our wanderings, our hardness of heart, our neglect of His Holy Word, His hand is stretched out still.

Grace is an attribute of God exercised toward undeserving human beings. We did not seek for it, but it was sent in search of us. God rejoices to bestow His grace upon us, not because we are worthy, but because we are so utterly unworthy. Our only claim to His mercy is our great need.

The Lord God through Jesus Christ holds out His hand all the day long in invitation to the sinful and fallen. He will receive all. He welcomes all. It is His glory to pardon the chief of sinners. He will take the prey from the mighty, He will deliver the captive, He will pluck the brand from the burning. He will lower the golden chain of His mercy to the lowest depths of human wretchedness, and lift up the debased soul contaminated with sin.

Every human being is the object of loving interest to Him who gave His life that He might bring men back to God. Souls guilty and helpless, liable to be destroyed by the arts and snares of Satan, are cared for as a shepherd cares for the sheep of his flock.

The Saviour's example is to be the standard of our service for the tempted and the erring. The same interest and tenderness and long-suffering that He has manifested toward us, we are to manifest toward others. "As I have loved you," He says, "that ye also love one another." John 13:34. If Christ dwells in us, we shall reveal His unselfish love toward all with whom we have to do. As we see men and women in need of sympathy and help, we shall not ask, "Are they worthy?" but "How can I benefit them?"

Rich and poor, high and low, free and bond, are God's heritage. He who gave His life to redeem man sees in every human being a value that exceeds finite computation. By the mystery and glory of the cross we are to discern His estimate of the value of the soul. When we do this, we shall feel that human beings, however degraded, have cost too much to be treated with coldness or contempt. We shall realize the importance of working for our fellow men, that they may be exalted to the throne of God.

The lost coin, in the Saviour's parable, though lying in the dirt and rubbish, was a piece of silver still. Its owner sought it because it was of value. So every soul, however degraded by sin, is in God's sight accounted precious. As the coin bore the image and superscription of the reigning power, so man at his creation bore the image and superscription of God. Though now marred and dim through the influence of sin, the traces of this inscription remain upon every soul. God desires to recover that soul and to retrace upon it His own image in righteousness and holiness.

How little do we enter into sympathy with Christ on that which should be the strongest bond of union between us and Him — compassion for depraved, guilty, suffering souls, dead in trespasses and sins! The inhumanity of man toward man is our greatest sin. Many think that they are representing the justice of God while they wholly fail of representing His tenderness and His great love. Often the ones whom they meet with sternness and severity are under the stress of temptation. Satan is wrestling with these souls, and harsh, unsympathetic words discourage them and cause them to fall a prey to the tempter's power.

It is a delicate matter to deal with minds. Only He who reads the heart knows how to bring men to repentance. Only His wisdom can give us success in reaching the lost. You may stand up stiffly, feeling, "I am holier than thou," and it matters not how correct your reasoning or how true your words; they will never touch hearts. The love of Christ, manifested in word and act, will win its way to the soul, when the reiteration of precept or argument would accomplish nothing.

We need more of Christlike sympathy; not merely sympathy for those who appear to us to be faultless, but sympathy for poor, suffering, struggling souls, who are often overtaken in fault, sinning and repenting, tempted and discouraged. We are to go to our fellow men, touched, like our merciful High Priest, with the feeling of their infirmities.

It was the outcast, the publican and sinner, the despised of the nations, that Christ called and by His loving-kindness compelled to come unto Him. The one class that He would never countenance was those who stood apart in their self-esteem and looked down upon others.

"Go out into the highways and hedges, and compel them to come in," Christ bids us, "that My house may be filled." In obedience to this word we must go to the heathen who are near us, and to those who are afar off. The "publicans and harlots" must hear the Saviour's invitation. Through the kindness and long-suffering of His messengers the invitation becomes a compelling power to uplift those who are sunken in the lowest depths of sin.

Christian motives demand that we work with a steady purpose, an undying interest, an ever-increasing importunity, for the souls whom Satan is seeking to destroy. Nothing is to chill the earnest, yearning energy for the salvation of the lost.

Mark how all through the word of God there is manifest the spirit of urgency, of imploring men and women to come to Christ. We must seize upon every opportunity, in private and in public, presenting every argument, urging every motive of infinite weight, to draw men to the Saviour. With all our power we must urge them to look unto Jesus and to accept His life of self-denial and sacrifice. We must show that we expect them to give joy to the heart of Christ by using every one of His gifts in honouring His name.

Saved by Hope

"We are saved by hope." Romans 8:24. The fallen must be led to feel that it is not too late for them to be men. Christ honoured man with His confidence and thus placed him on his honour. Even those who had fallen the lowest He treated with respect. It was a continual pain to Christ to be brought into contact with enmity, depravity, and impurity; but never did He utter one expression to show that His sensibilities were shocked or His refined tastes offended. Whatever the evil habits, the strong prejudices, or the overbearing passions of human beings, He met them all with pitying tenderness. As we partake of His Spirit, we shall regard all men as brethren, with similar temptations and trials, often falling and struggling to rise again, battling with discouragements and difficulties, craving sympathy and help. Then we shall meet them in such a way as not to discourage or repel them, but to awaken hope in their hearts. As they are thus encouraged, they can say with confidence, "Rejoice not against me, O mine enemy: when I fall, I shall arise; when I sit in darkness, the Lord shall be a light unto me." He will "plead my cause, and execute judgement for me: He will bring me forth to the light, and I shall behold His righteousness." Micah 7:8, 9.

> God "looketh upon all the inhabitants of the earth.
> He fashioneth their hearts alike."
> Psalm 33:14, 15.

He bids us, in dealing with the tempted and the erring, consider "thyself, lest thou also be tempted." Galatians 6:1. With a sense of our own infirmities, we shall have compassion for the infirmities of others.

"Who maketh thee to differ from another? and what hast thou that thou didst not receive? "One is your Master; . . . and all ye are brethren." "Why dost thou judge thy brother? or why dost thou set at nought thy brother?" "Let us not therefore judge one another: . . . but judge this rather, that no man put a stumbling block or an occasion to fall in his brother's way." 1 Corinthians 4:7; Matthew 23:8; Romans 14:10, 13.

It is always humiliating to have one's errors pointed out. None should make the experience more bitter by needless censure. No one was ever reclaimed by reproach; but many have thus been repelled and have been led to steel their hearts against conviction. A tender spirit, a gentle, winning deportment, may save the erring and hide a multitude of sins.

The apostle Paul found it necessary to reprove wrong, but how carefully he sought to show that he was a friend to the erring! How anxiously he explained to them the reason of his action! He made them understand that it cost him pain to give them pain. He showed his confidence and sympathy toward the ones who were struggling to overcome.

"Out of much affliction and anguish of heart," he said, "I wrote unto you with many tears; not that ye should be grieved, but that ye might know the love which I have more abundantly unto you." 2 Corinthians 2:4. "For though I made you sorry with my epistle, I do not regret it: though I did regret it, . . . I now rejoice, not that ye were made sorry, but that ye were made sorry unto repentance. . . . For behold, this selfsame thing, that ye were made sorry after a godly sort, what earnest care it wrought in you, yea what clearing of yourselves, yea what indignation, yea what fear, yea what longing, yea what zeal, yea what avenging! In everything ye approved yourselves to be pure in the matter. . . . Therefore we have been comforted." 2 Corinthians 7: 8-13, ARV.

"I rejoice that in everything I am of good courage concerning you." "I thank my God upon every remembrance of you, always in every prayer of mine for you all making request with joy, for your fellowship in the gospel from the first day until now;" "being confident of this very thing, that He who began a good work in you will perfect it until the day of Jesus Christ: even as it is right for me to be thus minded on behalf of you all, because I have you in my heart." "Therefore, my brethren dearly beloved and longed for, my joy and crown, so stand fast in the Lord, my dearly beloved." "Now we live, if ye stand fast in the Lord." Verse 16, ARV; Philippians 1:3-5; 1:6, 7, ARV; 4:1; 1 Thessalonians 3:8.

Paul wrote to these brethren as "saints in Christ Jesus;" but he was not writing to those who were perfect in character. He wrote to them as men and women who were striving against temptation and who were in danger of falling. He pointed them to "the God of peace, that brought again from the dead our Lord Jesus, that Great Shepherd of the sheep." He assured them that "through the blood of the everlasting covenant" He will "make you perfect in every good work to do His will, working in you that which is well pleasing in His sight, through Jesus Christ." Hebrews 13:20, 21.

When one at fault becomes conscious of his error, be careful not to destroy his self-respect. Do not discourage him by indifference or distrust. Do not say, "Before giving him my confidence, I will wait to see whether he will hold out." Often this very distrust causes the tempted one to stumble.

We should strive to understand the weakness of others. We know little of the heart trials of those who have been bound in chains of darkness and who lack resolution and moral power. Most pitiable is the condition of him who is suffering under remorse; he is as one stunned, staggering, sinking into the dust. He can see nothing clearly. The mind is beclouded, he knows not what steps to take. Many a poor soul is misunderstood, unappreciated, full of distress and agony – a lost, straying sheep. He cannot find God, yet he has an intense longing for pardon and peace.

Oh, let no word be spoken to cause deeper pain! To the soul weary of a life of sin, but knowing not where to find relief, present the compassionate Saviour. Take him by the hand, lift him up, speak to him words of courage and hope. Help him to grasp the hand of the Saviour.

We become too easily discouraged over the souls who do not at once respond to our efforts. Never should we cease to labour for a soul while there is one gleam of hope. Precious souls cost our self-sacrificing Redeemer too dear a price to be lightly given up to the tempter's power.

We need to put ourselves in the place of the tempted ones. Consider the power of heredity, the influence of evil associations and surroundings, the power of wrong habits. Can we wonder that under such influences many become degraded? Can we wonder that they should be slow to respond to efforts for their uplifting?

Often, when won to the gospel, those who appeared coarse and unpromising will be among its most loyal adherents and advocates. They are not altogether corrupt. Beneath the forbidding exterior there are good impulses that might be reached. Without a helping hand many would never recover themselves, but by patient, persistent effort they may be uplifted. Such need tender words, kind consideration, tangible help. They need that kind of counsel which will not extinguish the faint gleam of courage in the soul. Let the workers who come in contact with them consider this.

Some will be found whose minds have been so long debased that they will never in this life become what under more favourable circumstances they might have been. But the bright beams of the Sun of Righteousness may shine into the soul. It is their privilege to have the life that measures with the life of God. Plant in their minds uplifting, ennobling thoughts. Let your life make plain to them the difference between vice and purity, darkness and light. In your example let them read what it means to be a Christian. Christ is able to uplift the most sinful and place them where they will be acknowledged as children of God, joint heirs with Christ to the immortal inheritance.

By the miracle of divine grace, many may be fitted for lives of usefulness. Despised and forsaken, they have become utterly discouraged; they may appear stoical and stolid. But under the ministration of the Holy Spirit, the stupidity that makes their uplifting appear so hopeless will pass away. The dull, clouded mind will awake. The slave of sin will be set free. Vice will disappear, and ignorance will be overcome. Through the faith that works by love, the heart will be purified and the mind enlightened.

Working for the Intemperate

Every true reform has its place in the work of the gospel and tends to the uplifting of the soul to a new and nobler life. Especially does the temperance reform demand the support of Christian workers. They should call attention to this work and make it a living issue. Everywhere they should present to the people the principles of true temperance and call for signers to the temperance pledge. Earnest effort should be made in behalf of those who are in bondage to evil habits.

There is everywhere a work to be done for those who through intemperance have fallen. In the midst of churches, religious institutions, and professedly Christian homes, many of the youth are choosing the path to destruction. Through intemperate habits they bring upon themselves disease, and through greed to obtain money for sinful indulgence they fall into dishonest practices. Health and character are ruined. Aliens from God, outcasts from society, these poor souls feel that they are without hope either for this life or for the life to come. The hearts of the parents are broken. Men speak of these erring ones as hopeless; but not so does God regard them. He understands all the circumstances that have made them what they are, and He looks upon them with pity. This is a class that demand help. Never give them occasion to say, "No man cares for my soul."

Among the victims of intemperance are men of all classes and all professions. Men of high station, of eminent talents, of great attainments, have yielded to the indulgence of appetite until they are helpless to resist temptation. Some of them who were once in the possession of wealth are without home, without friends, in suffering, misery, disease, and degradation. They have lost their self-control. Unless a helping hand is held out to them, they will sink lower and lower. With these self-indulgence is not only a moral sin, but a physical disease.

Often in helping the intemperate we must, as Christ so often did, give first attention to their physical condition. They need wholesome, unstimulating food and drink, clean clothing, opportunity to secure physical cleanliness. They need to be surrounded with an atmosphere of helpful, uplifting Christian influence. In every city a place should be provided where the slaves of evil habit may receive help to break the chains that bind them. Strong drink is regarded by many as the only solace in trouble; but this need not be, if, instead of acting the part of the priest and Levite, professed Christians would follow the example of the good Samaritan.

In dealing with the victims of intemperance we must remember that we are not dealing with sane men, but with those who for the time being are under the power of a demon. Be patient and forbearing. Think not of the repulsive, forbidding appearance, but of the precious life that Christ died to redeem. As the drunkard awakens to a sense of his degradation, do all in your power to show that you are his friend. Speak no word of censure. Let no act or look express reproach or aversion. Very likely the poor soul curses himself. Help him to rise. Speak words that will encourage faith. Seek to strengthen every good trait in his character. Teach him how to reach upward. Show him that it is possible for him to live so as to win the respect of his fellow men. Help him to see the value of the talents which God has given him, but which he has neglected to improve.

Although the will has been depraved and weakened, there is hope for him in Christ. He will awaken in the heart higher impulses and holier desires. Encourage him to lay hold of the hope set before him in the gospel. Open the Bible before the tempted, struggling one, and over and over again read to him the promises of God. These promises will be to him as the leaves of the tree of life. Patiently continue your efforts, until with grateful joy the trembling hand grasps the hope of redemption through Christ.

You must hold fast to those whom you are trying to help, else victory will never be yours. They will be continually tempted to evil. Again and again they will be almost overcome by the craving for strong drink; again and again they may fall; but do not, because of this, cease your efforts.

They have decided to make an effort to live for Christ; but their will power is weakened, and they must be carefully guarded by those who watch for souls as they that must give an account. They have lost their manhood, and this they must win back. Many have to battle against strong hereditary tendencies to evil. Unnatural cravings, sensual impulses, were their inheritance from birth. These must be carefully guarded against. Within and without, good and evil are striving for the mastery. Those who have never passed through such experiences cannot know the almost overmastering power of appetite or the fierceness of the conflict between habits of self-indulgence and the determination to be temperate in all things. Over and over again the battle must be fought.

Many who are drawn to Christ will not have moral courage to continue the warfare against appetite and passion. But the worker must not be discouraged by this. Is it only those rescued from the lowest depths that backslide?

Remember that you do not work alone. Ministering angels unite in service with every truehearted son and daughter of God. And Christ is the restorer. The Great Physician Himself stands beside His faithful workers, saying to the repentant soul, "Child, thy sins be forgiven thee." Mark 2:5, ARV, margin.

Many are the outcasts who will grasp the hope set before them in the gospel and will enter the kingdom of heaven, while others who were blessed with great opportunities and great light which they did not improve will be left in outer darkness.

The victims of evil habit must be aroused to the necessity of making an effort for themselves. Others may put forth the most earnest endeavour to uplift them, the grace of God may be freely offered, Christ may entreat, His angels may minister; but all will be in vain unless they themselves are roused to fight the battle in their own behalf.

The last words of David to Solomon, then a young man, and soon to receive the crown of Israel, were, "Be . . . strong, . . . and show thyself a man." 1 Kings 2:2. To every child of humanity, the candidate for an immortal crown, are these words of inspiration spoken, "Be . . . strong, . . . and show thyself a man."

The self-indulgent must be led to see and feel that great moral renovation is necessary if they would be men. God calls upon them to arouse and in the strength of Christ win back the God-given manhood that has been sacrificed through sinful indulgence.

Feeling the terrible power of temptation, the drawing of desire that leads to indulgence, many a man cries in despair, "I cannot resist evil." Tell him that he can, that he must resist. He may have been overcome again and again, but it need not be always thus. He is weak in moral power, controlled by the habits of a life of sin. His promises and resolutions are like ropes of sand. The knowledge of his broken promises and forfeited pledges weakens his confidence in his own sincerity and causes him to feel that God cannot accept him or work with his efforts. But he need not despair.

Those who put their trust in Christ are not to be enslaved by any heredity or cultivated habit or tendency. Instead of being held in bondage to the lower nature, they are to rule every appetite and passion. God has not left us to battle with evil in our own finite strength. Whatever may be our inherited or cultivated tendencies to wrong, we can overcome through the power that He is ready to impart.

The Power of the Will

The tempted one needs to understand the true force of

the will. This is the governing power in the nature of man — the power of decision, of choice. Everything depends on the right action of the will. Desires for goodness and purity are right, so far as they go; but if we stop here, they avail nothing. Many will go down to ruin while hoping and desiring to overcome their evil propensities. They do not yield the will to God. They do not *choose* to serve Him.

God has given us the power of choice; it is ours to exercise. We cannot change our hearts, we cannot control our thoughts, our impulses, our affections. We cannot make ourselves pure, fit for God's service. But we can *choose* to serve God, we can give Him our will; then He will work in us to will and to do according to His good pleasure. Thus our whole nature will be brought under the control of Christ.

Through the right exercise of the will, an entire change may be made in the life. By yielding up the will to Christ, we ally ourselves with divine power. We receive strength from above to hold us steadfast. A pure and noble life, a life of victory over appetite and lust, is possible to everyone who will unite his weak, wavering human will to the omnipotent, unwavering will of God.

Those who are struggling against the power of appetite should be instructed in the principles of healthful living. They should be shown that violation of the laws of health, by creating diseased conditions and unnatural cravings, lays the foundation of the liquor habit. Only by living in obedience to the principles of health can they hope to be freed from the craving for unnatural stimulants. While they depend upon divine strength to break the bonds of appetite, they are to cooperate with God by obedience to His laws, both moral and physical.

Those who are endeavouring to reform should be provided with employment. None who are able to labour should be taught to expect food and clothing and shelter free of cost. For their own sake, as well as for the sake of others, some way should be devised whereby they may return an equivalent for what they receive.

Encourage every effort toward self-support. This will strengthen self-respect and a noble independence. And occupation of mind and body in useful work is essential as a safeguard against temptation.

Disappointments; Dangers

Those who work for the fallen will be disappointed in many who give promise of reform. Many will make but a superficial change in their habits and practices. They are moved by impulse, and for a time may seem to have reformed; but there is no real change of heart. They cherish the same self-love, have the same hungering for foolish pleasures, the same desire for self-indulgence. They have not a knowledge of the work of character building, and they cannot be relied upon as men of principle. They have debased their mental and spiritual powers by the gratification of appetite and passion, and this makes them weak. They are fickle and changeable. Their impulses tend toward sensuality. These persons are often a source of danger to others. Being looked upon as reformed men and women, they are trusted with responsibilities and are placed where their influence corrupts the innocent.

Even those who are sincerely seeking to reform are not beyond the danger of falling. They need to be treated with great wisdom as well as tenderness. The disposition to flatter and exalt those who have been rescued from the lowest depths sometimes proves their ruin. The practice of inviting men and women to relate in public the experience of their life of sin is full of danger to both speaker and hearers. To dwell upon scenes of evil is corrupting to mind and soul. And the prominence given to the rescued ones is harmful to them. Many are led to feel that their sinful life has given them a certain distinction. A love of notoriety and a spirit of self-trust are encouraged that prove fatal to the soul. Only in distrust of self and dependence on the mercy of Christ can they stand.

All who give evidence of true conversion should be encouraged to work for others. Let none turn away a soul who leaves the service of Satan for the service of Christ. When one gives evidence that the Spirit of God is striving with him, present every encouragement for entering the Lord's service. "Of some have compassion, making a difference." Jude 22. Those who are wise in the wisdom that comes from God will see souls in need of help, those who have sincerely repented, but who without encouragement would hardly dare to lay hold of hope. The Lord will put it into the hearts of His servants to welcome these trembling, repentant ones to their loving fellowship. Whatever may have been their besetting sins, however low they may have fallen, when in contrition they come to Christ, He receives them. Then give them something to do for Him. If they desire to labour in uplifting others from the pit of destruction from which they themselves were rescued, give them opportunity. Bring them into association with experienced Christians, that they may gain spiritual strength. Fill their hearts and hands with work for the Master.

When light flashes into the soul, some who appeared to be most fully given to sin will become successful workers for just such sinners as they themselves once were. Through faith in Christ some will rise to high places of service and be entrusted with responsibilities in the work of saving souls. They see where their own weakness lies, they realize the depravity of their nature. They know the strength of sin, the power of evil habit. They realize their inability to overcome without the help of Christ, and their constant cry is, "I cast my helpless soul on Thee."

These can help others. The one who has been tempted and tried, whose hope was well-nigh gone, but who was saved by hearing a message of love, can understand the science of soulsaving. He whose heart is filled with love for Christ because he himself has been sought for by the Saviour and brought back to the fold, knows how to seek the lost. He can point sinners to the Lamb of God. He has given himself without reserve to God and has been accepted in the Beloved. The hand that in weakness was held out for help has been grasped. By the ministry of such ones many prodigals will be brought to the Father.

For every soul struggling to rise from a life of sin to a life of purity, the great element of power abides in the only "name under heaven given among men, whereby we must be saved." Acts 4:12. "If any man thirst" for restful hope, for deliverance from sinful propensities, Christ says, "let him come unto Me, and drink." John 7:37. The only remedy for vice is the grace and power of Christ.

The good resolutions made in one's own strength avail nothing. Not all the pledges in the world will break the power of evil habit. Never will men practice temperance in all things until their hearts are renewed by divine grace. We cannot keep ourselves from sin for one moment. Every moment we are dependent upon God.

True reformation begins with soul cleansing. Our work for the fallen will achieve real success only as the grace of Christ reshapes the character and the soul is brought into living connection with God.

Christ lived a life of perfect obedience to God's law, and in this He set an example for every human being. The life that He lived in this world we are to live through His power and under His instruction.

In our work for the fallen the claims of the law of God and the need of loyalty to Him are to be impressed on mind and heart. Never fail to show that there is a marked difference between the one who serves God and the one who serves Him not. God is love, but He cannot excuse wilful disregard for His commands. The enactments of His government are such that men do not escape the consequences of disloyalty. Only those who honour Him can He honour. Man's conduct in this world decides his eternal destiny. As he has sown, so he must reap. Cause will be followed by effect.

Nothing less than perfect obedience can meet the standard of God's requirement. He has not left His requirements indefinite. He has enjoined nothing that is not necessary in order to bring man into harmony with

Him. We are to point sinners to His ideal of character and to lead them to Christ, by whose grace only can this ideal be reached.

The Saviour took upon Himself the infirmities of humanity and lived a sinless life, that men might have no fear that because of the weakness of human nature they could not overcome. Christ came to make us "partakers of the divine nature," and His life declares that humanity, combined with divinity, does not commit sin.

The Saviour overcame to show man how he may overcome. All the temptations of Satan, Christ met with the word of God. By trusting in God's promises, He received power to obey God's commandments, and the tempter could gain no advantage. To every temptation His answer was, "It is written." So God has given us His word wherewith to resist evil. Exceeding great and precious promises are ours, that by these we "might be partakers of the divine nature, having escaped the corruption that is in the world through lust." 2 Peter 1:4.

Bid the tempted one look not to circumstances, to the weakness of self, or to the power of temptation, but to the power of God's word. All its strength is ours. "Thy word," says the psalmist, "have I hid in mine heart, that I might not sin against Thee." "By the word of Thy lips I have kept me from the paths of the destroyer." Psalms 119:11, 17:4.

Talk courage to the people; lift them up to God in prayer. Many who have been overcome by temptation are humiliated by their failures, and they feel that it is in vain for them to approach unto God; but this thought is of the enemy's suggestion. When they have sinned, and feel that they cannot pray, tell them that it is then the time to pray. Ashamed they may be, and deeply humbled; but as they confess their sins, He who is faithful and just will forgive their sins and cleanse them from all unrighteousness.

Nothing is apparently more helpless, yet really more invincible, than the soul that feels its nothingness and relies wholly on the merits of the Saviour. By prayer, by the study of His word, by faith in His abiding presence, the weakest of human beings may live in contact with the living Christ, and He will hold them by a hand that will never let go.

These precious words every soul that abides in Christ may make his own. He may say:

> "I will look unto the Lord;
> I will wait for the God of my salvation:
> My God will hear me.
> Rejoice not against me, O mine enemy:
> When I fall, I shall arise;
> When I sit in darkness,
> The Lord shall be a light unto me."
> Micah 7:7, 8.
>
> "He will again have compassion on us,
> He will blot out our iniquities;
> Yea, Thou wilt cast all our sins into the depths of the sea!"
> Micah 7:19, Noyes.

God has promised:

> "I will make a man more precious than fine gold;
> Even a man than the golden wedge of Ophir."
> Isaiah 13:12.
>
> "Though ye have lain among the pots,
> Yet shall ye be as the wings of a dove covered with silver,
> And her feathers with yellow gold."
> Psalm 68:13.

Those whom Christ has forgiven most will love Him most. These are they who in the final day will stand nearest to His throne.

"They shall see His face; and His name shall be in their foreheads." Revelation 22:4.

Help for the Unemployed and the Homeless

There are largehearted men and women who are anxiously considering the condition of the poor and what means can be found for their relief. How the unemployed and the homeless can be helped to secure the common blessings of God's providence and to live the life He intended man to live, is a question to which many are earnestly endeavouring to find an answer. But there are not many, even among educators and statesmen, who comprehend the causes that underlie the present state of society. Those who hold the reins of government are unable to solve the problem of poverty, pauperism, and increasing crime. They are struggling in vain to place business operations on a more secure basis.

If men would give more heed to the teaching of God's word, they would find a solution of these problems that perplex them. Much might be learned from the Old Testament in regard to the labour question and the relief of the poor.

God's Plan for Israel

In God's plan for Israel every family had a home on the land, with sufficient ground for tilling. Thus were provided both the means and the incentive for a useful, industrious, and self-supporting life. And no devising of men has ever improved upon that plan. To the world's departure from it is owing, to a large degree, the poverty and wretchedness that exist today.

At the settlement of Israel in Canaan, the land was

divided among the whole people, the Levites only, as ministers of the sanctuary, being excepted from the equal distribution. The tribes were numbered by families, and to each family, according to its numbers, was apportioned an inheritance.

And although one might for a time dispose of his possession, he could not permanently barter away the inheritance of his children. When able to redeem his land, he was at liberty at any time to do so. Debts were remitted every seventh year, and in the fiftieth, or year of jubilee, all landed property reverted to the original owner.

"The land shall not be sold forever," was the Lord's direction; "for the land is Mine; for ye are strangers and sojourners with Me. And in all the land of your possession ye shall grant a redemption for the land. If thy brother be waxen poor, and hath sold away some of his possession, and if any of his kin come to redeem it, then shall he redeem that which his brother sold. And if the man . . . himself be able to redeem it; . . . he may return unto his possession. But if he be not able to restore it to him, then that which is sold shall remain in the hand of him that hath bought it until the year of jubilee." Leviticus 25:23-28.

"Ye shall hallow the fiftieth year, and proclaim liberty throughout all the land unto all the inhabitants thereof: it shall be a jubilee unto you; and ye shall return every man unto his possession, and ye shall return every man unto his family." Verse 10.

Thus every family was secured in its possession, and a safeguard was afforded against the extremes of either wealth or want.

Industrial Training

In Israel, industrial training was regarded as a duty. Every father was required to teach his sons some useful trade. The greatest men in Israel were trained to industrial pursuits. A knowledge of the duties pertaining to housewifery was considered essential for every woman.

And skill in these duties was regarded as an honour to women of the highest station.

Various industries were taught in the schools of the prophets, and many of the students sustained themselves by manual labour.

Consideration for the Poor

These arrangements did not, however, wholly do away with poverty. It was not God's purpose that poverty should wholly cease. It is one of His means for the development of character. "The poor," He says, "shall never cease out of the land: therefore I command thee, saying, Thou shalt open thine hand wide unto thy brother, to thy poor, and to thy needy, in thy land." Deuteronomy 15:11.

"If there be among you a poor man of one of thy brethren within any of thy gates in thy land which the Lord thy God giveth thee, thou shalt not harden thine heart, nor shut thine hand from thy poor brother. But thou shalt open thine hand wide unto him, and shalt surely lend him sufficient for his need, in that which he wanteth." Verses 7, 8.

"If thy brother be waxen poor, and fallen in decay with thee; then thou shalt relieve him: yea, though he be a stranger, or a sojourner; that he may live with thee." Leviticus 25:35.

"When ye reap the harvest of your land, thou shalt not wholly reap the corners of thy field." "When thou cuttest down thine harvest in thy field, and hast forgot a sheaf in the field, thou shalt not go again to fetch it. . . . When thou beatest thine olive tree, thou shalt not go over the boughs again. . . . When thou gatherest the grapes of thy vineyard, thou shalt not glean it afterward: it shall be for the stranger, for the fatherless, and for the widow." Leviticus 19:9; Deuteronomy 24:19-21.

None need fear that their liberality would bring them to want. Obedience to God's commandments would surely result in prosperity. "For this thing," God said, "the Lord thy God shall bless thee in all thy works, and in all that thou puttest thine hand unto." "Thou shalt lend unto many nations, but thou shalt not borrow; and thou shalt reign over many nations, but they shall not reign over thee." Deuteronomy 15:10, 6.

Business Principles

God's word sanctions no policy that will enrich one class by the oppression and suffering of another. In all our business transactions it teaches us to put ourselves in the place of those with whom we are dealing, to look not only on our own things, but also on the things of others. He who would take advantage of another's misfortunes in order to benefit himself, or who seeks to profit himself through another's weakness or incompetence, is a transgressor both of the principles and of the precepts of the word of God.

"Thou shalt not pervert the judgement of the stranger, nor of the fatherless; nor take a widow's raiment to pledge." "When thou dost lend thy brother anything, thou shalt not go into his house to fetch his pledge. Thou shalt stand abroad, and the man to whom thou dost lend shall bring out the pledge abroad unto thee. And if the man be poor, thou shalt not sleep with his pledge." "If thou at all take thy neighbour's raiment to pledge, thou shalt deliver it unto him by that the sun goeth down: for that is his covering only: . . . wherein shall he sleep? and it shall come to pass, when he crieth unto Me, that I will hear; for I am gracious." "If thou sell aught unto thy neighbour, or buyest aught of thy neighbour's hand, ye shall not oppress one another" Deuteronomy 24:17, 10-12; Exodus 22:26, 27; Leviticus 25:14.

"Ye shall do no unrighteousness in judgement, in measures of length, of weight, or of quantity." "Thou shalt not have in thy bag diverse weights, a great and a small. Thou shalt not have in thy house diverse measures, a great and a small." "Just balances, just weights, a just ephah, and a just hin, shall ye have." Leviticus 19:35, ARV; Deuteronomy 25:13, 14, ARV; Leviticus 19:36, ARV.

"Give to him that asketh thee, and from him that

would borrow of thee turn not thou away." "The wicked borroweth, and payeth not again: but the righteous showeth mercy, and giveth." Matthew 5:42; Psalm 37:21.

"Give counsel, execute justice; make thy shade as the night in the midst of the noonday; hide the outcasts; betray not the fugitive." "Let Mine outcasts dwell with thee; . . . be thou a covert to them from the face of the spoiler." Isaiah 16:3 (ARV), 4.

The plan of life that God gave to Israel was intended as an object lesson for all mankind. If these principles were carried out today, what a different place this world would be!

Within the vast boundaries of nature there is still room for the suffering and needy to find a home. Within her bosom there are resources sufficient to provide them with food. Hidden in the depths of the earth are blessings for all who have courage and will and perseverance to gather her treasures.

The tilling of the soil, the employment that God appointed to man in Eden, opens a field in which there is opportunity for multitudes to gain a subsistence.

> "Trust in the Lord, and do good;
> So shalt thou dwell in the land, and verily thou shalt be fed."
>
> Psalm 37:3.

Thousands and tens of thousands might be working upon the soil who are crowded into the cities, watching for a chance to earn a trifle. In many cases this trifle is not spent for bread, but is put into the till of the liquor seller, to obtain that which destroys soul and body.

Many look upon labour as drudgery, and they try to obtain a livelihood by scheming rather than by honest toil. This desire to get a living without work opens the door to wretchedness and vice and crime almost without limit.

The City Slums

In the great cities are multitudes who receive less

care and consideration than are given to dumb animals. Think of the families herded together in miserable tenements, many of them dark basements, reeking with dampness and filth. In these wretched places children are born and grow up and die. They see nothing of the beauty of natural things that God has created to delight the senses and uplift the soul. Ragged and half-starved, they live amid vice and depravity, moulded in character by the wretchedness and sin that surround them. Children hear the name of God only in profanity. Foul speech, imprecations, and revilings fill their ears. The fumes of liquor and tobacco, sickening stenches, moral degradation, pervert their senses. Thus multitudes are trained to become criminals, foes to society that has abandoned them to misery and degradation.

Not all the poor in the city slums are of this class. God-fearing men and women have been brought to the depths of poverty by illness or misfortune, often through the dishonest scheming of those who live by preying upon their fellows. Many who are upright and well-meaning become poor through lack of industrial training. Through ignorance they are unfitted to wrestle with the difficulties of life. Drifting into the cities, they are often unable to find employment. Surrounded by the sights and sounds of vice, they are subjected to terrible temptation. Herded and often classed with the vicious and degraded, it is only by a superhuman struggle, a more than finite power, that they can be preserved from sinking to the same depths. Many hold fast their integrity, choosing to suffer rather than to sin. This class especially demand help, sympathy, and encouragement.

If the poor now crowded into the cities could find homes upon the land, they might not only earn a livelihood, but find health and happiness now unknown to them. Hard work, simple fare, close economy, often hardship and privation, would be their lot. But what a blessing would be theirs in leaving the city, with its enticements to evil, its turmoil and crime, misery and foulness, for the country's quiet and peace and purity.

To many of those living in the cities who have not a spot of green grass to set their feet upon, who year after year have looked out upon filthy courts and narrow alleys, brick walls and pavements, and skies clouded with dust and smoke – if these could be taken to some farming district, surrounded with the green fields, the woods and hills and brooks, the clear skies and the fresh, pure air of the country, it would seem almost like heaven.

Cut off to a great degree from contact with and dependence upon men, and separated from the world's corrupting maxims and customs and excitements, they would come nearer to the heart of nature. God's presence would be more real to them. Many would learn the lesson of dependence upon Him. Through nature they would hear His voice speaking to their hearts of His peace and love, and mind and soul and body would respond to the healing, life-giving power.

If they ever become industrious and self-supporting, very many must have assistance, encouragement, and instruction. There are multitudes of poor families for whom no better missionary work could be done than to assist them in settling on the land and in learning how to make it yield them a livelihood.

The need for such help and instruction is not confined to the cities. Even in the country, with all its possibilities for a better life, multitudes of the poor are in great need. Whole communities are devoid of education in industrial and sanitary lines. Families live in hovels, with scant furniture and clothing, without tools, without books, destitute both of comforts and conveniences and of means of culture. Imbruted souls, bodies weak and ill-formed, reveal the results of evil heredity and of wrong habits. These people must be educated from the very foundation. They have led shiftless, idle, corrupt lives, and they need to be trained to correct habits.

How can they be awakened to the necessity of improvement? How can they be directed to a higher ideal of life? How can they be helped to rise? What can be done where poverty prevails and is to be contended with at every step? Certainly the work is difficult. The necessary reformation will never be made unless men and women are assisted by a power outside of themselves. It is God's purpose that the rich and the poor shall be closely bound together by the ties of sympathy and helpfulness. Those who have means, talents, and capabilities are to use these gifts in blessing their fellow men.

Christian farmers can do real missionary work in helping the poor to find homes on the land and in teaching them how to till the soil and make it productive. Teach them how to use the implements of agriculture, how to cultivate various crops, how to plant and care for orchards.

Many who till the soil fail to secure adequate returns because of their neglect. Their orchards are not properly cared for, the crops are not put in at the right time, and a mere surface work is done in cultivating the soil. Their ill success they charge to the unproductiveness of the land. False witness is often borne in condemning land that, if properly worked, would yield rich returns. The narrow plans, the little strength put forth, the little study as to the best methods, call loudly for reform.

Let proper methods be taught to all who are willing to learn. If any do not wish you to speak to them of advanced ideas, let the lessons be given silently. Keep up the culture of your own land. Drop a word to your neighbours when you can, and let the harvest be eloquent in favour of right methods. Demonstrate what can be done with the land when properly worked.

Attention should be given to the establishment of various industries so that poor families can find employment. Carpenters, blacksmiths, and indeed everyone who understands some line of useful labour, should feel a responsibility to teach and help the ignorant and the unemployed.

In ministry to the poor there is a wide field of service for women as well as for men. The efficient cook, the housekeeper, the seamstress, the nurse — the help of all is needed. Let the members of poor households be taught how to cook, how to make and mend their own clothing, how to nurse the sick, how to care properly for the home. Let boys and girls be thoroughly taught some useful trade or occupation.

Missionary Families

Missionary families are needed to settle in the waste places. Let farmers, financiers, builders, and those who are skilled in various arts and crafts, go to neglected fields, to improve the land, to establish industries, to prepare humble homes for themselves, and to help their neighbours.

The rough places of nature, the wild places, God has made attractive by placing beautiful things among the most unsightly. This is the work we are called to do. Even the desert places of the earth, where the outlook appears to be forbidding, may become as the garden of God.

"In that day shall the deaf hear the words of the book,
And the eyes of the blind shall see out of obscurity, and out of darkness.
The meek also shall increase their joy in the Lord,
And the poor among men shall rejoice in the Holy One of Israel."
Isaiah 29:18, 19.

By instruction in practical lines we can often help the poor most effectively. As a rule, those who have not been trained to work do not have habits of industry, perseverance, economy, and self-denial. They do not know how to manage. Often through lack of carefulness and right judgement there is wasted that which would maintain their families in decency and comfort if it were carefully and economically used. "Much food is in the tillage of the poor: but there is that is destroyed for want of judgement." Proverbs 13:23.

We may give to the poor, and harm them, by teaching them to be dependent. Such giving encourages selfishness and helplessness. Often it leads to idleness, extravagance, and intemperance. No man who can earn his own livelihood has a right to depend on others. The proverb "The world owes me a living" has in it the essence of falsehood, fraud, and robbery. The world owes no man a living who is able to work and gain a living for himself.

Real charity helps men to help themselves. If one comes to our door and asks for food, we should not turn him away hungry; his poverty may be the result of misfortune. But true beneficence means more than mere gifts. It means a genuine interest in the welfare of others. We should seek to understand the needs of the poor and distressed, and to give them the help that will benefit them most. To give thought and time and personal effort costs far more than merely to give money. But it is the truest charity.

Those who are taught to earn what they receive will more readily learn to make the most of it. And in learning to be self-reliant, they are acquiring that which will not only make them self-sustaining, but will enable them to help others. Teach the importance of life's duties to those who are wasting their opportunities. Show them that Bible religion never makes men idlers. Christ always encouraged industry. "Why stand ye here all the day idle?" He said to the indolent. "I must work . . . while it is day: the night cometh, when no man can work." Matthew 20:6; John 9:4.

It is the privilege of all to give to the world in their home life, in their customs and practices and order, an evidence of what the gospel can do for those who obey it. Christ came to our world to give us an example of what we may become. He expects His followers to be models of correctness in all the relations of life. He desires the divine touch to be seen upon outward things.

Our own homes and surroundings should be object lessons, teaching ways of improvement, so that industry, cleanliness, taste, and refinement may take the place of idleness, uncleanness, coarseness, and disorder. By our lives and example we can help others to discern that which is repulsive in their character or their surroundings, and with Christian courtesy we may encourage improvement. As we manifest an interest in them, we shall find opportunity to teach them how to put their energies to the best use.

Hope and Courage

We can do nothing without courage and perseverance. Speak words of hope and courage to the poor and the disheartened. If need be, give tangible proof of your interest by helping them when they come into strait places. Those who have had many advantages should remember that they themselves still err in many things, and that it is painful to them when their errors are pointed out and there is held up before them a comely pattern of what they should be. Remember that kindness will accomplish more than censure. As you try to teach others, let them see that you wish them to reach the highest standard, and that you are ready to give them help. If in some things they fail, be not quick to condemn them.

Simplicity, self-denial, economy, lessons so essential for the poor to learn, often seem to them difficult and unwelcome. The example and spirit of the world is constantly exciting and fostering pride, love of display, self-indulgence, prodigality, and idleness. These evils bring thousands to penury and prevent thousands more from rising out of degradation and wretchedness. Christians are to encourage the poor to resist these influences.

Jesus came to this world in humility. He was of lowly birth. The Majesty of heaven, the King of glory, the Commander of all the angel host, He humbled Himself to accept humanity, and then He chose a life of poverty and humiliation. He had no opportunities that the poor do not have. Toil, hardship, and privation were a part of every day's experience. "Foxes have holes," He said, "and birds of the air have nests; but the Son of man hath not where to lay His head." Luke 9:58.

Jesus did not seek the admiration or the applause of men. He commanded no army. He ruled no earthly kingdom. He did not court the favour of the wealthy and honoured of the world. He did not claim a position among the leaders of the nation. He dwelt among the lowly. He set at nought the artificial distinctions of society. The aristocracy of birth, wealth, talent, learning, rank, He ignored.

He was the Prince of heaven, yet He did not choose His disciples from among the learned lawyers, the rulers, the scribes, or the Pharisees. He passed these by, because they prided themselves on their learning and position. They were fixed in their traditions and superstitions. He who could read all hearts chose humble fishermen who were willing to be taught. He ate with publicans and sinners, and mingled with the common people, not to become low and earthly with them, but in order by precept and example to present to them right principles, and to uplift them from their earthliness and debasement.

Jesus sought to correct the world's false standard of judging the value of men. He took His position with the poor, that He might lift from poverty the stigma that the world had attached to it. He has stripped from it forever the reproach of scorn, by blessing the poor, the inheritors of God's kingdom. He points us to the path He trod, saying, "If any man will come after Me, let him deny himself, and take up his cross daily, and follow Me." Verse 23.

Christian workers are to meet the people where they are, and educate them, not in pride, but in character building. Teach them how Christ worked and denied Himself. Help them to learn from Him the lessons of self-denial and sacrifice. Teach them to beware of self-indulgence in conforming to fashion. Life is too valuable, too full of solemn, sacred responsibilities, to be wasted in pleasing self.

Life's Best Things

Men and women have hardly begun to understand the true object of life. They are attracted by glitter and show. They are ambitious for worldly pre-eminence. To this the true aims of life are sacrificed. Life's best things — simplicity, honesty, truthfulness, purity, integrity — cannot be bought or sold. They are as free to the ignorant as to the educated, to the humble labourer as to the honoured statesman. For everyone God has provided pleasure that may be enjoyed by rich and poor alike — the pleasure found in cultivating pureness of thought and unselfishness of action, the pleasure that comes from speaking sympathizing words and doing kindly deeds. From those who perform such service the light of Christ shines to brighten lives darkened by many shadows.

While helping the poor in temporal things, keep always in view their spiritual needs. Let your own life testify to the Saviour's keeping power. Let your character reveal the high standard to which all may attain. Teach the gospel in simple object lessons. Let everything with which you have to do be a lesson in character building.

In the humble round of toil, the very weakest, the most obscure, may be workers together with God and may have the comfort of His presence and sustaining grace. They are not to weary themselves with busy anxieties and needless cares. Let them work on from day to day, accomplishing faithfully the task that God's providence assigns, and He will care for them. He says:

"In nothing be anxious; but in everything by prayer and supplication with thanksgiving let your requests be made known unto God." "And the peace of God, which passeth all understanding, shall keep your hearts and minds through Christ Jesus." Philippians 4:6, ARV; 4:7.

The Lord's care is over all His creatures. He loves them all and makes no difference, except that He has the most tender pity for those who are called to bear life's heaviest burdens. God's children must meet trials and difficulties. But they should accept their lot with a cheerful spirit, remembering that for all that the world neglects to bestow, God Himself will make up to them in the best of favours.

It is when we come into difficult places that He reveals His power and wisdom in answer to humble prayer. Have confidence in Him as a prayer-hearing, prayer-answering God. He will reveal Himself to you as One who can help in every emergency. He who created man, who gave him his wonderful physical, mental, and spiritual faculties, will not withhold that which is necessary to sustain the life He has given. He who has given us His word — the leaves of the tree of life — will not withhold from us a knowledge of how to provide food for His needy children.

How can wisdom be obtained by him who holds the plough and drives the oxen? By seeking her as silver, and searching for her as for hid treasure. "For his God doth instruct him to discretion, and doth teach him." Isaiah 28:26. "This also cometh forth from Jehovah of hosts, who is wonderful in counsel, and excellent in wisdom." Verse 29, ARV.

He who taught Adam and Eve in Eden how to tend the garden, desires to instruct men today. There is wisdom for him who drives the plough and sows the seed. Before those who trust and obey Him, God will open ways of advance. Let them move forward courageously, trusting in Him to supply their needs according to the riches of His goodness.

He who fed the multitude with five loaves and two small fishes is able today to give us the fruit of our labour. He who said to the fishers of Galilee, "Let down your nets for a draft," and who, as they obeyed, filled their nets till they broke, desires His people to see in this an evidence of what He will do for them today. The God who in the wilderness gave the children of Israel manna from heaven still lives and reigns. He will guide His people and give skill and understanding in the work they are called to do. He will give wisdom to those who strive to do their duty conscientiously and intelligently. He who owns the world is rich in resources, and will bless everyone who is seeking to bless others.

We need to look heavenward in faith. We are not to be discouraged because of apparent failure, nor should we be disheartened by delay. We should work cheerfully, hopefully, gratefully, believing that the earth holds in her bosom rich treasures for the faithful worker to garner, stores richer than gold or silver. The mountains and hills are changing; the earth is waxing old like a garment; but the blessing of God, which spreads for His people a table in the wilderness, will never cease.

The Helpless Poor

When all has been done that can be done in helping the poor to help themselves, there still remain the widow and the fatherless, the aged, the helpless, and the sick, that claim sympathy and care. Never should these be neglected. They are committed by God Himself to the mercy, the love, and the tender care of all whom He has made His stewards.

The Household of Faith

"As we have therefore opportunity, let us do good unto all men, especially unto them who are of the household of faith." Galatians 6:10.

In a special sense, Christ has laid upon His church the duty of caring for the needy among its own members. He suffers His poor to be in the borders of every church. They are always to be among us, and He places upon the members of the church a personal responsibility to care for them.

As the members of a true family care for one another, ministering to the sick, supporting the weak, teaching the ignorant, training the inexperienced, so is "the household of faith" to care for its needy and helpless ones. Upon no consideration are these to be passed by.

Widows and Orphans

The widow and the fatherless are the objects of the Lord's special care.

> "A Father of the fatherless, and a Judge of the widows,
> Is God in His holy habitation."
>
> "Thy Maker is thy husband;
> Jehovah of hosts is His name:

And the Holy One of Israel is thy Redeemer;
The God of the whole earth shall He be called."

"Leave thy fatherless children, I will preserve them
alive;
And let thy widows trust in Me."

Psalm 68:5; Isaiah 54:5, ARV; Jeremiah 49:11.

Many a father, when called upon to part from his loved ones, has died resting in faith upon God's promise to care for them. The Lord provides for the widow and the fatherless, not by a miracle in sending manna from heaven, not by sending ravens to bring them food; but by a miracle upon human hearts, expelling selfishness, and unsealing the fountains of Christlike love. The afflicted and bereaved ones He commits to His followers as a precious trust. They have the very strongest claim upon our sympathy.

In homes supplied with life's comforts, in bins and granaries filled with the yield of abundant harvests, in warehouses stocked with the products of the loom, and vaults stored with gold and silver, God has supplied means for the sustenance of these needy ones. He calls upon us to be channels of His bounty.

Many a widowed mother with her fatherless children is bravely striving to bear her double burden, often toiling far beyond her strength in order to keep her little ones with her and to provide for their needs. Little time has she for their training and instruction, little opportunity to surround them with influences that would brighten their lives. She needs encouragement, sympathy, and tangible help.

God calls upon us to supply to these children, so far as we can, the want of a father's care. Instead of standing aloof, complaining of their faults, and of the trouble they may cause, help them in every way possible. Seek to aid the careworn mother. Lighten her burdens.

Then there are the multitudes of children who have been wholly deprived of the guidance of parents and the subduing influence of a Christian home. Let Christians open their hearts and homes to these helpless ones. The work that God has committed to them as an individual duty should not be turned over to some benevolent institution or left to the chances of the world's charity. If the children have no relatives able to give them care, let the members of the church provide homes for them. He who made us ordained that we should be associated in families, and the child nature will develop best in the loving atmosphere of a Christian home.

Many who have no children of their own could do a good work in caring for the children of others. Instead of giving attention to pets, lavishing affection upon dumb animals, let them give their attention to little children, whose characters they may fashion after the divine similitude. Place your love upon the homeless members of the human family. See how many of these children you can bring up in the nurture and admonition of the Lord. Many would thus be greatly benefited themselves.

The Aged

The aged also need the helpful influences of the family. In the home of brethren and sisters in Christ can most nearly be made up to them the loss of their own home. If encouraged to share in the interests and occupations of the household, it will help them to feel that their usefulness is not at an end. Make them feel that their help is valued, that there is something yet for them to do in ministering to others, and it will cheer their hearts and give interest to their lives.

So far as possible let those whose whitening heads and failing steps show that they are drawing near to the grave remain among friends and familiar associations. Let them worship among those whom they have known and loved. Let them be cared for by loving and tender hands.

Whenever they are able to do so, it should be the privilege of the members of every family to minister to their own kindred. When this cannot be, the work belongs to the church, and it should be accepted both as a privilege and as a duty. All who possess Christ's spirit will have a tender regard for the feeble and the aged.

The presence in our homes of one of these helpless ones is a precious opportunity to co-operate with Christ in His ministry of mercy and to develop traits of character like His. There is a blessing in the association of the old and the young. The young may bring sunshine into the hearts and lives of the aged. Those whose hold on life is weakening need the benefit of contact with the hopefulness and buoyancy of youth. And the young may be helped by the wisdom and experience of the old. Above all, they need to learn the lesson of unselfish ministry. The presence of one in need of sympathy and forbearance and self-sacrificing love would be to many a household a priceless blessing. It would sweeten and refine the home life, and call forth in old and young those Christlike graces that would make them beautiful with a divine beauty and rich in heaven's imperishable treasure.

A Test of Character

"Ye have the poor with you always," Christ said, "and whensoever ye will ye may do them good." "Pure religion and undefiled before God and the Father is this, To visit the fatherless and widows in their affliction, and to keep himself unspotted from the world." Mark 14:7; James 1:27.

In placing among them the helpless and the poor, to be dependent upon their care, Christ tests His professed followers. By our love and service for His needy children we prove the genuineness of our love for Him. To neglect them is to declare ourselves false disciples, strangers to Christ and His love.

If all were done that could be done in providing homes in families for orphan children, there would still remain very many requiring care. Many of them have received an inheritance of evil. They are unpromising, unattractive, perverse, but they are the purchase of the blood of Christ, and in His sight are just as precious as are our own little ones. Unless a helping hand is held out to them, they will grow up in ignorance and drift into vice and crime. Many of these children could be rescued through the work of orphan asylums.

Such institutions, to be most effective, should be modelled as closely as possible after the plan of a Christian home. Instead of large establishments, bringing great numbers together, let there be small institutions in different places. Instead of being in or near some town or large city, they should be in the country where land can be secured for cultivation and the children can be brought into contact with nature and can have the benefits of industrial training.

Those in charge of such a home should be men and women who are largehearted, cultured, and self-sacrificing; men and women who undertake the work from love to Christ and who train the children for Him. Under such care many homeless and neglected ones may be prepared to become useful members of society, an honour to Christ themselves, and in their turn helping others.

Many despise economy, confounding it with stinginess and narrowness. But economy is consistent with the broadest liberality. Indeed, without economy, there can be no true liberality. We are to save, that we may give.

No one can practice real benevolence without self-denial. Only by a life of simplicity, self-denial, and close economy is it possible for us to accomplish the work appointed us as Christ's representatives. Pride and worldly ambition must be put out of our hearts. In all our work the principle of unselfishness revealed in Christ's life is to be carried out. Upon the walls of our homes, the pictures, the furnishings, we are to read, "Bring the poor that are cast out to thy house." On our wardrobes we are to see written, as with the finger of God, "Clothe the naked." In the dining room, on the table laden with abundant food, we should see traced, "Is it not to deal thy bread to the hungry?" Isaiah 58:7.

A thousand doors of usefulness are open before us. Often we lament the scanty resources available, but were Christians thoroughly in earnest, they could multiply the resources a thousandfold. It is selfishness, self-indulgence, that bars the way to our usefulness.

How much means is expended for things that are mere idols, things that engross thought and time and strength which should be put to a higher use! How much money is wasted on expensive houses and furniture, on selfish pleasures, luxurious and unwholesome food, hurtful indulgences! How much is squandered on gifts that benefit no one! For things that are needless, often harmful, professed Christians are today spending more, many times more, than they spend in seeking to rescue souls from the tempter.

Many who profess to be Christians spend so much on dress that they have nothing to spare for the needs of others. Costly ornaments and expensive clothing they think they must have, regardless of the needs of those who can with difficulty provide themselves with even the plainest clothing.

My sisters, if you would bring your manner of dressing into conformity with the rules given in the Bible, you would have an abundance with which to help your poorer sisters. You would have not only means, but time. Often this is most needed. There are many whom you might help with your suggestions, your tact and skill. Show them how to dress simply and yet tastefully. Many a woman remains away from the house of God because her shabby, ill-fitting garments are in such striking contrast to the dress of others. Many a sensitive spirit cherishes a sense of bitter humiliation and injustice because of this contrast. And because of it many are led to doubt the reality of religion and to harden their hearts against the gospel.

Christ bids us, "Gather up the fragments that remain, that nothing be lost." While thousands are every day perishing from famine, bloodshed, fire, and plague, it becomes every lover of his kind to see that nothing is wasted, that nothing is needlessly expended, whereby he might benefit a human being.

It is wrong to waste our time, wrong to waste our

thoughts. We lose every moment that we devote to self-seeking. If every moment were valued and rightly employed, we should have time for everything that we need to do for ourselves or for the world. In the expenditure of money, in the use of time, strength, opportunities, let every Christian look to God for guidance. "If any of you lack wisdom, let him ask of God, that giveth to all men liberally, and upbraideth not; and it shall be given him." James 1:5.

"Give, and it shall be given unto you."

"Do good, and lend, hoping for nothing again; and your reward shall be great, and ye shall be the children of the Highest: for He is kind unto the unthankful and to the evil." Luke 6:35.

"He that hideth his eyes shall have many a curse;" but "he that giveth unto the poor shall not lack." Proverbs 28:27.

"Give, and it shall be given unto you; good measure, pressed down, and shaken together, and running over, shall men give into your bosom." Luke 6:38.

Ministry to the Rich

Cornelius, the Roman centurion, was a man of wealth and of noble birth. His position was one of trust and honour. A heathen by birth, training, and education, through contact with the Jews he had gained a knowledge of the true God, and he worshipped Him, showing the sincerity of his faith by compassion to the poor. He gave "alms to the people, and prayed to God always." Acts 10:2, ARV.

Cornelius had not a knowledge of the gospel as revealed in the life and death of Christ, and God sent a message direct from heaven to him, and by another message directed the apostle Peter to visit and instruct him. Cornelius was not united with the Jewish church, and he would have been looked upon by the rabbis as a heathen and unclean; but God read the sincerity of his heart, and sent messengers from His throne to unite with His servant on earth in teaching the gospel to this officer of Rome.

So today God is seeking for souls among the high as well as the low. There are many like Cornelius, men whom He desires to connect with His church. Their sympathies are with the Lord's people. But the ties that bind them to the world hold them firmly. It requires moral courage for these men to take their position with the lowly ones. Special effort should be made for these souls, who are in so great danger because of their responsibilities and associations.

Much is said concerning our duty to the neglected poor; should not some attention be given to the neglected rich? Many look upon this class as hopeless, and they do little to open the eyes of those, who, blinded and dazed by the glitter of earthly glory, have lost eternity out of their reckoning. Thousands of wealthy men have gone to their graves unwarned. But indifferent as they may appear, many among the rich are soul-burdened. "He that loveth silver shall not be satisfied with silver; nor he that loveth abundance with increase." He that says to fine gold, "Thou art my confidence," has "denied the God that is above." "None of them can by any means redeem his brother, nor give to God a ransom for him: (For the redemption of their soul is precious, and it ceaseth forever)." Ecclesiastes 5:10; Job 31:24, 28; Psalm 49:7, 8.

Riches and worldly honour cannot satisfy the soul. Many among the rich are longing for some divine assurance, some spiritual hope. Many long for something that will bring to an end the monotony of their aimless lives. Many in official life feel their need of something which they have not. Few among them go to church; for they feel that they receive little benefit. The teaching they hear does not touch the heart. Shall we make no personal appeal to them?

Among the victims of want and sin are found those who were once in possession of wealth. Men of different vocations and different stations in life have been overcome by the pollutions of the world, by the use of strong drink, by the indulgence of lust, and have fallen under temptation. While these fallen ones demand pity and help, should not some attention be given to those who have not yet descended to these depths, but who are setting their feet in the same path?

Thousands in positions of trust and honour are indulging habits that mean ruin to soul and body. Ministers of the gospel, statesmen, authors, men of wealth and talent, men of vast business capacity and power for usefulness, are in deadly peril because they do not see the necessity of self-control in all things. They need to have their attention called to the principles of temperance, not in a narrow or arbitrary way, but in the light of God's great purpose for humanity. Could the principles of true temperance thus be brought before them, there are very many of the higher classes who would recognize their value and give them a hearty acceptance.

We should show these persons the result of harmful indulgences in lessening physical, mental, and moral power. Help them to realize their responsibility as stewards of God's gifts. Show them the good they could do with the money they now spend for that which does them only harm. Present the total abstinence pledge, asking that the money they would otherwise spend for liquor, tobacco, or like indulgences be devoted to the relief of the sick poor or for the training of children and youth for usefulness in the world. To such an appeal not many would refuse to listen.

There is another danger to which the wealthy are especially exposed, and here is also a field for the medical missionary. Multitudes who are prosperous in the world, and who never stoop to the common forms of vice, are yet brought to destruction through the love of riches. The cup most difficult to carry is not the cup that is empty, but the cup that is full to the brim. It is this that needs to be most carefully balanced. Affliction and adversity bring disappointment and sorrow; but it is prosperity that is most dangerous to spiritual life.

Those who are suffering reverses are represented by the bush that Moses saw in the desert, which, though burning, was not consumed. The angel of the Lord was in the midst of the bush. So in deprivation and affliction the brightness of the presence of the Unseen is with us to comfort and sustain. Often prayer is solicited for those who are suffering from illness or adversity; but our prayers are most needed by the men entrusted with prosperity and influence.

In the valley of humiliation, where men feel their need and depend on God to guide their steps, there is comparative safety. But the men who stand, as it were, on a lofty pinnacle, and who, because of their position, are supposed to possess great wisdom — these are in greatest peril. Unless such men make God their dependence, they will surely fall.

The Bible condemns no man for being rich, if he has acquired his riches honestly. Not money, but the love of money, is the root of all evil. It is God who gives men power to get wealth; and in the hands of him who acts as God's steward, using his means unselfishly, wealth is a blessing, both to its possessor and to the world. But many, absorbed in their interest in worldly treasures, become insensible to the claims of God and the needs of their fellow men. They regard their wealth as a means of glorifying themselves. They add house to house, and land to land; they fill their homes with luxuries, while all about them are human beings in misery and crime, in disease and death. Those who thus give their lives to self-serving are developing in themselves, not the attributes of God, but the attributes of the wicked one.

These men are in need of the gospel. They need to have their eyes turned from the vanity of material things to behold the preciousness of the enduring riches. They need to learn the joy of giving, the blessedness of being co-workers with God.

The Lord bids us, "Charge them that are rich in this world" that they trust not "in uncertain riches, but in the living God, who giveth us richly all things to enjoy; that they do good, that they be rich in good works, ready to distribute, willing to communicate; laying up in store for themselves a good foundation against the time to come, that they may lay hold on eternal life." 1 Timothy 6:17-19.

It is by no casual, accidental touch that wealthy, world-loving, world-worshipping souls can be drawn to Christ. These persons are often the most difficult of access. Personal effort must be put forth for them by men and women imbued with the missionary spirit, those who will not fail or be discouraged.

Some are especially fitted to work for the higher classes. These should seek wisdom from God to know how to reach these persons, to have not merely a casual acquaintance with them, but by personal effort and living faith to awaken them to the needs of the soul, to lead them to a knowledge of the truth as it is in Jesus.

Many suppose that in order to reach the higher classes, a manner of life and method of work must be adopted that will be suited to their fastidious tastes. An appearance of wealth, costly edifices, expensive dress, equipage, and sorroundings, conformity to worldly customs, the artificial polish of fashionable society, classical culture, the graces of oratory, are thought to be essential. This is an error. The way of worldly policy is not God's way of reaching the higher classes. That which will reach them effectually is a consistent, unselfish presentation of the gospel of Christ.

The experience of the apostle Paul in meeting the philosophers of Athens has a lesson for us. In presenting the gospel before the court of the Areopagus, Paul met logic with logic, science with science, philosophy with philosophy. The wisest of his hearers were astonished and silenced. His words could not be controverted. But the effort bore little fruit. Few were led to accept the gospel. Henceforth Paul adopted a different manner of labour. He avoided elabourate arguments and discussion of theories, and in simplicity pointed men and women to Christ as the Saviour of sinners. Writing to the Corinthians of his work among them, he said:

"I, brethren, when I came to you, came not with excellency of speech or of wisdom, declaring unto you the testimony of God. For I determined not to know anything among you, save Jesus Christ, and Him crucified. . . . My speech and my preaching was not with enticing words of man's wisdom, but in demonstration of the Spirit and of power: that your faith should not stand in the wisdom of men, but in the power of God." 1 Corinthians 2:1-5.

Again, in his letter to the Romans, he says:

"I am not ashamed of the gospel of Christ: for it is the power of God unto salvation to everyone that believeth; to the Jew first, and also to the Greek." Romans 1:16.

Let those who work for the higher classes bear themselves with true dignity, remembering that angels are their companions. Let them keep the treasure house of mind and heart filled with, "It is written." Hang in memory's hall the precious words of Christ. They are to be valued far above gold or silver.

Christ has said that it is easier for a camel to go through the eye of a needle than for a rich man to enter the kingdom of God. In the work for this class many discouragements will be presented, many heart-sickening revelations will be made. But all things are possible with God. He can and will work through human agencies upon the minds of men whose lives have been devoted to money getting.

There are miracles to be wrought in genuine conversion, miracles that are not now discerned. The greatest men of the earth are not beyond the power of a wonder-working God. If those who are workers together with Him will do their duty bravely and faithfully, God will convert men who occupy responsible places, men of intellect and influence. Through the power of the Holy Spirit, many will be led to accept the divine principles.

When it is made plain that the Lord expects them as His representatives to relieve suffering humanity, many will respond and will give of their means and their sympathies for the benefit of the poor. As their minds are thus drawn away from their own selfish interests, many will surrender themselves to Christ. With their talents of influence and means they will gladly unite in the work of beneficence with the humble missionary who was God's agent in their conversion. By a right use of their earthly treasures they will lay up for themselves "a treasure in the heavens that faileth not, where no thief approacheth, neither moth corrupteth."

When converted to Christ, many will become agencies in the hand of God to work for others of their own class. They will feel that a dispensation of the gospel is committed to them for those who have made this world their all. Time and money will be consecrated to God, talent and influence will be devoted to the work of winning souls to Christ.

Only eternity will reveal what has been accomplished

by this kind of ministry — how many souls, sick with doubt and tired of worldliness and unrest, have been brought to the great Restorer, who longs to save to the uttermost all that come unto Him. Christ is a risen Saviour, and there is healing in His wings.

THE CARE OF THE SICK

In the Sickroom

Those who minister to the sick should understand the importance of careful attention to the laws of health. Nowhere is obedience to these laws more important than in the sickroom. Nowhere does so much depend upon faithfulness in little things on the part of the attendants. In cases of serious illness, a little neglect, a slight inattention to a patient's special needs or dangers, the manifestation of fear, excitement, or petulance, even a lack of sympathy, may turn the scale that is balancing life and death, and cause to go down to the grave a patient who otherwise might have recovered.

The efficiency of the nurse depends, to a great degree, upon physical vigour. The better the health, the better will she be able to endure the strain of attendance upon the sick, and the more successfully can she perform her duties. Those who care for the sick should give special attention to diet, cleanliness, fresh air, and exercise. Like carefulness on the part of the family will enable them also to endure the extra burdens brought upon them, and will help to prevent them from contracting disease.

Where the illness is serious, requiring the attendance of a nurse night and day, the work should be shared by at least two efficient nurses, so that each may have opportunity for rest and for exercise in the open air. This is especially important in cases where it is difficult to secure an abundance of fresh air in the sickroom. Through ignorance of the importance of fresh air, ventilation is sometimes restricted, and the lives of both patient and attendant are often in danger.

If proper precaution is observed, noncontagious

diseases need not be taken by others. Let the habits be correct, and by cleanliness and proper ventilation keep the sickroom free from poisonous elements. Under such conditions, the sick are much more likely to recover, and in most cases neither attendants nor the members of the family will contract the disease.

Sunlight, Ventilation, and Temperature

To afford the patient the most favourable conditions for recovery, the room he occupies should be large, light, and cheerful, with opportunity for thorough ventilation. The room in the house that best meets these requirements should be chosen as the sickroom. Many houses have no special provision for proper ventilation, and to secure it is difficult; but every possible effort should be made to arrange the sickroom so that a current of fresh air can pass through it night and day.

So far as possible an even temperature should be maintained in the sickroom. The thermometer should be consulted. Those who have the care of the sick, being often deprived of sleep or awakened in the night to attend to the patient, are liable to chilliness and are not good judges of a healthful temperature.

Diet

An important part of the nurse's duty is the care of the patient's diet. The patient should not be allowed to suffer or become unduly weakened through lack of nourishment, nor should the enfeebled digestive powers be overtaxed. Care should be taken so to prepare and serve the food that it will be palatable, but wise judgement should be used in adapting it to the needs of the patient, both in quantity and quality. In times of convalescence especially, when the appetite is keen, before the digestive organs have recovered strength, there is great danger of injury from errors in diet.

Duties of Attendants

Nurses, and all who have to do with the sickroom, should be cheerful, calm, and self-possessed. All hurry, excitement, or confusion, should be avoided. Doors should be opened and shut with care, and the whole household be kept quiet. In cases of fever, special care is needed when the crisis comes and the fever is passing away. Then constant watching is often necessary. Ignorance, forgetfulness, and recklessness have caused the death of many who might have lived had they received proper care from judicious, thoughtful nurses.

Visiting the Sick

It is misdirected kindness, a false idea of courtesy, that leads to much visiting of the sick. Those who are very ill should not have visitors. The excitement connected with receiving callers wearies the patient at a time when he is in the greatest need of quiet, undisturbed rest.

To a convalescent or a patient suffering from chronic disease, it is often a pleasure and a benefit to know that he is kindly remembered; but this assurance conveyed by a message of sympathy or by some little gift will often serve a better purpose than a personal visit, and without danger of harm.

Institutional Nursing

In sanitariums and hospitals, where nurses are constantly associated with large numbers of sick people, it requires a decided effort to be always pleasant and cheerful, and to show thoughtful consideration in every word and act. In these institutions it is of the utmost importance that the nurses strive to do their work wisely and well. They need ever to remember that in the discharge of their daily duties they are serving the Lord Christ.

The sick need to have wise words spoken to them. Nurses should study the Bible daily, that they may be able to speak words that will enlighten and help the suffering. Angels of God are in the rooms where these suffering ones are being ministered to, and the atmosphere surrounding the soul of the one giving treatment should be pure and fragrant. Physicians and nurses are to cherish the principles of Christ. In their lives His virtues are to be seen. Then, by what they do and say, they will draw the sick to the Saviour.

The Christian nurse, while administering treatment for the restoration of health, will pleasantly and successfully draw the mind of the patient to Christ, the healer of the soul as well as of the body. The thoughts presented, here a little and there a little, will have their influence. The older nurses should lose no favourable opportunity of calling the attention of the sick to Christ. They should be ever ready to blend spiritual healing with physical healing.

In the kindest and tenderest manner nurses are to teach that he who would be healed must cease to transgress the law of God. He must cease to choose a life of sin. God cannot bless the one who continues to bring upon himself disease and suffering by a wilful violation of the laws of heaven. But Christ, through the Holy Spirit, comes as a healing power to those who cease to do evil and learn to do well.

Those who have no love for God will work constantly against the best interests of soul and body. But those who awake to the importance of living in obedience to God in this present evil world will be willing to separate from every wrong habit. Gratitude and love will fill their hearts. They know that Christ is their friend. In many cases the realization that they have such a friend means more to the suffering ones in their recovery from sickness than the best treatment that can be given. But both lines of ministry are essential. They are to go hand in hand.

Prayer for the Sick

The Scripture says that "men ought always to pray, and not to faint" (Luke 18:1); and if ever there is a time when they feel their need of prayer, it is when strength fails and life itself seems slipping from their grasp. Often those who are in health forget the wonderful mercies continued to them day by day, year after year, and they render no tribute of praise to God for His benefits. But when sickness comes, God is remembered. When human strength fails, men feel their need of divine help. And never does our merciful God turn from the soul that in sincerity seeks Him for help. He is our refuge in sickness as in health.

> "Like as a father pitieth his children,
> So the Lord pitieth them that fear Him.
> For He knoweth our frame;
> He remembereth that we are dust."
> Psalm 103:13, 14.

> "Because of their transgression,
> And because of their iniquities, (men) are afflicted.
> Their soul abhorreth all manner of food;
> And they draw near unto the gates of death."
> Psalm 107:17, 18, ARV.

> "Then they cry unto the Lord in their trouble,
> And He saveth them out of their distresses.
> He sendeth His word, and healeth them,
> And delivereth them from their destructions."
> Verses 19, 20, RV.

God is just as willing to restore the sick to health now as when the Holy Spirit spoke these words through the psalmist. And Christ is the same compassionate physician now that He was during His earthly ministry. In Him there is healing balm for every disease, restoring power for every infirmity. His disciples in this time are to pray for the sick as verily as the disciples of old prayed. And recoveries will follow; for "the prayer of faith shall save the sick." We have the Holy Spirit's power, the calm assurance of faith, that can claim God's promises. The Lord's promise, "They shall lay hands on the sick, and they shall recover" (Mark 16:18), is just as trustworthy now as in the days of the apostles. It presents the privilege of God's children, and our faith should lay hold of all that it embraces. Christ's servants are the channel of His working, and through them He desires to exercise His healing power. It is our work to present the sick and suffering to God in the arms of our faith. We should teach them to believe in the Great Healer.

The Saviour would have us encourage the sick, the hopeless, the afflicted, to take hold upon His strength. Through faith and prayer the sickroom may be transformed into a Bethel. In word and deed, physicians and nurses may say, so plainly that it cannot be misunderstood, "God is in this place" to save, and not to destroy. Christ desires to manifest His presence in the sickroom, filling the hearts of physicians and nurses with the sweetness of His love. If the life of the attendants upon the sick is such that Christ can go with them to the bedside of the patient, there will come to him the conviction that the compassionate Saviour is present, and this conviction will itself do much for the healing of both the soul and the body.

And God hears prayer. Christ has said, "If ye shall ask anything in My name, I will do it." Again He says, "If any man serve Me, him will My Father honour." John 14:14; 12:26. If we live according to His word, every precious promise He has given will be fulfilled to us. We are undeserving of His mercy, but as we give ourselves to Him, He receives us. He will work for and through those who follow Him.

But only as we live in obedience to His word can we claim the fulfilment of His promises. The psalmist says, "If I regard iniquity in my heart, the Lord will not hear me." Psalm 66:18. If we render to Him only a partial, halfhearted obedience, His promises will not be fulfilled to us.

In the word of God we have instruction relative to special prayer for the recovery of the sick. But the offering of such prayer is a most solemn act, and should not be entered upon without careful consideration. In many cases of prayer for the healing of the sick, that which is called faith is nothing less than presumption.

Many persons bring disease upon themselves by their self-indulgence. They have not lived in accordance with natural law or the principles of strict purity. Others have disregarded the laws of health in their habits of eating and drinking, dressing, or working. Often some form of vice is the cause of feebleness of mind or body. Should these persons gain the blessing of health, many of them would continue to pursue the same course of heedless transgression of God's natural and spiritual laws, reasoning that if God heals them in answer to prayer, they are at liberty to continue their unhealthful practices and to indulge perverted appetite without restraint. If God were to work a miracle in restoring these persons to health, He would be encouraging sin.

It is labour lost to teach people to look to God as a healer of their infirmities, unless they are taught also to lay aside unhealthful practices. In order to receive His blessing in answer to prayer, they must cease to do evil and learn to do well. Their surroundings must be sanitary, their habits of life correct. They must live in harmony with the law of God, both natural and spiritual.

Confession of Sin

To those who desire prayer for their restoration to health, it should be made plain that the violation of God's law, either natural or spiritual, is sin, and that in order for them to receive His blessing, sin must be confessed and forsaken.

The Scripture bids us, "Confess your faults one to another, and pray one for another, that ye may be healed." James 5:16. To the one asking for prayer, let thoughts like these be presented: "We cannot read the heart, or know the secrets of your life. These are known only to yourself and to God. If you repent of your sins, it is your duty to make confession of them." Sin of a private character is to be confessed to Christ, the only mediator between God and man. For "if any man sin, we have an advocate with the Father, Jesus Christ the righteous." 1 John 2:1. Every sin is an offence against God and is to be confessed to Him through Christ. Every open sin should be as openly confessed. Wrong done to a fellow being should be made right with the one who has been offended. If any who are seeking health have been guilty of evilspeaking, if they have sowed discord in the home, the neighbourhood, or the church, and have stirred up alienation and dissension, if by any wrong practice they have led others into sin, these things should be confessed before God and before those who have been offended. "If we confess our sins, He is faithful and just to forgive us our sins, and to cleanse us from all unrighteousness." 1 John 1:9.

When wrongs have been righted, we may present the needs of the sick to the Lord in calm faith, as His Spirit may indicate. He knows each individual by name, and cares for each as if there were not another upon the earth for whom He gave His beloved Son. Because God's love is so great and so unfailing, the sick should be encouraged to trust in Him and be cheerful. To be anxious about themselves tends to cause weakness and disease. If they will rise above depression and gloom, their prospect of recovery will be better; for "the eye of the Lord is upon them" "that hope in His mercy." Psalm 33:18.

In prayer for the sick it should be remembered that "we know not what we should pray for as we ought." Romans 8:26. We do not know whether the blessing we desire will be best or not. Therefore our prayers should include this thought: "Lord, thou knowest every secret of the soul. Thou art acquainted with these persons. Jesus, their Advocate, gave His life for them. His love for them is greater than ours can possibly be. If, therefore, it is for Thy glory and the good of the afflicted ones, we ask, in the name of Jesus, that they may be restored to health. If it be not Thy will that they may be restored, we ask that Thy grace may comfort and Thy presence sustain them in their sufferings."

God knows the end from the beginning. He is acquainted with the hearts of all men. He reads every secret of the soul. He knows whether those for whom prayer is offered would or would not be able to endure the trials that would come upon them should they live. He knows whether their lives would be a blessing or a curse to themselves and to the world. This is one reason why, while presenting our petitions with earnestness, we should say, "Nevertheless not my will, but Thine, be done." Luke 22:42. Jesus added these words of submission to the wisdom and will of God when in the Garden of Gethsemane He pleaded, "O My Father, if it be possible, let this cup pass from Me." Matthew 26:39. And if they were appropriate for Him, the Son of God, how much more are they becoming on the lips of finite, erring mortals!

The consistent course is to commit our desires to our all-wise heavenly Father, and then, in perfect confidence, trust all to Him. We know that God hears us if we ask according to His will. But to press our petitions without a submissive spirit is not right; our prayers must take the form, not of command, but of intercession.

There are cases where God works decidedly by His divine power in the restoration of health. But not all the sick are healed. Many are laid away to sleep in Jesus. John on the Isle of Patmos was bidden to write: "Blessed are the dead which die in the Lord from henceforth: Yea, saith the Spirit, that they may rest from their labours; and their works do follow them." Revelation 14:13. From this we see that if persons are not raised to health, they should not on this account be judged as wanting in faith.

We all desire immediate and direct answers to our

prayers, and are tempted to become discouraged when the answer is delayed or comes in an unlooked-for form. But God is too wise and good to answer our prayers always at just the time and in just the manner we desire. He will do more and better for us than to accomplish all our wishes. And because we can trust His wisdom and love, we should not ask Him to concede to our will, but should seek to enter into and accomplish His purpose. Our desires and interests should be lost in His will. These experiences that test faith are for our benefit. By them it is made manifest whether our faith is true and sincere, resting on the word of God alone, or whether depending on circumstances, it is uncertain and changeable. Faith is strengthened by exercise. We must let patience have its perfect work, remembering that there are precious promises in the Scriptures for those who wait upon the Lord.

Not all understand these principles. Many who seek the Lord's healing mercy think that they must have a direct and immediate answer to their prayers or their faith is defective. For this reason, those who are weakened by disease need to be counselled wisely, that they may act with discretion. They should not disregard their duty to the friends who may survive them, or neglect to employ nature's agencies for the restoration of health.

Often there is danger of error here. Believing that they will be healed in answer to prayer, some fear to do anything that might seem to indicate a lack of faith. But they should not neglect to set their affairs in order as they would desire to do if they expected to be removed by death. Nor should they fear to utter words of encouragement or counsel which at the parting hour they wish to speak to their loved ones.

Those who seek healing by prayer should not neglect to make use of the remedial agencies within their reach. It is not a denial of faith to use such remedies as God has provided to alleviate pain and to aid nature in her work of restoration. It is no denial of faith to co-operate with God, and to place themselves in the condition most favourable to recovery. God has put it in our power to obtain a knowledge of the laws of life. This knowledge has been placed within our reach for use. We should employ every facility for the restoration of health, taking every advantage possible, working in harmony with natural laws. When we have prayed for the recovery of the sick, we can work with all the more energy, thanking God that we have the privilege of co-operating with Him, and asking His blessing on the means which He Himself has provided.

We have the sanction of the word of God for the use of remedial agencies. Hezekiah, king of Israel, was sick, and a prophet of God brought him the message that he should die. He cried unto the Lord, and the Lord heard His servant and sent him a message that fifteen years should be added to his life. Now, one word from God would have healed Hezekiah instantly; but special directions were given, "Let them take a lump of figs, and lay it for a plaster upon the boil, and he shall recover." Isaiah 38:21.

On one occasion Christ anointed the eyes of a blind man with clay and bade him, "Go, wash in the pool of Siloam. . . . He went his way therefore, and washed, and came seeing." John 9:7. The cure could be wrought only by the power of the Great Healer, yet Christ made use of the simple agencies of nature. While He did not give countenance to drug medication, He sanctioned the use of simple and natural remedies.

When we have prayed for the recovery of the sick, whatever the outcome of the case, let us not lose faith in God. If we are called upon to meet bereavement, let us accept the bitter cup, remembering that a Father's hand holds it to our lips. But should health be restored, it should not be forgotten that the recipient of healing mercy is placed under renewed obligation to the Creator. When the ten lepers were cleansed, only one returned to find Jesus and give Him glory. Let none of us be like the unthinking nine, whose hearts were untouched by the mercy of God. "Every good gift and every perfect gift is from above, and cometh down from the Father of lights, with whom is no variableness, neither shadow of turning." James 1:17.

The Use of Remedies

Disease never comes without a cause. The way is prepared, and disease invited, by disregard of the laws of health. Many suffer in consequence of the transgression of their parents. While they are not responsible for what their parents have done, it is nevertheless their duty to ascertain what are and what are not violations of the laws of health. They should avoid the wrong habits of their parents and, by correct living, place themselves in better conditions.

The greater number, however, suffer because of their own wrong course of action. They disregard the principles of health by their habits of eating, drinking, dressing, and working. Their transgression of nature's laws produces the sure result; and when sickness comes upon them, many do not credit their suffering to the true cause, but murmur against God because of their afflictions. But God is not responsible for the suffering that follows disregard of natural law.

God has endowed us with a certain amount of vital force. He has also formed us with organs suited to maintain the various functions of life, and He designs that these organs shall work together in harmony. If we carefully preserve the life force, and keep the delicate mechanism of the body in order, the result is health; but if the vital force is too rapidly exhausted, the nervous system borrows power for present use from its resources of strength, and when one organ is injured, all are affected. Nature bears much abuse without apparent resistance; she then arouses and makes a determined effort to remove the effects of the ill-treatment she has suffered. Her effort to correct these conditions is often manifest in fever and various other forms of sickness.

Rational Remedies

When the abuse of health is carried so far that sickness results, the sufferer can often do for himself what no one else can do for him. The first thing to be done is to ascertain the true character of the sickness and then go to work intelligently to remove the cause. If the harmonious working of the system has become unbalanced by overwork, overeating, or other irregularities, do not endeavour to adjust the difficulties by adding a burden of poisonous medicines.

Intemperate eating is often the cause of sickness, and what nature most needs is to be relieved of the undue burden that has been placed upon her. In many cases of sickness, the very best remedy is for the patient to fast for a meal or two, that the overworked organs of digestion may have an opportunity to rest. A fruit diet for a few days has often brought great relief to brain workers. Many times a short period of entire abstinence from food, followed by simple, moderate eating, has led to recovery through nature's own recuperative effort. An abstemious diet for a month or two would convince many sufferers that the path of self-denial is the path to health.

Rest as a Remedy

Some make themselves sick by overwork. For these, rest, freedom from care, and a spare diet, are essential to restoration of health. To those who are brain weary and nervous because of continual labour and close confinement, a visit to the country, where they can live a simple, carefree life, coming in close contact with the things of nature, will be most helpful. Roaming through the fields and the woods, picking the flowers, listening to the songs of the birds, will do far more that any other agency toward their recovery.

In health and in sickness, pure water is one of heaven's choicest blessings. Its proper use promotes health. It is the beverage which God provided to quench the thirst of animals and man. Drunk freely, it helps to supply the necessities of the system and assists nature to resist disease. The external application of water is one of the easiest and most satisfactory ways of regulating the circulation of the blood. A cold or cool bath is an excellent tonic. Warm baths open the pores and thus aid in the elimination of impurities. Both warm and neutral bath soothe the nerves and equalize the circulation.

But many have never learned by experience the beneficial effects of the proper use of water, and they are afraid of it. Water treatments are not appreciated as they should be, and to apply them skilfully requires work that many are unwilling to perform. But none should feel excused for ignorance or indifference on this subject. There are many ways in which water can be applied to relieve pain and check disease. All should become intelligent in its use in simple home treatments. Mothers, especially, should know how to care for their families in both health and sickness.

Action is a law of our being. Every organ of the body has its appointed work, upon the performance of which its development and strength depend. The normal action of all the organs gives strength and vigour, while the tendency of disuse is toward decay and death. Bind up an arm, even for a few weeks, then free it from its bands, and you will see that it is weaker than the one you have been using moderately during the same time. Inactivity produces the same effect upon the whole muscular system.

Inactivity is a fruitful cause of disease. Exercise quickens and equalizes the circulation of the blood, but in idleness the blood does not circulate freely, and the changes in it, so necessary to life and health, do not take place. The skin, too, becomes inactive. Impurities are not expelled as they would be if the circulation had been quickened by vigourous exercise, the skin kept in a healthy condition, and the lungs fed with plenty of pure, fresh air. This state of the system throws a double burden on the excretory organs, and disease is the result.

Invalids should not be encourage in inactivity. When there has been serious overtaxation in any direction, entire rest for a time will sometimes ward off serious illness; but in the case of confirmed invalids, it is seldom necessary to suspend all activity.

Those who have broken down from mental labour should have rest from wearing thought; but they should not be led to believe that it is dangerous to use their mental powers at all. Many are inclined to regard their condition as worse than it really is. This state of mind is unfavourable to recovery, and should not be encouraged.

Ministers, teachers, students, and other brain workers often suffer from illness as the result of severe mental taxation, unrelieved by physical exercise. What these persons need is a more active life. Strictly temperate habits, combined with proper exercise, would ensure both mental and physical vigour, and would give power of endurance to all brain workers.

Those who have overtaxed their physical powers should not be encouraged to forgo manual labour entirely. But labour, to be of the greatest advantage, should be systematic and agreeable. Outdoor exercise is the best; it should be so planned as to strengthen by use the organs that have become weakened; and the heart should be in it; the labour of the hands should never degenerate into mere drudgery.

When invalids have nothing to occupy their time and attention, their thoughts become centred upon themselves, and they grow morbid and irritable. Many times they dwell upon their bad feelings until they think themselves much worse than they really are and wholly unable to do anything.

In all these cases well-directed physical exercise would prove an effective remedial agent. In some cases it is indispensable to the recovery of health. The will goes with the labour of the hands; and what these invalids need is to have the will aroused. When the will is dormant, the imagination becomes abnormal, and it is impossible to resist disease.

Inactivity is the greatest curse that could come upon most invalids. Light employment in useful labour, while it does not tax mind or body, has a happy influence upon both. It strengthens the muscles, improves the circulation, and gives the invalid the satisfaction of knowing that he is not wholly useless in this busy world. He may be able to do but little at first, but he will soon find his strength increasing, and the amount of work done can be increased accordingly.

Exercise aids the dyspeptic by giving the digestive organs a healthy tone. To engage in severe study or violent physical exercise immediately after eating, hinders the work of digestion; but a short walk after a meal, with the head erect and the shoulders back, is a great benefit.

Notwithstanding all that is said and written concerning its importance, there are still many who neglect physical exercise. Some grow corpulent because the system is clogged; others become thin and feeble because their vital powers are exhausted in disposing of an excess of food. The liver is burdened in its effort to cleanse the blood of impurities, and illness is the result.

Those whose habits are sedentary should, when the weather will permit, exercise in the open air every day, summer or winter. Walking is preferable to riding or driving, for it brings more of the muscles into exercise. The lungs are forced into healthy action, since it is impossible to walk briskly without inflating them.

Such exercise would in many cases be better for the health than medicine. Physicians often advise their patients to take an ocean voyage, to go to some mineral spring, or to visit different places for change of climate, when in most cases if they would eat temperately, and take cheerful, healthful exercise, they would recover health and would save time and money.

Mind Cure

The relation that exists between the mind and the body is very intimate. When one is affected, the other sympathizes. The condition of the mind affects the health to a far greater degree than many realize. Many of the diseases from which men suffer are the result of mental depression. Grief, anxiety, discontent, remorse, guilt, distrust, all tend to break down the life forces and to invite decay and death.

Disease is sometimes produced, and is often greatly aggravated, by the imagination. Many are lifelong invalids who might be well if they only thought so. Many imagine that every slight exposure will cause illness, and the evil effect is produced because it is expected. Many die from disease the cause of which is wholly imaginary.

Courage, hope, faith, sympathy, love, promote health and prolong life. A contented mind, a cheerful spirit, is health to the body and strength to the soul. "A merry [rejoicing] heart doeth good like a medicine." Proverbs 17:22.

In the treatment of the sick the effect of mental influence should not be overlooked. Rightly used, this influence affords one of the most effective agencies for combating disease.

Control of Mind Over Mind

There is, however, a form of mind cure that is one of the most effective agencies for evil. Through this so-called science, one mind is brought under the control of another so that the individuality of the weaker is merged in that of the stronger mind. One person acts out the will of another. Thus it is claimed that the tenor of the thoughts may be changed, that health-giving impulses may be imparted, and patients may be enabled to resist and overcome disease.

This method of cure has been employed by persons who were ignorant of its real nature and tendency, and who believed it to be a means of benefit to the sick. But the so-called science is based upon false principles. It is foreign to the nature and spirit of Christ. It does not lead to Him who is life and salvation. The one who attracts minds to Himself leads them to separate from the true Source of their strength.

It is not God's purpose that any human being should yield his mind and will to the control of another, becoming a passive instrument in his hands. No one is to merge his individuality in that of another. He is not to look to any human being as the source of healing. His dependence must be in God. In the dignity of his God-given manhood he is to be controlled by God Himself, not by any human intelligence.

God desires to bring men into direct relation with Himself. In all His dealings with human beings He recognizes the principle of personal responsibility. He seeks to encourage a sense of personal dependence and to impress the need of personal guidance. He desires to bring the human into association with the divine, that men may be transformed into the divine likeness. Satan works to thwart this purpose. He seeks to encourage dependence upon men. When minds are turned away from God, the tempter can bring them under his rule. He can control humanity.

The theory of mind controlling mind was originated by Satan, to introduce himself as the chief worker, to put human philosophy where divine philosophy should be. Of all the errors that are finding acceptance among professedly Christian people, none is a more dangerous deception, none more certain to separate man from God, than is this. Innocent though it may appear, if exercised upon patients it will tend to their destruction, not to their restoration. It opens a door through which

Satan will enter to take possession both of the mind that is given up to be controlled by another, and of the mind that controls.

Fearful is the power thus given to evil-minded men and women. What opportunities it affords to those who live by taking advantage of other's weaknesses or follies! How many, through control of minds feeble or diseased, will find a means of gratifying lustful passion or greed of gain!

There is something better for us to engage in than the control of humanity by humanity. The physician should educate the people to look from the human to the divine. Instead of teaching the sick to depend upon human beings for the cure of soul and body, he should direct them to the One who can save to the uttermost all who come unto Him. He who made man's mind knows what the mind needs. God alone is the One who can heal. Those whose minds and bodies are diseased are to behold in Christ the restorer. "Because I live," He says, "ye shall live also." John 14:19. This is the life we are to present to the sick, telling them that if they have faith in Christ as the restorer, if they co-operate with Him, obeying the laws of health, and striving to perfect holiness in His fear, He will impart to them His life. When we present Christ to them in this way, we are imparting a power, a strength, that is of value; for it comes from above. This is the true science of healing for body and soul.

Sympathy

Great wisdom is needed in dealing with diseases caused through the mind. A sore, sick heart, a discouraged mind, needs mild treatment. Many times some living home trouble is, like a canker, eating to the very soul and weakening the life force. And sometimes it is the case that remorse for sin undermines the constitution and unbalances the mind. It is through tender sympathy that this class of invalids can be benefited. The physician should first gain their confidence and then point them to the Great Healer. If their faith can be directed to the True Physician, and they can have confidence that He has undertaken their case, this will bring relief to the mind and often give health to the body.

Sympathy and tact will often prove a greater benefit to the sick than will the most skilful treatment given in a cold, indifferent way. When a physician comes to the sickbed with a listless, careless manner, looks at the afflicted one with little concern, by word or action giving the impression that the case is not one requiring much attention, and then leaves the patient to his own reflections, he has done that patient positive harm. The doubt and discouragement produced by his indifference will often counteract the good effect of the remedies he may prescribe.

If physicians could put themselves in the place of the one whose spirit is humbled and whose will is weakened by suffering, and who longs for words of sympathy and assurance, they would be better prepared to appreciate his feelings. When the love and sympathy that Christ manifested for the sick is combined with the physician's knowledge, his very presence will be a blessing.

Frankness in dealing with a patient inspires him with confidence, and thus proves an important aid to recovery. There are physicians who consider it wise policy to conceal from the patient the nature and cause of the disease from which he is suffering. Many, fearing to excite or discourage a patient by stating the truth, will hold out false hopes of recovery, and even allow a patient to go down to the grave without warning him of his danger. All this is unwise. It may not always be safe or best to explain to the patient the full extent of his danger. This might alarm him and retard or even prevent recovery. Nor can the whole truth always be told to those whose ailments are largely imaginary. Many of these persons are unreasonable, and have not accustomed themselves to exercise self-control. They have peculiar fancies, and imagine many things that are false in regard to themselves and to others. To them these things are real, and those who care for them need to manifest constant kindness and unwearied patience and tact. If these patients were told the truth in regard to themselves, some would be offended, others discouraged. Christ said to His disciples, "I have yet many things to say unto you, but ye cannot bear them now." John 16:12. But though the truth may not all be spoken on all occasions, it is never necessary or justifiable to deceive. Never should the physician or the nurse stoop to prevarication. He who does this places himself where God cannot co-operate with him, and in forfeiting the confidence of his patients he is casting away one of the most effective human aids to their restoration.

The power of the will is not valued as it should be. Let the will be kept awake and rightly directed, and it will impart energy to the whole being and will be a wonderful aid in the maintenance of health. It is a power also in dealing with disease. Exercised in the right direction, it would control the imagination and be a potent means of resisting and overcoming disease of both mind and body. By the exercise of the will power in placing themselves in right relation to life, patients can do much to co-operate with the physician's efforts for their recovery. There are thousands who can recover health if they will. The Lord does not want them to be sick. He desires them to be well and happy, and they should make up their minds to be well. Often invalids can resist disease simply by refusing to yield to ailments and settle down in a state of inactivity. Rising above their aches and pains, let them engage in useful employment suited to their strength. By such employment and the free use of air and sunlight, many an emaciated invalid might recover health and strength.

Bible Principles of Cure

For those who would regain or preserve health there is a lesson in the words of Scripture, "Be not drunk with wine, wherein is excess; but be filled with the Spirit." Ephesians 5:18. Not through the excitement or oblivion produced by unnatural or unhealthful stimulants; not through indulgence of the lower appetites or passions, is to be found true healing or refreshment for the body or the soul. Among the sick are many who are without God and without hope. They suffer from ungratified desires, disordered passions, and the condemnation of their own consciences; they are losing their hold upon this life, and they have no prospect for the life to come. Let not the attendants upon the sick hope to benefit these patients by granting them frivolous, exciting indulgences. These have been the curse of their lives. The hungry, thirsting soul will continue to hunger and thirst so long as it seeks to find satisfaction here. Those who drink at the fountain of selfish pleasure are deceived. They mistake hilarity for strength, and when the excitement ceases, their inspiration ends, and they are left to discontent and despondency.

Abiding peace, true rest of spirit, has but one Source. It was of this that Christ spoke when He said, "Come unto Me, all ye that labour and are heavy-laden, and I will give you rest." Matthew 11:28. "Peace I leave with you, My peace I give unto you: not as the world giveth, give I unto you." John 14:27. This peace is not something that He gives apart from Himself. It is in Christ, and we can receive it only by receiving Him.

Christ is the wellspring of life. That which many need is to have a clearer knowledge of Him; they need to be patiently and kindly, yet earnestly, taught how the whole being may be thrown open to the healing agencies of heaven. When the sunlight of God's love illuminates the darkened chambers of the soul, restless weariness and dissatisfaction will cease, and satisfying joys will give vigour to the mind and health and energy to the body.

We are in a world of suffering. Difficulty, trial, and sorrow await us all along the way to the heavenly home. But there are many who make life's burdens doubly heavy by continually anticipating trouble. If they meet with adversity or disappointment they think that everything is going to ruin, that theirs is the hardest lot of all, that they are surely coming to want. Thus they bring wretchedness upon themselves and cast a shadow upon all around them. Life itself becomes a burden to them. But it need not be thus. It will cost a determined effort to change the current of their thought. But the change can be made. Their happiness, both for this life and for the life to come, depends upon their fixing their minds upon cheerful things. Let them look away from the dark picture, which is imaginary, to the benefits which God has strewn in their pathway, and beyond these to the unseen and eternal.

For every trial, God has provided help. When Israel in the desert came to the bitter waters of Marah, Moses cried unto the Lord. The Lord did not provide some new remedy; He called attention to that which was at hand. A shrub which He had created was to be cast into the fountain to make the water pure and sweet. When this was done, the people drank of the water and were refreshed. In every trial, if we seek Him, Christ will give us help. Our eyes will be opened to discern the healing promises recorded in His word. The Holy Spirit will teach us how to appropriate every blessing that will be an antidote to grief. For every bitter draft that is placed to our lips, we shall find a branch of healing.

We are not to let the future, with its hard problems, its unsatisfying prospects, make our hearts faint, our knees tremble, our hands hang down. "Let him take hold of My strength," says the Mighty One, "that he may make peace with Me; and he shall make peace with Me." Isaiah 27:5. Those who surrender their lives to His guidance and to His service will never be placed in a position for which He has not made provision. Whatever our situation, if we are doers of His word, we have a Guide to direct our way; whatever our perplexity, we have a sure Counsellor; whatever our sorrow, bereavement, or loneliness, we have a sympathizing Friend.

If in our ignorance we make missteps, the Saviour does not forsake us. We need never feel that we are alone. Angels are our companions. The Comforter that Christ promised to send in His name abides with us. In the way that leads to the City of God there are no difficulties which those who trust in Him may not overcome. There are no dangers which they may not escape. There is not a sorrow, not a grievance, not a human weakness, for which He has not provided a remedy.

None need abandon themselves to discouragement and despair. Satan may come to you with the cruel suggestion, "Yours is a hopeless case. You are irredeemable." But there is hope for you in Christ. God does not bid us overcome in our own strength. He asks us to come close to His side. Whatever difficulties we labour under, which weigh down soul and body, He waits to make us free.

He who took humanity upon Himself knows how to sympathize with the sufferings of humanity. Not only does Christ know every soul, and the peculiar needs and trials of that soul, but He knows all the circumstances that chafe and perplex the spirit. His hand is outstretched in pitying tenderness to every suffering child. Those who suffer most have most of His sympathy and pity. He is touched with the feeling of our infirmities, and He desires us to lay our perplexities and troubles at His feet and leave them there.

It is not wise to look to ourselves and study our emotions. If we do this, the enemy will present difficulties and temptations that weaken faith and destroy courage. Closely to study our emotions and give way to our feelings is to entertain doubt and entangle ourselves in perplexity. We are to look away from self to Jesus.

When temptations assail you, when care, perplexity, and darkness seem to surround your soul, look to the place where you last saw the light. Rest in Christ's love and under His protecting care. When sin struggles for the mastery in the heart, when guilt oppresses the soul and burdens the conscience, when unbelief clouds the mind, remember that Christ's grace is sufficient to subdue sin and banish the darkness. Entering into communion with the Saviour, we enter the region of peace.

The Healing Promises

"The Lord redeemeth the soul of His servants:
And none of them that trust in Him shall be desolate." Psalm 34:22.

"In the fear of the Lord is strong confidence:
And His children shall have a place of refuge."
Proverbs 14:26.

"Zion said, Jehovah hath forsaken me, and
The Lord hath forgotten me.
Can a woman forget her sucking child,
That she should not have compassion on the son of her womb?
Yea, these may forget, yet will not I forget thee.
Behold, I have graven thee upon the palms of My hands." Isaiah 49:14-16, ARV.

"Fear thou not; for I am with thee:
Be not dismayed; for I am thy God:
I will strengthen thee; yea, I will help thee;
Yea, I will uphold thee with the right hand of My righteousness."
Isaiah 41:10.

"Ye that have been borne by Me from your birth,
That have been carried by Me from your earliest breath,
Even to your old age I am the same;
Even to hoar hairs I will carry you;
I have done it, and I will still bear you;
I will carry, and I will deliver you."
Isaiah 46:3, 4, Noyes.

Nothing tends more to promote health of body and of soul than does a spirit of gratitude and praise. It is a positive duty to resist melancholy, discontented thoughts and feelings — as much a duty as it is to pray. If we are heaven-bound, how can we go as a band of mourners, groaning and complaining all along the way to our Father's house?

Those professed Christians who are constantly complaining, and who seem to think cheerfulness and happiness a sin, have not genuine religion. Those who take a mournful pleasure in all that is melancholy in the natural world, who choose to look upon dead leaves rather than to gather the beautiful living flowers, who see no beauty in grand mountain heights and in valleys clothed with living green, who close their senses to the joyful voice which speaks to them in nature, and which is sweet and musical to the listening ear — these are not in Christ. They are gathering to themselves gloom and darkness, when they might have brightness, even the Sun of Righteousness arising in their hearts with healing in His beams.

Often your mind may be clouded because of pain. Then do not try to think. You know that Jesus loves you. He understands your weakness. You may do His will by simply resting in His arms.

It is a law of nature that our thoughts and feelings are encouraged and strengthened as we give them utterance. While words express thoughts, it is also true that thoughts follow words. If we would give more expression to our faith, rejoice more in the blessings that we know we have — the great mercy and love of God — we should have more faith and greater joy. No tongue can express, no finite mind can conceive, the blessing that results from appreciating the goodness and love of God. Even on earth we may have joy as a wellspring, never failing, because fed by the streams that flow from the throne of God.

Then let us educate our hearts and lips to speak the praise of God for His matchless love. Let us educate our souls to be hopeful and to abide in the light shining from the cross of Calvary. Never should we forget that we are children of the heavenly King, sons and daughters of the Lord of hosts. It is our privilege to maintain a calm repose in God.

"Let the peace of God rule in your hearts; . . . and be ye thankful." Colossians 3:15. Forgetting our own difficulties and troubles, let us praise God for an opportunity to live for the glory of His name. Let the fresh blessings of each new day awaken praise in our hearts for these tokens of His loving care. When you open your eyes in the morning, thank God that He has kept you through the night. Thank Him for His peace in your heart. Morning, noon, and night, let gratitude as a sweet perfume ascend to heaven.

When someone asks how you are feeling, do not try to think of something mournful to tell in order to gain sympathy. Do not talk of your lack of faith and your sorrows and sufferings. The tempter delights to hear such words. When talking on gloomy subjects, you are glorifying him. We are not to dwell on the great power of Satan to overcome us. Often we give ourselves into his hands by talking of his power. Let us talk instead of the great power of God to bind up all our interests with His own. Tell of the matchless power of Christ, and speak of His glory. All heaven is interested in our salvation. The angels of God, thousands upon thousands, and ten thousand times ten thousand, are commissioned to minister to those who shall be heirs of salvation. They guard us against evil and press back the powers of darkness that are seeking our destruction. Have we not reason to be thankful every moment, thankful even when there are apparent difficulties in our pathway?

Sing Praises

Let praise and thanksgiving be expressed in song. When tempted, instead of giving utterance to our feelings, let us by faith lift up a song of thanksgiving to God.

> We praise Thee, O God, for the Son of Thy love —
> For Jesus who died and is now gone above.
>
> We praise Thee, O God, for Thy Spirit of light,
> Who has shown us our Saviour, and scattered our night.
>
> All glory and praise to the Lamb that was slain,
> Who has borne all our sins, and has cleansed every stain.
>
> All glory and praise to the God of all grace,
> Who has bought us, and sought us, and guided our ways.
>
> Revive us again; fill each heart with Thy love;
> May each soul be rekindled with fire from above.

Chorus:
Hallelujah! Thine the glory, Hallelujah! amen;
Hallelujah! Thine the glory, Revive us again.

Song is a weapon that we can always use against discouragement. As we thus open the heart to the sunlight of the Saviour's presence, we shall have health and His blessing.

"Give thanks unto the Lord, for He is good:
For His mercy endureth forever.
Let the redeemed of the Lord say so,
Whom He hath redeemed from the hand of the enemy."

"Sing unto Him, sing psalms unto Him:
Talk ye of all His wondrous works.
Glory ye in His holy name:
Let the heart of them rejoice that seek the Lord."

"For He satisfieth the longing soul,
And filleth the hungry soul with goodness.
Such as sit in darkness and in the shadow of death,
Being bound in affliction and iron; . . .
They cried unto the Lord in their trouble,
And He saved them out of their distresses.
He brought them out of darkness and the shadow of death,
And brake their bands in sunder.
Oh that men would praise the Lord for His goodness,
And for His wonderful works to the children of men!"

"Why art thou cast down, O my soul?
And why art thou disquieted within me?
Hope thou in God:
For I shall yet praise Him,
Who is the health of my countenance,
And my God."

Psalms 107:1, 2; 105:2, 3; 107:9-15; 42:11.

"In everything give thanks: for this is the will of God in Christ Jesus concerning you." 1 Thessalonians 5:18. This command is an assurance that even the things which appear to be against us will work for our good. God would not bid us be thankful for that which would do us harm.

"The Lord is my light and my salvation;
Whom shall I fear?
The Lord is the strength of my life;
Of whom shall I be afraid?"

"In the day of trouble He shall keep me secretly in His pavilion:
In the covert of His tabernacle shall He hide me; . . .
And I will offer in His tabernacle sacrifices of joy;
I will sing, yea, I will sing praises unto the Lord."

"I waited patiently for the Lord;
And He inclined unto me, and heard my cry.
He brought me up also out of an horrible pit, out of the miry clay,
And set my feet upon a rock, and established my goings.
And He hath put a new song in my mouth, even praise unto our God."

"The Lord is my strength and my shield;
My heart trusted in Him, and I am helped:
Therefore my heart greatly rejoiceth;
And with my song will I praise Him."

Psalms 27:1; 27:5, 6, RV; 40:1-3; 28:7.

One of the surest hindrances to the recovery of the sick is the centring of attention upon themselves. Many invalids feel that everyone should give them sympathy and help, when what they need is to have their attention turned away from themselves, to think of and care for others.

Often prayer is solicited for the afflicted, the sorrowful, the discouraged; and this is right. We should pray that God will shed light into the darkened mind and comfort the sorrowful heart. But God answers prayer for those who place themselves in the channel of His blessings. While we offer prayer for these sorrowful ones, we should encourage them to try to help those more needy than themselves. The darkness will be dispelled from their own hearts as they try to help others. As we seek to comfort others with the comfort wherewith we are comforted, the blessing comes back to us.

The fifty-eight chapter of Isaiah is a prescription for

maladies of the body and of the soul. If we desire health and the true joy of life we must put into practice the rules given in this scripture. Of the service acceptable to Him, and its blessings, the Lord says:

> "Is it not to deal thy bread to the hungry,
> And that thou bring the poor that are cast out to thy house?
> When thou seest the naked, that thou cover him;
> And that thou hide not thyself from thine own flesh?
> Then shall thy light break forth as the morning,
> And thine health shall spring forth speedily:
> And thy righteousness shall go before thee;
> The glory of the Lord shall be thy rearward.
> Then shalt thou call, and the Lord shall answer;
> Thou shalt cry, and He shall say, Here I am.
> If thou take away from the midst of thee the yoke,
> The putting forth of the finger, and speaking vanity;
> And if thou draw out thy soul to the hungry,
> And satisfy the afflicted soul;
> Then shall thy light rise in obscurity,
> And thy darkness be as the noonday:
> And the Lord shall guide thee continually,
> And satisfy thy soul in drought,
> And make fat thy bones:
> And thou shalt be like a watered garden,
> And like a spring of water,
> Whose waters fail not."
>
> Isaiah 58:7-11.

Good deeds are twice a blessing, benefiting both the giver and the receiver of the kindness. The consciousness of right-doing is one of the best medicines for diseased bodies and minds. When the mind is free and happy from a sense of duty well done and the satisfaction of giving happiness to others, the cheering, uplifting influence brings new life to the whole being.

Let the invalid, instead of constantly requiring sympathy, seek to impart it. Let the burden of your own weakness and sorrow and pain be cast upon the compassionate Saviour. Open your heart to His love, and let it flow out to others. Remember that all have trials hard to bear, temptations hard to resist, and you may do something to lighten these burdens. Express gratitude for the blessings you have; show appreciation of the attentions you receive. Keep the heart full of the precious promises of God, that you may bring forth from this treasure, words that will be a comfort and strength to others. This will surround you with an atmosphere that will be helpful and uplifting. Let it be your aim to bless those around you, and you will find ways of being helpful, both to the members of your own family and to others.

If those who are suffering from ill-health would forget self in their interest for others; if they would fulfil the Lord's command to minister to those more needy than themselves, they would realize the truthfulness of the prophetic promise, "Then shall thy light break forth as the morning, and thine health shall spring forth speedily."

Marah and Elim

Today 'tis Elim with its palms and wells,
  And happy shade for desert weariness;
'Twas Marah yesterday, all rock and sand,
  Unshaded solitude and dreariness.
Yet the same desert holds them both, the same
  Hot breezes wander o'er the lonely ground;
The same low stretch of valley shelters both,
  And the same mountains compass them around.

So it is here with us on earth, and so
  I do remember it has ever been;
The bitter and the sweet, the grief and joy,
  Lie near together, but a day between.

Sometimes God turns our bitter into sweet,
  Sometimes He gives us pleasant watersprings;
Sometimes He shades us with His pillar cloud,
  And sometimes to a blessed palm shade brings.

What matters it? The time will not be long;
  Marah and Elim will alike be passed;
Our desert wells and palms will soon be done,
  We reach the "City of our God" at last.
O happy land! beyond these lonely hills,
  Where gush in joy the everlasting springs;
O holy Paradise! above these heavens,
  Where we shall end our desert wanderings.

— Horatius Bonar.

Blessed Assurance

Blessed assurance, Jesus is mine!
Oh, what a foretaste of glory divine!
Heir of salvation, purchase of God,
Born of His Spirit, washed in His blood.

Chorus:
This is my story, this is my song,
Praising my Saviour all the day long;
This is my story, this is my song,
Praising my Saviour all the day long.

Perfect submission, perfect delight,
Visions of rapture now burst on my sight.
Angels descending bring from above
Echoes of mercy, whispers of love.

Perfect submission, all is at rest,
I in my Saviour am happy and blest,
Watching and waiting, looking above,
Filled with His goodness, lost in His love.

— Fanny J. Crosby.

In Contact With Nature

The Creator chose for our first parents the surroundings best adapted for their health and happiness. He did not place them in a palace or surround them with the artificial adornments and luxuries that so many today are struggling to obtain. He placed them in close touch with nature and in close communion with the holy ones of heaven.

In the garden that God prepared as a home for His children, graceful shrubs and delicate flowers greeted the eye at every turn. There were trees of every variety, many of them laden with fragrant and delicious fruit. On their branches the birds caroled their songs of praise. Under their shadow the creatures of the earth sported together without a fear.

Adam and Eve, in their untainted purity, delighted in the sights and sounds of Eden. God appointed them their work in the garden, "to dress it and to keep it." Genesis 2:15. Each day's labour brought them health and gladness, and the happy pair greeted with joy the visits of their Creator, as in the cool of the day He walked and talked with them. Daily God taught them His lessons.

The plan of life which God appointed for our first parents has lessons for us. Although sin has cast its shadow over the earth, God desires His children to find delight in the works of His hands. The more closely His plan of life is followed, the more wonderfully will He work to restore suffering humanity. The sick need to be brought into close touch with nature. An outdoor life amid natural surroundings would work wonders for many a helpless and almost hopeless invalid.

The noise and excitement and confusion of the cities, their constrained and artificial life, are most wearisome and exhausting to the sick. The air, laden with smoke and dust, with poisonous gases, and with germs of disease, is a peril to life. The sick, for the most part shut within four walls, come almost to feel as if they were prisoners in their rooms. They look out on houses and pavements and hurrying crowds, with perhaps not even a glimpse of blue sky or sunshine, of grass or flower or tree. Shut up in this way, they brood over their suffering and sorrow, and become a prey to their own sad thoughts.

And for those who are weak in moral power, the cities abound in dangers. In them, patients who have unnatural appetites to overcome are continually exposed to temptation. They need to be placed amid new surroundings where the current of their thoughts will be changed; they need to be placed under influences wholly different from those that have wrecked their lives. Let them for a season be removed from those influences that lead away from God, into a purer atmosphere.

Institutions for the care of the sick would be far more successful if they could be established away from the cities. And so far as possible, all who are seeking to recover health should place themselves amid country surroundings where they can have the benefit of out door life. Nature is God's physician. The pure air, the glad sunshine, the flowers and trees, the orchards and vineyards, and outdoor exercise amid these surroundings, are health-giving, life-giving.

Physicians and nurses should encourage their patients to be much in the open air. Outdoor life is the only remedy that many invalids need. It has a wonderful power to heal diseases caused by the excitements and excesses of fashionable life, a life that weakens and destroys the powers of body, mind, and soul.

How grateful to the invalids weary of city life, the glare of many lights, and the noise of the streets, are the quiet and freedom of the country! How eagerly do they turn to the scenes of nature! How glad would they be to sit in the open air, rejoice in the sunshine, and breathe the fragrance of tree and flower! There are life-giving properties in the balsam of the pine, in the fragrance of the cedar and the fir, and other trees also have properties that are health restoring.

To the chronic invalid, nothing so tends to restore health and happiness as living amid attractive country surroundings. Here the most helpless ones can sit or lie in the sunshine or in the shade of the trees. They have only to lift their eyes to see above them the beautiful foliage. A sweet sense of restfulness and refreshing comes over them as they listen to the murmuring of the breezes. The drooping spirits revive. The waning strength is recruited. Unconsciously the mind becomes peaceful, the fevered pulse more calm and regular. As the sick grow stronger, they will venture to take a few steps to gather some of the lovely flowers, precious messengers of God's love to His afflicted family here below.

Plans should be devised for keeping patients out of doors. For those who are able to work, let some pleasant, easy employment be provided. Show them how agreeable and helpful this outdoor work is. Encourage them to breathe the fresh air. Teach them to breathe deeply, and in breathing and speaking to exercise the abdominal muscles. This is an education that will be invaluable to them.

Exercise in the open air should be prescribed as a life-giving necessity. And for such exercises there is nothing better than the cultivation of the soil. Let patients have flower beds to care for, or work to do in the orchard or vegetable garden. As they are encouraged to leave their rooms and spend time in the open air, cultivating flowers or doing some other light, pleasant work, their attention will be diverted from themselves and their sufferings.

The more the patient can be kept out of doors, the less care will he require. The more cheerful his surroundings, the more helpful will he be. Shut up in the house, be it ever so elegantly furnished, he will grow fretful and gloomy. Surround him with the beautiful things of nature; place him where he can see the flowers growing and hear the birds singing, and his heart will break into song in harmony with the songs of the birds. Relief will come to body and mind. The intellect will be awakened, the imagination quickened, and the mind prepared to appreciate the beauty of God's word.

In nature may always be found something to divert the attention of the sick from themselves and direct their thoughts to God. Surrounded by His wonderful works, their minds are uplifted from the things that are seen to the things that are unseen. The beauty of nature leads them to think of the heavenly home, where there will be nothing to mar the loveliness, nothing to taint or destroy, nothing to cause disease or death.

Let physicians and nurses draw from the things of nature, lessons teaching of God. Let them point the patients to Him whose hand has made the lofty trees, the grass, and the flowers, encouraging them to see in every bud and flower an expression of His love for His children. He who cares for the birds and the flowers will care for the beings formed in His own image.

Out of doors, amid the things that God has made, breathing the fresh, health-giving air, the sick can best be told of the new life in Christ. Here God's word can be read. Here the light of Christ's righteousness can shine into hearts darkened by sin.

> O, could I find, from day to day,
> A nearness to my God,
> Then would my hours glide sweet away,
> While leaning on His word.
>
> Lord, I desire with Thee to live
> Anew from day to day,
> In joys the world can never give,
> Nor ever take away.
>
> Blest Jesus, come, and rule my heart,
> And make me wholly Thine,

That I may nevermore depart,
Nor grieve Thy love divine.
— Benjamin Cleveland.

Men and women in need of physical and spiritual healing are to be thus brought into contact with those whose words and acts will draw them to Christ. They are to be brought under the influence of the great Medical Missionary, who can heal both soul and body. They are to hear the story of the Saviour's love, of the pardon freely provided for all who come to Him confessing their sins.

Under such influences as these, many suffering ones will be guided into the way of life. Angels of heaven co-operate with human instrumentalities in bringing encouragement and hope and joy and peace to the hearts of the sick and suffering. Under such conditions the sick are doubly blessed, and many find health. The feeble step recovers its elasticity. The eye regains its brightness. The hopeless become hopeful. The once despondent countenance wears an expression of joy. The complaining tones of the voice give place to tones of cheerfulness and content.

As physical health is regained, men and women are better able to exercise that faith in Christ which secures the health of the soul. In the consciousness of sins forgiven there is inexpressible peace and joy and rest. The clouded hope of the Christian is brightened. The words express the belief, "God is our refuge and strength, a very pleasant help in trouble." "Yea, though I walk through the valley of the shadow of death, I will fear no evil: for Thou art with me; Thy rod and Thy staff they comfort me." "He giveth power to the faint; and to them that have no might He increaseth strength." Psalms 46:1; 23:4; Isaiah 40:29.

My faith looks up to Thee,
Thou Lamb of Calvary,
Saviour divine;
Now hear me while I pray,

Take all my guilt away,
O let me from this day
  Be wholly Thine.

May Thy rich grace impart
Strength to my fainting heart,
  My zeal inspire;
As Thou hast died for me,
O may my love to Thee
Pure, warm, and changeless be,
  A living fire.

While life's dark maze I tread,
And griefs around me spread,
  Be Thou my Guide;
Bid darkness turn to day,
Wipe sorrow's tears away,
Nor let me ever stray
  From Thee aside.

— Ray Palmer.

HEALTH PRINCIPLES

General Hygiene

The knowledge that man is to be a temple for God, a habitation for the revealing of His glory, should be the highest incentive to the care and development of our physical powers. Fearfully and wonderfully has the Creator wrought in the human frame, and He bids us make it our study, understand its needs, and act our part in preserving it from harm and defilement.

The Circulation of the Blood

In order to have good health, we must have good blood; for the blood is the current of life. It repairs waste and nourishes the body. When supplied with the proper food elements and when cleansed and vitalized by contact with pure air, it carries life and vigour to every part of the system. The more perfect the circulation, the better will this work be accomplished.

At every pulsation of the heart the blood should make its way quickly and easily to all parts of the body. Its circulation should not be hindered by tight clothing or bands, or by insufficient clothing of the extremities. Whatever hinders the circulation forces the blood back to the vital organs, producing congestion. Headache, cough, palpitation of the heart, or indigestion is often the result.

Respiration

In order to have good blood, we must breathe well. Full, deep inspirations of pure air, which fill the lungs with oxygen, purify the blood. They impart to it a bright colour and send it, a life-giving current, to every part of the body. A good respiration soothes the nerves; it stimulates the appetite and renders digestion more perfect; and it induces sound, refreshing sleep.

The lungs should be allowed the greatest freedom possible. Their capacity is developed by free action; it diminishes if they are cramped and compressed. Hence the ill effects of the practice so common, especially in sedentary pursuits, of stooping at one's work. In this position it is impossible to breathe deeply. Superficial breathing soon becomes a habit, and the lungs lose their power to expand. A similar effect is produced by tight lacing. Sufficient room is not given to the lower part of the chest; the abdominal muscles, which were designed to aid in breathing, do not have full play, and the lungs are restricted in their action.

Thus an insufficient supply of oxygen is received. The blood moves sluggishly. The waste, poisonous matter, which should be thrown off in the exhalations from the lungs, is retained, and the blood becomes impure. Not only the lungs, but the stomach, liver, and brain are affected. The skin becomes sallow, digestion is retarded; the heart is depressed; the brain is clouded; the thoughts are confused; gloom settles upon the spirits; the whole system becomes depressed and inactive, and peculiarly susceptible to disease.

The lungs are constantly throwing off impurities, and they need to be constantly supplied with fresh air. Impure air does not afford the necessary supply of oxygen, and the blood passes to the brain and other organs without being vitalized. Hence the necessity of thorough ventilation. To live in close, ill-ventilated rooms, where the air is dead and vitiated, weakens the entire system. It becomes peculiarly sensitive to the influence of cold, and a slight exposure induces disease. It is close confinement indoors that makes many women pale and feeble. They breathe the same air over and over until it becomes laden with poisonous matter thrown off through the lungs and pores, and impurities are thus conveyed back to the blood.

Ventilation and Sunlight

In the construction of buildings, whether for public purposes or as dwellings, care should be taken to provide for good ventilation and plenty of sunlight. Churches and schoolrooms are often faulty in this respect. Neglect of proper ventilation is responsible for much of the drowsiness and dullness that destroy the effect of many a sermon and make the teacher's work toilsome and ineffective.

So far as possible, all buildings intended for human habitation should be placed on high, well-drained ground. This will ensure a dry site and prevent the danger of disease from dampness and miasma. This matter is often too lightly regarded. Continuous ill-health, serious diseases, and many deaths result from the dampness and malaria of low-lying, ill-drained situations.

In the building of houses it is especially important to secure thorough ventilation and plenty of sunlight. Let there be a current of air and an abundance of light in every room in the house. Sleeping rooms should be so arranged as to have a free circulation of air day and night. No room is fit to be occupied as a sleeping room unless it can be thrown open daily to the air and sunshine. In most countries bedrooms need to be supplied with conveniences for heating, that they may be thoroughly warmed and dried in cold or wet weather.

The guestchamber should have equal care with the rooms intended for constant use. Like the other bedrooms, it should have air and sunshine, and should be provided with some means of heating, to dry out the dampness that always accumulates in a room not in constant use. Whoever sleeps in a sunless room, or occupies a bed that has not been thoroughly dried and aired, does so at the risk of health, and often of life.

In building, many make careful provision for their plants and flowers. The greenhouse or window devoted to their use is warm and sunny; for without warmth, air, and sunshine, plants would not live and flourish. If these conditions are necessary to the life of plants, how much more necessary are they for our own health and that of our families and guests!

If we would have our homes the abiding place of health and happiness we must place them above the miasma and fog of the lowlands, and give free entrance to heaven's life-giving agencies. Dispense with heavy curtains, open the windows and the blinds, allow no vines, however beautiful, to shade the windows, and permit no trees to stand so near the house as to shut out the sunshine. The sunlight may fade the drapery and the carpets, and tarnish the picture frames; but it will bring a healthy glow to the cheeks of the children.

Those who have the aged to provide for should remember that these especially need warm, comfortable rooms. Vigour declines as years advance, leaving less vitality with which to resist unhealthful influences; hence the greater necessity for the aged to have plenty of sunlight, and fresh, pure air.

Scrupulous cleanliness is essential to both physical and mental health. Impurities are constantly thrown off from the body through the skin. Its millions of pores are quickly clogged unless kept clean by frequent bathing, and the impurities which should pass off through the skin become an additional burden to the other eliminating organs.

Most persons would receive benefit from a cool or tepid bath every day, morning or evening. Instead of increasing the liability to take cold, a bath, properly taken, fortifies against cold, because it improves the circulation; the blood is brought to the surface, and a more easy and regular flow is obtained. The mind and the body are alike invigourated. The muscles become more flexible, the intellect is made brighter. The bath is a soother of the nerves. Bathing helps the bowels, the stomach, and the liver, giving health and energy to each, and it promotes digestion.

It is important also that the clothing be kept clean. The garments worn absorb the waste matter that passes off through the pores; if they are not frequently changed and washed, the impurities will be reabsorbed.

Every form of uncleanliness tends to disease. Death-producing germs abound in dark, neglected corners, in decaying refuse, in dampness and mould and must. No waste vegetables or heaps of fallen leaves should be allowed to remain near the house to decay and poison the air. Nothing unclean or decaying should be tolerated within the home. In towns or cities regarded perfectly healthful, many an epidemic of fever has been traced to decaying matter about the dwelling of some careless householder.

Perfect cleanliness, plenty of sunlight, careful attention to sanitation in every detail of the home life, are essential to freedom from disease and to the cheerfulness and vigour of the inmates of the home.

Hygiene Among the Israelites

In the teaching that God gave to Israel, the preservation of health received careful attention. The people who had come from slavery with the uncleanly and unhealthful habits which it engenders, were subjected to the strictest training in the wilderness before entering Canaan. Health principles were taught and sanitary laws enforced.

Prevention of Disease

Not only in their religious service, but in all the affairs of daily life was observed the distinction between clean and unclean. All who came in contact with contagious or contaminating diseases were isolated from the encampment, and they were not permitted to return without thorough cleansing of both the person and the clothing. In the case of one afflicted with a contaminating disease, the direction was given:

"Every bed, whereon he lieth, . . . is unclean: and everything, whereon he sitteth, shall be unclean. And whosoever toucheth his bed shall wash his clothes, and bathe himself in water, and be unclean until the even. And he that sitteth on anything whereon he sat . . . shall wash his clothes, and bathe himself in water, and be unclean until the even. And he that toucheth the flesh of him . . . shall wash his clothes, and bathe himself in water, and be unclean until the even. . . . And whosoever toucheth anything that was under him shall be unclean until the even: and he that beareth any of those things shall wash his clothes, and bathe himself in water, and be unclean until the even. And whomsoever he toucheth . . . and hath not rinsed his hands in water, he shall wash his clothes, and bathe himself in water, and be unclean until the even. And the vessel of earth, that he toucheth, . . . shall be broken: and every vessel of wood shall be rinsed in water." Leviticus 15:4-12.

The law concerning leprosy is also an illustration of the thoroughness with which these regulations were to be enforced:

"All the days wherein the plague shall be in him (the leper) he shall be defiled; he is unclean: he shall dwell alone; without the camp shall his habitation be. The garment also that the plague of leprosy is in, whether it be a woollen garment, or a linen garment; whether it be in the warp, or woof; of linen, or of woollen; whether in a skin, or in anything made of skin; . . . the priest shall look upon the plague: . . . if the plague be spread in the garment, either in the warp, or in the woof, or in a skin, or in any work that is made of skin; the plague is a fretting leprosy; it is unclean. He shall therefore burn that garment, whether warp or woof, in woollen or in linen, or anything of skin, wherein the plague is: for it is a fretting leprosy; it shall be burnt in the fire." Leviticus 13:46-52.

So, too, if a house gave evidence of conditions that rendered it unsafe for habitation, it was destroyed. The priest was to "break down the house, the stones of it, and the timber thereof, and all the mortar of the house; and he shall carry them forth out of the city into an unclean place. Moreover he that goeth into the house all the while that it is shut up shall be unclean until the even. And he that lieth in the house shall wash his clothes; and he that eateth in the house shall wash his clothes." Leviticus 14:45-47.

Cleanliness

The necessity of personal cleanliness was taught in the most impressive manner. Before gathering at Mount Sinai to listen to the proclamation of the law by the voice of God, the people were required to wash both their persons and their clothing. This direction was enforced on pain of death. No impurity was to be tolerated in the presence of God.

During the sojourn in the wilderness the Israelites were almost continually in the open air, where impurities would have a less harmful effect than upon the dwellers in close houses. But the strictest regard to cleanliness was required both within and without their tents. No refuse was allowed to remain within or about the encampment. The Lord said:

"The Lord thy God walketh in the midst of thy camp, to deliver thee, and to give up thine enemies before thee; therefore shall thy camp be holy." Deuteronomy 23:14.

Diet

The distinction between clean and unclean was made in all matters of diet:

"I am the Lord thy God, which have separated you from other people. Ye shall therefore put difference between clean beasts and unclean, and between unclean fowls and clean: and ye shall not make your souls abominable by beast, or by fowl, or by any manner of living thing, . . . which I have separated from you as unclean." Leviticus 20:24, 25.

Many articles of food eaten freely by the heathen about them were forbidden to the Israelites. It was no arbitrary distinction that was made. The things prohibited were unwholesome. And the fact that they were pronounced unclean taught the lesson that the use of injurious foods is defiling. That which corrupts the body tends to corrupt the soul. It unfits the user for communion with God, unfits him for high and holy service.

In the Promised Land the discipline begun in the wilderness was continued under circumstances favourable to the formation of right habits. The people were not crowded together in cities, but each family had its own landed possession, ensuring to all the health-giving blessings of a natural, unperverted life.

Concerning the cruel, licentious practices of the

Canaanites, who were dispossessed by Israel, the Lord said:

"Ye shall not walk in the manners of the nation, which I cast out before you: for they committed all these things, and therefore I abhorred them." Verse 23. "Neither shalt thou bring an abomination into thine house, lest thou be a cursed thing like it." Deuteronomy 7:26.

In all the affairs of their daily life, the Israelites were taught the lesson set forth by the Holy Spirit:

"Know ye not that ye are the temple of God, and that the Spirit of God dwelleth in you? If any man defile the temple of God, him shall God destroy; for the temple of God is holy, which temple ye are." 1 Corinthians 3:16, 17.

Rejoicing

"A merry [rejoicing] heart doeth good like a medicine." Proverbs 17:22. Gratitude, rejoicing, benevolence, trust in God's love and care — these are health's greatest safeguard. To the Israelites they were to be the very keynote of life.

The journey made three times a year to the annual feasts at Jerusalem, the week's sojourn in booths during the Feast of Tabernacles, were opportunities for outdoor recreation and social life. These feasts were occasions of rejoicing, made sweeter and more tender by the hospitable welcome given to the stranger, the Levite, and the poor.

"Rejoice in every good thing which the Lord thy God hath given unto thee, and unto thine house, thou, and the Levite, and the stranger that is among you." Deuteronomy 26:11.

So, in later years, when the law of God was read in Jerusalem to the captives returned from Babylon, and the people wept because of their transgressions, the gracious words were spoken:

"Mourn not. . . . Go your way, eat the fat, and drink the sweet, and send portions unto them for whom nothing is prepared: for this day is holy unto our Lord:

neither be ye sorry; for the joy of the Lord is your strength." Nehemiah 8:9, 10.

And it was published and proclaimed "in all their cities, and in Jerusalem, saying, Go forth unto the mount, and fetch olive branches, and pine branches, and myrtle branches, and palm branches, and branches of thick trees, to make booths, as it is written. So the people went forth, and brought them, and made themselves booths, everyone upon the roof of his house, and in their courts, and in the courts of the house of God, and in the street of the water gate, and in the street of the gate of Ephraim. And all the congregation of them that were come again out of the captivity made booths, and sat under the booths. . . . And there was very great gladness." Verses 15-17.

God gave to Israel instruction in all the principles essential to physical as well as to moral health, and it was concerning these principles no less than concerning those of the moral law that He commanded them:

"These words, which I command thee this day, shall be in thine heart: and thou shalt teach them diligently unto thy children, and shalt talk of them when thou sittest in thine house, and when thou walkest by the way, and when thou liest down, and when thou risest up. And thou shalt bind them for a sign upon thine hand, and they shall be as frontlets between thine eyes. And thou shalt write them upon the posts of thy house, and on thy gates." Deuteronomy 6:6-9.

"And when thy son asketh thee in time to come, saying, What mean the testimonies, and the statutes, and the judgements, which the Lord our God hath commanded you? Then thou shalt say unto thy son, . . . The Lord commanded us to do all these statutes, to fear the Lord our God, for our good always, that He might preserve us alive, as it is at this day." Verses 20-24.

Had the Israelites obeyed the instruction they received, and profited by their advantages, they would have been the world's object lesson of health and prosperity. If as a people they had lived according to God's plan, they would have been preserved from the diseases that afflicted other nations. Above any other people they would have possessed physical strength and vigour of intellect. They would have been the mightiest nation on the earth. God said:

"Thou shalt be blessed above all people." Deuteronomy 7:14.

"The Lord hath avouched thee this day to be His peculiar people, as He hath promised thee, and that thou shouldest keep all His commandments; and to make thee high above all nations which He hath made, in praise, and in name, and in honour; and that thou mayest be an holy people unto the Lord thy God, as He hath spoken." Deuteronomy 26:18, 19.

"And all these blessings shall come on thee, and overtake thee, if thou shalt hearken unto the voice of the Lord thy God. Blessed shalt thou be in the city, and blessed shalt thou be in the field. Blessed shall be the fruit of thy body, and the fruit of thy ground, and the fruit of thy cattle, the increase of thy kine, and the flocks of thy sheep. Blessed shall be thy basket and thy store. Blessed shalt thou be when thou comest in, and blessed shalt thou be when thou goest out." Deuteronomy 28:2-6.

"The Lord shall command the blessing upon thee in thy storehouses, and in all that thou settest thine hand unto; and He shall bless thee in the land which the Lord thy God giveth thee. The Lord shall establish thee an holy people unto Himself, as He hath sworn unto thee, if thou shalt keep the commandments of the Lord thy God, and walk in His ways. And all people of the earth shall see that thou art called by the name of the Lord; and they shall be afraid of thee. And the Lord shall make thee plenteous in goods, in the fruit of thy body, and in the fruit of thy cattle, and in the fruit of thy ground, in the land which the Lord sware unto thy fathers to give thee. The Lord shall open unto thee His good treasure, the heaven to give the rain unto thy land in his season, and to bless all the work of thine hand. . . . And the Lord shall make thee the head, and not the tail; and thou shalt be above only, and thou shalt not be beneath; if that thou hearken unto the commandments of the Lord thy God, which I command thee this day, to observe and to do them." Verses 8-13.

To Aaron the high priest and his sons the direction was given:

"On this wise ye shall bless the children of Israel, saying unto them,

> "Jehovah bless thee, and keep thee:
> Jehovah make His face to shine upon thee,
> And be gracious unto thee:
> Jehovah lift up His countenance upon thee,
> And give thee peace.
> So shall they put My name upon the children of
> Israel;
> And I will bless them."
>
> "As thy days, so shall thy strength be.
> There is none like unto God, O Jeshurun,
> Who rideth upon the heaven for thy help,
> And in His excellency on the skies.
> The eternal God is thy dwelling place,
> And underneath are the everlasting arms. . . .
> Israel dwelleth in safety,
> The fountain of Jacob alone,
>
> "In a land of corn and wine;
> Yea, His heavens drop down dew.
> Happy art thou, O Israel:
> Who is like unto thee, a people saved by the Lord,
> The shield of thy help,
> And that is the sword of thy excellency!"
>
> Numbers 6:23; 6:24-27, ARV;
> Deuteronomy 33:25-29, RV.

The Israelites failed of fulfilling God's purpose, and thus failed of receiving the blessings that might have been theirs. But in Joseph and Daniel, in Moses and Elisha, and many others, we have noble examples of the results of the true plan of living. Like faithfulness today will produce like results. To us it is written:

"Ye are a chosen generation, a royal priesthood, an holy nation, a peculiar people; that ye should show forth the praises of Him who hath called you out of darkness into His marvellous light." 1 Peter 2:9.

"Blessed is the man that trusteth in the Lord,
And whose hope the Lord is."
He "shall flourish like the palm tree:
He shall grow like a cedar in Lebanon.
Those that be planted in the house of the Lord
Shall flourish in the courts of our God.
They shall still bring forth fruit in old age."
"They shall be vigorous and covered with foliage."

"Let thine heart keep My commandments:
For length of days, and long life,
And peace, shall they add to thee."
"Then shalt thou walk in thy way safely,
And thy foot shall not stumble.
When thou liest down, thou shalt not be afraid:
Yea, thou shalt lie down, and thy sleep shall be sweet.
Be not afraid of sudden fear,
Neither of the desolation of the wicked, when it cometh.
For the Lord shall be thy confidence,
And shall keep thy foot from being taken."

Jeremiah 17:7; Psalm 92:12-14;
92:15, Leeser; Proverbs 3:1, 2, 23-26.

Dress

The Bible teaches modesty in dress. "In like manner also, that women adorn themselves in modest apparel." 1 Timothy 2:9. This forbids display in dress, gaudy colours, profuse ornamentation. Any device designed to attract attention to the wearer or to excite admiration, is excluded from the modest apparel which God's word enjoins.

Our dress is to be inexpensive — not with "gold, or pearls, or costly array." Verse 9.

Money is a trust from God. It is not ours to expend for the gratification of pride or ambition. In the hands of God's children it is food for the hungry, and clothing for the naked. It is a defence to the oppressed, a means of health to the sick, a means of preaching the gospel to the poor. You could bring happiness to many hearts by using wisely the means that is now spent for show. Consider the life of Christ. Study His character, and be partakers with Him in His self-denial.

In the professed Christian world enough is expended for jewels and needlessly expensive dress to feed all the hungry and to clothe the naked. Fashion and display absorb the means that might comfort the poor and the suffering. They rob the world of the gospel of the Saviour's love. Missions languish. Multitudes perish for want of Christian teaching. Beside our own doors and in foreign lands the heathen are untaught and unsaved. While God has laden the earth with His bounties and filled its storehouses with the comforts of life, while He has so freely given to us a saving knowledge of His truth, what excuse can we offer for permitting the cries of the widow and the fatherless, the sick and the suffering, the untaught and the unsaved, to ascend to heaven? In the day of God, when brought face to face with Him who gave His life for these needy ones, what excuse will those offer who are spending their time and money upon indulgences that God has forbidden? To such will not Christ say, "I was anhungered, and ye gave Me no meat: I was thirsty, and ye gave Me no drink: . . . naked, and ye clothed Me not: sick, and in prison, and ye visited Me not"? Matthew 25:42, 43.

But our clothing, while modest and simple, should be of good quality, of becoming colours, and suited for service. It should be chosen for durability rather than display. It should provide warmth and proper protection. The wise woman described in the Proverbs "is not afraid of the snow for her household: for all her household are clothed with double garments." Proverbs 31:21, margin.

Our dress should be cleanly. Uncleanliness in dress is unhealthful, and thus defiling to the body and to the soul. "Ye are the temple of God. . . . If any man defile the temple of God, him shall God destroy." 1 Corinthians 3:16, 17.

In all respects the dress should be healthful. "Above all things," God desires us to "be in health" — health of body and of soul. And we are to be workers together with Him for the health of both soul and body. Both are promoted by healthful dress.

It should have the grace, the beauty, the appropriateness of natural simplicity. Christ has warned us against the pride of life, but not against its grace and natural beauty. He pointed to the flowers of the field, to the lily unfolding in its purity, and said, "Even Solomon in all his glory was not arrayed like one of these." Matthew 6:29. Thus by the things of nature Christ illustrates the beauty that heaven values, the modest grace, the simplicity, the purity, the appropriateness, that would make our attire pleasing to Him.

The most beautiful dress He bids us wear upon the soul. No outward adorning can compare in value or loveliness with that "meek and quiet spirit" which in His sight is "of great price." 1 Peter 3:4.

To those who make the Saviour's principles their guide, how precious His words of promise:

"Why are ye anxious concerning raiment? . . . If God doth so clothe the grass of the field, which today is, and tomorrow is cast into the oven, shall He not much more clothe you? . . . Be not therefore anxious, saying, . . . Wherewithal shall we be clothed? . . . For your heavenly Father knoweth that ye have need of all these things. But seek ye first His kingdom, and His righteousness; and all these things shall be added unto you." Matthew 6:28-33, RV.

"Thou wilt keep him in perfect peace, whose mind is stayed on Thee: because he trusteth in Thee." Isaiah 26:3.

What a contrast is this to the weariness, the unrest, the disease and wretchedness, that result from the rule of fashion! How contrary to the principles given in the Scriptures are many of the modes of dress that fashion prescribes! Think of the styles that have prevailed for the last few hundreds of years or even for the last few decades. How many of them, when not in fashion, would be declared immodest; how many would be pronounced inappropriate for a refined, God-fearing, self-respecting woman.

The making of changes in apparel for the sake of fashion merely is not sanctioned by the word of God. Changing styles and elaborate, costly ornamentation squander the time and means of the rich, and lay waste the energies of mind and soul. They impose a heavy burden on the middle and poorer classes. Many who can hardly earn a livelihood, and who with simple modes might make their own clothing, are compelled to resort to the dressmaker in order to be in fashion. Many a poor girl, for the sake of a stylish gown, has deprived herself of warm underwear, and paid the penalty with her life. Many another, coveting the display and elegance of the rich, has been enticed into paths of dishonesty and shame. Many a home is deprived of comforts, many a man is driven to embezzlement or bankruptcy, to satisfy the extravagant demands of the wife or children.

Many a woman, forced to prepare for herself or her children the stylish costumes demanded by fashion, is doomed to ceaseless drudgery. Many a mother with throbbing nerves and trembling fingers toils far into the night to add to her children's clothing ornamentation that contributes nothing to healthfulness, comfort, or real beauty. For the sake of fashion she sacrifices health and that calmness of spirit so essential to the right guidance of her children. The culture of mind and heart is neglected. The soul is dwarfed.

The mother has no time to study the principles of physical development, that she may know how to care for the health of her children. She has no time for ministering to their mental or spiritual needs, no time to sympathize with them in their little disappointments and trials, or to share in their interests and pursuits.

Almost as soon as they come into the world the children are subjected to fashion's influence. They hear more of dress than of their Saviour. They see their mothers consulting the fashion plates more earnestly than the Bible. The display of dress is treated as of greater importance than the development of character. Parents and children are robbed of that which is best and sweetest and truest in life. For fashion's sake they are cheated out of a preparation for the life to come.

It was the adversary of all good who instigated the invention of the ever-changing fashions. He desires nothing so much as to bring grief and dishonour to God by working the misery and ruin of human beings. One of the means by which he most effectually accomplishes this is the devices of fashion that weaken the body as well as enfeeble the mind and belittle the soul.

Women are subject to serious maladies, and their sufferings are greatly increased by their manner of dress. Instead of preserving their health for the trying emergencies that are sure to come, they by their wrong habits too often sacrifice not only health but life, and leave to their children a legacy of woe in a ruined constitution, perverted habits, and false ideas of life.

One of fashion's wasteful and mischievous devices is the skirt that sweeps the ground. Uncleanly, uncomfortable, inconvenient, unhealthful — all this and more is true of the trailing skirt. It is extravagant, both because of the superfluous material required and because of the needless wear on account of its length. And whoever has seen a woman in a trailing skirt, with hands filled with parcels, attempt to go up or down stairs, to enter a streetcar, to walk through a crowd, to walk in the rain or on a muddy road, needs no other proof of its inconvenience and discomfort.

Another serious evil is the wearing of skirts so that their weight must be sustained by the hips. This heavy weight, pressing upon the internal organs, drags them downward and causes weakness of the stomach and a feeling of lassitude, inclining the wearer to stoop, which further cramps the lungs, making correct breathing more difficult.

Of late years the dangers resulting from compression of the waist have been so fully discussed that few can be ignorant in regard to them; yet so great is the power of fashion that the evil continues. By this practice, women and young girls are doing themselves untold harm. It is essential to health that the chest have room to expand to its fullest extent in order that the lungs may be enabled to take full inspiration. When the lungs are restricted, the quantity of oxygen received into them is lessened. The blood is not properly vitalized, and the waste, poisonous matter which should be thrown off through the lungs is retained. In addition to this the circulation is hindered, and the internal organs are so cramped and crowded out of place that they cannot perform their work properly.

Tight lacing does not improve the form. One of the chief elements in physical beauty is symmetry, the harmonious proportion of parts. And the correct model for physical development is to be found, not in the figures displayed by French modistes, but in the human form as developed according to the laws of God in nature. God is the author of all beauty, and only as we conform to His ideal shall we approach the standard of true beauty.

Another evil which custom fosters is the unequal distribution of the clothing, so that while some parts of the body have more than is required, others are insufficiently clad. The feet and limbs, being remote from the vital organs, should be especially guarded from cold by abundant clothing. It is impossible to have health when the extremities are habitually cold; for if there is too little blood in them there will be too much in other portions of the body. Perfect health requires a perfect circulation; but this cannot be had while three or four times as much clothing is worn upon the body, where the vital organs are situated, as upon the feet and limbs.

A multitude of women are nervous and careworn because they deprive themselves of the pure air that would make pure blood, and of the freedom of motion that would send the blood bounding through the veins, giving life, health, and energy. Many women have become confirmed invalids when they might have enjoyed health, and many have died of consumption and other diseases when they might have lived their allotted term of life had they dressed in accordance with health principles and exercised freely in the open air.

In order to secure the most healthful clothing, the needs of every part of the body must be carefully studied. The character of the climate, the surroundings, the condition of health, the age, and the occupation must all be considered. Every article of dress should fit easily, obstructing neither the circulation of the blood nor a free, full, natural respiration. Everything worn should be so loose that when the arms are raised the clothing will be correspondingly lifted.

Women who are in failing health can do much for themselves by sensible dressing and exercise. When suitably dressed for outdoor enjoyment, let them exercise in the open air, carefully at first, but increasing the amount of exercise as they can endure it. By taking this course, many might regain health and live to take their share in the world's work.

Independent of Fashion

Let women themselves, instead of struggling to meet the demands of fashion, have the courage to dress healthfully and simply. Instead of sinking into a mere household drudge, let the wife and mother take time to read, to keep herself well informed, to be a companion to her husband, and to keep in touch with the developing minds of her children. Let her use wisely the opportunities now hers to influence her dear ones for the higher life. Let her take time to make the dear Saviour a daily companion and familiar friend. Let her take time for the study of His word, take time to go with the children into the fields, and learn of God through the beauty of His works.

Let her keep cheerful and buoyant. Instead of spending every moment in endless sewing, make the evening a pleasant social season, a family reunion after the day's duties. Many a man would thus be led to choose the society of his home before that of the clubhouse or the saloon. Many a boy would be kept from the street or the corner grocery. Many a girl would be saved from frivolous, misleading associations. The influence of the home would be to parents and children what God designed it should be, a lifelong blessing.

Diet and Health

Our bodies are built up from the food we eat. There is a constant breaking down of the tissues of the body; every movement of every organ involves waste, and this waste is repaired from our food. Each organ of the body requires its share of nutrition. The brain must be supplied with its portion; the bones, muscles, and nerves demand theirs. It is a wonderful process that transforms the food into blood and uses this blood to build up the varied parts of the body; but this process is going on continually, supplying with life and strength each nerve, muscle, and tissue.

Selection of Food

Those foods should be chosen that best supply the elements needed for building up the body. In this choice, appetite is not a safe guide. Through wrong habits of eating, the appetite has become perverted. Often it demands food that impairs health and causes weakness instead of strength. We cannot safely be guided by the customs of society. The disease and suffering that everywhere prevail are largely due to popular errors in regard to diet.

In order to know what are the best foods, we must study God's original plan for man's diet. He who created man and who understands his needs appointed Adam his food. "Behold," He said, "I have given you every herb yielding seed, . . . and every tree, in which is the fruit of a tree yielding seed; to you it shall be for food." Genesis 1:29, ARV. Upon leaving Eden to gain his livelihood by tilling the earth under the curse of sin, man received permission to eat also "the herb of the field." Genesis 3:18.

Grains, fruits, nuts, and vegetables constitute the diet chosen for us by our Creator. These foods, prepared in as simple and natural a manner as possible, are the most healthful and nourishing. They impart a strength, a power of endurance, and a vigour of intellect that are not afforded by a more complex and stimulating diet.

But not all foods wholesome in themselves are equally suited to our needs under all circumstances. Care should be taken in the selection of food. Our diet should be suited to the season, to the climate in which we live, and to the occupation we follow. Some foods that are adapted for use at one season or in one climate are not suited to another. So there are different foods best suited for persons in different occupations. Often food that can be used with benefit by those engaged in hard physical labour is unsuitable for persons of sedentary pursuits or intense mental application. God has given us an ample variety of healthful foods, and each person should choose from it the things that experience and sound judgement prove to be best suited to his own necessities.

Nature's abundant supply of fruits, nuts, and grains is ample, and year by year the products of all lands are more generally distributed to all, by the increased facilities for transportation. As a result many articles of food which a few years ago were regarded as expensive luxuries are now within the reach of all as foods for everyday use. This is especially the case with dried and canned fruits.

Nuts and nut foods are coming largely into use to take the place of flesh meats. With nuts may be combined grains, fruits, and some roots, to make foods that are healthful and nourishing. Care should be taken, however, not to use too large a proportion of nuts. Those who realize ill effects from the use of nut foods may find the difficulty removed by attending to this precaution. It should be remembered, too, that some nuts are not so wholesome as others. Almonds are preferable to peanuts, but peanuts in limited quantities, used in connection with grains, are nourishing and digestible.

When properly prepared, olives, like nuts, supply the place of butter and flesh meats. The oil, as eaten in the olive, is far preferable to animal oil or fat. It serves as a laxative. Its use will be found beneficial to consumptives, and it is healing to an inflamed, irritated stomach.

Persons who have accustomed themselves to a rich, highly stimulating diet have an unnatural taste, and they cannot at once relish food that is plain and simple. It will take time for the taste to become natural and for the stomach to recover from the abuse it has suffered. But those who persevere in the use of wholesome food will, after a time, find it palatable. Its delicate and delicious flavours will be appreciated, and it will be eaten with greater enjoyment than can be derived from unwholesome dainties. And the stomach, in a healthy condition, neither fevered nor overtaxed, can readily perform its task.

In order to maintain health, a sufficient supply of good, nourishing food is needed.

If we plan wisely, that which is most conducive to health can be secured in almost every land. The various preparations of rice, wheat, corn, and oats are sent abroad everywhere, also beans, peas, and lentils. These, with native or imported fruits, and the variety of vegetables that grow in each locality, give an opportunity to select a dietary that is complete without the use of flesh meats.

Wherever fruit can be grown in abundance, a liberal supply should be prepared for winter, by canning or drying. Small fruits, such as currants, gooseberries, strawberries, raspberries, and blackberries, can be grown to advantage in many places where they are but little used and their cultivation is neglected.

For household canning, glass, rather than tin cans, should be used whenever possible. It is especially necessary that the fruit for canning should be in good condition. Use little sugar, and cook the fruit only long enough to ensure its preservation. Thus prepared, it is an excellent substitute for fresh fruit.

Wherever dried fruits, such as raisins, prunes, apples, pears, peaches, and apricots are obtainable at moderate prices, it will be found that they can be used as staple articles of diet much more freely than is customary, with the best results to the health and vigour of all classes of workers.

There should not be a great variety at any one meal, for this encourages overeating and causes indigestion.

It is not well to eat fruit and vegetables at the same meal. If the digestion is feeble, the use of both will often cause distress and inability to put forth mental effort. It is better to have the fruit at one meal and the vegetables at another.

The meals should be varied. The same dishes, prepared in the same way, should not appear on the table meal after meal and day after day. The meals are eaten with greater relish, and the system is better nourished, when the food is varied.

Preparation of Food

It is wrong to eat merely to gratify the appetite, but no indifference should be manifested regarding the quality of the food or the manner of its preparation. If the food eaten is not relished, the body will not be so well nourished. The food should be carefully chosen and prepared with intelligence and skill.

For use in breadmaking, the superfine white flour is not the best. Its use is neither healthful nor economical. Fine-flour bread is lacking in nutritive elements to be found in bread made from the whole wheat. It is a frequent cause of constipation and other unhealthful conditions.

The use of soda or baking powder in breadmaking is harmful and unnecessary. Soda causes inflammation of the stomach and often poisons the entire system. Many housewives think that they cannot make good bread without soda, but this is an error. If they would take the trouble to learn better methods, their bread would be more wholesome, and, to a natural taste, it would be more palatable.

In the making of raised or yeast bread, milk should not be used in place of water. The use of milk is an additional expense, and it makes the bread much less wholesome. Milk bread does not keep sweet so long after baking as does that made with water, and it ferments more readily in the stomach.

Bread should be light and sweet. Not the least taint of sourness should be tolerated. The loaves should be small and so thoroughly baked that, so far as possible, the yeast germs shall be destroyed. When hot or new, raised bread of any kind is difficult of digestion. It should never appear on the table. This rule does not, however, apply to unleavened bread. Fresh rolls made of wheaten meal without yeast or leaven, and baked in a well-heated oven, are both wholesome and palatable.

Grains used for porridge or "mush" should have several hours' cooking. But soft or liquid foods are less wholesome than dry foods, which require thorough mastication. Zwieback, or twice-baked bread, is one of the most easily digested and most palatable of foods. Let ordinary raised bread be cut in slices and dried in a warm oven till the last trace of moisture disappears. Then let it be browned slightly all the way through. In a dry place this bread can be kept much longer than ordinary bread, and, if reheated before using, it will be as fresh as when new.

Far too much sugar is ordinarily used in food. Cakes, sweet puddings, pastries, jellies, jams, are active causes of indigestion. Especially harmful are the custards and puddings in which milk, eggs, and sugar are the chief ingredients. The free use of milk and sugar taken together should be avoided.

If milk is used, it should be thoroughly sterilized; with this precaution, there is less danger of contracting disease from its use. Butter is less harmful when eaten on cold bread than when used in cooking; but, as a rule, it is better to dispense with it altogether.

Cheese is still more objectionable; it is wholly unfit for food.*

Scanty, ill-cooked food depraves the blood by weakening the blood-making organs. It deranges the system and brings on disease, with its accompaniment of irritable nerves and bad tempers. The victims of poor cookery are numbered by thousands and tens of thousands. Over many graves might be written: "Died because of poor cooking;" "Died of an abused stomach."

It is a sacred duty for those who cook to learn how to prepare healthful food. Many souls are lost as the result of poor cookery. It takes thought and care to make good bread; but there is more religion in a loaf of good bread than many think. There are few really good cooks. Young women think that it is menial to cook and do other kinds of housework, and for this reason many girls who marry and have the care of families have little idea of the duties devolving upon a wife and mother.

Cooking is no mean science, and it is one of the most essential in practical life. It is a science that all women should learn, and it should be taught in a way to benefit the poorer classes. To make food appetizing and at the same time simple and nourishing, requires skill; but it can be done. Cooks should know how to prepare simple food in a simple and healthful manner, and so

---

* The safeguarding of the purity of all foods of dairy origin is a matter of prime importance. While frequent testing of dairy herds, together with thorough pasturization and refrigeration, serves to this end, such foods, if from uncertain sources, or if carelessly handled, constitute a serious menace to health; for, as stated in US Department of Agriculture Farmers' Bulletin No. 1705 by a Government expert, Rowena Schmidt Carpenter: "The same chemical constituents and physical properties that recommend milk as a human food make it an excellent food for bacteria." The reader will understand that the reference to cheese *does not* include cottage cheese or foods of a similar character, which were ever recognized by the author as wholesome. — Publishers.

that it will be found more palatable, as well as more wholesome, because of its simplicity.

Every woman who is at the head of a family and yet does not understand the art of healthful cookery should determine to learn that which is so essential to the well-being of her household. In many places hygienic cooking schools afford opportunity for instruction in this line. She who has not the help of such facilities should put herself under the instruction of some good cook and persevere in her efforts for improvement until she is mistress of the culinary art.

Regularity in eating is of vital importance. There should be a specified time for each meal. At this time let everyone eat what the system requires and then take nothing more until the next meal. There are many who eat when the system needs no food, at irregular intervals, and between meals, because they have not sufficient strength of will to resist inclination. When travelling, some are constantly nibbling if anything eatable is within their reach. This is very injurious. If travellers would eat regularly of food that is simple and nutritious, they would not feel so great weariness nor suffer so much from sickness.

Another pernicious habit is that of eating just before bedtime. The regular meals may have been taken; but because there is a sense of faintness, more food is eaten. By indulgence this wrong practice becomes a habit and often so firmly fixed that it is thought impossible to sleep without food. As a result of eating late suppers, the digestive process is continued through the sleeping hours. But though the stomach works constantly, its work is not properly accomplished. The sleep is often disturbed with unpleasant dreams, and in the morning the person awakes unrefreshed and with little relish for breakfast. When we lie down to rest, the stomach should have its work all done, that it, as well as the other organs of the body, may enjoy rest. For persons of sedentary habits, late suppers are particularly harmful. With them the disturbance created is often the beginning of disease that ends in death.

In many cases the faintness that leads to a desire for food is felt because the digestive organs have been too severely taxed during the day. After disposing of one meal, the digestive organs need rest. At least five or six hours should intervene between the meals, and most persons who give the plan a trial will find that two meals a day are better than three.

Wrong Conditions of Eating

Food should not be eaten very hot or very cold. If food is cold, the vital force of the stomach is drawn upon in order to warm it before digestion can take place. Cold drinks are injurious for the same reason; while the free use of hot drinks is debilitating. In fact, the more liquid there is taken with the meals, the more difficult it is for the food to digest; for the liquid must be absorbed before digestion can begin. Do not eat largely of salt, avoid the use of pickles and spiced foods, eat an abundance of fruit, and the irritation that calls for so much drink at mealtime will largely disappear.

Food should be eaten slowly and should be thoroughly masticated. This is necessary in order that the saliva may be properly mixed with the food and the digestive fluids be called into action.

Another serious evil is eating at improper times, as after violent or excessive exercise, when one is much exhausted or heated. Immediately after eating there is a strong draft upon the nervous energies; and when mind or body is heavily taxed just before or just after eating, digestion is hindered. When one is excited, anxious, or hurried, it is better not to eat until rest or relief is found.

The stomach is closely related to the brain; and when the stomach is diseased, the nerve power is called from the brain to the aid of the weakened digestive organs. When these demands are too frequent, the brain becomes congested. When the brain is constantly taxed, and there is lack of physical exercise, even plain food should be eaten sparingly. At mealtime cast off care and anxious thought; do not feel hurried, but eat slowly and with cheerfulness, with your heart filled with gratitude to God for all His blessings.

Many who discard flesh meats and other gross and injurious articles think that because their food is simple and wholesome they may indulge appetite without restraint, and they eat to excess, sometimes to gluttony. This is an error. The digestive organs should not be burdened with a quantity or quality of food which it will tax the system to appropriate.

Custom has decreed that the food shall be placed upon the table in courses. Not knowing what is coming next, one may eat a sufficiency of food which perhaps is not the best suited to him. When the last course is brought on, he often ventures to overstep the bounds, and take the tempting dessert, which, however, proves anything but good for him. If all the food intended for a meal is placed on the table at the beginning, one has opportunity to make the best choice.

Sometimes the result of overeating is felt at once. In other cases there is no sensation of pain; but the digestive organs lose their vital force, and the foundation of physical strength is undermined.

The surplus food burdens the system and produces morbid, feverish conditions. It calls an undue amount of blood to the stomach, causing the limbs and extremities to chill quickly. It lays a heavy tax on the digestive organs, and when these organs have accomplished their task, there is a feeling of faintness or languor. Some who are continually overeating call this all-gone feeling hunger; but it is caused by the over-worked condition of the digestive organs. At times there is numbness of the brain, with disinclination to mental or physical effort.

These unpleasant symptoms are felt because nature has accomplished her work at an unnecessary outlay of vital force and is thoroughly exhausted. The stomach is saying, "Give me rest." But with many the faintness is interpreted as a demand for more food; so instead of giving the stomach rest, another burden is placed upon it. As a consequence the digestive organs are often worn out when they should be capable of doing good work.

We should not provide for the Sabbath a more liberal supply or a greater variety of food than for other days. Instead of this the food should be more simple, and less should be eaten in order that the mind may be clear and vigorous to comprehend spiritual things. A clogged stomach means a clogged brain. The most precious words may be heard and not appreciated because the mind is confused by an improper diet. By overeating on the Sabbath, many do more than they think to unfit themselves for receiving the benefit of its sacred opportunities.

Cooking on the Sabbath should be avoided; but it is not therefore necessary to eat cold food. In cold weather the food prepared the day before should be heated. And let the meals, however simple, be palatable and attractive. Especially in families where there are children, it is well, on the Sabbath, to provide something that will be regarded as a treat, something the family do not have every day.

Where wrong habits of diet have been indulged, there should be no delay in reform. When dyspepsia has resulted from abuse of the stomach, efforts should be made carefully to preserve the remaining strength of the vital forces by removing every overtaxing burden. The stomach may never entirely recover health after long abuse; but a proper course of diet will save further debility, and many will recover more or less fully. It is not easy to prescribe rules that will meet every case; but, with attention to right principles in eating, great reforms may be made, and the cook need not be continually toiling to tempt the appetite.

Abstemiousness in diet is rewarded with mental and moral vigour; it also aids in the control of the passions. Overeating is especially harmful to those who are sluggish in temperament; these should eat sparingly and take plenty of physical exercise. There are men and women of excellent natural ability who do not accomplish half what they might if they would exercise self-control in the denial of appetite.

Many writers and speakers fail here. After eating heartily, they give themselves to sedentary occupations, reading, study, or writing, allowing no time for physical exercise. As a consequence the free flow of thought and words is checked. They cannot write or speak with the force and intensity necessary in order to reach the heart; their efforts are tame and fruitless.

Those upon whom rest important responsibilities, those, above all, who are guardians of spiritual interests, should be men of keen feeling and quick perception. More than others, they need to be temperate in eating. Rich and luxurious food should have no place upon their tables.

Every day men in positions of trust have decisions to make upon which depend results of great importance. Often they have to think rapidly, and this can be done successfully by those only who practice strict temperance. The mind strengthens under the correct treatment of the physical and mental powers. If the strain is not too great, new vigour comes with every taxation. But often the work of those who have important plans to consider and important decisions to make is affected for evil by the results of improper diet. A disordered stomach produces a disordered, uncertain state of mind. Often it causes irritability, harshness, or injustice. Many a plan that would have been a blessing to the world has been set aside, many unjust, oppressive, even cruel measures have been carried, as the result of diseased conditions due to wrong habits of eating.

Here is a suggestion for all whose work is sedentary or chiefly mental; let those who have sufficient moral courage and self-control try it: At each meal take only two or three kinds of simple food, and eat no more than is required to satisfy hunger. Take active exercise every day, and see if you do not receive benefit.

Strong men who are engaged in active physical labour are not compelled to be as careful as to the quantity or quality of their food as are persons of sedentary habits;

but even these would have better health if they would practice self-control in eating and drinking.

Some wish that an exact rule could be prescribed for their diet. They overeat, and then regret it, and so they keep thinking about what they eat and drink. This is not as it should be. One person cannot lay down an exact rule for another. Everyone should exercise reason and self-control, and should act from principle.

Our bodies are Christ's purchased possession, and we are not at liberty to do with them as we please. All who understand the laws of health should realize their obligation to obey these laws which God has established in their being. Obedience to the laws of health is to be made a matter of personal duty. We ourselves must suffer the results of violated law. We must individually answer to God for our habits and practices. Therefore the question with us is not, "What is the world's practice?" but, "How shall I as an individual treat the habitation that God has given me?"

Flesh as Food

The diet appointed man in the beginning did not include animal food. Not till after the Flood, when every green thing on the earth had been destroyed, did man receive permission to eat flesh.

In choosing man's food in Eden, the Lord showed what was the best diet; in the choice made for Israel He taught the same lesson. He brought the Israelites out of Egypt and undertook their training, that they might be a people for His own possession. Through them He desired to bless and teach the world. He provided them with the food best adapted for this purpose, not flesh, but manna, "the bread of heaven." It was only because of their discontent and their murmuring for the fleshpots of Egypt that animal food was granted them, and this only for a short time. Its use brought disease and death to thousands. Yet the restriction to a nonflesh diet was never heartily accepted. It continued to be the cause of discontent and murmuring, open or secret, and it was not made permanent.

Upon their settlement in Canaan, the Israelites were permitted the use of animal food, but under careful restrictions which tended to lessen the evil results. The use of swine's flesh was prohibited, as also of other animals and of birds and fish whose flesh was pronounced unclean. Of the meats permitted, the eating of the fat and the blood was strictly forbidden.

Only such animals could be used for food as were in good condition. No creature that was torn, that had died of itself, or from which the blood had not been carefully drained, could be used as food.

By departing from the plan divinely appointed for

their diet, the Israelites suffered great loss. They desired a flesh diet, and they reaped its results. They did not reach God's ideal of character or fulfil His purpose. The Lord "gave them their request; but sent leanness into their soul." Psalm 106:15. They valued the earthly above the spiritual, and the sacred pre-eminence which was His purpose for them they did not attain.

Reasons for Discarding Flesh Foods

Those who eat flesh are but eating grains and vegetables at second hand; for the animal receives from these things the nutrition that produces growth. The life that was in the grains and vegetables passes into the eater. We receive it by eating the flesh of the animal. How much better to get it direct, by eating the food that God provided for our use!

Flesh was never the best food; but its use is now doubly objectionable, since disease in animals is so rapidly increasing. Those who use flesh foods little know what they are eating. Often if they could see the animals when living and know the quality of the meat they eat, they would turn from it with loathing. People are continually eating flesh that is filled with tuberculous and cancerous germs. Tuberculosis, cancer, and other fatal diseases are thus communicated.

The tissues of the swine swarm with parasites. Of the swine God said, "It is unclean unto you: ye shall not eat of their flesh, nor touch their dead carcass." Deuteronomy 14:8. This command was given because swine's flesh is unfit for food. Swine are scavengers, and this is the only use they were intended to serve. Never, under any circumstances, was their flesh to be eaten by human beings. It is impossible for the flesh of any living creature to be wholesome when filth is its natural element and when it feeds upon every detestable thing.

Often animals are taken to market and sold for food when they are so diseased that their owners fear to keep them longer. And some of the processes of fattening them for market produce disease. Shut away from the light and pure air, breathing the atmosphere of filthy stables, perhaps fattening on decaying food, the entire body soon becomes contaminated with foul matter.

Animals are often transported long distances and subjected to great suffering in reaching a market. Taken from the green pastures, and travelling for weary miles over the hot, dusty roads, or crowded into filthy cars, feverish and exhausted, often for many hours deprived of food and water, the poor creatures are driven to their death, that human beings may feast on the carcasses.

In many places fish become so contaminated by the filth on which they feed as to be a cause of disease. This is especially the case where the fish come in contact with the sewage of large cities. The fish that are fed on the contents of the drains may pass into distant waters and may be caught where the water is pure and fresh. Thus when used as food they bring disease and death on those who do not suspect the danger.

The effects of a flesh diet may not be immediately realized; but this is no evidence that it is not harmful. Few can be made to believe that it is the meat they have eaten which has poisoned their blood and caused their suffering. Many die of diseases wholly due to meat eating, while the real cause is not suspected by themselves or by others.

The moral evils of a flesh diet are not less marked than are the physical ills. Flesh food is injurious to health, and whatever affects the body has a corresponding effect on the mind and the soul. Think of the cruelty to animals that meat eating involves, and its effect on those who inflict and those who behold it. How it destroys the tenderness with which we should regard these creatures of God!

The intelligence displayed by many dumb animals approaches so closely to human intelligence that it is a mystery. The animals see and hear and love and fear and suffer. They use their organs far more faithfully than many human beings use theirs. They manifest sympathy and tenderness toward their companions in suffering. Many animals show an affection for those who have charge of them, far superior to the affection shown by some of the human race. They form attachments for man which are not broken without great suffering to them.

What man with a human heart, who has ever cared for domestic animals, could look into their eyes, so full of confidence and affection, and willingly give them over to the butcher's knife? How could he devour their flesh as a sweet morsel?

It is a mistake to suppose that muscular strength depends on the use of animal food. The needs of the system can be better supplied, and more vigorous health can be enjoyed, without its use. The grains, with fruits, nuts, and vegetables, contain all the nutritive properties necessary to make good blood. These elements are not so well or so fully supplied by a flesh diet. Had the use of flesh been essential to health and strength, animal food would have been included in the diet appointed man in the beginning.

When the use of flesh food is discontinued, there is often a sense of weakness, a lack of vigour. Many urge this as evidence that flesh food is essential; but it is because foods of this class are stimulating, because they fever the blood and excite the nerves, that they are so missed. Some will find it as difficult to leave off flesh eating as it is for the drunkard to give up his dram; but they will be the better for the change.

When flesh food is discarded, its place should be supplied with a variety of grains, nuts, vegetables, and fruits that will be both nourishing and appetizing. This is especially necessary in the case of those who are weak or who are taxed with continuous labour. In some countries where poverty abounds, flesh is the cheapest food. Under these circumstances the change will be made with greater difficulty; but it can be effected. We should, however, consider the situation of the people and the power of lifelong habit, and should be careful not to urge even right ideas unduly. None should be urged to make the change abruptly. The place of meat should be supplied with wholesome foods that are inexpensive. In this matter very much depends on the cook. With care and skill, dishes may be prepared that will be both nutritious and appetizing, and will, to a great degree, take the place of flesh food.

In all cases educate the conscience, enlist the will, supply good, wholesome food, and the change will be readily made, and the demand for flesh will soon cease.

Is it not time that all should aim to dispense with flesh foods? How can those who are seeking to become pure, refined, and holy, that they may have the companionship of heavenly angels, continue to use as food anything that has so harmful an effect on soul and body? How can they take the life of God's creatures that they may consume the flesh as a luxury? Let them, rather, return to the wholesome and delicious food given to man in the beginning, and themselves practice, and teach their children to practice, mercy toward the dumb creatures that God has made and has placed under our dominion.

Extremes in Diet

Not all who profess to believe in dietetic reform are really reformers. With many persons the reform consists merely in discarding certain unwholesome foods. They do not understand clearly the principles of health, and their tables, still loaded with harmful dainties, are far from being an example of Christian temperance and moderation.

Another class, in their desire to set a right example, go to the opposite extreme. Some are unable to obtain the most desirable foods, and, instead of using such things as would best supply the lack, they adopt an impoverished diet. Their food does not supply the elements needed to make good blood. Their health suffers, their usefulness is impaired, and their example tells against, rather than in favour of, reform in diet.

Others think that since health requires a simple diet, there need be little care in the selection or the preparation of food. Some restrict themselves to a very meager diet, not having sufficient variety to supply the needs of the system, and they suffer in consequence.

Those who have but a partial understanding of the principles of reform are often the most rigid, not only in carrying out their views themselves, but in urging them on their families and their neighbours. The effect of their mistaken reforms, as seen in their own ill-health, and their efforts to force their views upon others, give many a false idea of dietetic reform, and lead them to reject it altogether.

Those who understand the laws of health and who are governed by principle, will shun the extremes, both of indulgence and of restriction. Their diet is chosen, not for the mere gratification of appetite, but for the upbuilding of the body. They seek to preserve every power in the best condition for highest service to God and man. The appetite is under the control of reason and conscience, and they are rewarded with health of body and mind. While they do not urge their views offensively upon others, their example is a testimony in favour of right principles. These persons have a wide influence for good.

There is real common sense in dietetic reform. The subject should be studied broadly and deeply, and no one should criticize others because their practice is not, in all things, in harmony with his own. It is impossible to make an unvarying rule to regulate everyone's habits, and no one should think himself a criterion for all. Not all can eat the same things. Foods that are palatable and wholesome to one person may be distasteful, and even harmful, to another. Some cannot use milk, while others thrive on it. Some persons cannot digest peas and beans; others find them wholesome. For some the coarser grain preparations are good food, while others cannot use them.

Those who live in new countries or in poverty-stricken districts, where fruits and nuts are scarce, should not be urged to exclude milk and eggs from their dietary. It is true that persons in full flesh and in whom the animal passions are strong need to avoid the use of stimulating foods. Especially in families of children who are given to sensual habits, eggs should not be used. But in the case of persons whose blood-making organs are feeble — especially if other foods to supply the needed elements cannot be obtained — milk and eggs should not be wholly discarded. Great care should be taken, however, to obtain milk from healthy cows, and eggs from healthy fowls, that are well fed and well cared for; and the eggs should be so cooked as to be most easily digested.

The diet reform should be progressive. As disease in animals increases, the use of milk and eggs will become more and more unsafe. An effort should be made to supply their place with other things that are healthful and inexpensive. The people everywhere should be taught how to cook without milk and eggs, so far as possible, and yet have their food wholesome and palatable.

The practice of eating but two meals a day is generally found a benefit to health; yet under some circumstances persons may require a third meal. This should, however, if taken at all, be very light, and of food most easily digested. "Crackers" – the English biscuit – or zwieback, and fruit, or cereal coffee, are the foods best suited for the evening meal.

Some are continually anxious lest their food, however simple and healthful, may hurt them. To these let me say, Do not think that your food will injure you; do not think about it at all. Eat according to your best judgement; and when you have asked the Lord to bless the food for the strengthening of your body, believe that He hears your prayer, and be at rest.

Because principle requires us to discard those things that irritate the stomach and impair health, we should remember that an impoverished diet produces poverty of the blood. Cases of disease most difficult to cure result from this cause. The system is not sufficiently nourished, and dyspepsia and general debility are the result. Those who use such a diet are not always compelled by poverty to do so, but they choose it through ignorance or negligence, or to carry out their erroneous ideas of reform.

God is not honoured when the body is neglected or abused and is thus unfitted for His service. To care for the body by providing for it food that is relishable and strengthening is one of the first duties of the householder. It is far better to have less expensive clothing and furniture than to stint the supply of food.

Some householders stint the family table in order to provide expensive entertainment for visitors. This is unwise. In the entertainment of guests there should be greater simplicity. Let the needs of the family have first attention.

Unwise economy and artificial customs often prevent the exercise of hospitality where it is needed and would be a blessing. The regular supply of food for our tables should be such that the unexpected guest can be made welcome without burdening the housewife to make extra preparation.

All should learn what to eat and how to cook it. Men, as well as women, need to understand the simple, healthful preparation of food. Their business often calls them where they cannot obtain wholesome food; then, if they have a knowledge of cookery, they can use it to good purpose.

Carefully consider your diet. Study from cause to effect. Cultivate self-control. Keep appetite under the control of reason. Never abuse the stomach by overeating, but do not deprive yourself of the wholesome, palatable food that health demands.

The narrow ideas of some would-be health reformers have been a great injury to the cause of hygiene. Hygienists should remember that dietetic reform will be judged, to a great degree, by the provision they make for their tables; and instead of taking a course that will bring discredit upon it, they should so exemplify its principles as to commend them to candid minds. There is a large class who will oppose any reform movement, however reasonable, if it places a restriction on the appetite. They consult taste instead of reason or the laws of health. By this class, all who leave the beaten track of custom and advocate reform will be accounted radical, no matter how consistent their course. That these persons may have no ground for criticism, hygienists should not try to see how different they can be from others, but should come as near to them as possible without the sacrifice of principle.

When those who advocate hygienic reform go to extremes, it is no wonder that many who regard these persons as representing health principles reject the reform altogether. These extremes frequently do more harm in a short time than could be undone by a lifetime of consistent living.

Hygienic reform is based upon principles that are broad and far-reaching, and we should not belittle it by narrow views and practices. But no one should permit opposition or ridicule, or a desire to please or influence others, to turn him from true principles, or cause him lightly to regard them. Those who are governed by principle will be firm and decided in standing for the right; yet in all their associations they will manifest a generous, Christlike spirit and true moderation.

Stimulants and Narcotics

Under the head of stimulants and narcotics is classed a great variety of articles that, altogether used as food or drink, irritate the stomach, poison the blood, and excite the nerves. Their use is a positive evil. Men seek the excitement of stimulants, because, for the time, the results are agreeable. But there is always a reaction. The use of unnatural stimulants always tends to excess, and it is an active agent in promoting physical degeneration and decay.

Condiments

In this fast age, the less exciting the food, the better. Condiments are injurious in their nature. Mustard, pepper, spices, pickles, and other things of a like character, irritate the stomach and make the blood feverish and impure. The inflamed condition of the drunkard's stomach is often pictured as illustrating the effect of alcoholic liquors. A similarly inflamed condition is produced by the use of irritating condiments. Soon ordinary food does not satisfy the appetite. The system feels a want, a craving, for something more stimulating.

Tea and Coffee

Tea acts as a stimulant and, to a certain extent, produces intoxication. The action of coffee and many other popular drinks is similar. The first effect is exhilarating. The nerves of the stomach are excited; these convey irritation to the brain, and this in turn is aroused to impart increased action to the heart and short-lived energy to the entire system. Fatigue is forgotten; the strength seems to be increased. The intellect is aroused, the imagination becomes more vivid.

Because of these results, many suppose that their tea or coffee is doing them great good. But this is a mistake. Tea and coffee do not nourish the system. Their effect is produced before there has been time for digestion and assimilation, and what seems to be strength is only nervous excitement. When the influence of the stimulant is gone, the unnatural force abates, and the result is a corresponding degree of languor and debility.

The continued use of these nerve irritants is followed by headache, wakefulness, palpitation of the heart, indigestion, trembling, and many other evils; for they wear away the life forces. Tired nerves need rest and quiet instead of stimulation and overwork. Nature needs time to recuperate her exhausted energies. When her forces are goaded on by the use of stimulants, more will be accomplished for a time; but, as the system becomes debilitated by their constant use, it gradually becomes more difficult to rouse the energies to the desired point. The demand for stimulants becomes more difficult to control, until the will is overborne and there seems to be no power to deny the unnatural craving. Stronger and still stronger stimulants are called for, until exhausted nature can no longer respond.

The Tobacco Habit

Tobacco is a slow, insidious, but most malignant poison. In whatever form it is used, it tells upon the constitution; it is all the more dangerous because its effects are slow and at first hardly perceptible. It excites and then paralyses the nerves. It weakens and clouds the brain. Often it affects the nerves in a more powerful manner than does intoxicating drink. It is more subtle, and its effects are difficult to eradicate from the system. Its use excites a thirst for strong drink and in many cases lays the foundation for the liquor habit.

The use of tobacco is inconvenient, expensive, uncleanly, defiling to the user, and offensive to others. Its devotees are encountered everywhere. You rarely pass through a crowd but some smoker puffs his poisoned breath in your face. It is unpleasant and unhealthful to remain in a railway carriage or in a room where the atmosphere is laden with the fumes of liquor and tobacco. Though men persist in using these poisons themselves, what right have they to defile the air that others must breathe?

Among children and youth the use of tobacco is working untold harm. The unhealthful practices of past generations affect the children and youth of today. Mental inability, physical weakness, disordered nerves, and unnatural cravings are transmitted as a legacy from parents to children. And the same practices, continued by the children, are increasing and perpetuating the evil results. To this cause in no small degree is owing the physical, mental, and moral deterioration which is becoming such a cause of alarm.

Boys begin the use of tobacco at a very early age. The habit thus formed when body and mind are especially susceptible to its effects, undermines the physical strength, dwarfs the body, stupefies the mind, and corrupts the morals.

But what can be done to teach children and youth the evils of a practice of which parents, teachers, and ministers set them the example? Little boys, hardly emerged from babyhood, may be seen smoking their cigarettes. If one speaks to them about it, they say, "My father uses tobacco." They point to the minister or the Sunday-school superintendent and say, "Such a man smokes; what harm for me to do as he does?" Many workers in the temperance cause are addicted to the use of tobacco. What power can such persons have to stay the progress of intemperance?

I appeal to those who profess to believe and obey the word of God: Can you as Christians indulge a habit that is paralyzing your intellect and robbing you of power rightly to estimate eternal realities? Can you consent daily to rob God of service which is His due, and to rob your fellow men, both of service you might render and of the power of example?

Have you considered your responsibility as God's stewards, for the means in your hands? How much of the Lord's money do you spend for tobacco? Reckon up what you have thus spent during your lifetime. How does the amount consumed by this defiling lust compare with what you have given for the relief of the poor and the spread of the gospel?

No human being needs tobacco, but multitudes are perishing for want of the means that by its use is worse than wasted. Have you not been misappropriating the Lord's goods? Have you not been guilty of robbery toward God and your fellow men? "Know ye not that . . . ye are not your own? For ye are bought with a price: therefore glorify God in your body, and in your spirit, which are God's." 1 Corinthians 6:19, 20.

Intoxicating Drinks

> "Wine is a mocker, strong drink is raging:
> And whosoever is deceived thereby is not wise."
> "Who hath woe? who hath sorrow? who hath contentions? who hath babbling? who hath wounds without cause?
> Who hath redness of eyes?
> They that tarry long at the wine;
> They that go to seek mixed wine.
> Look not thou upon the wine when it is red,
> When it giveth his colour in the cup,
> When it moveth itself aright.
> At the last it biteth like a serpent,
> And stingeth like an adder."
> Proverbs 20:1; 23:29-32.

Never was traced by human hand a more vivid picture of the debasement and the slavery of the victim of intoxicating drink. Enthralled, degraded, even when awakened to a sense of his misery, he has no power to break from the snare; he "will seek it yet again." Verse 35.

No argument is needed to show the evil effects of intoxicants on the drunkard. The bleared, besotted wrecks of humanity — souls for whom Christ died, and over whom angels weep — are everywhere. They are a blot on our boasted civilization. They are the shame and curse and peril of every land.

And who can picture the wretchedness, the agony, the despair, that are hidden in the drunkard's home? Think of the wife, often delicately reared, sensitive, cultured, and refined, linked to one whom drink transforms into a sot or a demon. Think of the children, robbed of home comforts, education, and training, living in terror of him who should be their pride and protection, thrust into the world, bearing the brand of shame, often with the hereditary curse of the drunkard's thirst.

Think of the frightful accidents that are every day occurring through the influence of drink. Some official on a railway train neglects to heed a signal or misinterprets an order. On goes the train; there is a collision, and many lives are lost. Or a steamer is run aground, and passengers and crew find a watery grave. When the matter is investigated, it is found that someone at an important post was under the influence of drink. To what extent can one indulge the liquor habit and be safely trusted with the lives of human beings? He can be trusted only as he totally abstains.

The Milder Intoxicants

Persons who have inherited an appetite for unnatural stimulants should by no means have wine, beer, or cider in their sight, or within their reach; for this keeps the temptation constantly before them. Regarding sweet cider as harmless, many have no scruples in purchasing it freely. But it remains sweet for a short time only; then fermentation begins. The sharp taste which it then acquires makes it all the more acceptable to many palates, and the user is loath to admit that it has become hard, or fermented.

There is danger to health in the use of even sweet cider as ordinarily produced. If people could see what the microscope reveals in regard to the cider they buy, few would be willing to drink it. Often those who manufacture cider for the market are not careful as to the condition of the fruit used, and the juice of wormy and decayed apples is expressed. Those who would not think of using the poisonous, rotten apples in any other way, will drink the cider made from them, and call it a luxury; but the microscope shows that even when fresh from the press, this pleasant beverage is wholly unfit for use.*

Intoxication is just as really produced by wine, beer, and cider as by stronger drinks. The use of these drinks awakens the taste for those that are stronger, and thus the liquor habit is established. Moderate drinking is the school in which men are educated for the drunkard's career. Yet so insidious is the work of these milder stimulants that the highway to drunkenness is entered before the victim suspects his danger.

Some who are never considered really drunk are always under the influence of mild intoxicants. They are feverish, unstable in mind, unbalanced. Imagining themselves secure, they go on and on, until every barrier is broken down, every principle sacrificed. The strongest resolutions are undermined, the highest considerations are not sufficient to keep the debased appetite under the control of reason.

The Bible nowhere sanctions the use of intoxicating wine. The wine that Christ made from water at the marriage feast of Cana was the pure juice of the grape. This is the "new wine . . . found in the cluster," of which the Scripture says, "Destroy it not; for a blessing is in it." Isaiah 65:8.

It was Christ who, in the Old Testament, gave the warning to Israel, "Wine is a mocker, strong drink is raging: and whosoever is deceived thereby is not wise." Proverbs 20:1. He Himself provided no such beverage. Satan tempts men to indulgence that will becloud

---

(*When this statement was made in 1905, it was common practice to manufacture cider as here described by the author. Today, in places where the purity of foods is not controlled, apple cider may still be made the same way. But where cider is produced under sanitary conditions, using good, sound fruit, obviously the objections disappear. – Publishers.)

reason and benumb the spiritual perceptions, but Christ teaches us to bring the lower nature into subjection. He never places before men that which would be a temptation. His whole life was an example of self-denial. It was to break the power of appetite that in the forty days' fast in the wilderness He suffered in our behalf the severest test that humanity could endure. It was Christ who directed that John the Baptist should drink neither wine nor strong drink. It was He who enjoined similar abstinence upon the wife of Manoah. Christ did not contradict His own teaching. The unfermented wine that He provided for the wedding guests was a wholesome and refreshing drink. This is the wine that was used by our Saviour and His disciples in the first Communion. It is the wine that should always be used on the Communion table as a symbol of the Saviour's blood. The sacramental service is designed to be soul-refreshing and life-giving. There is to be connected with it nothing that could minister to evil.

In the light of what the Scriptures, nature, and reason teach concerning the use of intoxicants, how can Christians engage in the raising of hops for beer making, or in the manufacture of wine or cider for the market? If they love their neighbour as themselves, how can they help to place in his way that which will be a snare to him?

Often intemperance begins in the home. By the use of rich, unhealthful food the digestive organs are weakened, and a desire is created for food that is still more stimulating. Thus the appetite is educated to crave continually something stronger. The demand for stimulants becomes more frequent and more difficult to resist. The system becomes more or less filled with poison, and the more debilitated it becomes, the greater is the desire for these things. One step in the wrong direction prepares the way for another. Many who would not be guilty of placing on their table wine or liquor of any kind will load their table with food which creates such a thirst for strong drink that to resist the temptation is almost impossible. Wrong habits of eating and drinking destroy the health and prepare the way for drunkenness.

There would soon be little necessity for temperance crusades if in the youth who form and fashion society, right principles in regard to temperance could be implanted. Let parents begin a crusade against intemperance at their own firesides, in the principles they teach their children to follow from infancy, and they may hope for success.

There is work for mothers in helping their children to form correct habits and pure tastes. Educate the appetite; teach the children to abhor stimulants. Bring your children up to have moral stamina to resist the evil that surrounds them. Teach them that they are not to be swayed by others, that they are not to yield to strong influences, but to influence others for good.

Great efforts are made to put down intemperance; but there is much effort that is not directed to the right point. The advocates of temperance reform should be awake to the evils resulting from the use of unwholesome food, condiments, tea, and coffee. We bid all temperance workers Godspeed; but we invite them to look more deeply into the cause of the evil they war against and to be sure that they are consistent in reform.

It must be kept before the people that the right balance of the mental and moral powers depends in a great degree on the right condition of the physical system. All narcotics and unnatural stimulants that enfeeble and degrade the physical nature tend to lower the tone of the intellect and morals. Intemperance lies at the foundation of the moral depravity of the world. By the indulgence of perverted appetite, man loses his power to resist temptation.

Temperance reformers have a work to do in educating the people in these lines. Teach them that health, character, and even life, are endangered by the use of stimulants, which excite the exhausted energies to unnatural, spasmodic action.

In relation to tea, coffee, tobacco, and alcoholic drinks, the only safe course is to touch not, taste not, handle not. The tendency of tea, coffee, and similar drinks is in the same direction as that of alcoholic liquor and tobacco, and in some cases the habit is as difficult to break as it is for the drunkard to give up intoxicants. Those who attempt to leave off these stimulants will for a time feel a loss and will suffer without them. But by persistence they will overcome the craving and cease to feel the lack. Nature may require a little time to recover from the abuse she has suffered; but give her a chance, and she will again rally and perform her work nobly and well.

Liquor Traffic and Prohibition

"Woe unto him that buildeth his house by unrighteousness, and his chambers by wrong; . . . that saith, I will build me a wide house and large chambers, and cutteth him out windows; and it is ceiled with cedar, and painted with vermilion. Shalt thou reign, because thou closest thyself in cedar? . . . Thine eyes and thine heart are not but for thy covetousness, and for to shed innocent blood, and for oppression, and for violence, to do it." Jeremiah 22:13-17.

The Work of the Liquor Seller

This scripture pictures the work of those who manufacture and who sell intoxicating liquor. Their business means robbery. For the money they receive, no equivalent is returned. Every dollar they add to their gains has brought a curse to the spender.

With a liberal hand, God has bestowed His blessings upon men. If His gifts were wisely used, how little the world would know of poverty or distress! It is the wickedness of men that turns His blessings into a curse. It is through the greed of gain and the lust of appetite that the grains and fruits given for our sustenance are converted into poisons that bring misery and ruin.

Every year millions upon millions of gallons of intoxicating liquors are consumed. Millions upon millions of dollars are spent in buying wretchedness, poverty, disease, degradation, lust, crime, and death. For the sake of gain, the liquor seller deals out to his victims that which corrupts and destroys mind and body. He entails on the drunkard's family poverty and wretchedness.

When his victim is dead, the rum seller's exactions do not cease. He robs the widow and brings children to beggary. He does not hesitate to take the very necessaries of life from the destitute family, to pay the drink bill of the husband and father. The cries of the suffering children, the tears of the agonized mother, serve only to exasperate him. What is it to him if these suffering ones starve? What is it to him if they, too, are driven to degradation and ruin? He grows rich on the pittances of those whom he is leading to perdition.

Houses of prostitution, dens of vice, criminal courts, prisons, almshouses, insane asylums, hospitals, all are, to a great degree, filled as a result of the liquor seller's work. Like the mystic Babylon of the Apocalypse, he is dealing in "slaves, and souls of men." Behind the liquor seller stands the mighty destroyer of souls, and every art which earth or hell can devise is employed to draw human beings under his power. In the city and the country, on the railway trains, on the great steamers, in places of business, in the halls of pleasure, in the medical dispensary, even in the church, on the sacred Communion table, his traps are set. Nothing is left undone to create and to foster the desire for intoxicants. On almost every cornor stands the public house, with its brilliant lights, its welcome and good cheer, inviting the working man, the wealthy idler, and the unsuspecting youth.

In private lunchrooms and fashionable resorts, ladies are supplied with popular drinks, under some pleasing name, that are really intoxicants. For the sick and the exhausted, there are the widely advertised bitters, consisting largely of alcohol.

To create the liquor appetite in little children, alcohol is introduced into confectionery. Such confectionery is sold in the shops. And by the gift of these candies the liquor seller entices children into his resorts.

Day by day, month by month, year by year, the work goes on. Fathers and husbands and brothers, the stay and hope and pride of the nation, are steadily passing into the liquor dealer's haunts, to be sent back wrecked and ruined.

More terrible still, the curse is striking the very heart of the home. More and more, women are forming the liquor habit. In many a household, little children, even in the innocence and helplessness of babyhood, are in daily peril through the neglect, the abuse, the vileness of drunken mothers. Sons and daughters are growing up under the shadow of this terrible evil. What outlook for their future but that they will sink even lower than their parents?

From so-called Christian lands the curse is carried to the regions of idolatry. The poor, ignorant savages are taught the use of liquor. Even among the heathen, men of intelligence recognize and protest against it as a deadly poison; but in vain have they sought to protect their lands from its ravages. By civilized peoples, tobacco, liquor, and opium are forced upon the heathen nations. The ungoverned passions of the savage, stimulated by drink, drag him down to degradation before unknown, and it becomes an almost hopeless undertaking to send missionaries to these lands.

Through their contact with peoples who should have given them a knowledge of God, the heathen are led into vices which are proving the destruction of whole tribes and races. And in the dark places of the earth the men of civilized nations are hated because of this.

The Responsibility of the Church

The liquor interest is a power in the world. It has on its side the combined strength of money, habit, appetite. Its power is felt even in the church. Men whose money has been made, directly or indirectly, in the liquor traffic, are members of churches, "in good and regular standing." Many of them give liberally to popular charities. Their contributions help to support the enterprises of the church and to sustain its ministers. They command the consideration shown to the money power. Churches that accept such members are virtually sustaining the liquor traffic. Too often the minister has not the courage to stand for the right. He does not declare to his people what God has said concerning the work of the liquor seller. To speak plainly would mean the offending of his congregation, the sacrifice of his popularity, the loss of his salary.

But above the tribunal of the church is the tribunal of God. He who declared to the first murderer, "The voice of thy brother's blood crieth unto Me from the ground" (Genesis 4:10), will not accept for His altar the gifts of the liquor dealer. His anger is kindled against those who attempt to cover their guilt with a cloak of liberality. Their money is stained with blood. A curse is upon it.

> "To what purpose is the multitude of your sacrifices
> unto Me? saith the Lord. . . .
> When ye come to appear before Me,
> Who hath required this at your hand, to tread My
> courts?
> Bring no more vain oblation . . . .
> When ye spread forth your hands,
> I will hide Mine eyes from you:
> Yea, when ye make many prayers, I will not hear:
> Your hands are full of blood."
> Isaiah 1:11-15.

The drunkard is capable of better things. He has been entrusted with talents with which to honour God and bless the world; but his fellow men have laid a snare for his soul and built themselves up by his degradation. They have lived in luxury while the poor victims whom they have robbed, lived in poverty and wretchedness. But God will require for this at the hand of him who has helped to speed the drunkard on to ruin. He who rules in the heavens has not lost sight of the first cause or the last effect of drunkenness. He who has a care for the sparrow and clothes the grass of the field, will not pass by those who have been formed in His own image, purchased with His own blood, and pay no heed to their cries. God marks all this wickedness that perpetuates crime and misery.

The world and the church may have approval for the man who has gained wealth by degrading the human soul. They may smile upon him by whom men are led down step by step in the path of shame and degradation. But God notes it all and renders a just judgement. The liquor seller may be termed by the world a good businessman; but the Lord says, "Woe unto him." He will be charged with the hopelessness, the misery, the suffering, brought into the world by the liquor traffic. He will have to answer for the want and woe of the mothers and children who have suffered for food and clothing and shelter, and who have buried all hope and joy. He will have to answer for the souls he has sent unprepared into eternity. And those who sustain the liquor seller in his work are sharers in his guilt. To them God says, "Your hands are full of blood."

License Laws

The licensing of the liquor traffic is advocated by many as tending to restrict the drink evil. But the licensing of the traffic places it under the protection of law. The government sanctions its existence, and thus fosters the evil which it professes to restrict. Under the protection of license laws, breweries, distilleries, and wineries are planted all over the land, and the liquor seller plies his work beside our very doors.

Often he is forbidden to sell intoxicants to one who is drunk or who is known to be a confirmed drunkard; but the work of making drunkards of the youth goes steadily forward. Upon the creating of the liquor appetite in the youth the very life of the traffic depends. The youth are led on, step by step, until the liquor habit is established and the thirst is created that at any cost demands satisfaction. Less harmful would it be to grant liquor to the confirmed drunkard, whose ruin, in most cases, is already determined, than to permit the flower of our youth to be lured to destruction through this terrible habit.

By the licencing of the liquor traffic, temptation is kept constantly before those who are trying to reform.

Institutions have been established where the victims of intemperance may be helped to overcome their appetite. This is a noble work; but so long as the sale of liquor is sanctioned by law, the imtemperate receive little benefit from inebriate asylums. They cannot remain there always. They must again take their place in society. The appetite for intoxicating drink, though subdued, is not wholly destroyed; and when temptation assails them, as it does on every hand, they too often fall an easy prey.

The man who has a vicious beast and who, knowing its disposition, allows it liberty, is by the laws of the land held accountable for the evil the beast may do. In the laws given to Israel the Lord directed that when a beast known to be vicious caused the death of a human being, the life of the owner should pay the price of his carelessness or malignity. On the same principle the government that licenses the liquor seller should be held responsible for the results of his traffic. And if it is a crime worthy of death to give liberty to a vicious beast, how much greater is the crime of sanctioning the work of the liquor seller!

Licences are granted on the plea that they bring a revenue to the public treasury. But what is this revenue when compared with the enormous expense incurred for the criminals, the insane, the paupers, that are the fruit of the liquor traffic! A man under the influence of liquor commits a crime; he is brought into court; and those who legalized the traffic are forced to deal with the result of their own work. They authorized the sale of a draft that would make a sane man mad; and now it is necessary for them to send the man to prison or to the gallows, while often his wife and children are left destitute to become the charge of the community in which they live.

Considering only the financial aspect of the question, what folly it is to tolerate such a business! But what revenue can compensate for the loss of human reason, for the defacing and deforming of the image of God in man, for the ruin of children, reduced to pauperism and degradation, to perpetuate in their children the evil tendencies of their drunken fathers?

Prohibition

The man who has formed the habit of using intoxicants is in a desperate situation. His brain is diseased, his will power is weakened. So far as any power in himself is concerned, his appetite is uncontrollable. He cannot be reasoned with or persuaded to deny himself. Drawn into the dens of vice, one who has resolved to quit drink is led to seize the glass again, and with the first taste of the intoxicant every good resolution is overpowered, every vestige of will destroyed. One taste of the maddening draft, and all thought of its results has vanished. The heartbroken wife is forgotten. The debauched father no longer cares that his children are hungry and naked. By legalizing the traffic, the law gives its sanction to this downfall of the soul and refuses to stop the trade that fills the world with evil.

Must this always continue? Will souls always have to struggle for victory, with the door of temptation wide open before them? Must the curse of intemperance forever rest like a blight upon the civilized world? Must it continue to sweep, every year, like a devouring fire over thousands of happy homes? When a ship is wrecked in sight of shore, people do not idly look on. They risk their lives in the effort to rescue men and women from a watery grave. How much greater the demand for effort in rescuing them from the drunkard's fate!

It is not the drunkard and his family alone who are imperiled by the work of the liquor seller, nor is the burden of taxation the chief evil which his traffic brings on the community. We are all woven together in the web of humanity. The evil that befalls any part of the great human brotherhood brings peril to all.

Many a man who through love of gain or ease would have nothing to do with restricting the liquor traffic has found, too late, that the traffic had to do with him. He has seen his own children besotted and ruined. Lawlessness runs riot. Property is in danger. Life is unsafe.

Accidents by sea and by land multiply. Diseases that breed in the haunts of filth and wretchedness make their way to lordly and luxurious homes. Vices fostered by the children of debauchery and crime infect the sons and daughters of refined and cultured households.

There is no man whose interests the liquor traffic does not imperil. There is no man who for his own safeguard should not set himself to destroy it.

Above all other places having to do with secular interests only, legislative halls and courts of justice should be free from the curse of intemperance. Governors, senators, representatives, judges, men who enact and administer a nation's laws, men who hold in their hands the lives, the fair fame, the possessions of their fellows, should be men of strict temperance. Only thus can their minds be clear to discriminate between right and wrong. Only thus can they possess firmness of principle, and wisdom to administer justice and to show mercy. But how does the record stand? How many of these men have their minds beclouded, their sense of right and wrong confused, by strong drink! How many are the oppressive laws enacted, how many the innocent persons condemned to death, through the injustice of drinking lawmakers, witnesses, jurors, lawyers, and even judges! Many there are, "mighty to drink wine," and "men of strength to mingle strong drink," "that call evil good, and good evil;" that "justify the wicked for reward, and take away the righteousness of the righteous from him!" Of such God says:

"Woe unto them. . . .
As the fire devoureth the stubble,
And the flame consumeth the chaff,
So their root shall be as rottenness,
And their blossom shall go up as dust:
Because they have cast away the law of the Lord of hosts,
And despised the word of the Holy One of Israel."
Isaiah 5:22-24.

The honour of God, the stability of the nation, the well-being of the community, of the home, and of the individual, demand that every possible effort be made in arousing the people to the evil of intemperance. Soon we shall see the result of this terrible evil as we do not see it now. Who will put forth a determined effort to stay the work of destruction? As yet the contest has hardly begun. Let an army be formed to stop the sale of the drugged liquors that are making men mad. Let the danger from the liquor traffic be made plain and a public sentiment be created that shall demand its prohibition. Let the drink-maddened men be given an opportunity to escape from their thralldom. Let the voice of the nation demand of its lawmakers that a stop be put to this infamous traffic.

> "If thou forbear to deliver them that are drawn unto death,
> And those that are ready to be slain;
> If thou sayest, Behold, we knew it not;
> Doth not He that pondereth the heart consider it?
> And He that keepeth thy soul, doth not He know it?"
> And "what wilt thou say when He shall punish thee?"
> Proverbs 24:11, 12; Jeremiah 13:21.

THE HOME

Ministry of the Home

The restoration and uplifting of humanity begins in the home. The work of parents underlies every other. Society is composed of families, and is what the heads of families make it. Out of the heart are "the issues of life" (Proverbs 4:23); and the heart of the community, of the church, and of the nation is the household. The well-being of society, the success of the church, the prosperity of the nation, depend upon home influences.

The importance and the opportunities of the home life are illustrated in the life of Jesus. He who came from heaven to be our example and teacher spent thirty years as a member of the household at Nazareth. Concerning these years the Bible record is very brief. No mighty miracles attracted the attention of the multitude. No eager throngs followed His steps or listened to His words. Yet during all these years He was fulfilling His divine mission. He lived as one of us, sharing the home life, submitting to its discipline, performing its duties, bearing its burdens. In the sheltering care of a humble home, participating in the experiences of our common lot, He "increased in wisdom and stature, and in favour with God and man." Luke 2:52.

During all these secluded years His life flowed out in currents of sympathy and helpfulness. His unselfishness and patient endurance, His courage and faithfulness, His resistance of temptation, His unfailing peace and quiet joyfulness, were a constant inspiration. He brought a pure, sweet atmosphere into the home, and His life was as leaven working amidst the elements of society. None said that He had wrought a miracle;

yet virtue — the healing, life-giving power of love — went out from Him to the tempted, the sick, and the disheartened. In an unobtrusive way, from His very childhood, He ministered to others, and because of this, when He began His public ministry, many heard Him gladly.

The Saviour's early years are more than an example to the youth. They are a lesson, and should be an encouragement, to every parent. The circle of family and neighbourhood duties is the very first field of effort for those who would work for the uplifting of their fellow men. There is no more important field of effort than that committed to the founders and guardians of the home. No work entrusted to human beings involves greater or more far-reaching results than does the work of fathers and mothers.

It is by the youth and children of today that the future of society is to be determined, and what these youth and children shall be depends upon the home. To the lack of right home training may be traced the larger share of the disease and misery and crime that curse humanity. If the home life were pure and true, if the children who went forth from its care were prepared to meet life's responsibilities and dangers, what a change would be seen in the world!

Great efforts are put forth, time and money and labour almost without limit are expended, in enterprises and institutions for reforming the victims of evil habits. And even these efforts are inadequate to meet the great necessity. Yet how small is the result! How few are permanently reclaimed!

Multitudes long for a better life, but they lack courage and resolution to break away from the power of habit. They shrink from the effort and struggle and sacrifice demanded, and their lives are wrecked and ruined. Thus even men of the brightest minds, men of high aspirations and noble powers, otherwise fitted by nature and education to fill positions of trust and responsibility, are degraded and lost for this life and for the life to come.

For those who do reform, how bitter the struggle to regain their manhood! And all their life long, in a shattered constitution, a wavering will, impaired intellect, and weakened soul power, many reap the harvest of their evil sowing. How much more might be accomplished if the evil were dealt with at the beginning!

This work rests, in a great degree, with parents. In the efforts put forth to stay the progress of intemperance and of other evils that are eating like a cancer in the social body, if more attention were given to teaching parents how to form the habits and character of their children, a hundredfold more good would result. Habit, which is so terrible a force for evil, it is in their power to make a force for good. They have to do with the stream at its source, and it rests with them to direct it rightly.

Parents may lay for their children the foundation for a healthy, happy life. They may send them forth from their homes with moral stamina to resist temptation, and courage and strength to wrestle successfully with life's problems. They may inspire in them the purpose and develop the power to make their lives an honour to God and a blessing to the world. They may make straight paths for their feet, through sunshine and shadow, to the glorious heights above.

The mission of the home extends beyond its own members. The Christian home is to be an object lesson, illustrating the excellence of the true principles of life. Such an illustration will be a power for good in the world. Far more powerful than any sermon that can be preached is the influence of a true home upon human hearts and lives. As the youth go out from such a home, the lessons they have learned are imparted. Nobler principles of life are introduced into other households, and an uplifting influence works in the community.

There are many others to whom we might make our homes a blessing. Our social entertainments should not be governed by the dictates of worldly custom, but by the Spirit of Christ and the teaching of His word. The Israelites, in all their festivities, included the poor, the stranger, and the Levite, who was both the assistant of the priest in the sanctuary, and a religious teacher and missionary. These were regarded as the guests of the people, to share their hospitality on all occasions of social and religious rejoicing, and to be tenderly cared for in sickness or in need. It is such as these whom we should make welcome to our homes. How much such a welcome might do to cheer and encourage the missionary nurse or the teacher, the care-burdened, hard-working mother, or the feeble and aged, so often without a home, and struggling with poverty and many discouragements.

"When thou makest a dinner or a supper," Christ says, "call not thy friends, nor thy brethren, neither thy kinsmen, nor thy rich neighbours; lest they also bid thee again, and a recompense be made thee. But when thou makest a feast, call the poor, the maimed, the lame, the blind: and thou shalt be blessed; for they cannot recompense thee: for thou shalt be recompensed at the resurrection of the just." Luke 14:12-14.

These are guests whom it will lay on you no great burden to receive. You will not need to provide for them elaborate or expensive entertainment. You will need to make no effort at display. The warmth of a genial welcome, a place at your fireside, a seat at your home table, the privilege of sharing the blessing of the hour prayer, would to many of these be like a glimpse of heaven.

Our sympathies are to overflow the boundaries of self and the enclosure of family walls. There are precious opportunities for those who will make their homes a blessing to others. Social influence is a wonderful power. We can use it if we will as a means of helping those about us.

Our homes should be a place of refuge for the tempted youth. Many there are who stand at the parting of the ways. Every influence, every impression, is determining the choice that shapes their destiny both here and hereafter. Evil invites them. Its resorts are made bright and attractive. They have a welcome for every comer. All about us are youth who have no home, and many whose homes have no helpful, uplifting power, and the youth drift into evil. They are going down to ruin within the very shadow of our own doors.

These youth need a hand stretched out to them in sympathy. Kind words simply spoken, little attentions simply bestowed, will sweep away the clouds of temptation which gather over the soul. The true expression of heaven-born sympathy has power to open the door of hearts that need the fragrance of Christlike words, and the simple, delicate touch of the spirit of Christ's love. If we would show an interest in the youth, invite them to our homes, and surround them with cheering, helpful influences, there are many who would gladly turn their steps into the upward path.

Life's Opportunities

Our time here is short. We can pass through this world but once; as we pass along, let us make the most of life. The work to which we are called does not require wealth or social position or great ability. It requires a kindly, self-sacrificing spirit and a steadfast purpose. A lamp, however small, if kept steadily burning, may be the means of lighting many other lamps. Our sphere of influence may seem narrow, our ability small, our opportunities few, our acquirements limited; yet wonderful possibilities are ours through a faithful use of the opportunities of our own homes. If we will open our hearts and homes to the divine principles of life we shall become channels for currents of life-giving power. From our homes will flow streams of healing, bringing life and beauty and fruitfulness where now are barrenness and dearth.

The Builders of the Home

He who gave Eve to Adam as a helpmeet, performed His first miracle at a marriage festival. In the festal hall where friends and kindred rejoiced together, Christ began His public ministry. Thus He sanctioned marriage, recognizing it as an institution that He Himself had established. He ordained that men and women should be united in holy wedlock, to rear families whose members, crowned with honour, should be recognized as members of the family above.

Christ honoured the marriage relation by making it also a symbol of the union between Him and His redeemed ones. He Himself is the Bridegroom; the bride is the church, of which, as His chosen one, He says, "Thou art all fair, My love; there is no spot in thee." Canticles 4:7.

Christ "loved the church, and gave Himself for it; that He might sanctify and cleanse it; . . . that it should be holy and without blemish." "So ought men to love their wives." Ephesians 5:25-28.

The family tie is the closest, the most tender and sacred, of any on earth. It was designed to be a blessing to mankind. And it is a blessing wherever the marriage covenant is entered into intelligently, in the fear of God, and with due consideration for its responsibilities.

Those who are contemplating marriage should consider what will be the character and influence of the home they are founding. As they become parents, a sacred trust is committed to them. Upon them depends in a great measure the well-being of their children in this world, and their happiness in the world to come. To a great extent they determine both the physical and the moral stamp that the little ones receive. And upon the character of the home depends the condition of society; the weight of each family's influence will tell in the upward or the downward scale.

The choice of a life companion should be such as best to secure physical, mental, and spiritual well-being for parents and for their children — such as will enable both parents and children to bless their fellow men and to honour their Creator.

Before assuming the responsibilities involved in marriage, young men and young women should have such an experience in practical life as will prepare them for its duties and its burdens. Early marriages are not to be encouraged. A relation so important as marriage and so far-reaching in its results should not be entered upon hastily, without sufficient preparation, and before the mental and physical powers are well developed.

The parties may not have worldly wealth, but they should have the far greater blessing of health. And in most cases there should not be a great disparity in age. A neglect of this rule may result in seriously impairing the health of the younger. And often the children are robbed of physical and mental strength. They cannot receive from an aged parent the care and companionship which their young lives demand, and they may be deprived by death of the father or the mother at the very time when love and guidance are most needed.

It is only in Christ that a marriage alliance can be safely formed. Human love should draw its closest bonds from divine love. Only where Christ reigns can there be deep, true, unselfish affection.

Love is a precious gift, which we receive from Jesus. Pure and holy affection is not a feeling, but a principle. Those who are actuated by true love are neither unreasonable nor blind. Taught by the Holy Spirit, they love God supremely, and their neighbour as themselves.

Let those who are contemplating marriage weigh every sentiment and watch every development of character in the one with whom they think to unite their life destiny. Let every step toward a marriage alliance be characterized by modesty, simplicity, sincerity, and an earnest purpose to please and honour God. Marriage affects the afterlife both in this world and in the world to come. A sincere Christian will make no plans that God cannot approve.

If you are blessed with God-fearing parents, seek counsel of them. Open to them your hopes and plans, learn the lessons which their life experiences have taught, and you will be saved many a heartache. Above all, make Christ your counsellor. Study His word with prayer.

Under such guidance let a young woman accept as a life companion only one who possesses pure, manly traits of character, one who is diligent, aspiring, and honest, one who loves and fears God. Let a young man seek one to stand by his side who is fitted to bear her share of life's burdens, one whose influence will ennoble and refine him, and who will make him happy in her love.

"A prudent wife is from the Lord." "The heart of her husband doth safely trust in her. . . . She will do him good and not evil all the days of her life." "She openeth her mouth with wisdom; and in her tongue is the law of kindness. She looketh well to the ways of her household, and eateth not the bread of idleness. Her children arise up, and call her blessed; her husband also, and he praiseth her," saying, "Many daughters have done virtuously, but thou excellest them all." He who gains such a wife "findeth a good thing, and obtaineth favour of the Lord." Proverbs 19:14; 31:11, 12, 26-29; 18:22.

However carefully and wisely marriage may have been entered into, few couples are completely united when the marriage ceremony is performed. The real union of the two in wedlock is the work of the after years.

As life with its burden of perplexity and care meets the newly wedded pair, the romance with which imagination so often invests marriage disappears. Husband and wife learn each other's character as it was impossible to learn it in their previous association. This is a most critical period in their experience. The happiness and usefulness of their whole future life depend upon their taking a right course now. Often they discern in each other unsuspected weaknesses and defects; but the hearts that love has united will discern excellencies also heretofore unknown. Let all seek to discover the excellencies rather than the defects. Often it is our own attitude, the atmosphere that surrounds ourselves, which determines what will be revealed to us in another. There are many who regard the expression of love as a weakness, and they maintain a reserve that repels others. This spirit checks the current of sympathy. As the social and generous impulses are repressed, they wither, and the heart becomes desolate and cold. We should beware of this error. Love cannot long exist without expression. Let not the heart of one connected with you starve for the want of kindness and sympathy.

Though difficulties, perplexities, and discouragements may arise, let neither husband nor wife harbour the thought that their union is a mistake or a disappointment. Determine to be all that it is possible to be to each other. Continue the early attentions. In every way encourage each other in fighting the battles of life. Study to advance the happiness of each other. Let there be mutual love, mutual forbearance. Then marriage, instead of being the end of love, will be as it were the very beginning of love. The warmth of true friendship, the love that binds heart to heart, is a foretaste of the joys of heaven.

Around every family there is a sacred circle that should be kept unbroken. Within this circle no other person has a right to come. Let not the husband or the wife permit another to share the confidences that belong solely to themselves.

Let each give love rather than exact it. Cultivate that which is noblest in yourselves, and be quick to recognize the good qualities in each other. The consciousness of being appreciated is a wonderful stimulus and satisfaction. Sympathy and respect encourage the striving after excellence, and love itself increases as it stimulates to nobler aims.

Neither the husband nor the wife should merge his or her individuality in that of the other. Each has a personal relation to God. Of Him each is to ask, "What is right?" "What is wrong?" "How may I best fulfil life's purpose?" Let the wealth of your affection flow forth to Him who gave His life for you. Make Christ first and last and best in everything. As your love for Him becomes deeper and stronger, your love for each other will be purified and strengthened.

The spirit that Christ manifests toward us is the spirit that husband and wife are to manifest toward each other. "As Christ also hath loved us," "walk in love." "As the church is subject unto Christ, so let the wives be to their own husbands in everything. Husbands, love your wives, even as Christ also loved the church, and gave Himself for it." Ephesians 5:2, 24, 25.

Neither the husband nor the wife should attempt to exercise over the other an arbitrary control. Do not try to compel each other to yield to your wishes. You cannot do this and retain each other's love. Be kind, patient, and forbearing, considerate, and courteous. By the grace of God you can succeed in making each other happy, as in your marriage vow you promised to do.

Happiness in Unselfish Service

But remember that happiness will not be found in shutting yourselves up to yourselves, satisfied to pour out all your affection upon each other. Seize upon every opportunity for contributing to the happiness of those around you. Remember that true joy can be found only in unselfish service.

Forbearance and unselfishness mark the words and acts of all who live the new life in Christ. As you seek to live His life, striving to conquer self and selfishness and to minister to the needs of others, you will gain victory after victory. Thus your influence will bless the world.

Men and women can reach God's ideal for them if they will take Christ as their helper. What human wisdom cannot do, His grace will accomplish for those who give themselves to Him in loving trust. His providence can unite hearts in bonds that are of heavenly origin. Love will not be a mere exchange of soft and flattering words. The loom of heaven weaves with warp and woof finer, yet more firm, than can be woven by the looms of earth. The result is not a tissue fabric, but a texture that will bear wear and test and trial. Heart will be bound to heart in the golden bonds of a love that is enduring.

Better than gold is a peaceful home,
Where all the fireside charities come;
The shrine of love and the heaven of life,
Hallowed by mother, or sister, or wife.
However humble the home may be,
Or tried with sorrows by heaven's decree,
The blessings that never were bought or sold,
And centre there, are better than gold.

— Anon.

Choice and Preparation of the Home

The gospel is a wonderful simplifier of life's problems. Its instruction, heeded, would make plain many a perplexity and save us from many an error. It teaches us to estimate things at their true value and to give the most effort to the things of greatest worth — the things that will endure. This lesson is needed by those upon whom rests the responsibility of selecting a home. They should not allow themselves to be diverted from the highest aim. Let them remember that the home on earth is to be a symbol of and a preparation for the home in heaven. Life is a training school, from which parents and children are to be graduated to the higher school in the mansions of God. As the location for a home is sought, let this purpose direct the choice. Be not controlled by the desire for wealth, the dictates of fashion, or the customs of society. Consider what will tend most to simplicity, purity, health, and real worth.

The world over, cities are becoming hotbeds of vice. On every hand are the sights and sounds of evil. Everywhere are enticements to sensuality and dissipation. The tide of corruption and crime is continually swelling. Every day brings the record of violence — robberies, murders, suicides, and crimes unnamable.

Life in the cities is false and artificial. The intense passion for money getting, the whirl of excitement and pleasure seeking, the thirst for display, the luxury and extravagance, all are forces that, with the great masses of mankind, are turning the mind from life's true purpose. They are opening the door to a thousand evils.

Upon the youth they have almost irresistible power.

One of the most subtle and dangerous temptations that assail the children and youth in the cities is the love of pleasure. Holidays are numerous; games and horse racing draw thousands, and the whirl of excitement and pleasure attracts them away from the sober duties of life. Money that should have been saved for better uses is frittered away for amusements.

Through the working of trusts, and the results of labour unions and strikes, the conditions of life in the city are constantly becoming more and more difficult. Serious troubles are before us; and for many families removal from the cities will become a necessity.

The physical surroundings in the cities are often a peril to health. The constant liability to contact with disease, the prevalence of foul air, impure water, impure food, the crowded, dark, unhealthful dwellings, are some of the many evils to be met.

It was not God's purpose that people should be crowded into cities, huddled together in terraces and tenements. In the beginning He placed our first parents amidst the beautiful sights and sounds He desires us to rejoice in today. The more nearly we come into harmony with God's original plan, the more favourable will be our position to secure health of body, and mind, and soul.

An expensive dwelling, elabourate furnishings, display, luxury, and ease, do not furnish the conditions essential to a happy, useful life. Jesus came to this earth to accomplish the greatest work ever accomplished among men. He came as God's ambassador, to show us how to live so as to secure life's best results. What were the conditions chosen by the infinite Father for His Son? A secluded home in the Galilean hills; a household sustained by honest, self-respecting labour; a life of simplicity; daily conflict with difficulty and hardship; self-sacrifice, economy, and patient, gladsome service; the hour of study at His mother's side, with the open scroll of Scripture; the quiet of dawn or twilight in the green valley; the holy ministries of nature; the study of creation and providence; and the soul's communion with God — these were the conditions and opportunities of the early life of Jesus.

So with the great majority of the best and noblest men of all ages. Read the history of Abraham, Jacob, and Joseph, of Moses, David, and Elisha. Study the lives of men of later times who have most worthily filled positions of trust and responsibility, the men whose influence has been most effective for the world's uplifting.

How many of these were reared in country homes. They knew little of luxury. They did not spend their youth in amusement. Many were forced to struggle with poverty and hardship. They early learned to work, and their active life in the open air gave vigour and elasticity to all their faculties. Forced to depend upon their own resources, they learned to combat difficulties and to surmount obstacles, and they gained courage and perseverance. They learned the lessons of self-reliance and self-control. Sheltered in a great degree from evil associations, they were satisfied with natural pleasures and wholesome companionships. They were simple in their tastes and temperate in their habits. They were governed by principle, and they grew up pure and strong and true. When called to their lifework, they brought to it physical and mental power, buoyancy of spirit, ability to plan and execute, and steadfastness in resisting evil, that made them a positive power for good in the world.

Better than any other inheritance of wealth you can give to your children will be the gift of a healthy body, a sound mind, and a noble character. Those who understand what constitutes life's true success will be wise betimes. They will keep in view life's best things in their choice of a home.

Instead of dwelling where only the works of men can be seen, where the sights and sounds frequently suggest thoughts of evil, where turmoil and confusion bring weariness and disquietude, go where you can look upon the works of God. Find rest of spirit in the beauty and quietude and peace of nature. Let the eye rest on the green fields, the groves, and the hills. Look up to the blue sky, unobscured by the city's dust and smoke, and breathe the invigorating air of heaven. Go where, apart from the distractions and dissipations of city life, you can give your children your companionship, where you can teach them to learn of God through His works, and train them for lives of integrity and usefulness.

Simplicity in Furnishing

Our artificial habits deprive us of many blessings and much enjoyment, and unfit us for living the most useful lives. Elabourate and expensive furnishings are a waste not only of money, but of that which is a thousandfold more precious. They bring into the home a heavy burden of care and labour and perplexity.

What are the conditions in many homes, even where resources are limited and the work of the household rests chiefly on the mother? The best rooms are furnished in a style beyond the means of the occupants and unsuited to their convenience and enjoyment. There are expensive carpets, elabourately carved and daintily upholstered furniture, and delicate drapery. Tables, mantels, and every other available space are crowded with ornaments, and the walls are covered with pictures, until the sight becomes wearying. And what an amount of work is required to keep all these in order and free from dust! This work, and the other artificial habits of the family in its conformity to fashion, demand of the housewife unending toil.

In many a home the wife and mother has no time to read, to keep herself well informed, no time to be a companion to her husband, no time to keep in touch with the developing minds of her children. There is no time or place for the precious Saviour to be a close, dear companion. Little by little she sinks into a mere household drudge, her strength and time and interest absorbed in the things that perish with the using. Too late she awakes to find herself almost a stranger in her own home. The precious opportunities once hers to influence her dear ones for the higher life, unimproved, have passed away forever.

Let the homemakers resolve to live on a wiser plan. Let it be your first aim to make a pleasant home. Be sure to provide the facilities that will lighten labour and promote health and comfort. Plan for the entertainment of the guests whom Christ has bidden us welcome, and of whom He says, "Inasmuch as ye have done it unto one of the least of these My brethren, ye have done it unto Me." Matthew 25:40.

Furnish your home with things plain and simple, things that will bear handling, that can be easily kept clean, and that can be replaced without great expense. By exercising taste, you can make a very simple home attractive and inviting, if love and contentment are there.

Beautiful Surroundings

God loves the beautiful. He has clothed the earth and the heavens with beauty, and with a Father's joy He watches the delight of His children in the things that He has made. He desires us to surround our homes with the beauty of natural things.

Nearly all dwellers in the country, however poor, could have about their homes a bit of grassy lawn, a few shade trees, flowering shrubbery, or fragrant blossoms. And far more than any artificial adorning will they minister to the happiness of the household. They will bring into the home life a softening, refining influence, strengthening the love of nature, and drawing the members of the household nearer to one another and nearer to God.

The Mother

What the parents are, that, to a great extent, the children will be. The physical conditions of the parents, their dispositions and appetites, their mental and moral tendencies, are, to a greater or less degree, reproduced in their children.

The nobler the aims, the higher the mental and spiritual endowments, and the better developed the physical powers of the parents, the better will be the life equipment they give their children. In cultivating that which is best in themselves, parents are exerting an influence to mould society and to uplift future generations.

Fathers and mothers need to understand their responsibility. The world is full of snares for the feet of the young. Multitudes are attracted by a life of selfish and sensual pleasure. They cannot discern the hidden dangers or the fearful ending of the path that seems to them the way of happiness. Through the indulgence of appetite and passion, their energies are wasted, and millions are ruined for this world and for the world to come. Parents should remember that their children must encounter these temptations. Even before the birth of the child, the preparation should begin that will enable it to fight successfully the battle against evil.

Especially does responsibility rest upon the mother. She, by whose lifeblood the child is nourished and its physical frame built up, imparts to it also mental and spiritual influences that tend to the shaping of mind and character. It was Jochebed, the Hebrew mother, who, strong in faith, was "not afraid of the king's commandment" (Hebrews 11:23), of whom was born Moses, the deliverer of Israel. It was Hannah, the woman of prayer and self-sacrifice and heavenly inspiration, who gave birth to Samuel, the heaven-instructed child, the incorruptible judge, the founder of Israel's sacred schools. It was Elizabeth the kinswoman and kindred spirit of Mary of Nazareth, who was the mother of the Saviour's herald.

Temperance and Self-control

The carefulness with which the mother should guard her habits of life is taught in the Scriptures. When the Lord would raise up Samson as a deliverer for Israel, "the angel of Jehovah" appeared to the mother, with special instruction concerning her habits, and also for the treatment of her child. "Beware," he said, "and now drink no wine nor strong drink, neither eat any unclean thing." Judges 13:13, 7.

The effect of prenatal influences is by many parents looked upon as a matter of little moment; but heaven does not so regard it. The message sent by an angel of God, and twice given in the most solemn manner, shows it to be deserving of our most careful thought.

In the words spoken to the Hebrew mother, God speaks to all mothers in every age. "Let her beware," the angel said; "all that I commanded her let her observe." The well-being of the child will be affected by the habits of the mother. Her appetites and passions are to be controlled by principle. There is something for her to shun, something for her to work against, if she fulfils God's purpose for her in giving her a child. If before the birth of her child she is self-indulgent, if she is selfish, impatient, and exacting, these traits will be reflected in the disposition of the child. Thus many children have received as a birthright almost unconquerable tendencies to evil.

But if the mother unswervingly adheres to right principles, if she is temperate and self-denying, if she is kind, gentle, and unselfish, she may give her child these same precious traits of character. Very explicit was the command prohibiting the use of wine by the mother. Every drop of strong drink taken by her to gratify appetite endangers the physical, mental, and moral health of her child, and is a direct sin against her Creator.

Many advisers urge that every wish of the mother should be gratified; that if she desires any article of food, however harmful, she should freely indulge her appetite. Such advice is false and mischievous. The mother's physical needs should in no case be neglected. Two lives are depending upon her, and her wishes should be tenderly regarded, her needs generously supplied. But at this time above all others she should avoid, in diet and in every other line, whatever would lessen physical or mental strength. By the command of God Himself she is placed under the most solemn obligation to exercise self-control.

Overwork

The strength of the mother should be tenderly cherished. Instead of spending her precious strength in exhausting labour, her care and burdens should be lessened. Often the husband and father is unacquainted with the physical laws which the well-being of his family requires him to understand. Absorbed in the struggle for a livelihood, or bent on acquiring wealth and pressed with cares and perplexities, he allows to rest upon the wife and mother burdens that overtax her strength at the most critical period and cause feebleness and disease.

Many a husband and father might learn a helpful lesson from the carefulness of the faithful shepherd. Jacob, when urged to undertake a rapid and difficult journey, made answer:

"The children are tender, and the flocks and herds with young are with me: and if men should overdrive them one day, all the flock will die. . . . I will lead on softly, according as the cattle that goeth before me and the children be able to endure." Genesis 33:13, 14.

In life's toilsome way let the husband and father "lead on softly," as the companion of his journey is able to endure. Amidst the world's eager rush for wealth and power, let him learn to stay his steps, to comfort and support the one who is called to walk by his side.

Cheerfulness

The mother should cultivate a cheerful, contented, happy disposition. Every effort in this direction will be abundantly repaid in both the physical well-being and the moral character of her children. A cheerful spirit will promote the happiness of her family and in a very great degree improve her own health.

Let the husband aid his wife by his sympathy and unfailing affection. If he wishes to keep her fresh and gladsome, so that she will be as sunshine in the home, let him help her bear her burdens. His kindness and loving courtesy will be to her a precious encouragement, and the happiness he imparts will bring joy and peace to his own heart.

The husband and father who is morose, selfish, and overbearing, is not only unhappy himself, but he casts gloom upon all the inmates of his home. He will reap the result in seeing his wife dispirited and sickly, and his children marred with his own unlovely temper.

If the mother is deprived of the care and comforts she should have, if she is allowed to exhaust her strength through overwork or through anxiety and gloom, her children will be robbed of the vital force and of the mental elasticity and cheerful buoyancy they should inherit. Far better will it be to make the mother's life bright and cheerful, to shield her from want, wearing labour, and depressing care, and let the children inherit good constitutions, so that they may battle their way through life with their own energetic strength.

Great is the honour and the responsibility placed upon fathers and mothers, in that they are to stand in the place of God to their children. Their character, their daily life, their methods of training, will interpret His words to the little ones. Their influence will win or repel the child's confidence in the Lord's assurances.

The Privilege of Parents in Child Training

Happy are the parents whose lives are a true reflection of the divine, so that the promises and commands of God awaken in the child gratitude and reverence; the parents whose tenderness and justice and long-suffering interpret to the child the love and justice and long-suffering of God; and who, by teaching the child to love and trust and obey them, are teaching him to love and trust and obey his Father in heaven. Parents who impart to a child such a gift have endowed him with a treasure more precious than the wealth of all the ages — a treasure as enduring as eternity.

In the children committed to her care, every mother has a sacred charge from God. "Take this son, this daughter," He says; "train it for Me; give it a character polished after the similitude of a palace, that it may shine in the courts of the Lord forever."

The mother's work often seems to her an unimportant service. It is a work that is rarely appreciated. Others know little of her many cares and burdens. Her days are occupied with a round of little duties, all calling for patient effort, for self-control, for tact, wisdom, and self-sacrificing love; yet she cannot boast of what she has done as any great achievement. She has only kept things in the home running smoothly; often weary and perplexed, she has tried to speak kindly to the children, to keep them busy and happy, and to guide the little feet in the right path. She feels that she has accomplished nothing. But it is not so. Heavenly angels watch the care-worn mother, noting the burdens she carries day by day. Her name may not have been heard in the world, but it is written in the Lamb's book of life.

The Mother's Opportunity

There is a God above, and the light and glory from His throne rests upon the faithful mother as she tries to educate her children to resist the influence of evil. No other work can equal hers in importance. She has not, like the artist, to paint a form of beauty upon canvas, nor, like the sculptor, to chisel it from marble. She has not, like the author, to embody a noble thought in words of power, nor, like the musician, to express a beautiful sentiment in melody. It is hers, with the help of God, to develop in a human soul the likeness of the divine.

The mother who appreciates this will regard her opportunities as priceless. Earnestly will she seek, in her own character and by her methods of training, to present before her children the highest ideal. Earnestly, patiently, courageously, she will endeavour to improve her own abilities, that she may use aright the highest powers of the mind in the training of her children. Earnestly will she inquire at every step, "What hath God spoken?" Diligently she will study His word. She will keep her eyes fixed upon Christ, that her own daily experience, in the lowly round of care and duty, may be a true reflection of the one true Life.

The Child

Not only the habits of the mother, but the training of the child were included in the angel's instruction to the Hebrew parents. It was not enough that Samson, the child who was to deliver Israel, should have a good legacy at his birth. This was to be followed by careful training. From infancy he was to be trained to habits of strict temperance.

Similar instruction was given in regard to John the Baptist. Before the birth of the child, the message sent from heaven to the father was:

"Thou shalt have joy and gladness; and many shall rejoice at his birth. For he shall be great in the sight of the Lord, and he shall drink no wine nor strong drink; and he shall be filled with the Holy Spirit." Luke 1:14, 15, ARV.

On heaven's record of noble men the Saviour declared that there stood not one greater than John the Baptist. The work committed to him was one demanding not only physical energy and endurance, but the highest qualities of mind and soul. So important was right physical training as a preparation for this work that the highest angel in heaven was sent with a message of instruction to the parents of the child.

The directions given concerning the Hebrew children teach us that nothing which affects the child's physical well-being is to be neglected. Nothing is unimportant. Every influence that affects the health of the body has its bearing upon mind and character.

Too much importance cannot be placed upon the early training of children. The lessons learned, the habits formed, during the years of infancy and childhood, have more to do with the formation of the character and the direction of the life than have all the instruction and training of after years.

Parents need to consider this. They should understand the principles that underlie the care and training of children. They should be capable of rearing them in physical, mental, and moral health. Parents should study the laws of nature. They should become acquainted with the organism of the human body. They need to understand the functions of the various organs, and their relation and dependence. They should study the relation of the mental to the physical powers, and the conditions required for the healthy action of each. To assume the responsibilities of parenthood without such preparation is a sin.

Far too little thought is given to the causes underlying the mortality, the disease and degeneracy, that exist today even in the most civilized and favoured lands. The human race is deteriorating. More than one third die in infancy;* of those who reach manhood and womanhood, by far the greater number suffer from disease in some form, and but few reach the limit of human life.

Most of the evils that are bringing misery and ruin to the race might be prevented, and the power to deal with them rests to a great degree with parents. It is not a "mysterious providence" that removes the little children. God does not desire their death. He gives them to the parents to be trained for usefulness here, and for heaven hereafter. Did fathers and mothers do what they might to give their children a good inheritance, and then by right management endeavour to remedy any wrong conditions of their birth, what a change for the better the world might see!

---

*The statement concerning infant mortality was correct at the time it was written in 1905. However, modern medicine and proper child care have greatly reduced the mortality rate in infancy and childhood. — Publishers.)

The Care of Infants

The more quiet and simple the life of the child, the more favourable it will be to both physical and mental development. At all times the mother should endeavour to be quiet, calm, and self-possessed. Many infants are extremely susceptible to nervous excitement, and the mother's gentle, unhurried manner will have a soothing influence that will be of untold benefit to the child.

Babies require warmth, but a serious error is often committed in keeping them in overheated rooms, deprived to a great degree of fresh air. The practice of covering the infant's face while sleeping is harmful, since it prevents free respiration.

The baby should be kept free from every influence that would tend to weaken or to poison the system. The most scrupulous care should be taken to have everything about it sweet and clean. While it may be necessary to protect the little ones from sudden or too great changes of temperature, care should be taken, that, sleeping or waking, day or night, they breathe a pure, invigorating atmosphere.

In the preparation of the baby's wardrobe, convenience, comfort, and health should be sought before fashion or a desire to excite admiration. The mother should not spend time in embroidery and fancywork to make the little garments beautiful, thus taxing herself with unnecessary labour at the expense of her own health and the health of her child. She should not bend over sewing that severely taxes eyes and nerves, at a time when she needs much rest and pleasant exercise. She should realize her obligation to cherish her strength, that she may be able to meet the demands that will be made upon her.

If the dress of the child combines warmth, protection, and comfort, one of the chief causes of irritation and restlessness will be removed. The little one will have better health, and the mother will not find the care of the child so heavy a tax upon her strength and time.

Tight bands or waists hinder the action of the heart

and lungs, and should be avoided. No part of the body should at any time be made uncomfortable by clothing that compresses any organ or restricts its freedom of movement. The clothing of all children should be loose enough to admit of the freest and fullest respiration, and so arranged that the shoulders will support its weight.

In some countries the custom of leaving bare the shoulders and limbs of little children still prevails. This custom cannot be too severely condemned. The limbs being remote from the centre of circulation, demand greater protection than the other parts of the body. The arteries that convey the blood to the extremities are large, providing for a sufficient quantity of blood to afford warmth and nutrition. But when the limbs are left unprotected or are insufficiently clad, the arteries and veins become contracted, the sensitive portions of the body are chilled, and the circulation of the blood hindered.

In growing children all the forces of nature need every advantage to enable them to perfect the physical frame. If the limbs are insufficiently protected, children, and especially girls, cannot be out of doors unless the weather is mild. So they are kept in for fear of the cold. If children are well clothed, it will benefit them to exercise freely in the open air, summer or winter.

Mothers who desire their boys and girls to possess the vigour of health should dress them properly and encourage them in all reasonable weather to be much in the open air. It may require effort to break away from the chains of custom, and dress and educate the children with reference to health; but the result will amply repay the effort.

The Child's Diet

The best food for the infant is the food that nature provides. Of this it should not be needlessly deprived. It is a heartless thing for a mother, for the sake of convenience or social enjoyment, to seek to free herself from the tender office of nursing her little one.

The mother who permits her child to be nourished by another should consider well what the result may be. To a greater or less degree the nurse imparts her own temper and temperament to the nursing child.

The importance of training children to right dietetic habits can hardly be overestimated. The little ones need to learn that they eat to live, not live to eat. The training should begin with the infant in its mother's arms. The child should be given food only at regular intervals, and less frequently as it grows older. It should not be given sweets, or the food of older persons, which it is unable to digest. Care and regularity in the feeding of infants will not only promote health, and thus tend to make them quiet and sweet-tempered, but will lay the foundation of habits that will be a blessing to them in after years.

As children emerge from babyhood, great care should still be taken in educating their tastes and appetite. Often they are permitted to eat what they choose and when they choose, without reference to health. The pains and money so often lavished upon unwholesome dainties lead the young to think that the highest object in life, and that which yields the greatest amount of happiness, is to be able to indulge the appetite. The result of this training is gluttony, then comes sickness, which is usually followed by dosing with poisonous drugs.

Parents should train the appetites of their children and should not permit the use of unwholesome foods. But in the effort to regulate the diet, we should be careful not to err in requiring children to eat that which is distasteful, or to eat more than is needed. Children have rights, they have preferences, and when these preferences are reasonable they should be respected.

Regularity in eating should be carefully observed. Nothing should be eaten between meals, no confectionery, nuts, fruits, or food of any kind. Irregularities in eating destroy the healthful tone of the digestive organs, to the detriment of health and cheerfulness. And when the children come to the table, they do not relish wholesome food; their appetites crave that which is hurtful for them.

Mothers who gratify the desires of their children at the expense of health and happy tempers, are sowing seeds of evil that will spring up and bear fruit. Self-indulgence grows with the growth of the little ones, and both mental and physical vigour are sacrificed. Mothers who do this work reap with bitterness the seed they have sown. They see their children grow up unfitted in mind and character to act a noble and useful part in society or in the home. The spiritual as well as the mental and physical powers suffer under the influence of unhealthful food. The conscience becomes stupefied, and the susceptibility to good impressions is impaired.

While the children should be taught to control the appetite and to eat with reference to health; let it be made plain that they are denying themselves only that which would do them harm. They give up hurtful things for something better. Let the table be made inviting and attractive, as it is supplied with the good things which God has so bountifully bestowed. Let mealtime be a cheerful, happy time. As we enjoy the gifts of God, let us respond by grateful praise to the Giver.

The Care of Children in Sickness

In many cases the sickness of children can be traced to errors in management. Irregularities in eating, insufficient clothing in the chilly evening, lack of vigorous exercise to keep the blood in healthy circulation, or lack of abundance of air for its purification, may be the cause of the trouble. Let the parents study to find the causes of the sickness, and then remedy the wrong conditions as soon as possible.

All parents have it in their power to learn much concerning the care and prevention, and even the treatment, of disease. Especially ought the mother to know what to do in common cases of illness in her family. She should know how to minister to her sick child. Her love and insight should fit her to perform services for it which could not so well be trusted to a stranger's hand.

The Study of Physiology

Parents should early seek to interest their children in the study of physiology and should teach them its simpler principles. Teach them how best to preserve the physical, mental, and spiritual powers, and how to use their gifts so that their lives may bring blessing to one another and honour to God. This knowledge is invaluable to the young. An education in the things that concern life and health is more important to them than a knowledge of many of the sciences taught in the schools.

Parents should live more for their children, and less for society. Study health subjects, and put your knowledge to a practical use. Teach your children to reason from cause to effect. Teach them that if they desire health and happiness, they must obey the laws of nature. Though you may not see so rapid improvement as you desire, be not discouraged, but patiently and perseveringly continue your work.

Teach your children from the cradle to practice self-denial and self-control. Teach them to enjoy the beauties of nature and in useful employments to exercise systematically all the powers of body and mind. Bring them up to have sound constitutions and good morals, to have sunny dispositions and sweet tempers. Impress upon their tender minds the truth that God does not design that we should live for present gratification merely, but for our ultimate good. Teach them that to yield to temptation is weak and wicked; to resist, noble and manly. These lessons will be as seed sown in good soil, and they will bear fruit that will make your hearts glad.

Above all things else, let parents surround their children with an atmosphere of cheerfulness, courtesy, and love. A home where love dwells, and where it is expressed in looks, in words, and in acts, is a place where angels delight to manifest their presence.

Parents, let the sunshine of love, cheerfulness, and happy contentment enter your own hearts, and let its sweet, cheering influence pervade your home. Manifest a kindly, forbearing spirit; and encourage the same in your children, cultivating all the graces that will brighten the home life. The atmosphere thus created will be to the children what air and sunshine are to the vegetable world, promoting health and vigour of mind and body.

Home Influences

The home should be to the children the most attractive place in the world, and the mother's presence should be its greatest attraction. Children have sensitive, loving natures. They are easily pleased and easily made unhappy. By gentle discipline, in loving words and acts, mothers may bind their children to their hearts.

Young children love companionship and can seldom enjoy themselves alone. They yearn for sympathy and tenderness. That which they enjoy they think will please mother also, and it is natural for them to go to her with their little joys and sorrows. The mother should not wound their sensitive hearts by treating with indifference matters that, though trifling to her, are of great importance to them. Her sympathy and approval are precious. An approving glance, a word of encouragement or commendation, will be like sunshine in their hearts, often making the whole day happy.

Instead of sending her children from her, that she may not be annoyed by their noise or troubled by their little wants, let the mother plan amusement or light work to employ the active hands and minds.

By entering into their feelings and directing their amusements and employments, the mother will gain the confidence of her children, and she can the more effectually correct wrong habits, or check the manifestations of selfishness or passion. A word of caution or reproof spoken at the right time will be of great value. By patient, watchful love, she can turn the minds of the children in the right direction, cultivating in them beautiful and attractive traits of character.

Mothers should guard against training their children

to be dependent and self-absorbed. Never lead them to think that they are the centre, and that everything must revolve around them. Some parents give much time and attention to amusing their children, but children should be trained to amuse themselves, to exercise their own ingenuity and skill. Thus they will learn to be content with very simple pleasures. They should be taught to bear bravely their little disappointments and trials. Instead of calling attention to every trifling pain or hurt, divert their minds, teach them to pass lightly over little annoyances or discomforts. Study to suggest ways by which the children may learn to be thoughtful for others.

But let not the children be neglected. Burdened with many cares, mothers sometimes feel that they cannot take time patiently to instruct their little ones and give them love and sympathy. But they should remember that if the children do not find in their parents and in their home that which will satisfy their desire for sympathy and companionship, they will look to other sources, where both mind and character may be endangered.

For lack of time and thought, many a mother refuses her children some innocent pleasure, while busy fingers and weary eyes are diligently engaged on work designed only for adornment, something that, at best, will serve only to encourage vanity and extravagance in their young hearts. As the children approach manhood and womanhood, these lessons bear fruit in pride and moral worthlessness. The mother grieves over her children's faults, but does not realize that the harvest she is reaping is from seed which she herself planted.

Some mothers are not uniform in the treatment of their children. At times they indulge them to their injury, and again they refuse some innocent gratification that would make the childish heart very happy. In this they do not imitate Christ; He loved the children; He comprehended their feelings and sympathized with them in their pleasures and their trials.

The Father's Responsibility

The husband and father is the head of the household. The wife looks to him for love and sympathy, and for aid in the training of the children; and this is right. The children are his as well as hers, and he is equally interested in their welfare. The children look to their father for support and guidance; he needs to have a right conception of life and of the influences and associations that should surround his family; above all, he should be controlled by the love and fear of God and by the teaching of His word, that he may guide the feet of his children in the right way.

The father is the lawmaker of the household; and, like Abraham, he should make the law of God the rule of his home. God said of Abraham, "I know him, that he will command his children and his household." Genesis 18:19. There would be no sinful neglect to restrain evil, no weak, unwise, indulgent favouritism; no yielding of his conviction of duty to the claims of mistaken affection. Abraham would not only give right instruction, but he would maintain the authority of just and righteous laws. God has given rules for our guidance. Children should not be left to wander away from the safe path marked out in God's word, into ways leading to danger, which are open on every side. Kindly, but firmly, with persevering, prayerful effort, their wrong desires should be restrained, their inclinations denied.

The father should enforce in his family the sterner virtues — energy, integrity, honesty, patience, courage, diligence, and practical usefulness. And what he requires of his children he himself should practice, illustrating these virtues in his own manly bearing.

But, fathers, do not discourage your children. Combine affection with authority, kindness and sympathy with firm restraint. Give some of your leisure hours to your children; become acquainted with them; associate with them in their work and in their sports, and win their confidence. Cultivate friendship with them, especially with your sons. In this way you will be a strong influence for good.

The father should do his part toward making home happy. Whatever his cares and business perplexities, they should not be permitted to overshadow his family; he should enter his home with smiles and pleasant words.

In a sense the father is the priest of the household, laying upon the family altar the morning and evening sacrifice. But the wife and children should unite in prayer and join in the song of praise. In the morning before he leaves home for his daily labour, let the father gather his children about him and, bowing before God, commit them to the care of the Father in heaven. When the cares of the day are past, let the family unite in offering grateful prayer and raising the song of praise, in acknowledgment of divine care during the day.

Fathers and mothers, however pressing your business, do not fail to gather your family around God's altar. Ask for the guardianship of holy angels in your home. Remember that your dear ones are exposed to temptations. Daily annoyances beset the path of young and old. Those who would live patient, loving, cheerful lives must pray. Only by receiving constant help from God can we gain the victory over self.

Home should be a place where cheerfulness, courtesy, and love abide; and where these graces dwell, there will abide happiness and peace. Troubles may invade, but these are the lot of humanity. Let patience, gratitude, and love keep sunshine in the heart, though the day may be ever so cloudy. In such homes angels of God abide.

Let the husband and wife study each other's happiness, never failing in the small courtesies and little kindly acts that cheer and brighten the life. Perfect confidence should exist between husband and wife. Together they should consider their responsibilities. Together they should work for the highest good of their children. Never should they in the presence of the children criticize each other's plans or question each other's judgement. Let the wife be careful not to make the husband's work for the children more difficult. Let the husband hold up the hands of his wife, giving her wise counsel and loving encouragement.

No barrier of coldness and reserve should be allowed to arise between parents and children. Let parents become acquainted with their children, seeking to understand their tastes and dispositions, entering into their feelings, and drawing out what is in their hearts.

Parents, let your children see that you love them and will do all in your power to make them happy. If you do so, your necessary restrictions will have far greater weight in their young minds. Rule your children with tenderness and compassion, remembering that "their angels do always behold the face of My Father which is in heaven." Matthew 18:10. If you desire the angels to do for your children the work given them of God, co-operate with them by doing your part.

Brought up under the wise and loving guidance of a true home, children will have no desire to wander away in search of pleasure and companionship. Evil will not attract them. The spirit that prevails in the home will mold their characters; they will form habits and principles that will be a strong defence against temptation when they shall leave the home shelter and take their place in the world.

Children as well as parents have important duties in the home. They should be taught that they are a part of the home firm. They are fed and clothed and loved and cared for, and they should respond to these many mercies by bearing their share of the home burdens and bringing all the happiness possible into the family of which they are members.

Children are sometimes tempted to chafe under restraint; but in afterlife they will bless their parents for the faithful care and strict watchfulness that guarded and guided them in their years of inexperience.

True Education, a Missionary Training

True education is missionary training. Every son and daughter of God is called to be a missionary; we are called to the service of God and our fellow men; and to fit us for this service should be the object of our education.

Training for Service

This object should ever be kept in view by Christian parents and teachers. We know not in what line our children may serve. They may spend their lives within the circle of the home; they may engage in life's common vocations, or go as teachers of the gospel to heathen lands; but all are alike called to be missionaries for God, ministers of mercy to the world.

The children and youth, with their fresh talent, energy, and courage, their quick susceptibilities, are loved of God, and He desires to bring them into harmony with divine agencies. They are to obtain an education that will help them to stand by the side of Christ in unselfish service.

Of all His children to the close of time, no less than of the first disciples, Christ said, "As Thou hast sent Me into the world, even so have I also sent them into the world" (John 17:18), to be representatives of God, to reveal His Spirit, to manifest His character, to do His work.

Our children stand, as it were, at the parting of the ways. On every hand the world's enticements to self-seeking and self-indulgence call them away from the path cast up for the ransomed of the Lord. Whether their lives shall be a blessing or a curse depends upon the choice they make. Overflowing with energy, eager to test their untried capabilities, they must find some outlet for their superabounding life. Active they will be for good or for evil.

God's word does not repress activity, but guides it aright. God does not bid the youth to be less aspiring. The elements of character that make a man truly successful and honoured among men — the irrepressible desire for some greater good, the indomitable will, the strenuous application, the untiring perseverance — are not to be discouraged. By the grace of God they are to be directed to the attainment of objects as much higher than mere selfish and worldly interests as the heavens are higher than the earth.

With us as parents and as Christians it rests to give our children right direction. They are to be carefully, wisely, tenderly guided into paths of Christlike ministry. We are under sacred covenant with God to rear our children for His service. To surround them with such influences as shall lead them to choose a life of service, and to give them the training needed, is our first duty.

"God so loved, . . . that He gave," "gave His only-begotten Son," that we should not perish, but have everlasting life. "Christ . . . hath loved us, and hath given Himself for us." If we love we shall give. "Not to be ministered unto, but to minister" is the great lesson which we are to learn and to teach. John 3:16; Ephesians 5:2; Matthew 20:28.

Let the youth be impressed with the thought that they are not their own. They belong to Christ. They are the purchase of His blood, the claim of His love. They live because He keeps them by His power. Their time, their strength, their capabilities are His, to be developed, to be trained, to be used for Him.

Next to the angelic beings, the human family, formed in the image of God, are the noblest of His created works. God desires them to become all that He has made it possible for them to be, and to do their very best with the powers He has given them.

Life is mysterious and sacred. It is the manifestation of God Himself, the source of all life. Precious are its opportunities, and earnestly should they be improved. Once lost, they are gone forever.

Before us God places eternity, with its solemn realities, and gives us a grasp on immortal, imperishable themes. He presents valuable, ennobling truth, that we may advance in a safe and sure path, in pursuit of an object worthy of the earnest engagement of all our capabilities.

God looks into the tiny seed that He Himself has formed, and sees wrapped within it the beautiful flower, the shrub, or the lofty, wide-spreading tree. So does He see the possibilities in every human being. We are here for a purpose. God has given us His plan for our life, and He desires us to reach the highest standard of development.

He desires that we shall constantly be growing in holiness, in happiness, in usefulness. All have capabilities which they must be taught to regard as sacred endowments, to appreciate as the Lord's gifts, and rightly to employ. He desires the youth to cultivate every power of their being, and to bring every faculty into active exercise. He desires them to enjoy all that is useful and precious in this life, to be good and to do good, laying up a heavenly treasure for the future life.

It should be their ambition to excel in all things that are unselfish, high, and noble. Let them look to Christ as the pattern after which they are to be fashioned. The holy ambition that He revealed in His life they are to cherish — an ambition to make the world better for their having lived in it. This is the work to which they are called.

A Broad Foundation

The highest of all sciences is the science of soul saving. The greatest work to which human beings can aspire is the work of winning men from sin to holiness.

For the accomplishment of this work, a broad foundation must be laid. A comprehensive education is needed — an education that will demand from parents and teachers such thought and effort as mere instruction in the sciences does not require. Something more is called for than the culture of the intellect. Education is not complete unless the body, the mind, and the heart are equally educated. The character must receive proper discipline for its fullest and highest development. All the faculties of mind and body are to be developed and rightly trained. It is a duty to cultivate and to exercise every power that will render us more efficient workers for God.

True education includes the whole being. It teaches the right use of one's self. It enables us to make the best use of brain, bone, and muscle, of body, mind, and heart. The faculties of the mind, as the higher powers, are to rule the kingdom of the body. The natural appetites and passions are to be brought under the control of the conscience and the spiritual affections. Christ stands at the head of humanity, and it is His purpose to lead us, in His service, into high and holy paths of purity. By the wondrous working of His grace, we are to be made complete in Him.

Jesus secured His education in the home. His mother was His first human teacher. From her lips, and from the scrolls of the prophets, He learned of heavenly things. He lived in a peasant's home and faithfully and cheerfully acted His part in bearing the household burdens. He who had been the commander of heaven was a willing servant, a loving, obedient son. He learned a trade and with His own hands worked in the carpenter's shop with Joseph. In the garb of a common labourer He walked the streets of the little town, going to and returning from His humble work.

With the people of that age the value of things was estimated by outward show. As religion had declined in power, it had increased in pomp. The educators of the time sought to command respect by display and ostentation. To all this the life of Jesus presented a marked contrast. His life demonstrated the worthlessness of those things that men regarded as life's great essentials. The schools of His time, with their magnifying of things small and their belittling of things great, He did not seek. His education was gained from Heaven-appointed sources, from useful work, from the study of the Scriptures, from nature, and from the experiences of life — God's lesson books, full of instruction to all who bring to them the willing hand, the seeing eye, and the understanding heart.

"The Child grew, and waxed strong in spirit, filled with wisdom: and the grace of God was upon Him." Luke 2:40.

Thus prepared, He went forth to His mission, in every moment of His contact with men exerting upon them an influence to bless, a power to transform, such as the world had never witnessed.

The home is the child's first school, and it is here that the foundation should be laid for a life of service. Its principles are to be taught not merely in theory. They are to shape the whole life training.

Very early the lesson of helpfulness should be taught the child. As soon as strength and reasoning power are sufficiently developed, he should be given duties to perform in the home. He should be encouraged in trying to help father and mother, encouraged to deny and to control himself, to put other's happiness and convenience before his own, to watch for opportunities to cheer and assist brothers and sisters and playmates, and to show kindness to the aged, the sick, and the unfortunate. The more fully the spirit of true ministry pervades the home, the more fully it will be developed in the lives of the children. They will learn to find joy in service and sacrifice for the good of others.

The Work of the School

The home training should be supplemented by the work of the school. The development of the whole being, physical, mental, and spiritual, and the teaching of service and sacrifice, should be kept constantly in view.

Above any other agency, service for Christ's sake in the little things of everyday experience has power to mould the character and to direct the life into lines of unselfish ministry. To awaken this spirit, to encourage and rightly to direct it, is the parents' and the teacher's work. No more important work could be committed to them. The spirit of ministry is the spirit of heaven, and with every effort to develop and encourage it angels will co-operate.

Such an education must be based upon the word of God. Here only are its principles given in their fullness. The Bible should be made the foundation of study and of teaching. The essential knowledge is a knowledge of God and of Him whom He has sent.

Every child and every youth should have a knowledge of himself. He should understand the physical habitation that God has given him, and the laws by which it is kept in health. All should be thoroughly grounded in the common branches of education. And they should have industrial training that will make them men and women of practical ability, fitted for the duties of everyday life. To this should be added training and practical experience in various lines of missionary effort.

Learning by Imparting

Let the youth advance as fast and as far as they can in the acquisition of knowledge. Let their field of study be as broad as their powers can compass. And, as they learn, let them impart their knowledge. It is thus that their minds will acquire discipline and power. It is the use they make of knowledge that determines the value of their education. To spend a long time in study, with no effort to impart what is gained, often proves a hindrance rather than a help to real development. In both the home and the school it should be the student's effort to learn how to study and how to impart the knowledge gained. Whatever his calling, he is to be both a learner and a teacher as long as life shall last. Thus he may advance continually, making God his trust, clinging to Him who is infinite in wisdom, who can reveal the secrets hidden for ages, who can solve the most difficult problems for minds that believe in Him.

God's word places great stress upon the influence of association, even upon men and women. How much greater is its power on the developing mind and character of children and youth. The company they keep, the principles they adopt, the habits they form, will decide the question of their usefulness here and of their future, eternal interest.

It is a terrible fact, and one that should make the hearts of parents tremble, that in so many schools and colleges to which the youth are sent for mental culture and discipline, influences prevail which misshape the character, divert the mind from life's true aims, and debase the morals. Through contact with the irreligious, the pleasure loving, and the corrupt, many, many youth lose the simplicity and purity, the faith in God, and the spirit of self-sacrifice that Christian fathers and mothers have cherished and guarded by careful instruction and earnest prayer.

Many who enter school with the purpose of fitting themselves for some line of unselfish ministry become absorbed in secular studies. An ambition is aroused to win distinction in scholarship and to gain position and honour in the world. The purpose for which they entered school is lost sight of, and the life is given up to selfish and worldly pursuits. And often habits are formed that ruin the life both for this world and for the world to come.

As a rule, men and women who have broad ideas, unselfish purposes, noble aspirations, are those in whom these characteristics were developed by their associations in early years. In all His dealings with Israel, God urged upon them the importance of guarding the associations of their children. All the arrangements of civil, religious, and social life were made with a view to preserving the children from harmful companionship and making them, from their earliest years, familiar with the precepts and principles of the law of

God. The object lesson given at the birth of the nation was of a nature deeply to impress all hearts. Before the last terrible judgement came upon the Egyptians in the death of the first-born, God commanded His people to gather their children into their own homes. The door-post of every house was marked with blood, and within the protection assured by this token all were to abide. So today parents who love and fear God are to keep their children under "the bond of the covenant" — within the protection of those sacred influences made possible through Christ's redeeming blood.

Of His disciples Christ said, "I have given them Thy word; and . . . they are not of the world, even as I am not of the world." John 17:14.

"Be not conformed to this world," God bids us; "but be ye transformed by the renewing of your mind." Romans 12:2.

"Be ye not unequally yoked together with unbelievers: for what fellowship hath righteousness with unrighteousness? and what communion hath light with darkness? . . . and what agreement hath the temple of God with idols? for ye are the temple of the living God; as God hath said, I will dwell in them, and walk in them; and I will be their God, and they shall be My people. Wherefore

> "Come out from among them, and be ye separate, . . .
> And touch not the unclean; . . .
> And I will receive you,
> And will be a Father unto you,
> And ye shall be My sons and daughters,
> Saith the Lord Almighty."
>
> 2 Corinthians 6:14-18.

"Gather the children." "Make them know the statutes of God, and His laws." Joel 2:16; Exodus 18:16.

"Put My name upon the children of Israel; and I will bless them." Numbers 6:27.

"And all the peoples of the earth shall see that thou art called by the name of Jehovah." Deuteronomy 28:10, ARV.

"The remnant of Jacob shall be in the midst of many
people
As a dew from the Lord,
As the showers upon the grass,
That tarrieth not for man,
Nor waiteth for the sons of men."
Micah 5:7.

We are numbered with Israel. All the instruction given to the Israelites of old concerning the education and training of their children, all the promises of blessing through obedience, are for us.

God's word to us is, "I will bless thee, . . . and thou shalt be a blessing." Genesis 12:2.

Of the first disciples and of all who should believe on Him through their word Christ said, "The glory which Thou gavest Me I have given them; that they may be one, even as We are one: I in them, and Thou in Me, that they may be made perfect in one; and that the world may know that Thou hast sent Me, and hast loved them, as Thou hast loved Me." John 17:22, 23.

Wonderful, wonderful words, almost beyond the grasp of faith! The Creator of all worlds loves those who give themselves to His service, even as He loves His son. Even here and now His gracious favour is bestowed upon us to this marvellous extent. He has given us the Light and Majesty of heaven, and with Him He has bestowed all the heavenly treasure. Much as He has promised us for the life to come, He bestows princely gifts in this life. As subjects of His grace, He desires us to enjoy everything that will ennoble, expand, and elevate our characters. He is waiting to inspire the youth with power from above, that they may stand under the blood-stained banner of Christ, to work as He worked, to lead souls into safe paths, to plant the feet of many upon the Rock of Ages.

All who are seeking to work in harmony with God's plan of education will have His sustaining grace, His continual presence, His keeping power. To everyone He says:

"Be strong and of a good courage; be not afraid,

neither be thou dismayed: for the Lord thy God is with thee." "I will not fail thee, nor forsake thee." Joshua 1:9, 5.

> "As the rain cometh down, and the snow from heaven,
> And returneth not thither,
> But watereth the earth, and maketh it bring forth and bud,
> That it may give seed to the sower, and bread to the eater:
> So shall My word be that goeth forth out of My mouth:
> It shall not return unto Me void,
> But it shall accomplish that which I please,
> And it shall prosper in the thing whereto I sent it.
> For ye shall go out with joy,
> And be led forth with peace:
> The mountains and the hills shall break forth before you into singing,
> And all the trees of the field shall clap their hands.
> Instead of the thorn shall come up the fir tree,
> And instead of the brier shall come up the myrtle tree:
> And it shall be to the Lord for a name,
> For an everlasting sign that shall not be cut off."
> Isaiah 55:10-13.

Throughout the world, society is in disorder, and a thorough transformation is needed. The education given to the youth is to mould the whole social fabric.

> "They shall build the old wastes,
> They shall raise up the former desolations,
> And they shall repair the waste cities,
> The desolations of many generations."
> Men shall call them "the ministers of our God. . . .
> Everlasting joy shall be unto them.
> For I, Jehovah, love justice."
>
> "I will direct their work in truth,
> And I will make an everlasting covenant with them."
> "Their race shall be illustrious among the nations,
> And their offspring among the people;
> All that see them shall acknowledge

That they are a race which Jehovah hath
blessed. . . .
For as the earth putteth forth her shoots,
And as a garden causeth its plants to spring forth,
So shall the Lord Jehovah cause salvation to spring
forth,
And praise before all the nations."
Isaiah 61:4, 6-8, Noyes; 61:8; 61:9, 11, Noyes.

THE ESSENTIAL KNOWLEDGE

A True Knowledge of God

Like our Saviour, we are in this world to do service for God. We are here to become like God in character, and by a life of service to reveal Him to the world. In order to be co-workers with God, in order to become like Him and to reveal His character, we must know Him aright. We must know Him as He reveals Himself.

A knowledge of God is the foundation of all true education and of all true service. It is the only real safeguard against temptation. It is this alone that can make us like God in character.

This is the knowledge needed by all who are working for the uplifting of their fellow men. Transformation of character, purity of life, efficiency in service, adherence to correct principles, all depend upon a right knowledge of God. This knowledge is the essential preparation both for this life and for the life to come.

"The knowledge of the Holy is understanding." Proverbs 9:10.

Through a knowledge of Him are given unto us "all things that pertain unto life and godliness." 2 Peter 1:3.

"This is life eternal," said Jesus, "that they might know Thee the only true God, and Jesus Christ, whom Thou hast sent." John 17:3.

> "Thus saith the Lord,
> Let not the wise man glory in his wisdom,
> Neither let the mighty man glory in his might,
> Let not the rich man glory in his riches:
> But let him that glorieth glory in this,
> That he understandeth and knoweth Me,

That I am the Lord which exercise loving-kindness,
Judgement, and righteousness, in the earth:
For in these things I delight, saith the Lord."
Jeremiah 9:23, 24.

We need to study the revelations of Himself that God has given.

"Acquaint now thyself with Him,
And be at peace:
Thereby good shall come unto thee.
Receive, I pray thee, the law from His mouth,
And lay up His words in thy heart. . . .
And the Almighty will be thy treasure. . . .

"Then shalt thou delight thyself in the Almighty,
And shalt lift up thy face unto God.
Thou shalt make thy prayer unto Him,
And He will hear thee;
And thou shalt pay thy vows.
Thou shalt also decree a thing,
And it shall be established unto thee;
And light shall shine upon thy ways.
When they cast thee down, thou shalt say,
There is lifting up;
And the humble person He will save."
Job 22:21-29, ARV.

"The invisible things of Him since the creation of the world are clearly seen, being perceived through the things that are made, even His everlasting power and divinity." Romans 1:20, ARV.

The things of nature that we now behold give us but a faint conception of Eden's glory. Sin has marred earth's beauty; on all things may be seen traces of the work of evil. Yet much that is beautiful remains. Nature testifies that One infinite in power, great in goodness, mercy, and love, created the earth, and filled it with life and gladness. Even in their blighted state, all things reveal the handiwork of the great Master Artist. Wherever we turn, we may hear the voice of God, and see evidences of His goodness.

From the solemn roll of the deep-toned thunder and old ocean's ceaseless roar, to the glad songs that make the forests vocal with melody, nature's ten thousand voices speak His praise. In earth and sea and sky, with their marvellous tint and colour, varying in gorgeous contrast or blended in harmony, we behold His glory. The everlasting hills tell us of His power. The trees that wave their green banners in the sunlight, and the flowers in their delicate beauty, point to their Creator. The living green that carpets the brown earth tells of God's care for the humblest of His creatures. The caves of the sea and the depths of the earth reveal His treasures. He who placed the pearls in the ocean and the amethyst and chrysolite among the rocks, is a lover of the beautiful. The sun rising in the heavens is a representative of Him who is the life and light of all that He has made. All the brightness and beauty that adorn the earth and light up the heavens, speak of God.

> "His glory covered the heavens."
> "The earth is full of Thy riches."
>
> "Day unto day uttereth speech,
> And night unto night showeth knowledge.
> There is no speech nor language,
> Without these their voice is heard.
> Their line is gone out through all the earth,
> And their words to the end of the world."
>
> Habakkuk 3:3; Psalms 104:24; 19:2-4, margin.

All things tell of His tender, fatherly care and of His desire to make His children happy.

The mighty power that works through all nature and sustains all things is not, as some men of science represent, merely an all-pervading principle, an actuating energy. God is a Spirit; yet He is a personal Being; for so He has revealed Himself:

> "The Lord is the true God,
> He is the living God, and an everlasting King: . . .
> The gods that have not made the heavens and the earth,
> Even they shall perish from the earth, and from under these heavens."

"The portion of Jacob is not like them:
For He is the former of all things."

"He hath made the earth by His power,
He hath established the world by His wisdom,
And hath stretched out the heavens by His
discretion."

Jeremiah 10:10, 11, 16, 12.

Nature Is Not God

God's handiwork in nature is not God Himself in nature. The things of nature are an expression of God's character and power; but we are not to regard nature as God. The artistic skill of human beings produces very beautiful workmanship, things that delight the eye, and these things reveal to us something of the thought of the designer; but the thing made is not the maker. It is not the work, but the workman, that is counted worthy of honour. So while nature is an expression of God's thought, it is not nature, but the God of nature, that is to be exalted.

"Let us worship and bow down:
Let us kneel before the Lord."
"In His hand are the deep places of the earth;
The heights of the mountains are His also.
The sea is His, and He made it;
And His hands formed the dry land."

Psalm 95:6; 95:4, 5, ARV.

"Seek Him that maketh the Pleiades and Orion,
And turneth the shadow of death into the morning,
And maketh the day dark with night;"
"He that formeth the mountains, and createth the
wind,
And declareth unto man what is His thought;"
"He that buildeth His spheres in the heaven,
And hath founded His arch [Noyes's translation] in
the earth;"
"He that calleth for the waters of the sea,
And poureth them out upon the face of the earth;
Jehovah is His name."

Amos 5:8, ARV; 4:13, ARV;
9:6, margin; 9:6, ARV.

The Creation of the Earth

The work of creation cannot be explained by science. What science can explain the mystery of life?

"Through faith we understand that the worlds were framed by the word of God, so that things which are seen were not made of things which do appear." Hebrews 11:3.

> "I form the light, and create darkness: . . .
> I the Lord do all these things. . . .
> I have made the earth,
> And created man upon it:
> I, even My hands, have stretched out the heavens,
> And all their host have I commanded."
> "When I call unto them, they stand up together."
> Isaiah 45:7-12; 48:13.

In the creation of the earth, God was not indebted to pre-existing matter. "He spake, and it was; . . . He commanded, and it stood fast." Psalm 33:9. All things, material or spiritual, stood up before the Lord Jehovah at His voice and were created for His own purpose. The heavens and all the host of them, the earth and all things therein, came into existence by the breath of His mouth.

In the creation of man was manifest the agency of a personal God. When God had made man in His image, the human form was perfect in all its arrangements, but it was without life. Then a personal, self-existing God breathed into that form the breath of life, and man became a living, intelligent being. All parts of the human organism were set in action. The heart, the arteries, the veins, the tongue, the hands, the feet, the senses, the faculties of the mind, all began their work, and all were placed under law. Man became a living soul. Through Christ the Word, a personal God created man and endowed him with intelligence and power.

Our substance was not hid from Him when we were made in secret; His eyes saw our substance, yet being imperfect, and in His book all our members were written when as yet there were none of them.

Above all lower orders of being, God designed that man, the crowning work of His creation, should express His thought and reveal His glory. But man is not to exalt himself as God.

> "Make a joyful noise unto the Lord. . . .
> Serve the Lord with gladness:
> Come before His presence with singing.
> Know ye that the Lord He is God:
> It is He that hath made us, and His we are;
> We are His people, and the sheep of His pasture.
> Enter into His gates with thanksgiving,
> And into His courts with praise:
> Be thankful unto Him, and bless His name."
> "Exalt the Lord our God,
> And worship at His holy hill;
> For the Lord our God is holy."
>
> Psalms 100:1-4, margin; 99:9.

God is constantly employed in upholding and using as His servants the things that He has made. He works through the laws of nature, using them as His instruments. They are not self-acting. Nature in her work testifies of the intelligent presence and active agency of a Being who moves in all things according to His will.

> "Forever, O Lord,
> Thy word is settled in heaven.
> Thy faithfulness is unto all generations:
> Thou hast established the earth, and it abideth.
> They continue this day according to Thine ordinances:
> For all are Thy servants."
> "Whatsoever the Lord pleased, that did He
> In heaven, and in earth, in the seas, and all deep places."
> "He commanded, and they were created.
> He hath also established them for ever and ever:
> He hath made a decree which shall not pass."
>
> Psalms 119:89-91; 135:6; 148:5, 6.

It is not by inherent power that year by year the earth yields its bounties and continues its march around the sun. The hand of the Infinite One is perpetually at work guiding this planet. It is God's power continually exercised that keeps the earth in position in its rotation. It is God who causes the sun to rise in the heavens. He opens the windows of heaven and gives rain.

> "He giveth snow like wool:
> He scattereth the hoarfrost like ashes."
>
> "When He uttereth His voice, there is a multitude of waters in the heavens,
> And He causeth the vapours to ascend from the ends of the earth;
> He maketh lightnings with rain,
> And bringeth forth the wind out of His treasures."
>
> Psalm 147:16; Jeremiah 10:13.

It is by His power that vegetation is caused to flourish, that every leaf appears, every flower blooms, every fruit develops.

The mechanism of the human body cannot be fully understood; it presents mysteries that baffle the most intelligent. It is not as the result of a mechanism, which, once set in motion, continues its work, that the pulse beats and breath follows breath. In God we live and move and have our being. The beating heart, the throbbing pulse, every nerve and muscle in the living organism, is kept in order and activity by the power of an ever-present God.

The Bible shows us God in His high and holy place, not in a state of inactivity, not in silence and solitude, but surrounded by ten thousand times ten thousand and thousands of thousands of holy beings, all waiting to do His will. Through these messengers He is in active communication with every part of His dominion. By His Spirit He is everywhere present. Through the agency of His Spirit and His angels He ministers to the children of men.

Above the distractions of the earth He sits enthroned; all things are open to His divine survey; and from His great and calm eternity He orders that which His providence sees best.

> "The way of man is not in himself:
> It is not in man that walketh to direct his steps."

"Trust in the Lord with all thine heart. . . .
In all thy ways acknowledge Him,
And He shall direct thy paths."

"The eye of the Lord is upon them that fear Him,
Upon them that hope in His mercy;
To deliver their soul from death,
And to keep them alive in famine."

"How precious is Thy loving-kindness, O God! . . .
The children of men take refuge under the shadow of Thy wings."
"Happy is he that hath the God of Jacob for his help,
Whose hope is in the Lord his God."

"The earth, O Jehovah, is full of Thy loving-kindness."
Thou lovest "righteousness and justice."
Thou "art the confidence of all the ends of the earth,
And of them that are afar off upon the sea:
Who by His strength setteth fast the mountains,
Being girded about with might;
Who stilleth the roaring of the seas, . . .
And the tumult of the peoples."

"Thou makest the outgoings of the morning and evening to rejoice."
"Thou crownest the year with Thy goodness;
And Thy paths drop fatness."

"The Lord upholdeth all that fall,
And raiseth up all those that be bowed down.
The eyes of all wait upon Thee;
And Thou givest them their meat in due season.
Thou openest Thine hand,
And satisfiest the desire of every living thing."

Jeremiah 10:23; Proverbs 3:5, 6; Psalms 33:18, 19; 36:7, ARV; 146:5; 119:64, ARV; 33:5, ARV; 65:5-7, ARV; 65:8, 11; 145:14-16.

Personality of God Revealed in Christ

As a personal being, God has revealed Himself in His Son. The outshining of the Father's glory, "and the express image of His person," Jesus, as a personal Saviour, came to the world. As a personal Saviour He ascended on high. As a personal Saviour He intercedes in the heavenly courts. Before the throne of God in our behalf ministers "One like unto the Son of man." Hebrews 1:3; Revelation 1:13.

Christ, the Light of the world, veiled the dazzling splendour of His divinity and came to live as a man among men, that they might, without being consumed, become acquainted with their Creator. Since sin brought separation between man and his Maker, no man has seen God at any time, except as He is manifested through Christ.

"I and My Father are one," Christ declared. "No man knoweth the Son, but the Father; neither knoweth any man the Father, save the Son, and he to whomsoever the Son will reveal Him." John 10:30; Matthew 11:27.

Christ came to teach human beings what God desires them to know. In the heavens above, in the earth, in the broad waters of the ocean, we see the handiwork of God. All created things testify to His power, His wisdom, His love. Yet not from the stars or the ocean or the cataract can we learn of the personality of God as it was revealed in Christ.

God saw that a clearer revelation than nature was needed to portray both His personality and His character. He sent His Son into the world to manifest, so far as could be endured by human sight, the nature and the attributes of the invisible God.

Revealed to the Disciples

Let us study the words that Christ spoke in the upper chamber on the night before His crucifixion. He was nearing His hour of trial, and He sought to comfort His disciples, who were to be so severely tempted and tried.

"Let not your heart be troubled," He said. "Ye believe in God, believe also in Me. In My Father's house are many mansions: if it were not so, I would have told you. I go to prepare a place for you. . . .

"Thomas saith unto Him, Lord, we know not whither Thou goest; and how can we know the way? Jesus saith unto him, I am the way, the truth, and the life: no man cometh unto the Father, but by Me. If ye had known

Me, ye should have known My Father also: and from henceforth ye know Him, and have seen Him. . . .

"Lord, show us the Father," said Philip, "and it sufficeth us. Jesus saith unto him, Have I been so long time with you, and yet hast thou not known Me, Philip? he that hath seen Me hath seen the Father; and how sayest thou then, Show us the Father? Believest thou not that I am in the Father, and the Father in Me? the words that I speak unto you I speak not of Myself: but the Father that dwelleth in Me, He doeth the works." John 14:1-10.

The disciples did not yet understand Christ's words concerning His relation to God. Much of His teaching was still dark to them. Christ desired them to have a clearer, more distinct knowledge of God.

"These things have I spoken unto you in parables," He said; "but the time cometh, when I shall no more speak unto you in parables, but I shall show you plainly of the Father." John 16:25, margin.

When, on the Day of Pentecost, the Holy Spirit was poured out on the disciples, they understood more fully the truths that Christ had spoken in parables. Much of the teaching that had been a mystery to them was made clear. But not even then did the disciples receive the complete fulfilment of Christ's promise. They received all the knowledge of God that they could bear, but the complete fulfilment of the promise that Christ would show them plainly of the Father was yet to come. Thus it is today. Our knowledge of God is partial and imperfect. When the conflict is ended, and the Man Christ Jesus acknowledges before the Father His faithful workers, who in a world of sin have borne true witness for Him, they will understand clearly what now are mysteries to them.

Christ took with Him to the heavenly courts His glorified humanity. To those who receive Him He gives power to become the sons of God, that at last God may receive them as His, to dwell with Him throughout eternity. If during this life they are loyal to God, they will at last "see His face; and His name shall be in their foreheads." Revelation 22:4. And what is the happiness of heaven but to see God? What greater joy could come to the sinner saved by the grace of Christ than to look upon the face of God and know Him as Father?

The Scriptures clearly indicate the relation between God and Christ, and they bring to view as clearly the personality and individuality of each.

"God, who at sundry times and in divers manners spake in time past unto the fathers by the prophets, hath in these last days spoken unto us by His Son; . . . who being the brightness of His glory, and the express image of His person, and upholding all things by the word of His power, when He had by Himself purged our sins, sat down on the right hand of the Majesty on high; being made so much better than the angels, as He hath by inheritance obtained a more excellent name than they. For unto which of the angels said He at any time,

"Thou art My Son,
This day have I begotten Thee?
And again,
I will be to Him a Father,
And He shall be to Me a Son?"
Hebrews 1:1-5.

The personality of the Father and the Son, also the unity that exists between Them, are presented in the seventeenth chapter of John, in the prayer of Christ for His disciples:

"Neither pray I for these alone, but for them also which shall believe on Me through their word; that they all may be one; as Thou, Father, art in Me, and I in Thee, that they also may be one in Us: that the world may believe that Thou hast sent Me." John 17:20, 21.

The unity that exists between Christ and His disciples does not destroy the personality of either. They are one in purpose, in mind, in character, but not in person. It is thus that God and Christ are one.

Character of God Revealed in Christ

Taking humanity upon Him, Christ came to be one with humanity, and at the same time to reveal our heavenly Father to sinful human beings. He who had been in the presence of the Father from the beginning, He who was the express image of the invisible God, was alone able to reveal the character of the Deity to mankind. He was in all things made like unto His brethren. He became flesh even as we are. He was hungry and thirsty and weary. He was sustained by food and refreshed by sleep. He shared the lot of men; yet He was the blameless Son of God. He was a stranger and sojourner on the earth – in the world, but not of the world; tempted and tried as men and women today are tempted and tried, yet living a life free from sin. Tender, compassionate, sympathetic, ever considerate of others, He represented the character of God, and was constantly engaged in service for God and man.

"Jehovah hath anointed Me," He said,
"To preach good tidings unto the poor;
He hath sent Me to bind up the brokenhearted,
To proclaim liberty to the captives,"
"And recovering of sight to the blind;"
"To proclaim the year of Jehovah's favour; . . .
To comfort all that mourn."

Isaiah 61:1, ARV, margin;
Luke 4:18; Isaiah 61:2, ARV.

"Love your enemies," He bids us; "bless them that curse you, do good to them that hate you, and pray for them which despitefully use you, and persecute you; that ye may be the children of your Father which is in heaven;" "for He is kind unto the unthankful and to the evil." "He maketh His sun to rise on the evil and on the good, and sendeth rain on the just and on the unjust." "Be ye therefore merciful, as your Father also is merciful." Matthew 5:44, 45; Luke 6:35; Matthew 5:45; Luke 6:36.

"Through the tender mercy of our God; . . .
The Dayspring from on high hath visited us,
To give light to them that sit in darkness and in the shadow of death,
To guide our feet into the way of peace."
Luke 1:78, 79.

The Glory of the Cross

The revelation of God's love to man centres in the cross. Its full significance tongue cannot utter, pen cannot portray, the mind of man cannot comprehend. Looking upon the cross of Calvary, we can only say, "God so loved the world, that He gave His only-begotten Son, that whosoever believeth in Him should not perish, but have everlasting life." John 3:16.

Christ crucified for our sins, Christ risen from the dead, Christ ascended on high, is the science of salvation that we are to learn and to teach.

It Was Christ

"Who, existing in the form of God, counted not the being on an equality with God a thing to be grasped, but emptied Himself, taking the form of a servant, being made in the likeness of men; and being found in fashion as a man, He humbled Himself, becoming obedient even unto death, yea, the death of the cross." Philippians 2:6-8, ARV.

"It is Christ that died, yea rather, that is risen again, who is even at the right hand of God." "Wherefore He is able also to save them to the uttermost that come unto God by Him, seeing He ever liveth to make intercession for them." Romans 8:34; Hebrews 7:25.

"We have not a high priest that cannot be touched with the feeling of our infirmities; but One that hath been in all points tempted like as we are, yet without sin." Hebrews 4:15, ARV.

It is through the gift of Christ that we receive every blessing. Through that gift there comes to us day by day the unfailing flow of Jehovah's goodness. Every flower, with its delicate tints and its fragrance, is given for our enjoyment through that one Gift. The sun and the moon were made by Him. There is not a star which beautifies the heavens that He did not make. Every drop of rain that falls, every ray of light shed upon our unthankful world, testifies to the love of God in Christ. Everything is supplied to us through the one unspeakable Gift, God's only-begotten Son. He was nailed to the cross that all these bounties might flow to God's workmanship.

"Behold, what manner of love the Father hath bestowed upon us, that we should be called the sons of God." 1 John 3:1.

> "Men have not heard, nor perceived by the ear,
> Neither hath the eye seen a God besides Thee,
> Who worketh for him that waiteth for Him."
> Isaiah 64:4, ARV.

The Knowledge That Works Transformation

The knowledge of God as revealed in Christ is the knowledge that all who are saved must have. It is the knowledge that works transformation of character. This knowledge, received, will re-create the soul in the image of God. It will impart to the whole being a spiritual power that is divine.

"We all, with open face beholding as in a glass the glory of the Lord, are changed into the same image from glory to glory." 2 Corinthians 3:18.

Of His own life the Saviour said, "I have kept My Father's commandments." John 15:10. "The Father hath not left Me alone; for I do always those things that please Him." John 8:29. As Jesus was in human nature, so God means His followers to be. In His strength we are to live the life of purity and nobility which the Saviour lived.

"For this cause," Paul says, "I bow my knees unto the Father of our Lord Jesus Christ, of whom the whole family in heaven and earth is named, that He would grant you, according to the riches of His glory, to be strengthened with might by His Spirit in the inner man; that Christ may dwell in your hearts by faith; that ye, being rooted and grounded in love, may be able to comprehend with all saints what is the breadth, and length, and depth, and height; and to know the love of Christ, which passeth knowledge, that ye might be filled with all the fullness of God." Ephesians 3:14-19.

We "do not cease to pray for you, and to desire that ye might be filled with the knowledge of His will in all wisdom and spiritual understanding; that ye might walk worthy of the Lord unto all pleasing, being fruitful in every good work, and increasing in the knowledge of God; strengthened with all might, according to His glorious power, unto all patience and long-suffering with joyfulness." Colossians 1:9-11.

This is the knowledge which God is inviting us to receive, and beside which all else is vanity and nothingness.

Danger in Speculative Knowledge

One of the greatest evils that attends the quest for knowledge, the investigations of science, is the disposition to exalt human reasoning above its true value and its proper sphere. Many attempt to judge of the Creator and His works by their own imperfect knowledge of science. They endeavour to determine the nature and attributes and prerogatives of God, and indulge in speculative theories concerning the Infinite One. Those who engage in this line of study are treading upon forbidden ground. Their research will yield no valuable results and can be pursued only at the peril of the soul.

Our first parents were led into sin through indulging a desire for knowledge that God had withheld from them. In seeking to gain this knowledge, they lost all that was worth possessing. If Adam and Eve had never touched the forbidden tree, God would have imparted to them knowledge — knowledge upon which rested no curse of sin, knowledge that would have brought them everlasting joy. All that they gained by listening to the tempter was an acquaintance with sin and its results. By their disobedience, humanity was estranged from God and the earth was separated from heaven.

The lesson is for us. The field into which Satan led our first parents is the same to which he is alluring men today. He is flooding the world with pleasing fables. By every device at his command he tempts men to speculate in regard to God. Thus he seeks to prevent them from obtaining that knowledge of God which is salvation.

Pantheistic Theories

Today there are coming into educational institutions and into the churches everywhere spiritualistic teachings that undermine faith in God and in His word. The theory that God is an essence pervading all nature is received by many who profess to believe the Scriptures; but, however beautifully clothed, this theory is a most dangerous deception. It misrepresents God and is a dishonour to His greatness and majesty. And it surely tends not only to mislead, but to debase men. Darkness is its element, sensuality its sphere. The result of accepting it is separation from God. And to fallen human nature this means ruin.

Our condition through sin is unnatural, and the power that restores us must be supernatural, else it has no value. There is but one power that can break the hold of evil from the hearts of men, and that is the power of God in Jesus Christ. Only through the blood of the Crucified One is there cleansing from sin. His grace alone can enable us to resist and subdue the tendencies of our fallen nature. The spiritualistic theories concerning God make His grace of no effect. If God is an essence pervading all nature, then He dwells in all men; and in order to attain holiness, man has only to develop the power within him.

These theories, followed to their logical conclusion, sweep away the whole Christian economy. They do away with the necessity for the atonement and make man his own saviour. These theories regarding God make His word of no effect, and those who accept them are in great danger of being led finally to look upon the whole Bible as a fiction. They may regard virtue as better than vice; but, having shut out God from His rightful position of sovereignty, they place their dependence upon human power, which, without God, is worthless. The unaided human will has no real power to resist and overcome evil. The defences of the soul are broken down. Man has no barrier against sin. When once the restraints of God's word and His Spirit are rejected, we know not to what depths one may sink.

> "Every word of God is pure:
> He is a shield unto them that put their trust in Him.
> Add thou not unto His words,
> Lest He reprove thee, and thou be found a liar."
> "His own iniquities shall take the wicked himself,
> And he shall be holden with the cords of his sins."
> Proverbs 30:5, 6; 5:22.

Searching Into Divine Mysteries

"The secret things belong unto the Lord our God: but those things which are revealed belong unto us and to our children forever." Deuteronomy 29:29. The revelation of Himself that God has given in His word is for our study. This we may seek to understand. But beyond this we are not to penetrate. The highest intellect may tax itself until it is wearied out in conjectures regarding the nature of God, but the effort will be fruitless. This problem has not been given us to solve. No human mind can comprehend God. None are to indulge in speculation regarding His nature. Here silence is eloquence. The Omniscient One is above discussion.

Even the angels were not permitted to share the counsels between the Father and the Son when the plan of salvation was laid. And human beings are not to intrude into the secrets of the Most High. We are as ignorant of God as little children; but, as little children, we may love and obey Him. Instead of speculating in regard to His nature or His prerogatives, let us give heed to the words He has spoken:

> "Canst thou by searching find out God?
> Canst thou find out the Almighty unto perfection?
> It is as high as heaven; what canst thou do?
> Deeper than hell; what canst thou know?
> The measure thereof is longer than the earth,
> And broader than the sea."

> "Where shall wisdom be found?
> And where is the place of understanding?
> Man knoweth not the price thereof;

Neither is it found in the land of the living.
The depth saith, It is not in me:
And the sea saith, It is not with me.
It cannot be gotten for gold,
Neither shall silver be weighed for the price thereof.
It cannot be valued with the gold of Ophir,
With the precious onyx, or the sapphire.
The gold and the crystal cannot equal it:
And the exchange of it shall not be for jewels of fine gold.
No mention shall be made of coral, or of pearls:
For the price of wisdom is above rubies.
The topaz of Ethiopia shall not equal it,
Neither shall it be valued with pure gold.
Whence then cometh wisdom?
And where is the place of understanding? . . .
Destruction and death say,
We have heard the fame thereof with our ears.
God understandeth the way thereof,
And He knoweth the place thereof.

"For He looketh to the ends of the earth,
And seeth under the whole heaven. . . .
When He made a decree for the rain,
And a way for the lightning of the thunder:
Then did He see it, and declare it;
He prepared it, yea, and searched it out.
And unto man He said,
Behold, the fear of the Lord, that is wisdom;
And to depart from evil is understanding."
Job 11:7-9; 28:12-28.

Neither by searching the recesses of the earth nor in vain endeavours to penetrate the mysteries of God's being, is wisdom found. It is found, rather, in humbly receiving the revelation that He has been pleased to give, and in conforming the life to His will.

Men of the greatest intellect cannot understand the mysteries of Jehovah as revealed in nature. Divine inspiration asks many questions which the most profound scholar cannot answer. These questions were not asked that we might answer them, but to call our attention to the deep mysteries of God and to teach us that our wisdom is limited; that in the surroundings of our daily life there are many things beyond the comprehension of finite beings.

Sceptics refuse to believe in God because they cannot comprehend the infinite power by which He reveals Himself. But God is to be acknowledged as much from what He does not reveal of Himself, as from that which is open to our limited comprehension. Both in divine revelation and in nature, God has given mysteries to command our faith. This must be so. We may be ever searching, ever inquiring, ever learning, and yet there is an infinity beyond.

> "Who hath measured the waters in the hollow of His hand,
> And meted out heaven with the span,
> And comprehended the dust of the earth in a measure,
> And weighed the mountains in scales,
> And the hills in a balance?
> Who hath directed the Spirit of Jehovah,
> Or being His counsellor hath taught Him? . . .
> Behold, the nations are as a drop of a bucket,
> And are accounted as the small dust of the balance:
> Behold, He taketh up the isles as a very little thing.
> And Lebanon is not sufficient to burn,
> Nor the beasts thereof sufficient for a burnt offering.
> All the nations are as nothing before Him;
> They are accounted by Him as less than nothing, and vanity.
> "To whom then will ye liken God?
> Or what likeness will ye compare unto Him? . . .
> Have ye not known?
> Have ye not heard?
> Hath it not been told you from the beginning?
> Have ye not understood from the foundations of the earth?
> It is He that sitteth above the circle of the earth,
> And the inhabitants thereof are as grasshoppers;
> That stretcheth out the heavens as a curtain,
> And spreadeth them out as a tent to dwell in. . . .
> To whom then will ye liken Me? . . .
> Saith the Holy One.
> Lift up your eyes on high,
> And see who hath created these,
> That bringeth out their host by number;
> He calleth them all by name;

By the greatness of His might, and for that He is
strong in power,
Not one is lacking.

"Why sayest thou, O Jacob, and speakest, O Israel,
My way is hid from Jehovah,
And the justice due to me is passed away from my God?
Hast thou not known?
Hast thou not heard?
The everlasting God, Jehovah,
The Creator of the ends of the earth,
Fainteth not, neither is weary;
There is no searching of His understanding."
Isaiah 40:12-28, ARV.

From the representations given by the Holy Spirit to His prophets, let us learn the greatness of our God. The prophet Isaiah writes:

"In the year that King Uzziah died I saw the Lord sitting upon a throne, high and lifted up; and His train filled the temple. Above Him stood the seraphim: each one had six wings; with twain he covered his face, and with twain he covered his feet, and with twain he did fly. And one cried unto another, and said, Holy, holy, holy, is Jehovah of hosts: the whole earth is full of His glory. And the foundations of the thresholds shook at the voice of him that cried, and the house was filled with smoke.

"Then said I, Woe is me! for I am undone; because I am a man of unclean lips, and I dwell in the midst of a people of unclean lips: for mine eyes have seen the King, Jehovah of hosts.

"Then flew one of the seraphim unto me, having a live coal in his hand, which he had taken with the tongs from off the altar: and he touched my mouth with it, and said, Lo, this hath touched thy lips; and thine iniquity is taken away, and thy sin expiated." Isaiah 6:1-7, ARV, margin.

"There is none like unto Thee, O Lord;
Thou art great,
And Thy name is great in might.
Who would not fear Thee, O King of nations?"

"O Lord, Thou hast searched me, and known me.
Thou knowest my downsitting and mine uprising,
Thou understandest my thought afar off.
Thou compassest my path and my lying down,
And art acquainted with all my ways.
For there is not a word in my tongue,
But, lo, O Lord, Thou knowest it altogether.
Thou hast beset me behind and before,
And laid Thine hand upon me.
Such knowledge is too wonderful for me;
It is high, I cannot attain unto it."

Jeremiah 10:6, 7; Psalm 139:1-6.

"Great is our Lord, and of great power: His understanding is infinite." Psalm 147:5.

"The ways of man are before the eyes of the Lord, and He pondereth all his goings." Proverbs 5:21.

"He revealeth the deep and secret things: He knoweth what is in the darkness, and the light dwelleth with Him." Daniel 2:22.

"Known unto God are all His works from the beginning of the world." "Who hath known the mind of the Lord? or who hath been His counsellor? Or who hath first given to Him, and it shall be recompensed unto him again? For of Him, and through Him, and to Him, are all things: to whom be glory forever." Acts 15:18; Romans 11:34-36.

"Unto the King eternal, immortal, invisible," "who only hath immortality, dwelling in the light which no man can approach unto; whom no man hath seen, nor can see: to whom be honour and power everlasting." 1 Timothy 1:17; 6:16.

"Shall not His excellency make you afraid?
And His dread fall upon you?"

"Is not God in the height of heaven?
And behold the height of the stars, how high they are!"

"Is there any number of His armies?
And upon whom doth not His light arise?"

"Great things doeth He, which we cannot comprehend.
For He saith to the snow,
Fall thou on the earth;
Likewise to the shower of rain,

And to the showers of His mighty rain.
He sealeth up the hand of every man,
That all men whom He hath made may know it. . . .
He spreadeth abroad the cloud of His lightning:
And it is turned round about by His guidance,
That they may do whatsoever He commandeth them
Upon the face of the habitable world;
Whether it be for correction, or for His land,
Or for loving-kindness, that He cause it to come.

"Hearken unto this: . . .
Stand still, and consider the wondrous works of God.
Dost thou know how God layeth His charge upon them,
And causeth the lightning of His cloud to shine?
Dost thou know the balancings of the clouds,
The wondrous works of Him who is perfect in knowledge? . . .
Canst thou with Him spread out the sky,
Which is strong as a molten mirror?
Teach us what we shall say unto Him;
For we cannot set our speech in order by reason of darkness. . . .
And now men cannot look on the light when it is bright in the skies,

"When the wind hath passed, and cleared them.
Out of the north cometh golden splendour:
God hath upon Him terrible majesty.
Touching the Almighty, we cannot find Him out:
He is excellent in power;
And in justice and plenteous righteousness. . . .
Men do therefore fear Him."

"Who is like unto the Lord our God, who dwelleth on high,
Who humbleth Himself to behold the things that are in heaven, and in the earth!"

"The Lord hath His way in the whirlwind and in the storm,
And the clouds are the dust of His feet."

"Great is the Lord, and greatly to be praised;
And His greatness is unsearchable.
One generation shall praise Thy works to another,
And shall declare Thy mighty acts.
I will speak of the glorious honour of Thy majesty,
And of Thy wondrous works.
And men shall speak of the might of Thy terrible acts:
And I will declare Thy greatness.

They shall abundantly utter the memory of Thy great
goodness,
And shall sing of Thy righteousness. . . .
"All Thy works shall praise Thee, O Lord;
And Thy saints shall bless Thee.
They shall speak of the glory of Thy kingdom,
And talk of Thy power;
To make known to the sons of men His mighty acts,
And the glorious majesty of His kingdom.
Thy kingdom is an everlasting kingdom,
And Thy dominion endureth throughout all
generations. . . .
My mouth shall speak the praise of the Lord:
And let all flesh bless His holy name for ever and ever."

Job 13:11; 22:12; 25:3; 37:5-24, ARV, margin; Psalm 113:5, 6; Nahum 1:3; Psalm 145:3-21.

As we learn more and more of what God is, and of what we ourselves are in His sight, we shall fear and tremble before Him. Let men of today take warning from the fate of those who in ancient times presumed to make free with that which God had declared sacred. When the Israelites ventured to open the ark on its return from the land of the Philistines, their irreverent daring was signally punished.

Again, consider the judgement that fell upon Uzzah. As in David's reign the ark was being carried to Jerusalem, Uzzah put forth his hand to keep it steady. For presuming to touch the symbol of God's presence, he was smitten with instant death.

At the burning bush, when Moses, not recognizing God's presence, turned aside to behold the wonderful sight, the command was given:

"Draw not nigh hither: put off thy shoes from off thy feet, for the place whereon thou standest is holy ground. . . . And Moses hid his face; for he was afraid to look upon God." Exodus 3:5, 6.

"And Jacob went out from Beersheba, and went toward Haran. And he lighted upon a certain place, and tarried there all night, because the sun was set; and he took of the stones of that place, and put them for his pillows, and lay down in that place to sleep.

"And he dreamed, and behold a ladder set up on the earth, and the top of it reached to heaven: and behold the angels of God ascending and descending on it. And, behold, the Lord stood above it, and said,

"I am the Lord God of Abraham thy father, and the God of Isaac: the land whereon thou liest, to thee will I give it, and to thy seed. . . . And, behold, I am with thee, and will keep thee in all places whither thou goest, and will bring thee again into this land; for I will not leave thee, until I have done that which I have spoken to thee of.

"And Jacob awaked out of his sleep, and he said, Surely the Lord is in this place; and I knew it not. And he was afraid, and said, How dreadful is this place! this is none other but the house of God, and this is the gate of heaven." Genesis 28:10-17.

In the sanctuary of the wilderness tabernacle and of the temple that were the earthly symbols of God's dwelling place, one apartment was sacred to His presence. The veil inwrought with cherubim at its entrance was not to be lifted by any hand save one. To lift that veil, and intrude unbidden into the sacred mystery of the most holy place, was death. For above the mercy seat dwelt the glory of the Holiest — glory upon which no man might look and live. On the one day of the year appointed for ministry in the most holy place, the high priest with trembling entered God's presence, while clouds of incense veiled the glory from his sight. Throughout the courts of the temple every sound was hushed. No priests ministered at the altars. The host of worshippers, bowed in silent awe, offered their petitions for God's mercy.

"These things happened unto them for ensamples: and they are written for our admonition, upon whom the ends of the world are come." 1 Corinthians 10:11.

> "The Lord is in His holy temple:
> Let all the earth keep silence before Him."
>
> "The Lord reigneth; let the people tremble:
> He sitteth between the cherubims; let the earth be moved.

The Lord is great in Zion;
And He is high above all the people.
Let them praise Thy great and terrible name;
For it is holy."

"The Lord's throne is in heaven:
His eyes behold, His eyelids try, the children of men."
"From the height of His sanctuary" "He hath looked down;"
"From the place of His habitation He looketh
Upon all the inhabitants of the earth.
He fashioneth their hearts alike;
He considereth all their works."
"Let all the earth fear the Lord:
Let all the inhabitants of the world stand in awe of Him."

Habakkuk 2:20; Psalms 99:1-3; 11:4; 102:19; 33:14, 15, 8.

Man cannot by searching find out God. Let none seek with presumptuous hand to lift the veil that conceals His glory. "Unsearchable are His judgements, and His ways past finding out." Romans 11:33. It is a proof of His mercy that there is the hiding of His power; for to lift the veil that conceals the divine presence is death. No mortal mind can penetrate the secrecy in which the Mighty One dwells and works. Only that which He sees fit to reveal can we comprehend of Him. Reason must acknowledge an authority superior to itself. Heart and intellect must bow to the great I AM.

The False and the True in Education

The mastermind in the confederacy of evil is ever working to keep out of sight the words of God, and to bring into view the opinions of men. He means that we shall not hear the voice of God, saying, "This is the way, walk ye in it." Isaiah 30:21. Through perverted educational processes he is doing his utmost to obscure heaven's light.

Philosophical speculation and scientific research in which God is not acknowledged are making sceptic of thousands. In the schools of today the conclusions that learned men have reached as the result of their scientific investigations are carefully taught and fully explained; while the impression is distinctly given that if these learned men are correct, the Bible cannot be. Scepticism is attractive to the human mind. The youth see in it an independence that captivates the imagination, and they are deceived. Satan triumphs. He nourishes every seed of doubt that is sown in young hearts. He causes it to grow and bear fruit, and soon a plentiful harvest of infidelity is reaped.

It is because the human heart is inclined to evil that it is so dangerous to sow the seeds of scepticism in young minds. Whatever weakens faith in God robs the soul of power to resist temptation. It removes the only real safeguard against sin. We are in need of schools where the youth shall be taught that greatness consists in honouring God by revealing His character in daily life. Through His word and His works we need to learn of God, that our lives may fulfil His purpose.

Infidel Authors

In order to obtain an education, many think it essential to study the writings of infidel authors, because these works contain many bright gems of thought. But who was the originator of these gems of thought? It was God, and God only. He is the source of all light. Why then should we wade through the mass of error contained in the works of infidels for the sake of a few intellectual truths, when all truth is at our command.

How is it that men who are at war with the government of God come into possession of the wisdom which they sometimes display? Satan himself was educated in the heavenly courts, and he has a knowledge of good as well as of evil. He mingles the precious with the vile, and this is what gives him power to deceive. But because Satan has robed himself in garments of heavenly brightness, shall we receive him as an angel of light? The tempter has his agents, educated according to his methods, inspired by his spirit, and adapted to his work. Shall we co-operate with them? Shall we receive the works of his agents as essential to the acquirement of an education?

If the time and effort spent in seeking to grasp the bright ideas of infidels were given to studying the precious things of the word of God, thousands who now sit in darkness and in the shadow of death would be rejoicing in the glory of the Light of life.

Historical and Theological Lore

As a preparation for Christian work, many think it essential to acquire an extensive knowledge of historical and theological writings. They suppose that this knowledge will be an aid to them in teaching the gospel. But their laborious study of the opinions of men tends to the enfeebling of their ministry, rather than to its strengthening. As I see libraries filled with ponderous volumes of historical and theological lore, I think, Why spend money for that which is not bread? The sixth chapter of John tells us more than can be found in such works. Christ says: "I am the Bread of Life: he that cometh to Me shall never hunger; and he that believeth on Me shall never thirst." "I am the living Bread which came down from heaven: if any man eat of this Bread, he shall live forever." "He that believeth on Me hath everlasting life." "The words that I speak unto you, they are spirit, and they are life." John 6:35, 51, 47, 63.

There is a study of history that is not to be condemned. Sacred history was one of the studies in the schools of the prophets. In the record of His dealings with the nations were traced the footsteps of Jehovah. So today we are to consider the dealings of God with the nations of the earth. We are to see in history the fulfilment of prophecy, to study the workings of Providence in the great reformatory movements, and to understand the progress of events in the marshalling of the nations for the final conflict of the great controversy.

Such study will give broad, comprehensive views of life. It will help us to understand something of its relations and dependencies, how wonderfully we are bound together in the great brotherhood of society and nations, and to how great an extent the oppression and degradation of one member means loss to all.

But history, as commonly studied, is concerned with man's achievements, his victories in battle, his success in attaining power and greatness. God's agency in the affairs of men is lost sight of. Few study the working out of His purpose in the rise and fall of nations.

And, to a great degree, theology, as studied and taught, is but a record of human speculation, serving only to "darken counsel by words without knowledge." Too often the motive in accumulating these many books is not so much a desire to obtain food for mind and soul, as it is an ambition to become acquainted with philosophers and theologians, a desire to present Christianity to the people in learned terms and propositions.

Not all the books written can serve the purpose of a holy life. "'Learn of Me'," said the Great Teacher, "'take My yoke upon you,' learn My meekness and lowliness." Your intellectual pride will not aid you in communicating with souls that are perishing for want of the bread of life. In your study of these books you are allowing them to take the place of the practical lessons you should be learning from Christ. With the results of this study the people are not fed. Very little of the research which is so wearying to the mind furnishes that which will help one to be a successful labourer for souls.

The Saviour came "to preach the gospel to the poor." Luke 4:18. In His teaching He used the simplest terms and the plainest symbols. And it is said that "the common people heard Him gladly." Mark 12:37. Those who are seeking to do His work for this time need a deeper insight into the lessons He has given.

The words of the living God are the highest of all education. Those who minister to the people need to eat of the bread of life. This will give them spiritual strength; then they will be prepared to minister to all classes of people.

The Classics

In the colleges and universities thousands of youth devote a large part of the best years of life to the study of Greek and Latin. And while they are engaged in these studies, mind and character are moulded by the evil sentiments of pagan literature, the reading of which is generally regarded as an essential part of the study of these languages.

Those who are conversant with the classics declare that "the Greek tragedies are full of incest, murder, and human sacrifices to lustful and revengeful gods." Far better would it be for the world were the education gained from such sources to be dispensed with. "Can one go upon hot coals, and his feet not be burned?" Proverbs 6:28. "Who can bring a clean thing out of an unclean? not one." Job 14:4. Can we then expect the youth to develop Christian character while their education is moulded by the teaching of those who set at defiance the principles of the law of God?

In casting off restraint and plunging into reckless amusement, dissipation, and vice, students are but imitating that which is kept before their minds by these studies. There are callings in which a knowledge of Greek and Latin is needed. Some must study these languages. But the knowledge of them essential for practical uses might be gained without a study of literature that is corrupt and corrupting.

And a knowledge of Greek and Latin is not needed by many. The study of dead languages should be made secondary to a study of those subjects that teach the right use of all the powers of body and mind. It is folly for students to devote their time to the acquirement of dead languages or of book knowledge in any line, to the neglect of a training for life's practical duties.

What do students carry with them when they leave school? Where are they going? What are they to do? Have they the knowledge that will enable them to teach others? Have they been educated to be true fathers and mothers? Can they stand at the head of a family as wise instructors? The only education worthy of the name is that which leads young men and young women to be Christlike, which fits them to bear life's responsibilities, fits them to stand at the head of their families. Such an education is not to be acquired by a study of heathen classics.

Sensational Literature

Many of the popular publications of the day are filled with sensational stories that are educating the youth in wickedness and leading them in the path to perdition. Mere children in years are old in a knowledge of crime. They are incited to evil by the tales they read. In imagination they act over the deeds portrayed, until their ambition is aroused to see what they can do in committing crime and evading punishment.

To the active minds of children and youth the scenes pictured in imaginary revelations of the future are realities. As revolutions are predicted and all manner of proceedings described that break down the barriers of law and self-restraint, many catch the spirit of these representations. They are led to the commission of crimes even worse, if possible, than these sensational writers depict. Through such influences as these, society is becoming demoralized. The seeds of lawlessness are sown broadcast. None need marvel that a harvest of crime is the result.

Works of romance, frivolous, exciting tales, are, in hardly less degree, a curse to the reader. The author may profess to teach a moral lesson, throughout his work he may interweave religious sentiments; but often these serve only to veil the folly and worthlessness beneath.

The world is flooded with books that are filled with enticing error. The youth receive as truth that which the Bible denounces as falsehood, and they love and cling to deception that means ruin to the soul.

There are works of fiction that were written for the purpose of teaching truth or exposing some great evil. Some of these works have accomplished good. Yet they have also wrought untold harm. They contain statements and highly wrought pen pictures that excite the imagination and give rise to a train of thought which is full of danger, especially to the youth. The scenes described are lived over and over again in their thoughts. Such reading unfits the mind for usefulness and disqualifies it for spiritual exercise. It destroys interest in the Bible. Heavenly things find little place in the thoughts. As the mind dwells upon the scenes of impurity portrayed, passion is aroused, and the end is sin.

Even fiction which contains no suggestion of impurity, and which may be intended to teach excellent principles, is harmful. It encourages the habit of hasty and superficial reading merely for the story. Thus it tends to destroy the power of connected and vigorous thought; it unfits the soul to contemplate the great problems of duty and destiny.

By fostering love for mere amusement, the reading of fiction creates a distaste for life's practical duties. Through its exciting, intoxicating power it is not infrequently a cause of both mental and physical disease. Many a miserable, neglected home, many a lifelong invalid, many an inmate of the insane asylum, has become such through the habit of novel reading.

It is often urged that in order to win the youth from sensational or worthless literature, we should supply them with a better class of fiction. This is like trying to cure the drunkard by giving him, in the place of whisky or brandy, the milder intoxicants, such as wine, beer, or cider. The use of these would continually foster the appetite for stronger stimulants. The only safety for the inebriate, and the only safeguard for the temperate man, is total abstinence. For the lover of fiction the same rule holds true. Total abstinence is his only safety.

Myths and Fairy Tales

In the education of children and youth, fairy tales, myths, and fictitious stories are now given a large place. Books of this character are used in the schools, and they are to be found in many homes. How can Christian parents permit their children to use books so filled with falsehood? When the children ask the meaning of stories so contrary to the teaching of their parents, the answer is that the stories are not true; but this does not do away with the evil results of their use. The ideas presented in these books mislead the children. They impart false views of life and beget and foster a desire for the unreal.

The widespread use of such books at this time is one of the cunning devices of Satan. He is seeking to divert the minds of old and young from the great work of character building. He means that our children and youth shall be swept away by the soul-destroying deceptions with which he is filling the world. Therefore he seeks to divert their minds from the word of God and thus prevent them from obtaining a knowledge of those truths that would be their safeguard.

Never should books containing a perversion of truth be placed in the hands of children or youth. Let not our children, in the very process of obtaining an education, receive ideas that will prove to be seeds of sin. If those with mature minds had nothing to do with such books, they would themselves be far safer, and their example and influence on the right side would make it far less difficult to guard the youth from temptation.

We have an abundance of that which is real, that which is divine. Those who thirst for knowledge need not go to polluted fountains. The Lord says:

"Bow down thine ear, and hear the words of the wise,
And apply thine heart unto My knowledge. . . .
That thy trust may be in the Lord,
I have made known to thee this day, even to thee.
Have not I written to thee excellent things
In counsels and knowledge,
That I might make thee know the certainty of the words of truth;
That thou mightest answer the words of truth to them that send unto thee?"
"He established a testimony in Jacob,
And appointed a law in Israel,
Which He commanded our fathers,
That they should make them known to their children;"
"Showing to the generation to come the praises of the Lord,
And His strength, and His wonderful works that He hath done."
"That the generation to come might know them,
Even the children which should be born;
Who should arise and declare them to their children:
That they might set their hope in God."

"The blessing of the Lord, it maketh rich,
And He addeth no sorrow with it."

Proverbs 22:17-21; Psalm 78:5, 4, 6, 7; Proverbs 10:22.

Christ's Teaching

So also Christ presented the principles of truth in the gospel. In His teaching we may drink of the pure streams that flow from the throne of God. Christ could have imparted to men knowledge that would have surpassed any previous disclosures, and put in the background every other discovery. He could have unlocked mystery after mystery, and could have concentrated around these wonderful revelations the active, earnest thought of successive generations till the close of time. But He would not spare a moment from teaching the science of salvation. His time, His faculties, and His life were appreciated and used only as the means for working out the salvation of the souls of men. He had come to seek and to save that which was lost, and He would not be turned from His purpose. He allowed nothing to divert Him.

Christ imparted only that knowledge which could be utilized. His instruction of the people was confined to the needs of their own condition in practical life. The curiosity that led them to come to Him with prying questions, He did not gratify. All such questionings He made the occassion for solemn, earnest, vital appeals. To those who were so eager to pluck from the tree of knowledge, He offered the fruit of the tree of life. They found every avenue closed except the way that leads to God. Every fountain was sealed save the fountain of eternal life.

Our Saviour did not encourage any to attend the rabbinical schools of His day, for the reason that their minds would be corrupted with the continually repeated, "They say," or, "It has been said." Why, then, should we accept the unstable words of men as exalted wisdom, when a greater, a certain, wisdom is at our command?

That which I have seen of eternal things, and that which I have seen of the weakness of humanity, has deeply impressed my mind and influenced my lifework. I see nothing wherein man should be praised or glorified. I see no reason why the opinions of worldly-wise men and so-called great men should be trusted in and exalted. How can those who are destitute of divine enlightenment have correct ideas of God's plans and ways? They either deny Him altogether and ignore His existence, or they circumscribe His power by their own finite conceptions.

Let us choose to be taught by Him who created the heavens and the earth, by Him who set the stars in their order in the firmament and appointed the sun and the moon to do their work.

It is right for the youth to feel that they must reach the highest development of their mental powers. We would not restrict the education to which God has set no limit. But our attainments avail nothing if not put to use for the honour of God and the good of humanity.

It is not well to crowd the mind with studies that require intense application, but that are not brought into use in practical life. Such education will be a loss to the student. For these studies lessen his desire and inclination for the studies that would fit him for usefulness and enable him to fulfil his responsibilities. A practical training is worth far more than any amount of mere theorizing. It is not enough even to have knowledge. We must have ability to use the knowledge aright.

The time, means, and study that so many expend for a comparatively useless education should be devoted to gaining an education that would make them practical men and women, fitted to bear life's responsibilities. Such an education would be of the highest value.

What we need is knowledge that will strengthen mind and soul, that will make us better men and women. Heart education is of far more importance than mere book learning. It is well, even essential, to have a knowledge of the world in which we live; but if we leave eternity out of our reckoning, we shall make a failure from which we can never recover.

A student may devote all his powers to acquiring knowledge; but unless he has a knowledge of God, unless he obeys the laws that govern his own being, he will destroy himself. By wrong habits, he loses the power of self-appreciation; he loses self-control. He cannot reason correctly about matters that concern him most deeply. He is reckless and irrational in his treatment of mind and body. Through his neglect to cultivate right principles, he is ruined both for this world and for the world to come.

If the youth understood their own weakness, they would find in God their strength. If they seek to be taught by Him they will become wise in His wisdom, and their lives will be fruitful of blessing to the world. But if they give up their minds to mere worldly and speculative study, and thus separate from God, they will lose all that enriches life.

The Importance of Seeking True Knowledge

More clearly than we do we need to understand the issues at stake in the great conflict in which we are engaged. We need to understand more fully the value of the truths of the word of God and the danger of allowing our minds to be diverted from them by the great deceiver.

The infinite value of the sacrifice required for our redemption reveals the fact that sin is a tremendous evil. Through sin the whole human organism is deranged, the mind is perverted, the imagination corrupted. Sin has degraded the faculties of the soul. Temptations from without find an answering chord within the heart, and the feet turn imperceptibly toward evil.

As the sacrifice in our behalf was complete, so our restoration from the defilement of sin is to be complete. No act of wickedness will the law of God excuse; no unrighteousness can escape its condemnation. The ethics of the gospel acknowledge no standard but the perfection of the divine character. The life of Christ was a perfect fulfilment of every precept of the law. He said, "I have kept My Father's commandments." His life is our example of obedience and service. God alone can renew the heart. "It is God which worketh in you both to will and to do of His good pleasure." But we are bidden, "Work out your own salvation." John 15:10; Philippians 2:13, 12.

The Work That Requires Our Thought

Wrongs cannot be righted, nor can reformations in conduct be made by a few feeble, intermittent efforts. Character building is the work, not of a day, nor of a year, but of a lifetime. The struggle for conquest over self, for holiness and heaven, is a lifelong struggle. Without continual effort and constant activity, there can be no advancement in the divine life, no attainment of the victor's crown.

The strongest evidence of man's fall from a higher state is the fact that it costs so much to return. The way of return can be gained only by hard fighting, inch by inch, hour by hour. In one moment, by a hasty, unguarded act, we may place ourselves in the power of evil; but it requires more than a moment to break the fetters and attain to a holier life. The purpose may be formed, the work begun; but its accomplishment will require toil, time, perseverance, patience, and sacrifice.

We cannot allow ourselves to act from impulse. We cannot be off guard for a moment. Beset with temptations without number, we must resist firmly or be conquered. Should we come to the close of life with our work undone, it would be an eternal loss.

The life of the apostle Paul was a constant conflict with self. He said, "I die daily." 1 Corinthians 15:31. His will and his desires every day conflicted with duty and the will of God. Instead of following inclination, he did God's will, however crucifying to his nature.

At the close of his life of conflict, looking back over its struggles and triumphs, he could say, "I have fought a good fight, I have finished my course, I have kept the faith: henceforth there is laid up for me a crown of righteousness, which the Lord, the righteous Judge, shall give me at that day." 2 Timothy 4:7, 8.

The Christian life is a battle and a march. In this warfare there is no release; the effort must be continuous and persevering. It is by unceasing endeavour that we maintain the victory over the temptations of Satan. Christian integrity must be sought with resistless energy and maintained with a resolute fixedness of purpose.

No one will be borne upward without stern, persevering effort in his own behalf. All must engage in this warfare for themselves; no one else can fight our battles. Individually we are responsible for the issues of the struggle; though Noah, Job, and Daniel were in the land they could deliver neither son nor daughter by their righteousness.

The Science to Be Mastered

There is a science of Christianity to be mastered — a science as much deeper, broader, higher than any human science as the heavens are higher than the earth. The mind is to be disciplined, educated, trained; for we are to do service for God in ways that are not in harmony with inborn inclination. Hereditary and cultivated tendencies to evil must be overcome. Often the education and training of a lifetime must be discarded, that one may become a learner in the school of Christ. Our hearts must be educated to become steadfast in God. We are to form habits of thought that will enable us to resist temptation. We must learn to look upward. The principles of the word of God — principles that are as high as heaven, and that compass eternity — we are to understand in their bearing upon our daily life. Every act, every word, every thought, is to be in accord with these principles. All must be brought into harmony with, and subject to, Christ.

The precious graces of the Holy Spirit are not developed in a moment. Courage, fortitude, meekness, faith, unwavering trust in God's power to save, are acquired by the experience of years. By a life of holy endeavour and firm adherence to the right the children of God are to seal their destiny.

No Time to Lose

We have no time to lose. We know not how soon our probation may close. At the longest, we have but a brief lifetime here, and we know not how soon the arrow of death may strike our hearts. We know not how soon we may be called to give up the world and all its interests. Eternity stretches before us. The curtain is about to be lifted. But a few short years, and for everyone now numbered with the living the mandate will go forth:

"He that is unjust, let him be unjust still: . . . and he that is righteous, let him be righteous still: and he that is holy, let him be holy still." Revelation 22:11.

Are we prepared? Have we become acquainted with God, the Governor of heaven, the Lawgiver, and with Jesus Christ whom He sent into the world as His representative? When our lifework is ended, shall we be able to say, as did Christ our example:

"I have glorified Thee on the earth: I have finished the work which Thou gavest Me to do. . . . I have manifested Thy name"? John 17:4-6.

The angels of God are seeking to attract us from ourselves and from earthly things. Let them not labour in vain.

Minds that have been given up to loose thought need to change. "Gird up the loins of your mind, be sober, and hope to the end for the grace that is to be brought unto you at the revelation of Jesus Christ; as obedient children, not fashioning yourselves according to the former lusts in your ignorance: but as He which hath called you is holy, so be ye holy in all manner of conversation; because it is written, Be ye holy; for I am holy." 1 Peter 1:13-16.

The thoughts must be centred upon God. We must put forth earnest effort to overcome the evil tendencies of the natural heart. Our efforts, our self-denial and perseverance, must be proportionate to the infinite value of the object of which we are in pursuit. Only by overcoming as Christ overcame shall we win the crown of life.

The Need of Self-renunciation

Man's great danger is in being self-deceived, indulging self-sufficiency, and thus separating from God, the source of his strength. Our natural tendencies, unless corrected by the Holy Spirit of God, have in them the seeds of moral death. Unless we become vitally connected with God, we cannot resist the unhallowed effects of self-indulgence, self-love, and temptation to sin.

In order to receive help from Christ, we must realize our need. We must have a true knowledge of ourselves. It is only he who knows himself to be a sinner that Christ can save. Only as we see our utter helplessness and renounce all self-trust, shall we lay hold on divine power.

It is not only at the beginning of the Christian life that this renunciation of self is to be made. At every advance step heavenward it is to be renewed. All our good works are dependent on a power outside of ourselves; therefore there needs to be a continual reaching out of the heart after God, a constant, earnest confession of sin and humbling of the soul before Him. Perils surround us; and we are safe only as we feel our weakness and cling with the grasp of faith to our mighty Deliverer.

Christ the Fountainhead of True Knowledge

We must turn away from a thousand topics that invite attention. There are matters that consume time and arouse inquiry, but end in nothing. The highest interests demand the close attention and energy that are so often given to comparatively insignificant things.

Accepting new theories does not in itself bring new life to the soul. Even an acquaintance with facts and theories important in themselves is of little value unless put to a practical use. We need to feel our responsibility to give our souls food that will nourish and stimulate spiritual life.

> "Incline thine ear unto wisdom, . . .
> Apply thy heart to understanding; . . .
> Seek her as silver, . . .
> Search for her as hid treasures:
> Then shalt thou understand the fear of Jehovah,
> And find the knowledge of God. . . .

Then shalt thou understand righteousness and justice,
And equity, yea, every good path.
For wisdom shall enter into thy heart,
And knowledge shall be pleasant unto thy soul;
Discretion shall watch over thee;
Understanding shall keep thee."
Wisdom "is a tree of life to them that lay hold upon her:
And happy is everyone that retaineth her."

Proverbs 2:2-11, ARV; 3:18.

The question for us to study is, "What is truth — the truth that is to be cherished, loved, honoured, and obeyed?" The devotees of science have been defeated and disheartened in their efforts to find out God. What they need to inquire at this time is, "What is the truth that will enable us to win the salvation of our souls?"

"What think ye of Christ?" — this is the all-important question. Do you receive Him as a personal Saviour? To all who receive Him He gives power to become sons of God.

Christ revealed God to His disciples in a way that performed in their hearts a special work, such as He desires to do in our hearts. There are many who, in dwelling too largely upon theory, have lost sight of the living power of the Saviour's example. They have lost sight of Him as the humble, self-denying worker. What they need is to behold Jesus. Daily we need the fresh revealing of His presence. We need to follow more closely His example of self-renunciation and self-sacrifice.

We need the experience that Paul had when he wrote: "I am crucified with Christ: nevertheless I live; yet not I, but Christ liveth in me: and the life which I now live in the flesh I live by the faith of the Son of God, who loved me, and gave Himself for me." Galatians 2:20.

The knowledge of God and of Jesus Christ expressed in character is an exaltation above everything else that is esteemed on earth or in heaven. It is the very highest education. It is the key that opens the portals of the heavenly city. This knowledge it is God's purpose that all who put on Christ shall possess.

The Knowledge Received Through God's Word

The whole Bible is a revelation of the glory of God in Christ. Received, believed, obeyed, it is the great instrumentality in the transformation of character. It is the grand stimulus, the constraining force, that quickens the physical, mental, and spiritual powers, and directs the life into right channels.

The reason why the youth, and even those of mature years, are so easily led into temptation and sin, is that they do not study the word of God and meditate upon it as they should. The lack of firm, decided will power, which is manifest in life and character, results from neglect of the sacred instruction of God's word. They do not by earnest effort direct the mind to that which would inspire pure, holy thought and divert it from that which is impure and untrue. There are few who choose the better part, who sit at the feet of Jesus, as did Mary, to learn of the divine Teacher. Few treasure His words in the heart and practice them in the life.

The truths of the Bible, received, will uplift mind and soul. If the word of God were appreciated as it should be, both young and old would possess an inward rectitude, a strength of principle, that would enable them to resist temptation.

Let men teach and write the precious things of the Holy Scriptures. Let the thought, the aptitude, the keen exercise of brain power, be given to the study of the thoughts of God. Study not the philosophy of man's conjectures, but study the philosophy of Him who is truth. No other literature can compare with this in value.

The mind that is earthly finds no pleasure in contemplating the word of God; but for the mind renewed by the Holy Spirit, divine beauty and celestial light shine from the sacred page. That which to the earthly mind was a desolate wilderness, to the spiritual mind becomes a land of living streams.

The knowledge of God as revealed in His word is the knowledge to be given to our children. From the earliest dawn of reason they should be made familiar with the name and the life of Jesus. Their first lessons should teach them that God is their Father. Their first training should be that of loving obedience. Reverently and tenderly let the word of God be read and repeated to them in portions suited to their comprehension and adapted to awaken their interest. And, above all, let them learn of His love revealed in Christ, and its great lesson:

"If God so loved us, we ought also to love one another." 1 John 4:11.

Let the youth make the word of God the food of mind and soul. Let the cross of Christ be made the science of all education, the centre of all teaching and all study. Let it be brought into the daily experience in practical life. So will the Saviour become to the youth a daily companion and friend. Every thought will be brought into captivity to the obedience of Christ. With the apostle Paul they will be able to say:

"God forbid that I should glory, save in the cross of our Lord Jesus Christ, by whom the world is crucified unto me, and I unto the world." Galatians 6:14.

Thus through faith they come to know God by an experimental knowledge. They have proved for themselves the reality of His word, the truth of His promises. They have tasted, and they know that the Lord is good.

The beloved John had a knowledge gained through his own experience. He could testify:

"That which was from the beginning, which we have heard, which we have seen with our eyes, which we have looked upon, and our hands have handled, of the

Word of life; (for the life was manifested, and we have seen it, and bear witness, and show unto you that eternal life, which was with the Father, and was manifested unto us;) that which we have seen and heard declare we unto you, that ye also may have fellowship with us: and truly our fellowship is with the Father, and with His Son Jesus Christ." 1 John 1:1-3.

So everyone may be able, through his own experience, to "set his seal to this, that God is true." John 3:33, ARV. He can bear witness to that which he himself has seen and heard and felt of the power of Christ. He can testify:

"I needed help, and I found it in Jesus. Every want was supplied, the hunger of my soul was satisfied; the Bible is to me the revelation of Christ. I believe in Jesus because He is to me a divine Saviour. I believe the Bible because I have found it to be the voice of God to my soul."

He who has gained a knowledge of God and His word through personal experience is prepared to engage in the study of natural science. Of Christ it is written, "In Him was life; and the life was the light of men." John 1:4. Before the entrance of sin, Adam and Eve in Eden were surrounded with a clear and beautiful light, the light of God. This light illuminated everything which they approached. There was nothing to obscure their perception of the character or the works of God. But when they yielded to the tempter, the light departed from them. In losing the garments of holiness, they lost the light that had illuminated nature. No longer could they read it aright. They could not discern the character of God in His works. So today man cannot of himself read aright the teaching of nature. Unless guided by divine wisdom, he exalts nature and the laws of nature above nature's God. This is why mere human ideas in regard to science so often contradict the teaching of God's word. But for those who receive the light of the life of Christ, nature is again illuminated. In the light shining from the cross, we can rightly interpret nature's teaching.

He who has a knowledge of God and His word through personal experience has a settled faith in the divinity of the Holy Scriptures. He has proved that God's word is truth, and he knows that truth can never contradict itself. He does not test the Bible by men's ideas of science; he brings these ideas to the test of the unerring standard. He knows that in true science there can be nothing contrary to the teaching of the word; since both have the same Author, a correct understanding of both will prove them to be in harmony. Whatever in so-called scientific teaching contradicts the testimony of God's word is mere human guesswork.

To such a student, scientific research will open vast fields of thought and information. As he contemplates the things of nature, a new perception of truth comes to him. The book of nature and the written word shed light upon each other. Both make him better acquainted with God by teaching him of His character and of the laws through which He works.

The experience of the psalmist is the experience that all may gain by receiving God's word through nature and through revelation. He says:

> "Thou, Lord, hast made me glad through Thy work:
> I will triumph in the works of Thy hands."
> "Thy mercy, O Lord, is in the heavens;
> And Thy faithfulness reacheth unto the clouds.
> Thy righteousness is like the great mountains;
> Thy judgements are a great deep. . . .
>
> "How excellent is Thy loving-kindness, O God!"
> "The children of men take refuge under the shadow of Thy wings. . . .
> And Thou wilt make them drink of the river of Thy pleasures.
> For with Thee is the fountain of life:
> In Thy light shall we see light."
>
> "Blessed are they that are upright in way,
> Who walk in the law of Jehovah.
> Blessed are they that keep His testimonies,
> That seek Him with the whole heart."

"Wherewith shall a young man cleanse his way?
By taking heed thereto according to Thy word."
"I have chosen the way of faithfulness:
Thine ordinances have I set before Me."
"Thy word have I laid up in my heart,
That I might not sin against Thee."
"And I shall walk at liberty;
For I have sought Thy precepts."

"Open Thou mine eyes, that I may behold
Wondrous things out of Thy law."
"Thy testimonies also are my delight
And my counsellors."
"The law of Thy mouth is better unto me
Than thousands of gold and silver."

"Oh how love I Thy law!
It is my meditation all the day."
"Thy testimonies are wonderful;
Therefore doth my soul keep them."
"Thy statutes have been my songs
In the house of my pilgrimage."

"Thy word is very pure;
Therefore Thy servant loveth it."
"The sum of Thy word is truth;
And every one of Thy righteous ordinances endureth forever."

"Let my soul live, and it shall praise Thee;
And let Thine ordinances help me."
"Great peace have they that love Thy law;
And they have no occasion of stumbling.

"I have hoped for Thy salvation, O Jehovah,
And have done Thy commandments.
My soul hath observed Thy testimonies;
And I love them exceedingly."

"The opening of Thy words giveth light;
It giveth understanding unto the simple."
"Thy commandments make me wiser than mine enemies;
For they are ever with me.
I have more understanding than all my teachers;
For Thy testimonies are my meditation.
I understand more than the aged,
Because I have kept Thy precepts."
"Through Thy precepts I get understanding:
Therefore I hate every false way."

"Thy testimonies have I taken as a heritage forever;
For they are the rejoicing of my heart."
Psalms 92:4; 36:5-7; 36:7-9, ARV; 119:1, 2, 9, 30, ARV, margin; 119:11, 45, 18, 24, 72, 97, 129, 54, 140, 160, 175, 165-167, 130, 98-100, 104, 111, ARV.

Clearer Revealings of God

It is our privilege to reach higher and still higher for clearer revealings of the character of God. When Moses prayed, "I beseech Thee, show me Thy glory," the Lord did not rebuke him, but He granted his prayer. God declared to His servant, "I will make all My goodness pass before thee, and I will proclaim the name of the Lord before thee." Exodus 33:18, 19.

It is sin that darkens our minds and dims our perceptions. As sin is purged from our hearts, the light of the knowledge of the glory of God in the face of Jesus Christ, illuminating His word and reflected from the face of nature, more and more fully will declare Him "merciful and gracious, long-suffering, and abundant in goodness and truth." Exodus 34:6.

In His light shall we see light, until mind and heart and soul are transformed into the image of His holiness.

For those who thus lay hold of the divine assurances of God's word, there are wonderful possibilities. Before them lie vast fields of truth, vast resources of power. Glorious things are to be revealed. Privileges and duties which they do not even suspect to be in the Bible will be made manifest. All who walk in the path of humble obedience, fulfilling His purpose, will know more and more of the oracles of God.

Let the student take the Bible as his guide and stand firm for principle, and he may aspire to any height of attainment. All the philosophies of human nature have led to confusion and shame when God has not been recognized as all in all. But the precious faith inspired of God imparts strength and nobility of character. As His goodness, His mercy, and His love are dwelt upon, clearer and still clearer will be the perception of truth;

higher, holier, the desire for purity of heart and clearness of thought. The soul dwelling in the pure atmosphere of holy thought is transformed by intercourse with God through the study of His word. Truth is so large, so far-reaching, so deep, so broad, that self is lost sight of. The heart is softened and subdued into humility, kindness, and love.

And the natural powers are enlarged because of holy obedience. From the study of the word of life, students may come forth with minds expanded, elevated, ennobled. If they are, like Daniel, hearers and doers of the word of God, they may advance as he did in all branches of learning. Being pure-minded, they will become strong-minded. Every intellectual faculty will be quickened. They may so educate and discipline themselves that all within the sphere of their influence shall see what man can be, and what he can do, when connected with the God of wisdom and power.

Education in the Life Eternal

Our lifework here is a preparation for the life eternal. The education begun here will not be completed in this life; it will be going forward through all eternity — ever progressing, never completed. More and more fully will be revealed the wisdom and love of God in the plan of redemption. The Saviour, as He leads His children to the fountains of living waters, will impart rich stores of knowledge. And day by day the wonderful works of God, the evidences of His power in creating and sustaining the universe, will open before the mind in new beauty. In the light that shines from the throne, mysteries will disappear, and the soul will be filled with astonishment at the simplicity of the things that were never before comprehended.

Now we see through a glass, darkly; but then face to face; now we know in part; but then we shall know even as also we are known.

THE WORKER'S NEED

Help in Daily Living

There is an eloquence far more powerful than the eloquence of words in the quiet, consistent life of a pure, true Christian. What a man is has more influence than what he says.

The officers who were sent to Jesus came back with the report that never man spoke as He spoke. But the reason for this was that never man lived as He lived. Had His life been other than it was, He could not have spoken as He did. His words bore with them a convincing power, because they came from a heart pure and holy, full of love and sympathy, benevolence and truth.

It is our own character and experience that determine our influence upon others. In order to convince others of the power of Christ's grace, we must know its power in our own hearts and lives. The gospel we present for the saving of souls must be the gospel by which our own souls are saved. Only through a living faith in Christ as a personal Saviour is it possible to make our influence felt in a sceptical world. If we would draw sinners out of the swift-running current, our own feet must be firmly set upon the Rock, Christ Jesus.

The badge of Christianity is not an outward sign, not the wearing of a cross or a crown, but it is that which reveals the union of man with God. By the power of His grace manifested in the transformation of character the world is to be convinced that God has sent His Son as its Redeemer. No other influence that can surround the human soul has such power as the influence of an unselfish life. The strongest argument in favour of the gospel is a loving and lovable Christian.

The Discipline of Trial

To live such a life, to exert such an influence, costs at every step effort, self-sacrifice, discipline. It is because they do not understand this that many are so easily discouraged in the Christian life. Many who sincerely consecrate their lives to God's service are surprised and disappointed to find themselves, as never before, confronted by obstacles and beset by trials and perplexities. They pray for Christlikeness of character, for a fitness for the Lord's work, and they are placed in circumstances that seem to call forth all the evil of their nature. Faults are revealed of which they did not even suspect the existence. Like Israel of old they question, "If God is leading us, why do all these things come upon us?"

It is because God is leading them that these things come upon them. Trials and obstacles are the Lord's chosen methods of discipline and His appointed conditions of success. He who reads the hearts of men knows their characters better than they themselves know them. He sees that some have powers and susceptibilities which, rightly directed, might be used in the advancement of His work. In His providence He brings these persons into different positions and varied circumstances that they may discover in their character the defects which have been concealed from their own knowledge. He gives them opportunity to correct these defects and to fit themselves for His service. Often He permits the fires of affliction to assail them that they may be purified.

The fact that we are called upon to endure trial shows that the Lord Jesus sees in us something precious which He desires to develop. If He saw in us nothing whereby He might glorify His name, He would not spend time in refining us. He does not cast worthless stones into His furnace. It is valuable ore that He refines. The blacksmith puts the iron and steel into the fire that he may know what manner of metal they are. The Lord allows His chosen ones to be placed in the furnace of affliction to prove what temper they are of and whether they can be fashioned for His work.

The potter takes the clay and moulds it according to his will. He kneads it and works it. He tears it apart and presses it together. He wets it and then dries it. He lets it lie for a while without touching it. When it is perfectly pliable, he continues the work of making of it a vessel. He forms it into shape and on the wheel trims and polishes it. He dries it in the sun and bakes it in the oven. Thus it becomes a vessel fit for use. So the great Master Worker desires to mould and fashion us. And as the clay is in the hands of the potter, so are we to be in His hands. We are not to try to do the work of the potter. Our part is to yield ourselves to be moulded by the Master Worker.

"Beloved, think it not strange concerning the fiery trial which is to try you, as though some strange thing happened unto you: but rejoice, inasmuch as ye are partakers of Christ's sufferings; that, when His glory shall be revealed, ye may be glad also with exceeding joy." 1 Peter 4:12, 13.

In the full light of day, and in hearing of the music of other voices, the caged bird will not sing the song that his master seeks to teach him. He learns a snatch of this, a trill of that, but never a separate and entire melody. But the master covers the cage, and places it where the bird will listen to the one song he is to sing. In the dark, he tries and tries again to sing that song until it is learned, and he breaks forth in perfect melody. Then the bird is brought forth, and ever after he can sing that song in the light. Thus God deals with His children. He has a song to teach us, and when we have learned it amid the shadows of affliction we can sing it ever afterward.

Many are dissatisfied with their lifework. It may be that their surroundings are uncongenial; their time is occupied with commonplace work, when they think themselves capable of higher responsibilities; often their efforts seem to them to be unappreciated or fruitless; their future is uncertain.

Let us remember that while the work we have to do may not be our choice, it is to be accepted as God's choice for us. Whether pleasing or unpleasing, we are to do the duty that lies nearest. "Whatsoever thy hand findeth to do, do it with thy might; for there is no work, nor device, nor knowledge, nor wisdom, in the grave, whither thou goest." Ecclesiastes 9:10.

If the Lord desires us to bear a message to Nineveh, it will not be as pleasing to Him for us to go to Joppa or to Capernaum. He has reasons for sending us to the place toward which our feet have been directed. At that very place there may be someone in need of the help we can give. He who sent Philip to the Ethiopian councillor, Peter to the Roman centurion, and the little Israelitish maiden to the help of Naaman, the Syrian captain, sends men and women and youth today as His representatives to those in need of divine help and guidance.

God's Plans the Best

Our plans are not always God's plans. He may see that it is best for us and for His cause to refuse our very best intentions, as He did in the case of David. But of one thing we may be assured, He will bless and use in the advancement of His cause those who sincerely devote themselves and all they have to His glory. If He sees it best not to grant their desires He will counterbalance the refusal by giving them tokens of His love and entrusting to them another service.

In His loving care and interest for us, often He who understands us better than we understand ourselves refuses to permit us selfishly to seek the gratification of our own ambition. He does not permit us to pass by the homely but sacred duties that lie next us. Often these duties afford the very training essential to prepare us for a higher work. Often our plans fail that God's plans for us may succeed.

We are never called upon to make a real sacrifice for God. Many things He asks us to yield to Him, but in doing this we are but giving up that which hinders us in the heavenward way. Even when called upon to surrender those things which in themselves are good, we may be sure that God is thus working out for us some higher good.

In the future life the mysteries that here have annoyed and disappointed us will be made plain. We shall see that our seemingly unanswered prayers and disappointed hopes have been among our greatest blessings.

We are to look upon every duty, however humble, as sacred because it is a part of God's service. Our daily prayer should be, "Lord, help me to do my best. Teach me how to do better work. Give me energy and cheerfulness. Help me to bring into my service the loving ministry of the Saviour."

A Lesson From the Life of Moses

Consider the experience of Moses. The education he received in Egypt as the king's grandson and the prospective heir to the throne was very thorough. Nothing was neglected that was calculated to make him a wise man, as the Egyptians understood wisdom. He received the highest civil and military training. He felt that he was fully prepared for the work of delivering Israel from bondage. But God judged otherwise. His providence appointed Moses forty years of training in the wilderness as a keeper of sheep.

The education that Moses had received in Egypt was a help to him in many respects; but the most valuable preparation for his lifework was that which he received while employed as a shepherd. Moses was naturally of an impetuous spirit. In Egypt a successful military leader and a favourite with the king and the nation, he had been accustomed to receiving praise and flattery. He had attracted the people to himself. He hoped to accomplish by his own powers the work of delivering Israel. Far different were the lessons he had to learn as God's representative. As he led his flocks through the wilds of the mountains and into the green pastures of the valleys, he learned faith and meekness, patience, humility, and self-forgetfulness. He learned to care for the weak, to nurse the sick, to seek after the straying, to bear with the unruly, to tend the lambs, and to nurture the old and the feeble.

In this work Moses was drawn nearer to the Chief Shepherd. He became closely united to the Holy One of Israel. No longer did he plan to do a great work. He sought to do faithfully as unto God the work committed to his charge. He recognized the presence of God in his surroundings. All nature spoke to him of the Unseen One. He knew God as a personal God, and, in meditating upon His character he grasped more and more fully the sense of His presence. He found refuge in the everlasting arms.

After this experience, Moses heard the call from heaven to exchange his shepherd's crook for the rod of authority; to leave his flock of sheep and take the leadership of Israel. The divine command found him self-distrustful, slow of speech, and timid. He was overwhelmed with a sense of his incapacity to be a mouthpiece for God. But he accepted the work, putting his whole trust in the Lord. The greatness of his mission called into exercise the best powers of his mind. God blessed his ready obedience, and he became eloquent, hopeful, self-possessed, fitted for the greatest work ever given to man. Of him it is written: "There hath not arisen a prophet since in Israel like unto Moses, whom Jehovah knew face to face." Deuteronomy 34:10, ARV.

Let those who feel that their work is not appreciated, and who crave a position of greater responsibility, consider that "promotion cometh neither from the east, nor from the west, nor from the south. But God is the Judge: He putteth down one, and setteth up another." Psalm 75:6, 7. Every man has his place in the eternal plan of heaven. Whether we fill that place depends upon our own faithfulness in co-operating with God.

We need to beware of self-pity. Never indulge the

feeling that you are not esteemed as you should be, that your efforts are not appreciated, that your work is too difficult. Let the memory of what Christ has endured for us silence every murmuring thought. We are treated better than was our Lord. "Seekest thou great things for thyself? seek them not." Jeremiah 45:5. The Lord has no place in His work for those who have a greater desire to win the crown than to bear the cross. He wants men who are more intent upon doing their duty than upon receiving their reward — men who are more solicitous for principle than for promotion.

Those who are humble, and who do their work as unto God, may not make so great a show as do those who are full of bustle and self-importance; but their work counts for more. Often those who make a great parade call attention to self, interposing between the people and God, and their work proves a failure. "Wisdom is the principal thing; therefore get wisdom: and with all thy getting get understanding. Exalt her, and she shall promote thee: she shall bring thee to honour, when thou dost embrace her." Proverbs 4:7, 8.

Because they have not the determination to take themselves in hand and to reform, many become stereotyped in a wrong course of action. But this need not be. They may cultivate their powers to do the very best kind of service, and then they will be always in demand. They will be valued for all that they are worth.

If any are qualified for a higher position, the Lord will lay the burden, not alone on them, but on those who have tested them, who know their worth, and who can understandingly urge them forward. It is those who perform faithfully their appointed work day by day, who in God's own time will hear His call, "Come up higher."

While the shepherds were watching their flocks on the hills of Bethlehem, angels from heaven visited them. So today while the humble worker for God is following his employment, angels of God stand by his side, listening to his words, noting the manner in which his work is done, to see if larger responsibilities may be entrusted to his hands.

Not by their wealth, their education, or their position does God estimate men. He estimates them by their purity of motive and their beauty of character. He looks to see how much of His Spirit they possess and how much of His likeness their life reveals. To be great in God's kingdom is to be as a little child in humility, in simplicity of faith, and in purity of love.

"Ye know," Christ said, "that the rulers of the Gentiles lord it over them, and their great ones exercise authority over them. Not so shall it be among you: but whosoever would become great among you shall be your minister." Matthew 20:25, 26, ARV.

Of all the gifts that heaven can bestow upon men, fellowship with Christ in His sufferings is the most weighty trust and the highest honour. Not Enoch, who was translated to heaven, not Elijah, who ascended in a chariot of fire, was greater or more honoured than John the Baptist, who perished alone in the dungeon. "Unto you it is given in the behalf of Christ, not only to believe on Him, but also to suffer for His sake." Philippians 1:29.

Plans for the Future

Many are unable to make definite plans for the future. Their life is unsettled. They cannot discern the outcome of affairs, and this often fills them with anxiety and unrest. Let us remember that the life of God's children in this world is a pilgrim life. We have not wisdom to plan our own lives. It is not for us to shape our future. "By faith Abraham, when he was called to go out into a place which he should after receive for an inheritance, obeyed; and he went out, not knowing whither he went." Hebrews 11:8.

Christ in His life on earth made no plans for Himself. He accepted God's plans for Him, and day by day the Father unfolded His plans. So should we depend upon God, that our lives may be the simple outworking of

His will. As we commit our ways to Him, He will direct our steps.

Too many, in planning for a brilliant future, make an utter failure. Let God plan for you. As a little child, trust to the guidance of Him who will "keep the feet of His saints." 1 Samuel 2:9. God never leads His children otherwise than they would choose to be led, if they could see the end from the beginning and discern the glory of the purpose which they are fulfilling as co-workers with Him.

Wages

When Christ called His disciples to follow Him, He offered them no flattering prospects in this life. He gave them no promise of gain or worldly honour, nor did they make any stipulation as to what they should receive. To Matthew as he sat at the receipt of custom, the Saviour said, "Follow Me. And he left all, rose up, and followed Him." Luke 5:27, 28. Matthew did not, before rendering service, wait to demand a certain salary equal to the amount received in his former occupation. Without question or hesitation he followed Jesus. It was enough for him that he was to be with the Saviour, that he might hear His words and unite with Him in His work.

So it was with the disciples previously called. When Jesus bade Peter and his companions follow Him, immediately they left their boats and nets. Some of these disciples had friends dependent on them for support; but when they received the Saviour's invitation they did not hesitate and inquire, "How shall I live and sustain my family?" They were obedient to the call; and when afterward Jesus asked them, "When I sent you without purse, and scrip, and shoes, lacked ye anything?" they could answer, "Nothing." Luke 22:35.

Today the Saviour calls us, as He called Matthew and John and Peter, to His work. If our hearts are touched by His love, the question of compensation will not be uppermost in our minds. We shall rejoice to be co-workers with Christ, and we shall not fear to trust His care. If we make God our strength we shall have clear perceptions of duty, unselfish aspirations; our life will be actuated by a noble purpose which will raise us above sordid motives.

God Will Provide

Many who profess to be Christ's followers have an anxious, troubled heart because they are afraid to trust themselves with God. They do not make a complete surrender to Him, for they shrink from the consequences that such a surrender may involve. Unless they do make this surrender they cannot find peace.

There are many whose hearts are aching under a load of care because they seek to reach the world's standard. They have chosen its service, accepted its perplexities, adopted its customs. Thus their character is marred and their life made a weariness. The continual worry is wearing out the life forces. Our Lord desires them to lay aside this yoke of bondage. He invites them to accept His yoke; He says, "My yoke is easy, and My burden is light." Worry is blind and cannot discern the future; but Jesus sees the end from the beginning. In every difficulty He has His way prepared to bring relief. "No good thing will He withhold from them that walk uprightly." Matthew 11:30; Psalm 84:11.

Our heavenly Father has a thousand ways to provide for us of which we know nothing. Those who accept the one principle of making the service of God supreme, will find perplexities vanish and a plain path before their feet.

The faithful discharge of today's duties is the best preparation for tomorrow's trials. Do not gather together all tomorrow's liabilities and cares and add them to the burden of today. "Sufficient unto the day is the evil thereof." Matthew 6:34.

Let us be hopeful and courageous. Despondency in God's service is sinful and unreasonable. He knows our every necessity. To the omnipotence of the King of kings our covenant-keeping God unites the gentleness and care of the tender shepherd. His power is absolute, and it is the pledge of the sure fulfilment of His promises to all who trust in Him. He has means for the removal of every difficulty, that those who serve Him and respect the means He employs may be sustained. His love is as far above all other love as the heavens are above the earth. He watches over His children with a love that is measureless and everlasting.

In the darkest days, when appearances seem most forbidding, have faith in God. He is working out His will, doing all things well in behalf of His people. The strength of those who love and serve Him will be renewed day by day.

He is able and willing to bestow upon His servants all the help they need. He will give them the wisdom which their varied necessities demand.

Said the tried apostle Paul: "He said unto me, My grace is sufficient for thee: for My strength is made perfect in weakness. Most gladly therefore will I rather glory in my infirmities, that the power of Christ may rest upon me. Therefore I take pleasure in infirmities, in reproaches, in necessities, in persecutions, in distresses for Christ's sake: for when I am weak, then am I strong." 2 Corinthians 12:9, 10.

In Contact With Others

Every association of life calls for the exercise of self-control, forbearance, and sympathy. We differ so widely in disposition, habits, education, that our ways of looking at things vary. We judge differently. Our understanding of truth, our ideas in regard to the conduct of life, are not in all respects the same. There are no two whose experience is alike in every particular. The trials of one are not the trials of another. The duties that one finds light are to another most difficult and perplexing.

So frail, so ignorant, so liable to misconception is human nature, that each should be careful in the estimate he places upon another. We little know the bearing of our acts upon the experience of others. What we do or say may seem to us of little moment, when, could our eyes be opened, we should see that upon it depended the most important results for good or for evil.

Consideration for Burden Bearers

Many have borne so few burdens, their hearts have known so little real anguish, they have felt so little perplexity and distress in behalf of others, that they cannot understand the work of the true burden bearer. No more capable are they of appreciating his burdens than is the child of understanding the care and toil of his burdened father. The child may wonder at his father's fears and perplexities. These appear needless to him. But when years of experience shall have been added to his life, when he himself comes to bear its burdens, he will look back upon his father's life and understand that which was once so incomprehensible. Bitter experience has given him knowledge.

The work of many a burden bearer is not understood, his labours are not appreciated, until death lays him low. When others take up the burdens he has laid down, and meet the difficulties he encountered, they can understand how his faith and courage were tested. Often then the mistakes they were so quick to censure are lost sight of. Experience teaches them sympathy. God permits men to be placed in positions of responsibility. When they err, He has power to correct or to remove them. We should be careful not to take into our hands the work of judging that belongs to God.

The conduct of David toward Saul has a lesson. By command of God, Saul had been anointed as king over Israel. Because of his disobedience the Lord declared that the kingdom should be taken from him; and yet how tender and courteous and forbearing was the conduct of David toward him! In seeking the life of David, Saul came into the wilderness and, unattended, entered the very cave where David with his men of war lay hidden. "And the men of David said unto him, Behold the day of which the Lord said unto thee, . . . I will deliver thine enemy into thine hand, that thou mayest do to him as it shall seem good unto thee. . . . And he said unto his men, The Lord forbid that I should do this thing unto my master, the Lord's anointed, to stretch forth mine hand against him, seeing he is the anointed of the Lord." The Saviour bids us, "Judge not, that ye be not judged. For with what judgement ye judge, ye shall be judged: and with what measure ye mete, it shall be measured to you again." Remember that soon your life record will pass in review before God. Remember, too, that He has said, "Thou art inexcusable, O man, whosoever thou art that judgest: . . . for thou that judgest doest the same things." 1 Samuel 24:4-6; Matthew 7:1, 2; Romans 2:1.

Forbearance Under Wrong

We cannot afford to let our spirits chafe over any real or supposed wrong done to ourselves. Self is the enemy we most need to fear. No form of vice has a more baleful effect upon the character than has human passion not under the control of the Holy Spirit. No other victory we can gain will be so precious as the victory gained over self.

We should not allow our feelings to be easily wounded. We are to live, not to guard our feelings or our reputation, but to save souls. As we become interested in the salvation of souls we cease to mind the little differences that so often arise in our association with one another. Whatever others may think of us or do to us, it need not disturb our oneness with Christ, the fellowship of the Spirit. "What glory is it, if, when ye be buffeted for your faults, ye shall take it patiently? but if, when ye do well, and suffer for it, ye take it patiently, this is acceptable with God." 1 Peter 2:20.

Do not retaliate. So far as you can do so, remove all cause for misapprehension. Avoid the appearance of evil. Do all that lies in your power, without the sacrifice of principle, to conciliate others. "If thou bring thy gift to the altar, and there rememberest that thy brother hath aught against thee; leave there thy gift before the altar, and go thy way; first be reconciled to thy brother, and then come and offer thy gift." Matthew 5:23, 24.

If impatient words are spoken to you, never reply in the same spirit. Remember that "a soft answer turneth away wrath." Proverbs 15:1. And there is wonderful power in silence. Words spoken in reply to one who is angry sometimes serve only to exasperate. But anger met with silence, in a tender, forbearing spirit, quickly dies away.

Under a storm of stinging, faultfinding words, keep the mind stayed upon the word of God. Let mind and heart be stored with God's promises. If you are ill-treated or wrongfully accused, instead of returning an angry answer, repeat to yourself the precious promises:

"Be not overcome of evil, but overcome evil with good." Romans 12:21.

"Commit thy way unto the Lord; trust also in Him; and He shall bring it to pass. And He shall bring forth thy righteousness as the light, and thy judgement as the noonday." Psalm 37:5, 6.

"There is nothing covered, that shall not be revealed; neither hid, that shall not be known." Luke 12:2.

"Thou hast caused men to ride over our heads; we went through fire and through water: but Thou broughtest us out into a wealthy place." Psalm 66:12.

We are prone to look to our fellow men for sympathy and uplifting, instead of looking to Jesus. In His mercy and faithfulness God often permits those in whom we place confidence to fail us, in order that we may learn the folly of trusting in man and making flesh our arm. Let us trust fully, humbly, unselfishly in God. He knows the sorrows that we feel to the depths of our being, but which we cannot express. When all things seem dark and unexplainable, remember the words of Christ, "What I do thou knowest not now; but thou shalt know hereafter." John 13:7.

Study the history of Joseph and of Daniel. The Lord did not prevent the plottings of men who sought to do them harm; but He caused all these devices to work for good to His servants who amidst trial and conflict preserved their faith and loyalty.

So long as we are in the world, we shall meet with adverse influences. There will be provocations to test the temper; and it is by meeting these in a right spirit that the Christian graces are developed. If Christ dwells in us, we shall be patient, kind, and forbearing, cheerful amid frets and irritations. Day by day and year by year we shall conquer self, and grow into a noble heroism. This is our allotted task; but it cannot be accomplished without help from Jesus, resolute decision, unwavering purpose, continual watchfulness, and unceasing prayer. Each one has a personal battle to fight.

Not even God can make our characters noble or our lives useful, unless we become co-workers with Him. Those who decline the struggle lose the strength and joy of victory.

We need not keep our own record of trials and difficulties, griefs, and sorrows. All these things are written in the books, and heaven will take care of them. While we are counting up the disagreeable things, many things that are pleasant to reflect upon are passing from memory, such as the merciful kindness of God surrounding us every moment and the love over which angels marvel, that God gave His Son to die for us. If as workers for Christ you feel that you have had greater cares and trials than have fallen to the lot of others, remember that for you there is a peace unknown to those who shun these burdens. There is comfort and joy in the service of Christ. Let the world see that life with Him is no failure.

If you do not feel lighthearted and joyous, do not talk of your feelings. Cast no shadow upon the lives of others. A cold, sunless religion never draws souls to Christ. It drives them away from Him into the nets that Satan has spread for the feet of the straying. Instead of thinking of your discouragements, think of the power you can claim in Christ's name. Let your imagination take hold upon things unseen. Let your thoughts be directed to the evidences of the great love of God for you. Faith can endure trial, resist temptation, bear up under disappointment. Jesus lives as our advocate. All is ours that His mediation secures.

Think you not that Christ values those who live wholly for Him? Think you not that He visits those who, like the beloved John in exile, are for His sake in hard and trying places? God will not suffer one of His truehearted workers to be left alone, to struggle against great odds and be overcome. He preserves as a precious jewel everyone whose life is hid with Christ in Him. Of every such one He says: "I . . . will make thee as a signet: for I have chosen thee." Haggai 2:23.

Then talk of the promises; talk of Jesus' willingness

to bless. He does not forget us for one brief moment. When, notwithstanding disagreeable circumstances, we rest confidingly in His love, and shut ourselves in with Him, the sense of His presence will inspire a deep, tranquil joy. Of Himself Christ said: "I do nothing of Myself; but as My Father hath taught Me, I speak these things. And He that sent Me is with Me: the Father hath not left Me alone; for I do always those things that please Him." John 8:28, 29.

The Father's presence encircled Christ, and nothing befell Him but that which infinite love permitted for the blessing of the world. Here was His source of comfort, and it is for us. He who is imbued with the Spirit of Christ abides in Christ. Whatever comes to him comes from the Saviour, who surrounds him with His presence. Nothing can touch him except by the Lord's permission. All our sufferings and sorrows, all our temptations and trials, all our sadness and griefs, all our persecutions and privations, in short, all things work together for our good. All experiences and circumstances are God's workmen whereby good is brought to us.

If we have a sense of the long-suffering of God toward us, we shall not be found judging or accusing others. When Christ was living on the earth, how surprised His associates would have been, if, after becoming acquainted with Him, they had heard Him speak one word of accusation, of fault-finding, or of impatience. Let us never forget that those who love Him are to represent Him in character.

"Be kindly affectioned one to another with brotherly love; in honour preferring one another." "Not rendering evil for evil, or railing for railing: but contrariwise blessing; knowing that ye are thereunto called, that ye should inherit a blessing." Romans 12:10; 1 Peter 3:9.

The Lord Jesus demands our acknowledgement of the rights of every man. Men's social rights, and their rights as Christians, are to be taken into consideration. All are to be treated with refinement and delicacy, as the sons and daughters of God.

Christianity will make a man a gentleman. Christ was courteous, even to His persecutors; and His true followers will manifest the same spirit. Look at Paul when brought before rulers. His speech before Agrippa is an illustration of true courtesy as well as persuasive eloquence. The gospel does not encourage the formal politeness current with the world, but the courtesy that springs from real kindness of heart.

The most careful cultivation of the outward proprieties of life is not sufficient to shut out all fretfulness, harsh judgement, and unbecoming speech. True refinement will never be revealed so long as self is considered as the supreme object. Love must dwell in the heart. A thoroughgoing Christian draws his motives of action from his deep heart love for his Master. Up through the roots of his affection for Christ springs an unselfish interest in his brethren. Love imparts to its possessor grace, propriety, and comeliness of deportment. It illuminates the countenance and subdues the voice; it refines and elevates the whole being.

Life is chiefly made up, not of great sacrifices and wonderful achievements, but of little things. It is oftenest through the little things which seem so unworthy of notice that great good or evil is brought into our lives. It is through our failure to endure the tests that come to us in little things, that the habits are moulded, the character misshaped; and when the greater tests come, they find us unready. Only by acting upon principle in the tests of daily life can we acquire power to stand firm and faithful in the most dangerous and most difficult positions.

We are never alone. Whether we choose Him or not, we have a companion. Remember that wherever you are, whatever you do, God is there. Nothing that is said or done or thought can escape His attention. To your every word or deed you have a witness — the holy, sin-hating God. Before you speak or act, always think of this. As a Christian, you are a member of the royal family, a child of the heavenly King. Say no word, do no act, that shall bring dishonour upon "that worthy name by the which ye are called." James 2:7.

Study carefully the divine-human character, and constantly inquire, "What would Jesus do were He in my place?" This should be the measurement of our duty. Do not place yourselves needlessly in the society of those who by their arts would weaken your purpose to do right, or bring a stain upon your conscience. Do nothing among strangers, in the street, on the cars, in the home, that would have the least appearance of evil. Do something every day to improve, beautify, and ennoble the life that Christ has purchased with His own blood.

Always act from principle, never from impulse. Temper the natural impetuosity of your nature with meekness and gentleness. Indulge in no lightness or trifling. Let no low witticism escape your lips. Even the thoughts are not to be allowed to run riot. They must be restrained, brought into captivity to the obedience of Christ. Let them be placed upon holy things. Then, through the grace of Christ, they will be pure and true.

We need a constant sense of the ennobling power of pure thoughts. The only security for any soul is right thinking. As a man "thinketh in his heart, so is he." Proverbs 23:7. The power of self-restraint strengthens by exercise. That which at first seems difficult, by constant repetition grows easy, until right thoughts and actions become habitual. If we will we may turn away from all that is cheap and inferior, and rise to a high standard; we may be respected by men and beloved of God.

Cultivate the habit of speaking well of others. Dwell upon the good qualities of those with whom you associate, and see as little as possible of their errors and failings. When tempted to complain of what someone has said or done, praise something in that person's life or character. Cultivate thankfulness. Praise God for His wonderful love in giving Christ to die for us. It never pays to think of our grievances. God calls upon us to think of His mercy and His matchless love, that we may be inspired with praise.

Earnest workers have no time for dwelling upon the faults of others. We cannot afford to live on the husks of others' faults or failings. Evil speaking is a twofold curse, falling more heavily upon the speaker than upon the hearer. He who scatters the seeds of dissension and strife reaps in his own soul the deadly fruits. The very act of looking for evil in others develops evil in those who look. By dwelling upon the faults of others, we are changed into the same image. But by beholding Jesus, talking of His love and perfection of character, we become changed into His image. By contemplating the lofty ideal He has placed before us, we shall be uplifted into a pure and holy atmosphere, even the presence of God. When we abide here, there goes forth from us a light that irradiates all who are connected with us.

Instead of criticizing and condemning others, say, "I must work out my own salvation. If I co-operate with Him who desires to save my soul, I must watch myself diligently. I must put away every evil from my life. I must overcome every fault. I must become a new creature in Christ. Then, instead of weakening those who are striving against evil, I can strengthen them by encouraging words." We are too indifferent in regard to one another. Too often we forget that our fellow labourers are in need of strength and cheer. Take care to assure them of your interest and sympathy. Help them by your prayers, and let them know that you do it.

Not all who profess to be workers for Christ are true disciples. Among those who bear His name, and who are even numbered with His workers, are some who do not represent Him in character. They are not governed by His principles. These persons are often a cause of perplexity and discouragement to their fellow workers who are young in Christian experience; but none need be misled. Christ has given us a perfect example. He bids us follow Him.

Till the end of time there will be tares among the

wheat. When the servants of the householder, in their zeal for his honour, asked permission to root out the tares, the master said: "Nay; lest while ye gather up the tares, ye root up also the wheat with them. Let both grow together until the harvest." Matthew 13:29, 30.

In His mercy and long-suffering, God bears patiently with the perverse and even the falsehearted. Among Christ's chosen apostles was Judas the traitor. Should it then be a cause of surprise or discouragement that there are falsehearted ones among His workers today? If He who reads the heart could bear with him who He knew was to be His betrayer, with what patience should we bear with those at fault.

And not all, even of those who appear most faulty, are like Judas. Peter, impetuous, hasty, and self-confident, often appeared to far greater disadvantage than Judas did. He was oftener reproved by the Saviour. But what a life of service and sacrifice was his! What a testimony does it bear to the power of God's grace! So far as we are capable, we are to be to others what Jesus was to His disciples when He walked and talked with them on the earth.

Regard yourselves as missionaries, first of all, among your fellow workers. Often it requires a vast amount of time and labour to win one soul to Christ. And when a soul turns from sin to righteousness, there is joy in the presence of the angels. Think you that the ministering spirits who watch over these souls are pleased to see how indifferently they are treated by some who claim to be Christians? Should Jesus deal with us as we too often deal with one another, who of us could be saved?

Remember that you cannot read hearts. You do not know the motives which prompted the actions that to you look wrong. There are many who have not received a right education; their characters are warped, they are hard and gnarled, and seem to be crooked in every way. But the grace of Christ can transform them. Never cast them aside, never drive them to discouragement or despair by saying, "You have disappointed me, and I will not try to help you." A few words spoken hastily under provocation — just what we think they deserve — may cut the cords of influence that should have bound their hearts to ours.

The consistent life, the patient forbearance, the spirit unruffled under provocation, is always the most conclusive argument and the most solemn appeal. If you have had opportunities and advantages that have not fallen to the lot of others, consider this, and be ever a wise, careful, gentle teacher.

In order to have the wax take a clear, strong impression of the seal, you do not dash the seal upon it in a hasty, violent way; you carefully place the seal on the plastic wax and quietly, steadily press it down until it has hardened in the mould. In like manner deal with human souls. The continuity of Christian influence is the secret of its power, and this depends on the steadfastness of your manifestation of the character of Christ. Help those who have erred, by telling them of your experiences. Show how, when you made grave mistakes, patience, kindness, and helpfulness on the part of your fellow workers gave you courage and hope.

Until the judgement you will never know the influence of a kind, considerate course toward the inconsistent, the unreasonable, the unworthy. When we meet with ingratitude and betrayal of sacred trusts, we are roused to show our contempt or indignation. This the guilty expect; they are prepared for it. But kind forbearance takes them by surprise and often awakens their better impulses and arouses a longing for a nobler life.

"Brethren, if a man be overtaken in a fault, ye which are spiritual, restore such an one in the spirit of meekness; considering thyself, lest thou also be tempted. Bear ye one another's burdens, and so fulfil the law of Christ." Galatians 6:1, 2.

All who profess to be children of God should bear in mind that as missionaries they will be brought into contact with all classes of minds. There are the refined and the coarse, the humble and the proud, the religious and the sceptical, the educated and the ignorant, the rich and the poor. These varied minds cannot be treated alike; yet all need kindness and sympathy. By mutual contact our minds should receive polish and refinement. We are dependent upon one another, closely bound together by the ties of human brotherhood.

> "Heaven forming each on other to depend,
> A master or a servant or a friend,
> Bids each on other for assistance call,
> Till one man's weakness grows the strength of all."

It is through the social relations that Christianity comes in contact with the world. Every man or woman who has received the divine illumination is to shed light on the dark pathway of those who are unacquainted with the better way. Social power, sanctified by the Spirit of Christ, must be improved in bringing souls to the Saviour. Christ is not to be hid away in the heart as a coveted treasure, sacred and sweet, to be enjoyed solely by the possessor. We are to have Christ in us as a well of water, springing up into everlasting life, refreshing all who come in contact with us.

Development and Service

Christian life is more than many take it to be. It does not consist wholly in gentleness, patience meekness, and kindliness. These graces are essential; but there is need also of courage, force, energy, and perseverance. The path that Christ marks out is a narrow, self-denying path. To enter that path and press on through difficulties and discouragements requires men who are more than weaklings.

Force of Character

Men of stamina are wanted, men who will not wait to have their way smoothed and every obstacle removed, men who will inspire with fresh zeal the flagging efforts of dispirited workers, men whose hearts are warm with Christian love and whose hands are strong to do the Master's work.

Some who are engaged in missionary service are weak, nerveless, spiritless, easily discouraged. They lack push. They have not those positive traits of character that give power to do something — the spirit and energy that kindle enthusiasm. Those who would win success must be courageous and hopeful. They should cultivate not only passive but active virtues. While they are to give the soft answer that turns away wrath, they must possess the courage of a hero to resist evil. With the charity that endures all things, they need the force of character that will make their influence a positive power.

Some have no firmness of character. Their plans and purposes have no definite form and consistency. They are of but little practical use in the world. This weakness, indecision, and inefficiency should be overcome. There is in true Christian character an indomitableness that cannot be moulded or subdued by adverse circumstances. We must have moral backbone, an integrity that cannot be flattered, bribed, or terrified.

God desires us to make use of every opportunity for securing a preparation for His work. He expects us to put all our energies into its performance and to keep our hearts alive to its sacredness and its fearful responsibilities.

Many who are qualified to do excellent work accomplish little because they attempt little. Thousands pass through life as if they had no great object for which to live, no high standard to reach. One reason for this is the low estimate which they place upon themselves. Christ paid an infinite price for us, and according to the price paid He desires us to value ourselves.

Be not satisfied with reaching a low standard. We are not what we might be, or what is God's will that we should be. God has given us reasoning powers, not to remain inactive, not to be perverted to earthly and sordid pursuits, but that they may be developed to the utmost, refined, sanctified, ennobled, and used in advancing the interests of His kingdom.

None should consent to be mere machines, run by another man's mind. God has given us ability, to think and to act, and it is by acting with carefulness, looking to Him for wisdom that you will become capable of bearing burdens. Stand in your God-given personality. Be no other person's shadow. Expect that the Lord will work in and by and through you.

Never think that you have learned enough, and that you may now relax your efforts. The cultivated mind is the measure of the man. Your education should continue during your lifetime; every day you should be learning and putting to practical use the knowledge gained.

Remember that in whatever position you may serve you are revealing motive, developing character. Whatever your work, do it with exactness, with diligence; overcome the inclination to seek an easy task.

The same spirit and principles that one brings into the daily labour will be brought into the whole life. Those who desire a fixed amount to do and a fixed salary, who wish to prove an exact fit without the trouble of adaptation or training, are not the ones whom God calls to work in His cause. Those who study how to give as little as possible of their physical, mental, and moral power are not the workers upon whom He can pour out abundant blessings. Their example is contagious. Self-interest is the ruling motive. Those who need to be watched and who work only as every duty is specified to them, are not the ones who will be pronounced good and faithful. Workers are needed who manifest energy, integrity, diligence, those who are willing to do anything that needs to be done.

Many become inefficient by evading responsibilities for fear of failure. Thus they fail of gaining education which results from exerience, and which reading and study and all the advantages otherwise gained cannot give them.

Man can shape cicumstances, but circumstances should not be allowed to shape the man. We should seize upon circumstances as instruments by which to work. We are to master them, but should not permit them to master us.

Men of power are those who have been opposed, baffled, and thwarted. By calling their energies into action, the obstacles they meet prove to them positive blessings. They gain self-reliance. Conflict and perplexity call for the exercise of trust in God and for that firmness which develops power.

Christ gave no stinted service. He did not measure His work by hours. His time, His heart, His soul and strength, were given to labour for the benefit of humanity. Through weary days He toiled, and through long nights He bent in prayer for grace and enduruance that He might do a larger work. With strong crying and tears He sent His petitions to heaven, that His human nature might be strengthened, that He might be braced to meet the wily foe in all his deceptive workings, and fortified to fulfil His missions of uplifting humanity. To His workers He says, "I have given you an example, that ye should do as I have done." John 13:15.

"The love of Christ," said Paul, "constraineth us." 2 Corinthians 5:14. This was the actuating principle of his conduct; it was his motive power. If ever his ardour in the path of duty flagged for a moment, one glance at the cross caused him to gird up anew the loins of his mind and press forward in the way of self-denial. In his labours for his brethren he relied much upon the manifestation of infinite love in the sacrifice of Christ, with its subduing, constraining power.

How earnest, how touching, his appeal: "Ye know the grace of our Lord Jesus Christ, that, though He was rich, yet for your sakes He became poor, that ye through His poverty might be rich." 2 Corinthians 8:9. You know the height from which He stooped, the depth of humiliation to which He descended. His feet entered upon the path of sacrifice and turned not aside until He had given His life. There was no rest for Him between the throne in heaven and the cross. His love for man led Him to welcome every indignity and suffer every abuse.

Paul admonishes us to "look not every man on his own things, but every man also on the things of others." He bids us possess the mind "which was also in Christ Jesus: who, being in the form of God, thought it not robbery to be equal with God: but made Himself of no reputation, and took upon Him the form of a servant, and was made in the likeness of men: and being found in fashion as a man, He humbled Himself, and became obedient unto death, even the death of the cross." Philippians 2:4-8.

Paul was deeply anxious that the humiliation of Christ should be seen and realized. He was convinced that if men could be led to consider the amazing sacrifice made by the Majesty of heaven, selfishness would be banished from their hearts. The apostle lingers over point after point, that we may in some measure comprehend the wonderful condescension of the Saviour in behalf of sinners. He directs the mind first to the position which Christ occupied in heaven in the bosom of His Father; he reveals Him afterward as laying aside His glory, voluntarily subjecting Himself to the humbling conditions of man's life, assuming the responsibilities of a servant, and becoming obedient unto death, and that the most ignominious and revolting, the most agonizing — the death of the cross. Can we contemplate this wonderful manifestation of the love of God without gratitude and love, and a deep sense of the fact that we are not our own? Such a Master should not be served from grudging, selfish motives.

"Ye know," says Peter, "that ye were not redeemed with corruptible things, as silver and gold." 1 Peter 1:18. Oh, had these been sufficient to purchase the salvation of man, how easily it might have been accomplished by Him who says, "The silver is Mine, and the gold is Mine"! Haggai 2:8. But the sinner could be redeemed only by the precious blood of the Son of God. Those who, failing to appreciate this wonderful sacrifice, withhold themselves from Christ's service, will perish in their selfishness.

Singleness of Purpose

In the life of Christ, everything was made subordinate to His work, the great work of redemption which He came to accomplish. And the same devotion, the same self-denial and sacrifice, the same subjection to the claims of the word of God, is to be manifest in His disciples.

Everyone who accepts Christ as his personal Saviour will long for the privilege of serving God. Contemplating what heaven has done for him, his heart is moved with boundless love and adoring gratitude. He is eager to signalize his gratitude by devoting his abilities to God's service. He longs to show his love for Christ and for His purchased possession. He covets toil, hardship, sacrifice.

The true worker for God will do his best, because in so doing he can glorify his Master. He will do right in order to regard the requirements of God. He will endeavour to improve all his faculties. He will perform every duty as unto God. His one desire will be that Christ may receive homage and perfect service.

There is a picture representing a bullock standing between a plough and an altar, with the inscription, "Ready for either," ready to toil in the furrow or to be offered on the altar of sacrifice. This is the position of the true child of God — willing to go where duty calls, to deny self, to sacrifice for the Redeemer's cause.

A Higher Experience

We need constantly a fresh revelation of Christ, a daily experience that harmonizes with His teachings. High and holy attainments are within our reach. Continual progress in knowledge and virtue is God's purpose for us. His law is the echo of His own voice, giving to all the invitation, "Come up higher. Be holy, holier still." Every day we may advance in perfection of Christian character.

Those who are engaged in service for the Master need an experience much higher, deeper, broader, than many have yet thought of having. Many who are already members of God's great family know little of what it means to behold His glory and to be changed from glory to glory. Many have a twilight perception of Christ's excellence, and their hearts thrill with joy. They long for a fuller, deeper sense of the Saviour's love. Let these cherish every desire of the soul after God. The Holy Spirit works with those who will be worked, moulds those who will be moulded, fashions those who will be fashioned. Give yourselves the culture of spiritual thoughts and holy communings. You have seen but the first rays of the early dawn of His glory. As you follow on to know the Lord, you will know that "the path of the righteous is as the light of dawn, that shineth more and more unto the perfect day." Proverbs 4:18, RV, margin.

"These things have I spoken unto you," said Christ, "that My joy might remain in you, and that your joy might be full." John 15:11.

Ever before Him, Christ saw the result of His mission. His earthly life, so full of toil and self-sacrifice, was cheered by the thought that He would not have all this travail for nought. By giving His life for the life of men, He would restore in humanity the image of God. He would lift us up from the dust, reshape the character after the pattern of His own character, and make it beautiful with His own glory.

Christ saw of the travail of His soul and was satisfied. He viewed the expanse of eternity and saw the happiness of those who through His humiliation should receive pardon and everlasting life. He was wounded for their transgressions, bruised for their iniquities. The chastisement of their peace was upon Him, and with His stripes they were healed. He heard the shout of the redeemed. He heard the ransomed ones singing the song of Moses and the Lamb. Although the baptism of blood must first be received, although the sins of the world were to weigh upon His innocent soul, although the shadow of an unspeakable woe was upon Him; yet for the joy that was set before Him He chose to endure the cross and despised the shame.

This joy all His followers are to share. However great and glorious hereafter, our reward is not all to be reserved for the time of final deliverance. Even here we are by faith to enter into the Saviour's joy. Like Moses, we are to endure as seeing the Invisible.

Now the church is militant. Now we are confronted with a world in darkness, almost wholly given over to idolatry.

The Joy of the Lord

There were ninety and nine that safely lay
  In the shelter of the fold,
But one was out on the hills away,
  Far, far from the gates of gold —
Away on the mountains wild and bare,
Away from the tender Shepherd's care.

"Lord, Thou hast here Thy ninety and nine;
  Are they not enough for Thee?"
But the Shepherd made answer: "One of Mine
  Has wandered away from Me,
And although the road be rough and steep,
I go to the desert to find My sheep."

But none of the ransomed ever knew
  How deep were the waters crossed,
Nor how dark was the night that the Lord passed through
  Ere He found His sheep that was lost.
Far out in the desert He heard its cry —
Fainting and helpless, and ready to die.

"Lord, whence are these blood drops all the way
That mark out the mountain's track?"
"They were shed for one who had gone astray,
Ere the Shepherd could bring him back."
"Lord, why are Thy hands so rent and torn?"
"They were pierced tonight by many a thorn."

But all through the mountains, thunder-riven,
And up from the rocky steep,
There rose a cry to the gate of heaven,
"Rejoice, I have found My sheep!"
And the angels sang around the throne,
"Rejoice, for the Lord brings back His own!"
— Elizabeth C. Clephane.

But the day is coming when the battle will have been fought, the victory won. The will of God is to be done on earth as it is done in heaven. The nations of the saved will know no other law than the law of heaven. All will be a happy, united family, clothed with the garments of praise and thanksgiving — the robe of Christ's righteousness. All nature, in its surpassing loveliness, will offer to God a tribute of praise and adoration. The world will be bathed in the light of heaven. The light of the moon will be as the light of the sun, and the light of the sun will be sevenfold greater than it is now. The years will move on in gladness. Over the scene the morning stars will sing together, the sons of God will shout for joy, while God and Christ will unite in proclaiming, "There shall be no more sin, neither shall there be any more death."

These visions of future glory, scenes pictured by the hand of God, should be dear to His children.

Stand on the threshold of eternity and hear the gracious welcome given to those who in this life have co-operated with Christ, regarding it as a privilege and an honour to suffer for His sake. With the angels, they cast their crowns at the feet of the Redeemer, exclaiming, "Worthy is the Lamb that was slain to receive power, and riches, and wisdom, and strength, and honour, and glory, and blessing. . . . Honour, and glory, and power, be unto Him that sitteth upon the throne, and unto the Lamb for ever and ever." Revelation 5:12, 13.

There the redeemed ones greet those who directed

them to the uplifted Saviour. They unite in praising Him who died that human beings might have the life that measures with the life of God. The conflict is over. All tribulation and strife are at an end. Songs of victory fill all heaven, as the redeemed stand around the throne of God. All take up the joyful strain, "Worthy is the Lamb that was slain" and hath redeemed us to God.

"I beheld, and, lo, a great multitude, which no man could number, of all nations, and kindreds, and people, and tongues, stood before the throne, and before the Lamb, clothed with white robes, and palms in their hands; and cried with a loud voice, saying, Salvation to our God which sitteth upon the throne, and unto the Lamb." Revelation 7:9, 10.

"These are they which came out of great tribulation, and have washed their robes, and made them white in the blood of the Lamb. Therefore are they before the throne of God, and serve Him day and night in His temple: and He that sitteth on the throne shall dwell among them. They shall hunger no more, neither thirst any more; neither shall the sun light on them, nor any heat. For the Lamb which is in the midst of the throne shall feed them, and shall lead them unto living fountains of waters: and God shall wipe away all tears from their eyes." "And there shall be no more death, neither sorrow, nor crying, neither shall there be any more pain: for the former things are passed away." Verses 14-17; 21:4.

We need to keep ever before us this vision of things unseen. It is thus that we shall be able to set a right value on the things of eternity and the things of time. It is this that will give us power to influence others for the higher life.

In the Mount With God

"Come up to Me into the mount," God bids us. To Moses, before he could be God's instrument in delivering Israel, was appointed the forty years of communion with Him in the mountain solitudes. Before bearing God's message to Pharaoh, he spoke with the angel in the burning bush. Before receiving God's law as the representative of His people, he was called into the mount, and beheld His glory. Before executing justice on the idolaters, he was hidden in the cleft of the rock, and the Lord said, "I will proclaim the name of the Lord before thee," "merciful and gracious, slow to anger, and abundant in loving-kindness and truth; . . . and that will by no means clear the guilty." Exodus 33:19; 34:6, 7, ARV. Before he laid down, with his life, his burden for Israel, God called him to the top of Pisgah and spread out before him the glory of the Promised Land.

Before the disciples went forth on their mission, they were called up into the mount with Jesus. Before the power and glory of Pentecost, came the night of communion with the Saviour, the meeting on the mountain in Galilee, the parting scene upon Olivet, with the angel's promise, and the days of prayer and communion in the upper chamber.

Jesus, when preparing for some great trial or some important work, would resort to the solitude of the mountains and spend the night in prayer to His Father. A night of prayer preceded the ordination of the apostles and the Sermon on the Mount, the transfiguration, the agony of the judgement hall and the cross, and the resurrection glory.

The Privilege of Prayer

We, too, must have times set apart for meditation and prayer and for receiving spiritual refreshing. We do not value the power and efficacy of prayer as we should. Prayer and faith will do what no power on earth can accomplish. We are seldom, in all respects, placed in the same position twice. We continually have new scenes and new trials to pass through, where past experience cannot be a sufficient guide. We must have the continual light that comes from God.

Christ is ever sending messages to those who listen for His voice. On the night of the agony in Gethsemane, the sleeping disciples heard not the voice of Jesus. They had a dim sense of the angels' presence, but lost the power and glory of the scene. Because of their drowsiness and stupor they failed of receiving the evidence that would have strengthened their souls for the terrible scenes before them. Thus today the very men who most need divine instruction often fail of receiving it, because they do not place themselves in communion with heaven.

The temptations to which we are daily exposed make prayer a necessity. Dangers beset every path. Those who are seeking to rescue others from vice and ruin are especially exposed to temptation. In constant contact with evil, they need a strong hold upon God lest they themselves be corrupted. Short and decisive are the steps that lead men down from high and holy ground to a low level. In a moment decisions may be made that fix one's condition forever. One failure to overcome leaves the soul unguarded. One evil habit, if not firmly resisted, will strengthen into chains of steel, binding the whole man.

The reason why so many are left to themselves in places of temptation is that they do not set the Lord always before them. When we permit our communion with God to be broken, our defence is departed from us. Not all your good purposes and good intentions will enable you to withstand evil. You must be men and women of prayer. Your petitions must not be faint, occasional, and fitful, but earnest, persevering, and constant. It is not always necessary to bow upon your knees in order to pray. Cultivate the habit of talking with the Saviour when you are alone, when you are walking, and when you are busy with your daily labour. Let the heart be continually uplifted in silent petition for help, for light, for strength, for knowledge. Let every breath be a prayer.

As workers for God we must reach men where they are, surrounded with darkness, sunken in vice, and stained with corruption. But while we stay our minds upon Him who is our sun and our shield, the evil that surrounds us will not bring one stain upon our garments. As we work to save the souls that are ready to perish we shall not be put to shame if we make God our trust. Christ in the heart, Christ in the life, this is our safety. The atmosphere of His presence will fill the soul with abhorrence of all that is evil. Our spirit may be so identified with His that in thought and aim we shall be one with Him.

It was through faith and prayer that Jacob, from

being a man of feebleness and sin, became a prince with God. It is thus that you may become men and women of high and holy purpose, of noble life, men and women who will not for any consideration be swayed from truth, right, and justice. All are pressed with urgent cares, burdens, and duties, but the more difficult your position and the heavier your burdens, the more you need Jesus.

It is a serious mistake to neglect the public worship of God. The privileges of divine service should not be lightly regarded. Those who attend upon the sick are often unable to avail themselves of these privileges, but they should be careful not to absent themselves needlessly from the house of worship.

In ministering to the sick, more than in any merely secular business, success depends on the spirit of consecration and self-sacrifice with which the work is done. Those who bear responsibilities need to place themselves where they will be deeply impressed by the Spirit of God. You should have as much greater anxiety than do others for the aid of the Holy Spirit and for a knowledge of God as your position of trust is more responsible than that of others.

Nothing is more needed in our work than the practical results of communion with God. We should show by our daily lives that we have peace and rest in the Saviour. His peace in the heart will shine forth in the countenance. It will give to the voice a persuasive power. Communion with God will ennoble the character and the life. Men will take knowledge of us, as of the first disciples, that we have been with Jesus. This will impart to the worker a power that nothing else can give. Of this power he must not allow himself to be deprived.

We must live a twofold life — a life of thought and action, of silent prayer and earnest work. The strength received through communion with God, united with earnest effort in training the mind to thoughtfulness and caretaking, prepares one for daily duties and keeps the spirit in peace under all circumstances, however trying.

The Divine Counsellor

When in trouble, many think they must appeal to some earthly friend, telling him their perplexities, and begging for help. Under trying circumstances unbelief fills their hearts, and the way seems dark. And all the time there stands beside them the mighty Counsellor of the ages, inviting them to place their confidence in Him. Jesus, the great Burden Bearer, is saying, "Come unto Me, and I will give you rest." Shall we turn from Him to uncertain human beings, who are as dependent upon God as we ourselves are?

You may feel the deficiency of your character and the smallness of your ability in comparison with the greatness of the work. But if you had the greatest intellect ever given to man, it would not be sufficient for your work. "Without Me ye can do nothing," says our Lord and Saviour. John 15:5. The result of all we do rests in the hands of God. Whatever may betide, lay hold upon Him with steady, persevering confidence.

In your business, in companionship for leisure hours, and in alliance for life, let all the associations you form be entered upon with earnest, humble prayer. You will thus show that you honour God, and God will honour you. Pray when you are fainthearted. When you are desponding, close the lips firmly to men; do not shadow the path of others; but tell everything to Jesus. Reach up your hands for help. In your weakness lay hold of infinite strength. Ask for humility, wisdom, courage, increase of faith, that you may see light in God's light and rejoice in His love.

Consecration; Trust

When we are humble and contrite we stand where God can and will manifest Himself to us. He is well pleased when we urge past mercies and blessings as a reason why He should bestow on us greater blessings. He will more than fulfil the expectations of those who trust fully in Him. The Lord Jesus knows just what His children need, how much divine power we will appropriate for the blessing of humanity; and He bestows upon us all that we will employ in blessing others and ennobling our own souls.

We must have less trust in what we ourselves can do, and more trust in what the Lord can do for and through us. You are not engaged in your own work; you are doing the work of God. Surrender your will and way to Him. Make not a single reserve, not a single compromise with self. Know what it is to be free in Christ.

The mere hearing of sermons Sabbath after Sabbath, the reading of the Bible through and through, or the explanation of it verse by verse, will not benefit us or those who hear us, unless we bring the truths of the Bible into our individual experience. The understanding, the will, the affections, must be yielded to the control of the word of God. Then through the work of the Holy Spirit the precepts of the word will become the principles of the life.

As you ask the Lord to help you, honour your Saviour by believing that you do receive His blessing. All power, all wisdom, are at our command. We have only to ask.

Walk continually in the light of God. Meditate day and night upon His character. Then you will see His beauty and rejoice in His goodness. Your heart will glow with a sense of His love. You will be uplifted as if borne by everlasting arms. With the power and light that God imparts, you can comprehend more and accomplish more than you ever before deemed possible.

"Abide in Me."

Christ bids us: "Abide in Me, and I in you. As the branch cannot bear fruit of itself, except it abide in the vine; no more can ye, except ye abide in Me. . . . He that abideth in Me, and I in him, the same bringeth forth much fruit: for without Me ye can do nothing. . . . If ye abide in Me, and My words abide in you, ye shall ask what ye will, and it shall be done unto you. Herein is My Father glorified, that ye bear much fruit; so shall ye be My disciples.

"As the Father hath loved Me, so have I loved you: continue ye in My love. . . .

"Ye have not chosen Me, but I have chosen you, and ordained you, that ye should go and bring forth fruit, and that your fruit should remain: that whatsoever ye ask of the Father in My name, He may give it you." John 15:4-16.

"Behold, I stand at the door, and knock: if any man hear My voice, and open the door, I will come in to him, and will sup with him, and he with Me." Revelation 3:20.

"To him that overcometh will I give to eat of the hidden manna, and will give him a white stone, and in the stone a new name written, which no man knoweth saving he that receiveth it." Revelation 2:17.

"He that overcometh, . . . I will give him the Morning Star," "and I will write upon him the name of My God, and the name of the city of My God: . . . and I will write upon him My new name." Verses 26-28; 3:12.

"This One Thing I Do."

He whose trust is in God will with Paul be able to say, "I can do all things in Him that strengtheneth me." Philippians 4:13, RV. Whatever the mistakes or failures of the past, we may, with the help of God, rise above them. With the apostle we may say:

"This one thing I do, forgetting those things which are behind, and reaching forth unto those things which are before, I press toward the mark for the prize of the high calling of God in Christ Jesus." Philippians 3:13, 14.

Scriptural Index

Mark

Luke

John

Acts

Romans

1 Corinthians

General Index

Page numbers indicated here refer to those in brackets throughout the book.